A STRING IN THE HARP

When their father accepts a teaching post at the University of Wales, twelve-year-old Peter and ten-year-old Becky have to go with him. Soon their older sister, Jen, joins them, and together they try to adjust to life in a small Welsh village and make a new start after their mother's death. Things might have worked out, except for Peter— miserable and bitter—who discovers a strange, ancient object that he eventually identifies as the tuning key for the harp of Taliesin, the great sixth-century bard who had lived in that part of Wales. Gradually, the key draws Peter back in time and he finds himself experiencing important and dramatic events in Taliesin's life—and he is pulled farther and farther away from his family and the modern world.

"Bond deftly blends fantasy and realism.... The interweaving of Welsh background, the intermittently-told story of Taliesin, and the problems of family adjustment is adroit. The characters are drawn with depth." —*Bulletin of the Center for Children's Books*

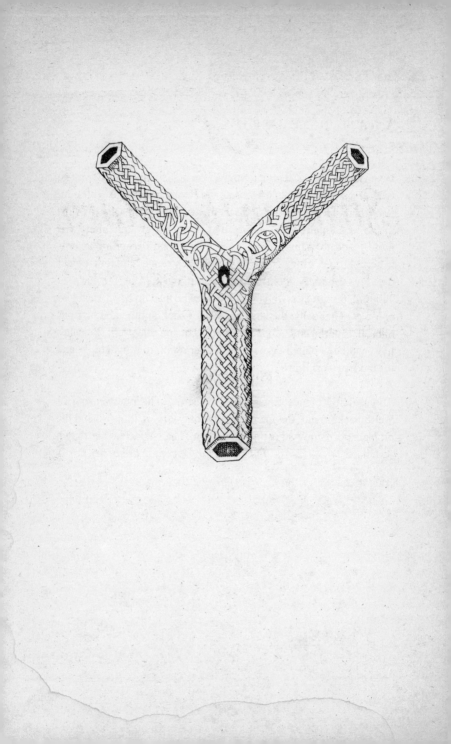

A
String in the Harp
by Nancy Bond

Puffin Books

Map and frontispiece drawing by Allen Davis

PUFFIN BOOKS
Viking Penguin Inc., 40 West 23rd Street, New York, New York 10010, U.S.A.
Penguin Books Ltd, 27 Wrights Lane, London W8 5TZ (Publishing & Editorial) and
Harmondsworth, Middlesex, England (Distribution & Warehouse)
Penguin Books Australia Ltd, Ringwood, Victoria, Australia
Penguin Books Canada Limited, 2801 John Street, Markham, Ontario, Canada L3R 1B4
Penguin Books (N.Z.) Ltd, 182-190 Wairau Road, Auckland 10, New Zealand

First published by Atheneum, 1976
Published in Puffin Books 1987
Copyright © Nancy Bond, 1976
All rights reserved
Printed in the United States of America by Offset Paperback Manufacturers, Inc.,
Dallas, Pennsylvania
Set in Times Roman

Library of Congress Cataloging-in-Publication Data
Bond, Nancy.   A string in the harp.
(Puffin Newberry library)
Reprint. Originally published: New York: Atheneum, 1981, c1976.
Summary: Relates what happens to three American
children, unwillingly transplanted to Wales for one year,
when one of them finds an ancient harp-tuning key that
takes him back to the time of the great sixth-century bard Taliesin.
1. Taliesin—Juvenile fiction.   [1. Taliesin—Fiction.
2. Space and time—Fiction.   3. Wales—Fictional]   I. Title.
[PZ7.B6384St 1987]   [Fic]   87-16919   ISBN 0-14-032376-7

FOR MY TWO PARENTS
AND FOUR GRANDPARENTS

Contents

1 · BORTH   3

2 · TALIESIN   24

3 · STORM AND FLOOD   47

4 · TO LLECHWEDD MELYN   80

5 · A NOT SO VERY MERRY
     CHRISTMAS   93

6 · BESIDE THE DOVEY   112

7 · A HARP KEY   134

8 · JEN ARGUES   156

9 · THE BATTLE OF CORS
     FOCHNO   168

10 · DR. RHYS   188

11 · ROAST CHICKEN AND
     MASHED POTATOES   199

12 · CARDIFF   214

13 · WOLF!   232

14 · A BIRTHDAY EXPEDITION   254

15 · DINNER PARTY   276

16 · A HOMECOMING   295

17 · CANNWYL CORPH   315

18 · GIVING IT BACK   346

19 · FAMILY DECISION   353

Author's Note   369

I have been a tear in the air,
I have been the dullest of stars,
I have been a word among letters,
I have been a book in the origin.
I have been the light of lanterns,
I have been a continuing bridge,
Over threescore Abers.
I have been a wolf, I have been an eagle.
I have been a coracle in the seas;
I have been a guest at the banquet.
I have been a drop in a shower;
I have been a sword in the grasp of the hand:
I have been a shield in battle.
I have been a string in the harp,
Disguised . . .

—from the Book of Taliesin, VIII

A
String in the Harp

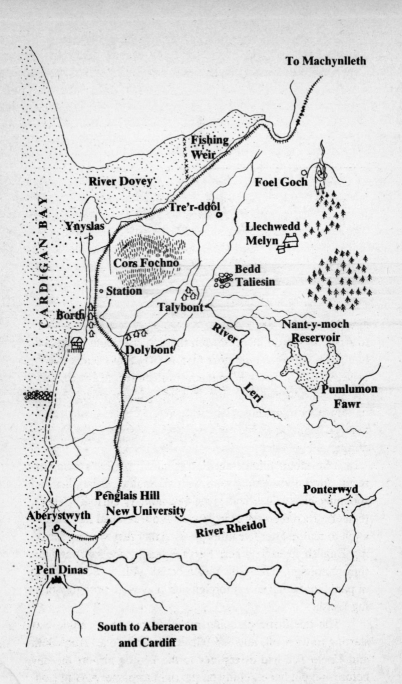

I

Borth

AN HOUR AND A QUARTER from Shrewsbury to Aberystwyth on the train. Jen thought she ought to feel exhausted—she'd been up more than twenty-four hours already, traveling by car, airplane, and now train, across Massachusetts, the Atlantic Ocean, and half of England. But it didn't seem like three thousand miles. She was shielded by a cocoon of unreality. Right now she only wanted to arrive and see the familiar faces of her family.

Two stout, middle-aged women shared Jen's compartment, littering the empty seats with all manner of bundles and shopping bags. They had given Jen politely curious glances, then absorbed themselves in conversation. Jen had had a bit of a jolt to realize after five minutes or so that they weren't speaking English to each other. For a moment she had thought, they're foreign. Then she remembered with a sudden surge of panic that no, *she* was foreign and they were probably talking Welsh.

The anesthetic of being managed by other people was starting to wear off, and Jen felt very much alone. Aunt Beth and Uncle Ted had driven her to the Boston airport the day before and put her carefully on the right airplane. And in London her father's friends, the Sullivans from Amherst, had met her and seen her across the city and onto the train for Shrewsbury. But at Shrewsbury there'd been no one waiting for her and she'd had to find the right train herself—not terribly difficult because the station wasn't large—and there wouldn't be anyone until her father, Becky, and Peter met her at Borth.

Beyond the train window a grudging December sun filtered through heavy drifts of cloud. Shrewsbury was practically on the Welsh border, Jen knew from studying a map before she'd left, so, presumably, they were now in Wales. Across the flat, green farmland ahead, suddenly and abruptly, rose mountains, the Welsh Marches Jen remembered from somewhere. And beyond them, what?

Jen glanced at her watch, willing the time to pass quickly. All had gone according to Aunt Beth's painstaking plans. She thought again of the round dining room table in Amherst covered with maps, schedules, an atlas, endless pieces of paper and pencils, the paper filled with Aunt Beth's neat but illegible writing: times and flight numbers, lists of clothing, emergency information, names and addresses. Most of the paper was now folded and clipped together in the huge new pocketbook, which Jen kept obediently hooked over her arm even while she sat in the train.

"For heaven's sake, dear, *don't* let it out of your hands! You just don't know what may happen and all your money and documents are in it." Aunt Beth had looked so worried in the Logan Airport waiting room that Jen almost decided not to go at the last minute, convinced by her aunt that the trip was impossible. But she had her father's letter in her pocket, the one that told her how much he was looking forward to seeing her, and Uncle Ted grinned reassuringly at her and said, "Send us a postcard when you arrive."

"Oh, I will," Jen promised. "A letter."

They were among the mountains now, the train following a valley between the great, stone-ribbed humps, patched with dead, rust-colored bracken. Jen had grown up among the hills of western Massachusetts, the Holyoke Range along the Connecticut River, and she loved them, but they had never given her the strange feeling these did. These seemed immensely ancient and wild. Without knowing their history, she knew they had one.

Welshpool was the first of a string of little stations they stopped at: a collection of low, gray stone houses and narrow streets. Jen couldn't begin to pronounce most of the names of the towns.

Not for the first time she wondered what Borth would look like. It was a tiny dot on the map beside the sea with nothing to make it different from hundreds of other tiny dots. She wondered if it were pretty and had gardens or if it were a fishing village with a harbor and boats; her father's letters had told her very little, really. Becky's notes were mostly concerned with school and the people she met, and Peter never wrote at all.

Aunt Beth had remarked on that and Jen could tell from her tone of voice that she still disapproved strongly of what her brother, Jen's father David, had done. Only five months after his wife's death he had accepted a teaching position at the University of Wales in Aberystwyth, and less than four months after that, he and his two youngest children had gone to live in Wales. Nothing Beth could say to him would change his mind. He was grimly determined to get away from Amherst, at least for a while, to fill his mind with something besides the automobile accident.

When Aunt Beth had realized it was pointless to argue with him over going, she had begun on his responsibility to his children instead. And David had finally relented. Jen could still see his set, white face as he told her that she was to stay in Amherst with Aunt Beth and Uncle Ted and continue high school. She had protested, but only half-heartedly. Secretly, she was relieved not to be leaving the town and school and friends she had known all her life. The horror of losing her mother was only compounded by the idea of leaving all that was safe and familiar, and she didn't understand why David felt he had to.

For Peter, twelve, and Becky, ten, there was never any choice. Their father stubbornly refused to leave them behind. Jen was only two years from college, and college was very important to David. Nothing must jeopardize her education. But a year in Welsh schools wouldn't harm the other two at all— it would, on the contrary, be a good experience. So Jen had helped sort and pack and store things in the attic of their Amherst house and had watched her father and brother and sister leave for Britain without her. Becky was excited, but Peter had fought against going every inch of the way. He was openly envious of Jen, rebellious and angry at being taken away from his school, friends, home. She knew he felt as she did about needing familiar things to hold on to.

And now, she wondered, how had he adjusted? Her father and Becky gave her no clue in what they wrote, they only said he was "fine" and "sends his love," which she rather doubted.

The sign on this station platform said "Machynlleth," which stirred something in Jen's mind. She hunted for her wad of papers and found what she was looking for: a note saying Machynlleth was only fifteen minutes from Borth. One of the two women got out here, gathering up her bags and bundles and continuing to talk as she went. The sun had gone into cloud for the last time and the early winter dusk was closing around the train. Jen glanced up at her suitcase in the rack over her head and decided she'd better get it down. She had a horror of being caught on the train at Borth, of seeing the station start to slide away before she had time to get out the carriage door. When she'd manhandled the case down—Aunt Beth had packed it with heavy, sensible clothes—she tried brushing the wrinkles out of her coat, her hands damp, her fingers nervous.

The train left Machynlleth and ran along the bank of a river. The valley it followed widened, pushing the mountains back on both sides. In the fading afternoon light the country looked bleak and unfriendly; wind rocked the train gently, and the glass of the window was cold. On the right through the windows beyond the corridor Jen could see the mud flat of the river stretching away from the train and to the left the mountains withdrew from a vast, grass-covered plain. Along its far edge was a thin row of lights, which came rapidly closer. The train turned and ran behind a low row of houses, the grass plain still beside it as it slowed.

Jen fumbled with her gloves, biting her lip in the way that irritated Aunt Beth. Where was her family? Would they be on the platform? What would she do it they weren't? Oh, God, let them be there! For a dreadful moment she couldn't see anybody at all. Then her father's slim familiar shape moved out of the shadow, beside him Peter, hunched inside his jacket, and Becky hopping up and down in a short skirt, her knees pink with cold.

The other woman in the compartment nodded to Jen as she struggled with her suitcase, airline bag, and pocketbook and held the carriage door for her. The wind and Becky hit her almost simultaneously, taking her breath away, as she stepped onto the platform.

"You've come! You've come! You've come!" shouted Becky, hugging her enthusiastically. "I thought the train would *never* get here!"

Over Becky's head, Jen grinned at Peter and he grinned back.

"Hello," said David. "We are glad to see you! Hope you had no trouble getting here." As soon as Becky let go, he gave Jen a slightly less breathless hug.

"Hey," said Peter, "have you got all your stuff? I'm freezing to the platform!"

Outside the station a short, dark-haired young man slung her bags into an elderly car.

"We've even got the taxi for you," Becky explained. "This is my sister, Jen. That's Billy-Davies-Taxi." The young man grinned pleasantly and nodded in agreement. "We don't usually have a taxi," Becky confided once they were squashed inside, "only when *we* came."

It was too dark to see much of Borth, even if Jen had had a chance to look around her as they drove, but she was much too busy answering questions and giving messages and relaying news about Amherst: Uncle Ted and Aunt Beth, the opening of the college, the blizzard on Thanksgiving, the tenants in their house, Peter's friends and Becky's two cats.

"And the Sullivans found you at the airport in London all right?" David wanted to know.

"Oh, yes, and they were very nice and bought me another breakfast at the station. They said to say hello to you. I didn't have any problems at all."

"I would have been surprised if you had. I gathered from your aunt's letters that the whole operation had been planned like a military campaign," David remarked dryly.

Jen didn't tell him Aunt Beth's elaborate emergency procedures: in case the plane were delayed; in case the Sullivans didn't meet her; in case there was trouble with Jen's passport; in case she missed the right train. . . .

"You must be over the 'flu or Beth would never have let you come."

"Mmm. A couple of weeks ago, and Dr. Harris said I was as well as ever."

"Little did he know what you were planning to do," said Peter darkly behind his upturned collar. "If you don't come down with pneumonia here in the first ten days . . ."

"It's a very healthy climate," said David flatly. "We've none of us been sick with anything since we came." Jen looked from her father to her brother; there was tension between them; she sensed it.

"Lots of fresh air . . ." David was saying.

Lots indeed. The taxi stopped abruptly and they all climbed out. The wind hit them immediately, strong and boisterous. Jen wasn't prepared and she almost lost her balance. She looked about her and discovered they were at the top of a cliff; below and to the right were the lights of Borth proper where the station was. To the left were empty miles of sea as gray as the clouds overhead. The horizon was lost somewhere between. Nothing shielded them from the wind.

She hadn't imagined this; she felt a bit overwhelmed. Peter said, still hunched, "Not even the last outpost of civilization." The tips of his ears were miserably red. "Civilization must have decided it wasn't worth coming out here."

Jen glanced at him doubtfully. He was inclined to relish his pessimism, exaggerating deliberately to wring the last drop from it, she was used to that. But this time he sounded decidedly down, no trace of pleasure in his remark.

Becky grabbed her arm then and pulled her toward one of the houses in the row behind them. It was a two-story, brown stucco house with a bow window and a gate and a tiny scrap of garden in front. It took the full buffeting of the wind, only the street and a strip of grass and scrub keeping it from the cliff.

At least, once the door was closed, most of the wind was shut outside. In the dark hallway Jen took off her coat and David hung it on a peg.

"You'll be sorry," Peter muttered at her.

"Sorry?"

"Wait and see."

"Well," said David, as if he wasn't quite sure what next, "this is Bryn Celyn, and I hope you'll like it while you're here."

"Bryn Celyn?" echoed Jen.

"Holly Bank in Welsh," Becky informed her. "All the houses here have names. Once you get used to it, it's much nicer than numbers. Let's have tea."

Peter still hadn't taken his jacket off, Jen noticed, not even when they sat down around the kitchen table. Someone had set it for a meal with plates and silver and a huge teapot, and Jen realized for the first time that she was tired and ravenously hungry. David put the kettle on to boil and Becky uncovered plates of sandwiches and tomatoes.

Listening with half her attention to Becky chatter about school, Jen looked at the kitchen. It was completely strange, totally unfamiliar except for her father and Becky and Peter. A little desperately she thought, yesterday morning I was *home* and *nothing* was strange. And now, outside this room, there is not one single person I know. I don't even know the language.

"Does everyone speak Welsh?" She interrupted Becky.

"Just about," said Peter, and "Not at all," said his father. "More people are learning it now, but most know English first and Welsh is a second language."

"There were two women on the train speaking it—at least I guess that's what it was."

"I'm learning it at school," said Becky. She was quite used to interruptions.

"You are?" Jen was surprised. "Why on earth—"

"Because it's taught in the state-run schools," said David, giving Peter a warning look, which Peter missed.

"It's stupid," he declared.

"You're learning it, too?"

He nodded. "Fat lot of good it'll do me."

David Morgan let out his breath crossly. "We have been over this countless times already. You go to school in Wales, you learn Welsh. You learn what everyone else does whether you see the point or not." The tension was even stronger. Jen could see the same stubbornness reflected on both David's and Peter's faces. They both had tempers and quick tongues and neither gave in gracefully. Her mother used to say they were too much alike not to argue, but then her mother had almost always been able to stop an argument between them. Now Peter's face was closed and angry, David's looked tired and older than she remembered.

"Well," she ventured in the uneasy silence, struggling to live up to her mother, "if learning Welsh teaches you how to say the names of towns, it has to be useful. I don't see where you put all the consonants."

Peter snorted but said nothing, and David smiled at her.

Becky was delighted to help Jen unpack. They were sharing one of the front bedrooms on the second floor. The view from their windows was the same Jen had seen when she'd gotten out of the taxi: the sea and the village and the great flat plain the train had skirted.

"Does it have a name?" Jen asked Becky. "Is it a huge field?"

"Behind Borth, you mean?" Becky shook her head. "That's the Borth Bog."

Jen stared out at the great dark void. She was too numb with weariness to question Becky further at the moment. She was also beginning to see what Peter had been hinting darkly at in the front hall. It was cold in the house; the wind seemed to find every crack around windows and doors, and the white net curtains in the bedroom stirred eerily. Chilly draughts gusted across the floor. Jen shivered involuntarily.

"Do you like it?" Becky asked, bouncing gently on Jen's bed. "What do you think?"

"I haven't seen much yet," Jen replied cautiously.

"I do. I like it," said Becky a little too firmly.

"Peter doesn't much, does he?"

"Right on the nose," agreed Peter, joining them. "I'd tell you why, but I expect you want to go to bed tonight!"

"It can't be *that* bad, Peter, really, or Dad wouldn't stay," said Jen, putting sweaters in a drawer, and blessing Aunt Beth for insisting on packing them.

Peter shrugged. "He's made up his mind to stay. I don't

think he even notices most of it, he's too busy. He's always working. But *I* notice and I don't like it one bit."

"But you didn't like it when we first got here," objected Becky. "You never tried to change your mind. It's different from home, but that's because it isn't home. It really isn't so bad."

"I'm glad to hear it!" Jen smiled at her sister. "But is it always this cold?"

"At least!" said Peter. "This house wasn't meant to be lived in year round, you know. They usually rent it out in the summer to people on vacation. I expect that's why we found it right away."

Jen sat down beside Becky. "Is this a summer resort?"

"In a manner of speaking. There's a beach out there and I think sometimes the sun comes out by mistake. But wait till you really see it to get excited. The town's one street wide and about two miles long with the ocean on one side and the great Borth Bog on the other—miles of one and acres of the other. I've never seen a place like it."

"It really is a bog, then."

"Oh, yes. You can sink in it. Maybe that isn't such a bad idea."

"Peter!" Becky sounded shocked, and Jen changed the subject quickly.

"How's Dad doing at the University."

"Who can tell? He usually spends his time there or shut in his study downstairs. I told you, he doesn't seem to notice very much, and he doesn't talk about work."

"Do you ask him?"

Peter shrugged.

Jen wasn't the least bit sorry to go off to bed with Becky at half-past eight as David insisted. But once the light in their room was out, she lay awake in the dark listening to the wind tear around the house.

"Jen?"

"Mmm."

"I'm really glad you're here," Becky whispered. "It'll be much nicer."

"I'm glad, too." At least I hope I am, she added to herself. Everything seemed unexpectedly complicated. It had been ever since their mother had been killed last December, and their family had seemed to come apart. She wasn't surprised to hear from Peter that David kept to himself; he'd done that for months before they'd come to Wales. Only in Amherst they'd still had Aunt Beth to fill in some of the gaps. It wasn't the same as having their own mother—Aunt Beth did her best to cope, but she'd never had children of her own and suddenly she was landed with three half-grown ones whose unhappiness and confusion she couldn't really fathom. But there was still school and there were friends and music lessons and Boy Scouts and all the usual activities to turn to.

But here David was all they had, and Jen felt rather bleak as she remembered Peter's words. She'd missed her family far more than she'd expected to once they'd gone. Her first semester at school hadn't been particularly successful. Even Aunt Beth had seen that. Everyone made allowances in the beginning: Jen had so many adjustments to make. But it didn't get better; it actually got worse, and she had finally admitted to herself she needed her father and Peter and Becky more than she needed home.

By November Aunt Beth was running out of patience, and when Jen had come down with 'flu and then a particularly violent cold, which sank her into depression and made her nearly impossible to live with, Aunt Beth had thrown in the towel. She wrote to her brother suggesting that his eldest daughter might like to be invited to Wales for Christmas vacation. And David had dutifully sent the invitation in one of his regular letters, those letters full of a determined cheerfulness and almost nothing else. They gave away very little. Jen realized what a sketchy preparation she'd had for Borth.

And for Peter. What in the world was wrong with him?

But she knew—he was every bit as miserable and bitter now as he had been before they'd come. At least Becky seemed to be her usual, cheerful self. Thank heaven for that! Jen wished suddenly and desperately that her mother was here and fell asleep, finally, wondering what it would be like if she were.

A cold, gray daylight filled the room when Jen woke, and Becky's bed was empty. The clock on the little night table said ten past ten, and everything in the room was unfamiliar: the shape of the windows, the white curtains, the cracks in the ceiling. Jen lay for a minute feeling depressed and unwelcome. Life at Bryn Celyn had started as usual this morning as if she weren't there. But that's silly, she told herself firmly, they're just letting me sleep because they knew I was tired.

Before she let herself go any further, she struggled upright to find the air beyond her bedclothes bitterly cold. She grimaced as her feet touched the icy floor and she dove for the pile of clothes she'd left out last night: jersey and jeans, her blue wool pullover and wool socks.

Bathroom's the door at the top of the stairs, she muttered, and remembered it was in two rooms—toilet and sink in a narrow little closet with a frosted glass window, tub and sink in the huge room next to it. The floor was a vast expanse of cold, pebbly linoleum and the bathtub stood on curved claw feet. When she turned on the hot water to wash her face, she was immediately enveloped in a cloud of steam, and the cold water could only have been a degree or two above ice. On her way out, Jen almost fell over a strange cylindrical object in the middle of the floor. It was about three feet high and balanced on little legs and she glared at it crossly.

"Damn," she said with feeling.

Peter and Becky were sprawled comfortably at the kitchen table surrounded by the usual Sunday morning debris of cereal boxes, jam jars, plates covered with toast crumbs, sticky knives, and mugs of milk and tea. An extra place had been set next to Becky, and Jen cheered up to find proof that she really was expected.

"Good morning!" Becky greeted her. "You must have really been asleep—you never even moved when I got up. Do you want some orange juice?"

Jen nodded. "Thank heaven it's warmer in here!"

Peter looked up from the book he was reading. "Noticed the cold, did you?" he said pleasantly.

"Isn't the heating on upstairs?"

"What heating?"

"But—" said Jen.

"Oh, there is some in the bathroom. You probably saw the paraffin heater? When Dad bought it, the man in the hardware shop told us it was the very newest model—you can even boil a kettle on the top if you need to."

"Paraffin heater?" said Jen blankly.

"Mmm. What we'd call a kerosene stove. You fill it with pink stuff, light the wick, and in ten minutes if you haven't blown up you have a room full of what they call 'pink warmth.'" Peter was gauging her reaction. "You have to be a little careful about asphyxiation, though, the man warned us."

"That's the heat?"

"That's it."

"But what about in the bedrooms?"

"Another tremendous advantage of that heater—you can move it from room to room, you see."

"Dad said we could get another one before Christmas," Becky broke in on Peter's relentless explanation. "And we really aren't in our bedrooms much except to go to bed."

"I can see why." Jen shivered involuntarily.

"Oh, you get used to it," Peter assured her. "At least that's what they *say*."

"What about the rest of the house, the downstairs?"

"The kitchen's nearly always warm because of the stove

and the hot water heater, and there's a gas fire in Dad's study and a coal fire in the lounge."

"*Very* efficient," said Peter, returning to his book.

Becky made a face at him which he didn't see. "You really do get used to it. It just means wearing more clothes," she said.

The kettle was boiling on the back of the gas stove, and Jen made herself a mug of instant coffee, half filling it with milk and sugar.

"Is there any toast?"

There were two slices, both stone cold. Jen sighed and said she'd make more, where was the toaster? But the toaster was a grill under the top of the stove, which Becky wasn't allowed to light and Peter claimed he didn't know how to, so Jen had to content herself with a couple of slices of bread and jam.

"Where's Dad?"

"He ate long ago," said Becky. "He's in his study."

"Working?"

"Grading papers."

"He hates being disturbed," warned Peter.

"This is ridiculous," said Jen looking around the kitchen. She felt a mixture of desperation and helplessness. This wasn't what she'd imagined, not at all.

"I've been saying that ever since we got to this awful place, but all *he* does is get furious."

"But what about meals? How do you manage?"

"Mrs. Davies," Becky said. "She lives next door and cleans and makes us supper, and dinner on weekends. She does cleaning for another professor down the way, too."

"Thank goodness for that! Is she nice?" Jen was relieved to find it wasn't quite as bad as she had, for a black moment, thought.

"Mmm. She is quite," Becky sounded a little cautious.

"She's a perfect witch," contradicted Peter.

"No, she isn't. Mr. Davies drives one of the buses, and

everyone calls him Hugh-the-Bus because there are so many other people named Davies, so you tell them apart by what they do, like Billy-Davies-Taxi. Hugh-the-Bus knows absolutely everyone and he tells me all about them when I go next door for lunch on school days."

Jen grinned with grudging admiration at her sister. Trust Becky to have stored away lots of information about people already. She always took great interest in whoever was around.

". . . and she has three children, but they're grown up now and only one's at home. Her daughters are married and one of them lives in Bow Street, which is very close. The other's gone to Birmingham, and Mrs. Davies says *she* can't see why anyone would want to live there. Gwilym's the one at home—he's still in school. You'll see Mrs. Davies when she comes to fix dinner."

"Well," said Jen, "what do you do on Sundays?"

"Homework," Peter said gloomily. "Try to keep warm. There isn't much else."

"I'll take you to get the newspapers," Becky volunteered. "You can see the shop."

"Don't get too excited," Peter advised.

"What about the dishes?"

"Leave them for Mrs. Davies."

Jen looked doubtful. "I don't think we should."

"We always do," said Peter irritably. "She gets paid for it anyway."

Becky shrugged. "It won't take long."

"Not me," said Peter, picking up his book. He paused at the door to say, "She'll expect us to do them every week now."

"No one will expect *you* to do anything," retorted Jen, flinging a handful of knives and forks into the dishpan.

Borth certainly was a peculiar-looking town. Jen had to agree with Peter. She'd never seen anything like it either. Becky paused in front of the house to point out the landmarks before they walked down to the shop, and Jen stared out over the cliff in fascination. Borth was, indeed, one street wide and about two miles long, shops and houses strung out on the street like beads on a cord. To the west was a wide margin of sandy beach and the cold-looking sheet of Cardigan Bay; to the east, the strange, desolate expanse of Borth Bog: dull patches of tan and wind-bitten green. She wondered if the town were there simply to show where the sea ended and the Bog began.

"And at the end is the Dovey River," Becky said, pointing. "You came along it in the train. The mountains are on the other side of it."

Today they were only a vague outline, lost in the gray, damp air. Jen began to realize just how far she was from Amherst. This was all outside her experience utterly. Wildness and isolation swept in over them on the salt-smelling wind.

"What're you thinking?" said Becky at last.

"I don't know. That it's awfully big and empty, I guess."

Becky nodded. "I felt that way, too, when we first came. I still do sometimes, and I don't think I'd like to stay here forever."

"But Dad never said you would."

"It would be a lot easier—" Becky hesitated.

"If what?" Jen prompted gently.

"Oh, if Dad and Peter didn't go at each other so much. Peter won't even try to get along. He just complains, and Dad gets really cross, then shuts himself up for hours and hours in his study, which doesn't help." She sighed.

"And what do *you* do?"

"Well, it's not so bad for me. I can go and visit Mrs. Davies, and Gwilym takes me for walks sometimes. He knows an awful lot about birds and plants and he doesn't mind if I go along when he goes looking for them. And there's school, too. I know a lot of people there."

"Does Peter? Know anyone, I mean?"

"Not that he ever talks about. He's as bad as Dad; he spends most of his time by himself reading."

"Peter?" said Jen in surprise. "That's new."

"I know, but he does."

Oh, help, thought Jen, what *is* happening? Back in Amherst, Peter had loads of friends, so had their parents. There were always extra people in the house and too many things to do. Peter had never been one for sitting still and reading; he hadn't been happy unless he was in the middle of some furious activity. And she could remember countless evenings when the living room of their house had been full of her father's colleagues deep in heated conversation. She wondered if Becky was as cheerful as she seemed. Her own thoughts were apprehensive.

The shop was at the bottom of the cliff road, a whitewashed building set on a crossroad and it announced with a sign over its door that it was both a shop and the Borth Post Office. Inside was a maze of little aisles between shelves piled high with the oddest assortment of stuff Jen had ever seen. Packages of biscuits and bins of apples and oranges stood next to piles of men's shirts and tennis shoes, jigsaw puzzles, flashlight batteries, paperback books, tins of soup, jars of jam and cases of milk bottles. Wellington boots, spades, and buckets hung from rope overhead, and in one corner was a little window covered with a grill that said "Closed" and gave the Post Office hours. How on earth do you find anything, Jen wondered, incredulous. But Becky had already sorted out the papers they wanted and was introducing her sister to Mr. Williams, the shopkeeper.

The shop was busy with people, half of whom were dressed somberly in what Jen guessed were church clothes: dark suits and coats, the women with hats and gloves on; the other half in jeans and jackets and old boots, rumpled-looking and chilly. Students, Becky told her when they were outside.

"There are lots of them in Borth. They rent the summer

cottages down by the railroad tracks or live in guest houses. There aren't very many dormitories at the University. Gwilym says they live in digs, but I'm not quite sure what that means."

"Sounds odd," Jen commented.

"Gwilym wants to go to the University himself when he finishes school, only he told me his mother doesn't see why he should."

Jen was shocked. "But she should *want* him to if he's smart enough."

"She says it just means three more years before he can get a job and earn some money. Hugh-the-Bus never went, neither did Gwilym's sisters."

"What does he want to do?"

"There's a place near here called the Plant Breeding Station."

"Plant Breeding Station?" Jen repeated. She felt a sense of unreality.

"It breeds plants."

"Are you serious?"

"Yes." Becky sounded a little impatient. "It's back in the hills, and there are a lot of botanists there who experiment with growing all kinds of crops, like clover and different kinds of grasses, to find out which are the best for feeding animals. Gwilym says crops discovered here are grown all over the world."

"And he wants to do that?"

"Mmm. But his mother thinks it's silly."

Mrs. Davies was in control of the kitchen by the time they got back. She was an angular woman with a sharp face and wiry gray hair, struggling out of a knot at the back of her head. She was scrubbing potatoes into submission at the sink.

"Hello," said Becky. "What's for dinner?"

"Roast, potatoes, and sprouts," said Mrs. Davies

shortly. She fixed Jen with pale blue eyes. "You'll be Jennifer then. I expect you can help out a bit now that you're here. Look after things once I've got them started, you can."

"Yes," said Jen, wondering what looking after things would involve. After all, this was her vacation.

"We did the dishes for you," Becky informed her, sitting on the edge of the table.

"So I noticed. Shouldn't think that brother of yours had much to do with it," she said tartly.

"He had homework." Becky covered for him.

"Shouldn't wonder," snorted Mrs. Davies. "I'll get the veg on"—it took Jen a moment to realize she meant "vegetables"—"then leave, if you don't mind. I've me daughter coming for dinner and your roast's in the oven. It's planned for one o'clock and all you need do is take it out when it's done." She dumped the potatoes, thoroughly subdued, into a pot of boiling water.

"Ah, Mrs. Davies. You've met Jen already. Good." David Morgan came in.

"Yes, Mr. Morgan. I was just saying that perhaps with your daughter here now I might be able to leave odds and ends to her if you don't mind."

David said he didn't see why not. "Dinner at one?"

"Yes, Mr. Morgan."

Jen's fate was sealed. She and Becky left Mrs. Davies to her inferno of boiling vegetables and followed David back into his study. That room at least looked more familiar, Jen found with relief; the same clutter of books and papers and notebooks and pencils she was used to in her father's study at home. Instead of a desk, he had covered what looked like a dining room table with his work and filled a small bookcase with volumes he'd brought from Amherst.

"Well," he said, as they all sat down. "Are you settled yet? Have you caught up with yourself? The time change is a bit hard to get used to."

Jen nodded. "It's funny to think how far I've come so quickly."

"I know, but you'll adjust. What's become of Peter? Did he go down to get the papers with you?"

"No," said Jen.

David frowned. "I don't know what's the matter with him for the life of me! He's been impossible since we got here. In fact, I've been hoping that with you around he might begin to show some sense again, but as it is, I can't talk to him without losing my temper completely."

Dinner was a determinedly cheerful meal. Peter turned up in time. Jen and Becky had got the roast out and the vegetables and potatoes off the stove just when they were supposed to, but the whole dinner was overdone. The sprouts were mushy, the potatoes fell apart, and the meat was leather-brown clear through. Jen was on the verge of apologizing when she realized that she was the only one who'd noticed. Everyone else ate without comment.

By the time the dishes had been cleared away, rain had closed like curtains across the windows, making it impossible to go out. David made up a fire in the room across from his study, which Becky called the lounge, and left his three children there to amuse themselves. Jen disliked the room on sight —it was a dreadful jumble of colors and patterns and ghastly furniture. The walls were papered in ships-and-harbors of green and blue, the carpet on the floor was wall-to-wall flowers of orange, brown, and black, and the sofa and two chairs were slipcovered in green and yellow. Over the green-tiled fireplace was an impressive collection of china horses and a large ashtray that said "Isle of Man" on it in gold. A large television set, an imitation wood coffee table, and one floor lamp completed the decor, leaving Jen breathless.

Becky followed her gaze around the improbable room. "It's the way they do things," she said with a giggle. "You should see Mrs. Davies's lounge."

"I don't think I'm ready."

"There's a fire, though." Becky settled down with her school books in front of it and Peter sank into one of the armchairs to read. Jen sat uneasily in a corner of the sofa and set herself to writing Aunt Beth and Uncle Ted the letter she'd promised. But from time to time she couldn't help looking up to convince herself the room really did look like that.

2

Taliesin

I F B O R T H W A S N ' T what Jen had imagined, her arrival wasn't exactly what Peter had hoped for either. He'd been foolish enough to expect everything to change when she came. She would, of course, be horrified at what their father had brought them to: a cold, bleak, comfortless country. Even David would have to see it then and he'd have to admit he was wrong to make them stay. Then they could all go home together. Peter had been counting on it, but it wasn't happening.

It was all very well for Jen, of course. She could go home after Christmas, Peter thought bitterly, watching her over the top of his book. She didn't have to stick it out for months and months. He stared drearily out the window at the rain. You wouldn't have thought there was that much water in the sky, but it came endlessly; he couldn't remember a day without some rain in it. He wished he could have swapped places with Jen—gone home while she came here, but *he* didn't have any choice.

No one understood how lonely and frustrated he was. Becky had already found friends of her own, and David was preoccupied with work. Peter hadn't made any friends at all. Many of the boys at school went straight home afterward to work in their fathers' shops or on their farms, and the ones who didn't all played games he didn't know, like cricket which looked silly, or more often something they called football that wasn't football at all. Peter stayed aloof and continued to feel strange.

And there was nowhere to go, nowhere at all. The house, Bryn Celyn, was cold and unwelcoming. No one was waiting there for him after school to give him a snack and hear how his day had been. Like as not Becky would be off at Mrs. Davies's or down in the village with girls her own age, and David never got back until suppertime. Then he shut himself away immediately afterward until time for Peter and Becky to go to bed.

If Peter didn't return to Bryn Celyn after school, he had the dismal choice of either wandering the sodden countryside, going nowhere in particular, or of hanging about the local shops, none of which amounted to anything.

School was no better, he reflected gloomily. Those subjects he knew weren't taught the way he was used to, and there were endless lessons in handwriting and dictation. They did what they called "maths" and read bits of Shakespeare and learned British history, which was full of kings and queens with the same names and hundreds of battles whose dates had to be learned by heart. And worst of all, they were taught Welsh. Peter simply could not get his father to see what a horrible waste of time it was for him to learn a language that meant absolutely nothing to anyone outside of one very tiny country. David only got cross and said that Peter and Becky were in the county schools in Borth, and for the year they were here they would participate in those schools and learn as much from them as possible. Peter hated it, every minute.

Often homesickness came upon him in great black, devouring waves, making him wretched, and he would hate everything and everyone: the bleak, wet country, the desolate village strung out along its one road, the cold sea, the people

who ignored him, the boys who played their own games without him, Becky because she was adjusting, Jen for being home
in Amherst, his mother for having died and let this happen,
and most of all his father, who had brought them to this place
and condemned them to a whole year of life in it.

Becky kept telling Peter it would get easier for him, but
it didn't because Peter wouldn't let it. He had to hang on to his
hardness and hate or he couldn't survive. Without the hate,
there were only the intolerable homesickness and the desperate longing for his mother. These hurt far too much for him
to bear alone.

Midway through the afternoon, Peter retreated from the
lounge, leaving it to the two girls, and holed up in his own little
room off the kitchen. He had, in all the world right now, one
small comfort: a secret that he had kept from everyone so
far. He had found it only about two weeks ago and he was
still a bit scared of it, unsure of what it was doing, but it fascinated and attracted him and he didn't like to be too long
without it.

In the top drawer of his bureau, hidden between his two
good shirts, as safe a place as any, he had decided, because he
never wore them, he kept what he called the Key. He called it
that because that's what it looked most like to him and he
didn't really know what it was.

Three Saturdays ago—the usual leaden, overcast sort of
day—Peter had found himself on his own. Becky had disappeared after breakfast and David was buried under stacks of
first year essays in the study. Peter was feeling restless, so he
pulled on his jacket and went out, down to the point of land
where the War Memorial stood, beyond the houses on the
Morgans' dead-end street. He sat for a while, aimlessly throwing pebbles over the cliff at the gray roughness of Cardigan
Bay. Finally he turned his collar up against the chilly wind,
and thrusting his hands in his pockets because he'd forgotten
gloves, he started out along the overgrown path that ran south

along the sea rim toward the town of Aberystwyth. He had no special destination in mind, no thought of walking to Aber, as Aberystwyth was called, which was seven miles over rough country. He just walked, shoulders hunched. He found he had to concentrate on where he put his feet. Under the rank grasses and dead bracken lay stones and holes and unexpected roots, and there were brambles that tore at his trousers. He had to be alert just to stay upright.

Once Peter had turned his back on Borth and gone around a bend in the path, he might have been on the edge of the world. To his left was a slope of grass, bracken, and gorse, to his right, the cliff with the sea at the bottom.

There is nothing, Peter thought a little desperately, nothing. A handful of gulls drifted past on the wind, their cries underlining the loneliness. The dampness blew up around him. He caught his foot under a tough, knotted gorse root and tripped. "Damn!" he said aloud and felt suddenly relieved. His father did not approve of swearing one bit. "Damn, damn, damn!" shouted Peter into the wind with conviction. It made him feel very much better. "I don't care," he called to the gulls. "I don't care *what* you think, dumb birds! You can go anywhere you want, but I'm stuck here. Don't you know how much better America is?" He stuck his tongue out at them.

Whenever he stopped walking, the wind cut through his jacket and made him shiver, so he kept on. No point in going back until he'd used up a good part of the day. Then he came over a rise and found himself looking down into a perfect little cove. A narrow valley, worn by a stream, lay below. On the near side was a small whitewashed house; on the far side, across a wooden footbridge, a stone hut with an overturned boat in the doorway. And spread like a yellow fan lay a triangle of sandy beach down which the stream ran to the ocean. He stood staring at it for a long moment it was so unexpected, and for just an instant Peter forgot how much he disliked the world. He was drawn to the cottage. But it was dark and empty, the door padlocked. No smoke wisped from its chimney; its curtains were drawn. Peter tried, but he couldn't find a crack to peer in. Someone must live here, though, Peter reasoned, the track down the valley by the stream looked well-used and he could see that the boat was in good repair.

He crossed the footbridge and walked out on the sand, which gave unpleasantly under his feet and got into his shoes. Toward the water it was firmer and damp. The tide had left a line of rubbery brown seaweed, bits of waterlogged wood, and odds and ends like light bulbs and disintegrating milk cartons. Peter looked without much interest. Beyond the sand, at the far edge of the cove, a tumble of rock stretched out into the waves: great chunks of stone, dropped at random from the cliff, Peter thought at first. They were bearded with green weed and crusted with barnacles, limpets, and snails. Peter climbed among them and gradually something peculiar about the rocks filtered through his mind. They hadn't been dropped at random at all: they ran out into the sea in a straight line. They must be a neglected causeway or a breakwater. Someone had deliberately piled them here, and in spite of himself, Peter felt a flicker of curiosity. Why? Had it been the man from the cottage? It seemed a strange place to go to so much trouble.

He chose a dry stone on the top of the breakwater and sat down. His interest was gone, he squelched it relentlessly. How long he stayed there he didn't afterward know, but when he began to feel chilled through, he got up and clambered gingerly out onto the rocks toward the sea. Between the dark, slimy stones were cracks and pools, dark places inhabited by heaven knew what ugly creatures. But out among the stones at the end that the sea was beginning to reclaim, Peter caught sight of a small dark object between two rocks. It was too regular in shape to be a pebble, and something made him look at it twice. It wasn't wood. Curious, Peter stooped and reached. It was cold and hard to the touch and wedged in securely. It was metal of some sort. He tugged and almost lost his balance, grew determined and pulled hard. With a sudden gritty, scraping sound, like fingernails being dragged across a blackboard, the thing came free in his hand.

Peter looked at it, frowning fiercely. He had no idea what it was, but he was sure it was old. It was shaped like a capital letter Y, about four inches across. Each arm of the Y was a hollow, six-sided shaft, and each had a slightly different diameter. There was a hole through it where the three arms came together, and it reminded Peter of an old-fashioned roller skate key. It was blackened and scratched, but not broken. He liked the feel of it. His fingers seemed to know its shape and curl around it by themselves. He crouched, looking at it, until a wave broke on the rock, splashing his shoes. Then he retreated along the causeway, holding the object firmly. He took it back to Bryn Celyn safely in his pocket.

A few days later, he had been sitting at the base of the War Memorial, where he came from time to time, with the Key again in his pocket, his right hand cupped around it. Without warning, he felt it begin to hum, a peculiar, tingling sensation like his hand falling asleep, which was what he had thought at first. But the humming had gotten stronger and a song had come to him, sweet and piercing, out of the air, nothing he could describe afterwards.

There had been a sudden, brilliant glimpse of something —sun on water, the sound of voices chanting—and Peter had pulled his hand out of his pocket as if he'd been stung, his heart thumping wildly. He was more frightened than he wanted to admit. Perhaps he was truly going crazy in this place. But a few days later, when it happened the second time—he was alone in the kitchen—he had managed to hang on a little longer. Yes, it *was* water, and the sun *was* shining. The water was all around—there was an island and there were boys on it. They were chanting . . .

Then Peter lost his nerve and put the Key down.

Now, today, on this rainy Sunday, he deliberately took it out of his drawer and sat on his bed, gripping it tightly, and waited. This time he'd find out more. The Key was warm in his hand, and after a few minutes he could feel it begin to vibrate almost imperceptibly with sound. He hung on and felt the room slip away from him, its walls melting into moving fragments of light: bright, dancing flecks that dazzled. Voices rose and fell in Welsh cadence, weaving together in patterns of rhythm that hung on the air.

Sunlight glistened on the surface of a huge lake. Peter saw it reflected in splinters on a sloping roof, that of a rough-hewn, open-sided shelter. Underlying the voices was the gentle sound of wavelets against the island's shores. He knew it was an island, for he could see bright water on all sides. The boys beneath the shelter were repeating phrases over and over in the summer afternoon, learning them by heart. *Triads*. The unfamiliar word came at once to Peter. He knew they were groups of three things: The Three Great Herdsmen; The Three Fearless Men; The Three Futile Battles. He felt the intensity of the sun and lake wind. The strange words conjured images in his mind, images the boys were being taught to remember. Peter was there, he saw it all, but no one took any notice of him. He seemed to be invisible.

Abruptly it all faded, the light and the lake, the island, the voices. Peter blinked at the window streaming with rain beside his bed. The Key was warm under his fingers, but it lay quite still. At least this time he had held onto it, and though he was bewildered and uncertain, he knew it hadn't hurt him in any way. But he couldn't tell anyone about it, he wouldn't know how. And why should he? They all had their own concerns. He would keep his secret. He put the Key carefully back in its hiding place.

"Here," said David. "You have to turn on the gas first, like that, then take a match and stick it in that hole." There was a popping noise, a whoosh, then a steady, vigorous roar that sounded like a blowtorch. "Nothing to it."

"Electricity is so much simpler," said Jen doubtfully.

"Oh, come now. You've been a Girl Scout, you know how to light fires. This isn't much different once you get the hang of it."

"Just don't singe your eyebrows," Peter said helpfully.

"You should talk," Becky chided. "You won't even try."

"I'm too young to die," her brother retorted.

David withdrew behind his morning paper and left them to bicker over the grill where the bread was toasted. "Just so long as I get some toast before I have to go."

Becky sawed chunks off a loaf of bread, while Jen made herself some coffee and watched the toast. It browned very fast under the gas, and she had only turned around to put milk in her mug when Becky yelled, "Smoke!"

The first two pieces were charred to crisps and had to be discarded, but at last Jen had a plateful, and they all sat down together.

"I still don't see why you have to go to the University to-day, even if it is Monday," said Becky. "It's Christmas vacation for everybody else. There won't be anyone to teach, will there?"

"Doesn't matter. I have lectures to work on, tests to grade, and a paper to write." David smiled at her. "You can manage on your own this week now that Jen's here, and Mrs. Davies is just next door if you need anything. You have a good time and I'll see you at supper."

"What do you want to do," Becky asked, when the beds were made and the dishes washed. "You should choose, Jen."

"We could go explore Borth, I guess. I haven't really seen it yet."

"Are you sure you're ready for it?" said Peter dryly. "It's a thrill."

"Well, you don't have to come," Becky exclaimed.

"Oh, let's have a good fight!" said Jen. "Nothing like it to begin Christmas vacation."

In the end they all went, for company and lack of anything better to do. The village began at Mr. Williams's shop and ran straight north. As Jen commented, there wasn't much chance of getting lost in Borth.

"If you did," Peter pointed out, "it would be fatal—you'd either drown or sink into the Bog."

The village wasn't very prepossessing, even Becky had to admit. The houses lining the street looked old and slightly decayed, their plaster flaking, stucco cracked, paint chipped by the rough salt wind and the sand that came stinging off the beach with it. More than half the buildings were blank and empty, shut up for the winter, looking derelict.

"It does seem kind of bleak," ventured Jen, after they'd been walking ten minutes.

"It wasn't quite this awful at the end of August," said Peter. "At least there were a few more people around and all the shops were open, but on its best days it isn't beautiful."

"What on earth do people *do* out here?"

"Run guest houses in the summer and keep students in the winter or have shops. And there are the ones like Hugh-the-Bus and Mr. Williams who work at regular jobs all year. Lots of professors from the University live out here, too, like Dad, and go into Aber every day," explained Becky. "Gwilym says he likes it better here in the winter when there aren't so many people. He says there are more birds."

Peter shook his head mournfully. "The Bog has gotten to him. It can be quite serious—Bog Fever. No cure."

Jen laughed. *That* sounded more like Peter. He seemed to have relaxed a bit.

Stuck in among the boarded-up buildings were shops that were still open and busy this morning. Jen looked in at each one with interest. There didn't seem to be any supermarket in Borth, just lots of little stores that each sold one kind of thing:

meat, or fruit and vegetables, or baked goods. They got sucked into a bakery by the lovely warm, sweet smell, as they stood looking at the cakes and pies in its window. Jen bought them each an eclair and they walked on, eating them and shamelessly licking their fingers.

Along the ocean, the houses suddenly ended and there was a great, gray cement sea wall instead, too high to see over from the road. On the right Becky pointed out the station where Jen had arrived. Was it really only two days ago? It hardly seemed possible. She remembered Aunt Beth saying, "It won't be anything like what you're used to, dear. I don't think there's much there." And Jen had answered confidently, "Dad and Becky and Peter will be there, and it'll be fun to live by the sea."

"Hey," Becky nudged her. "What are you thinking about?"

"Probably that in another three weeks she'll be on her way home again," said Peter, gloomy again.

"No," said Jen. "Just thinking how different from Amherst it is."

Peter snorted. "That's the kind of remark that always gets me into trouble!"

"Come on," Becky said, "let's go up on the sea wall."

There were steps to go up and a broad flat walk on top. On the other side was the sand beach. In spite of Peter's gloom, Jen was excited to be so close to the ocean. They lived too far from it at home to go often, but she had always loved it.

The steel-gray sea washed up and down the beach; the waves chipped white at the edges where they met the sand. Becky turned around to show Jen where their house was on the cliff behind them, but Peter refused to stop because it was too cold, so after a moment they followed him. Becky was too busy telling Jen about people and houses to notice when Peter did stop short, and she ran up his heels, Jen right in back.

"Do watch out," said Peter irritably, catching his balance. "You ought to say when you're going to stop."

"I didn't know I was. There's one of your friends, isn't it?" He pointed down the beach to a thin solitary figure wandering slowly toward them along the tide line.

"It's Gwilym," said Becky. "I wonder what he's been out looking for. Hey!" She waved her arms at him. "Hey, Gwilym!"

The figure turned in their direction and continued moving slowly.

"Maybe he'll ignore us," suggested Peter half-hopefully.

"What's the matter with him?" Jen asked in surprise.

"Nothing," said Becky flatly. "He just isn't interested in the things Peter likes, that's all. He's perfectly nice once you get to know him, but I think he's a bit shy." She jumped off the wall and ran over to Gwilym.

Jen and Peter followed slowly. Jen had heard too much from Becky about Gwilym not to be curious. He greeted Becky, glanced apprehensively at her brother and sister, and turned to point at something up the beach the way he'd come.

"There's a flock of ducks out there, Gwilym says. Can you see them? They're down near Ynyslas," Becky informed them as they came up. "He says they're scoters."

Oh, dear, thought Jen. Her first impression was of a tall, awkward boy, thin and brown-haired, wearing glasses. He looked uncomfortably like his mother. Gwilym blushed unbecomingly at Becky's excitement. "Scoters are really very common here," he said, not looking at Jen. There was a painful silence then he added, "They winter here every year."

"This is my sister, Jen," Becky said quickly.

Gwilym nodded. "Mum said you'd come Saturday. Just for the holidays, she said."

"Three weeks," said Jen, wondering what else Mrs. Davies had said.

"What did you see besides scoters?" Becky demanded.

Gwilym looked relieved; he was on safe ground. "Teal, widgeon, scaup, and a couple of pintails, mostly. All common this time of year." He managed to look straight at Jen this time. "It's good birding up at the estuary. Are you interested?"

"I'm afraid I really don't know anything about birds," she admitted.

"Oh." He was clearly disappointed. "People who aren't interested in natural history generally find Borth rather isolated."

"Yes, they do," declared Peter.

"Have you lived here always?" inquired Jen politely, with a frown at Peter.

"Yes." He put a full stop on it, and Jen began to search for something else she could ask, but then he went on. "I like it really. I like it this way, but in the season it gets too crowded."

Jen looked around at the vast empty sands and tried to imagine Borth crowded without much success: bodies stretched out on the sand, children building sandcastles, people swimming, eating ice cream, jostling on the sea wall. She shivered as the raw December wind gusted around them, and they began to move along the beach toward the cliff as if by mutual consent.

"After Bank Holiday in May or June all the rooms in town are booked solid, and the caravan parks south of here are full. It isn't much fun then."

"I should think it would be more cheerful," observed Jen.

Gwilym shrugged unenthusiastically. "Depends on what you like, I suppose. It's nicer without strangers in the house, too."

"Strangers? In your house?"

"I told you," said Becky. "Mrs. Davies takes in guests during the summer."

"Is it a hotel?"

"Just like yours," replied Gwilym. "A bit bigger perhaps. We've got three spare bedrooms with Susan and Sheila gone. Mum does your housekeeping because she hasn't anyone to look after at home this winter. She had a University student last year."

"It must be awful to have strange people staying in your house," said Peter.

"You get used to it. Mum's always done it. Her mum used to do it in Shrewsbury before. Lots of people around here do bed and breakfast in summer. Mum says it more than pays for itself, and it doesn't cost the trippers near as much as staying in a hotel would do."

"I would *hate* it," Peter declared.

"I don't know," said Becky thoughtfully. "It would be fun seeing who came. I don't think I'd mind."

"But suppose you don't like them? What if they leave a mess, or make lots of noise, or stay out late at night?" Jen could see all kinds of problems.

"You risk it," Gwilym answered, sounding mildly surprised that the Morgans considered bed-and-breakfast such a strange business. "Usually they're not bad—I hardly ever see them. Dad and I keep to the kitchen mostly, and guests have their bedrooms and the lounge for meals and like that. Don't you have bed-and-breakfast in America?"

"No way," said Peter.

"We have hotels and guest houses and motels," Jen amplified, "but I've never paid to stay in someone else's house."

Gwilym nodded wisely. He had opened up considerably and even seemed to be enjoying the conversation. "Dad says there are some motels in England and Scotland, but I've never stayed in one. They're very dear. Mind you, not all bed-and-breakfasts are very nice, but Mum keeps a good one and does a nice fried breakfast. Of course, last year—" They were all watching him with great interest. "Last year we did have a couple that left without Mum seeing them. But that's only happened the once to us."

"You mean they left without paying?" Becky asked.

"They did. They said they would stop the weekend till Monday morning, see. Then Sunday night we heard them come in—Dad said after it must just have been the man, but he made enough noise for two. When they didn't come down to breakfast in the morning, Mum went up to knock—she only serves until nine so she won't have to spend the morning over it—and the door was latched from the inside, see, and no one answered. Dad didn't get an answer either, speaking through the door, so I had to climb up the outside by the drain. The window was wide open, and there hadn't been anyone in the beds at all and the place was cleaned out. My mum was that mad, but Dad said they must have been truly hard up, not able to pay. We never did see them again, those two."

"But that's awful," exclaimed Becky in shocked tones. "What did your mother do?"

"Wasn't a thing she could do—gone is gone. Dad was sure they hadn't signed their proper names in our book. That's the risk of it, he says, but he took the latches off the insides of all the doors."

They absorbed this story of petty crime in silence, stopping together outside Mr. Williams's shop.

"Are you going up for lunch?" Jen inquired, avoiding Peter's eye.

"Well—" Gwilym hesitated. "I've to do some errands for Mum."

"Come by for tea," offered Becky promptly.

Gwilym glanced at Jen uncertainly.

"Sure," she said.

Gwilym smiled suddenly and Jen smiled back, glad to see his face lose some of its angularity.

"What did you do that for?" Peter demanded, as they started back up the hill.

"Don't be unpleasant," Jen said. "Just because you're antisocial, Becky and I needn't be. Besides, he may not even come, he didn't say he would."

But he did. Just after four he appeared at the kitchen door looking anxious. Becky pulled him in at once and made him take off his jacket. They'd kept the kitchen shut off from the rest of the house all afternoon, and it was quite cozy.

"Mum'll be in soon to start your dinner."

Jen set her teeth and lit the gas under the kettle.

"I told Jen you'd taken me walking with you," said Becky, piling biscuits on a plate. "We even went on the Bog once."

"His mistake was bringing you back again," remarked Peter.

"Peter!" said Jen sharply.

"I was just thinking," said Peter, sounding defensive, "that it would be a great opportunity to get rid of someone you didn't like. Slowly she sank into the trackless ooze, her cries growing fainter and fainter, lost in the emptiness."

"Beast," said Becky cheerfully. "You're wrong—Gwilym does like me in the first place. In the second, the Bog isn't trackless because we've been right across it; and in the third, someone would be bound to hear you if you yelled. Besides there are cattle grazing on it and they don't sink."

"Not much of a bog then, I must say."

"Oh, but it is." Gwilym protested seriously. "There are all kinds of rare plants on it, and scientists have found pollen from prehistoric ones in the peat. It's very old, you know. It's been called Cors Fochno for so long people have even forgotten what the name means."

"But if it's any kind of a bog why don't things sink into it, like in quicksand?" Peter persisted.

"They do, on parts of it. Every now and again someone loses a cow. But it's safe if you know where to walk."

"Unlimited possibilities." Peter grinned ghoulishly.

"What a morbid conversation!" Jen said. "I'd rather think of the prehistoric pollen!"

"It really is scientifically interesting," said Gwilym stiffly.

"No, I mean it," Jen assured him. "It's just that I don't know anything about birds or plants. But it would be fun to go out on the Bog. Would you take us sometime?"

He looked at her suspiciously, the steam from his tea fogging his spectacles mysteriously. "It's best early in the morning."

"How early?"

"Six o'clock or so."

Peter groaned. "You are *mad,*" he said. "Why are plants any better at six in the morning than at eleven?"

"It's birds at six."

Peter was about to make a sarcastic reply when Mrs. Davies opened the back door, letting in a blast of cold air.

"Oh, there you are," she said, seeing Gwilym. "I expected you'd be out wandering on them dunes."

"We met him this morning and asked him to tea," Becky explained.

"Much better, too." Mrs. Davies nodded in approval. "Spending time with kids your own age than out all day by yourself with them binoculars. Just what I've been telling you."

Gwilym looked dreadfully uncomfortable. He appeared to have taken an unusual interest in the arrangement of empty mugs on the table, and Jen sympathized silently. To have a mother like Mrs. Davies—but, no, it didn't do to think too much about mothers.

"Well, you can all lend a hand clearing up, so I can get your meal started."

When David came home at six, he found pots on the stove bubbling quietly and his three children sitting peacefully around the kitchen table reading. Mrs. Davies and Gwilym had gone home.

"Good day?"

"Mmm," said Jen, not looking up from her book. She'd

found a battered guide to Mid-Wales on a shelf in the lounge and was reading the part about Borth and Aberystwyth.

"We met Gwilym," said Becky. "Down on the beach. He told us about having tourists stay in their house."

"What's supper?"

"Well, you know it has to be either boiled or fried." Peter closed his book. "Boiled tonight."

David gave him an irritated glance.

"It certainly is a peculiar-looking area," Jen remarked hastily. "I mean all this flat land. The rest of Cardigan seems to be mountains."

"They call them hills here," corrected David with a smile. "You find anything interesting?"

"I do wonder why they built a town here." Jen showed her father a picture of Borth taken from their cliff top. "It isn't a very comfortable sort of place with the sea on one side and the Bog on the other."

"The beach," explained David briefly. "Good place for tourists. It isn't a very old town, but there's a lot of interest here."

Peter raised his eyebrows but kept still, to Jen's relief.

"Gwilym says he'll take us all out on the Bog," said Becky.

"That should be fascinating."

"I'm sure he'd take you, too."

Ruefully David shook his head. "I've got far too much work to do right now to go on expeditions. But you should be all right with Gwilym. He knows the country well, I understand. Is dinner ready?"

Jen glanced at her watch. "Oh, help! It should have been off the stove ten minutes ago!"

After a frantic scramble they all sat down to another overdone meal. Then Jen, Peter, and Becky sat on and played Hearts until Becky's bedtime.

"I don't see why I should have to go to bed earlier than anyone else during the holidays," she protested.

"The youngest person always goes to bed first—that's the rule," Peter told her callously. "Then you can get up first in the morning."

"Thank you very much!" retorted Becky. "It's a dumb rule!"

"They usually are," Peter replied.

When Becky had gone, Jen got out her book again. Peter sat watching her until she felt slightly uneasy. "Well?" she said at last, looking up.

"Can we talk?" he asked, his voice tense.

Jen wasn't at all sure she wanted to, but she nodded. "About what?"

"You know. This place."

"It doesn't seem too bad to me actually," she began cautiously.

"Oh, Jen!" Peter was agonized. "It's awful! It's a hole. Don't try to be cheerful about it."

Jen sighed. "Look, Peter, I know you didn't want to come. Everybody knew it. But Dad decided and he couldn't just have left you behind."

"He left you."

"That's different."

"Why?" he demanded. "I could have stayed with Aunt Beth and Uncle Ted, too."

"Then Becky would have been by herself." A vague, uncomfortable memory stirred in the back of Jen's mind, part of a conversation between her father and Aunt Beth she had overheard. Aunt Beth was saying, "Well, I really think Jennifer will be fine. After all she is grown-up and sensible. But, David, I wouldn't know where to begin with Peter. He needs a firm hand obviously, and Ted is so easygoing. Peter needs his father." David had answered, "All right, you needn't worry about Peter. I'll manage. I'm very grateful to you for offering to keep Jen. You're probably right about her school." But Jen couldn't very well tell Peter Aunt Beth hadn't wanted the responsibility for him.

". . . you know Becky," Peter was saying. "She'd be perfectly all right on her own. She's already got lots of friends."

"Haven't you got any?"

Peter gave an unhappy laugh. "Not likely. They're all too busy with themselves to care about me."

"Have you tried?" Before he could answer she went on, "I don't see why you go on fighting it, Peter. Now that you're actually here, there isn't much you can do, it seems to me, except give in and make the best of it."

"*Best* of it!" Peter exclaimed heatedly. "You don't know what you're talking about! Maybe it looks all right to you—you're only visiting and you can go home in three weeks and forget all the horrible parts. But just for a minute, look at it the way *I* have to—a dead-end town, most of it shut up tight, crumbling away. No decent stores, not even a movie. The closest one's in Aberystwyth and we hardly ever go there. Aberystwyth isn't much either, but after you've been in Borth for a while it doesn't look so bad! It rains all the time and it's cold—you can't even get warm indoors."

"What do you do all the time then?" asked Jen, a little shaken by the intensity of this outburst.

Peter glanced at her quickly, then away again. "Not much. Read, or go for walks by myself when it's dry enough."

It was hard for Jen to picture her popular, active younger brother wandering around alone or sitting still long enough to read a book. He'd always been the center of activity in Amherst, surrounded by friends his own age, constantly in motion. They were silent for a while, each thinking.

At last Peter said, "I was sure when we got here and saw the house and the town that Dad would come around. He'd have to understand we couldn't be expected to live here for a whole year in a place without heat in the middle of nowhere. But all he said was that he had a commitment and he didn't see why we couldn't manage perfectly well. And every time I open my mouth I get the 'Of-course-it's-different-but-we-all-have-to-be-willing-to-adjust' speech. You've heard it. He hasn't listened to anything anyone's said to him since—since Mom died."

"That's not fair," Jen protested. "It isn't easy for him either."

"But he's grown-up. He's responsible for us," countered Peter. "He's just made it harder, dumping us here." He pushed his hand through his coppery hair, making it stand on end, as he always did when he was upset or miserable. "I thought maybe—" He paused.

"What?" Jen thought she knew what was coming.

"Maybe you could talk to him for me. Tell him I can't stay."

"How? He won't send you back by yourself, I know he won't, and he's not going to leave in the middle of the year. I think you're just going to have to make up your mind to stick it out, Peter. It's only another six months."

"Six months!" he said bitterly. "And you can go home in three weeks."

Jen was growing impatient. "Grow up a little, Peter! If he won't listen to you, Dad's not going to listen to me, either. I'll just make him mad at me and that won't do anyone any good."

"Then you won't try?"

"I don't see how I can," she snapped.

"All right, then." Peter's face hardened, became impassive. "Do what you want, but don't count on me for anything." And with that he closed himself off. He might as well have gotten up and left the room, and she could only stare at him in irritated frustration. They said no more to each other, but Peter went off to bed shortly, saying a stiff good-night.

Well, honestly! Jen thought to herself after his door closed. No one can be as difficult as Peter. She was baffled by Peter's complete refusal to accept a situation he must have realized he couldn't possibly change. All he did was to make everyone cross and unhappy. Jen was glad Becky seemed to have decided to stay clear of the arguments, but then she hated family disputes. It was no good trying to stay up any longer, Jen decided, and turned off the kitchen light. There goes our good day.

It hadn't worked. It wasn't fair. Peter lay awake glaring into the dark, long after he heard his father go upstairs. There was silence in Bryn Celyn, and outside the never-ending noises of wind and surf. So he'd spent the whole day being cooperative —really trying to be pleasant—and it had gotten him nowhere. And he'd come to bed angry without even brushing his teeth: his mouth tasted awful.

He had no idea how long he'd lain there before he was aware of a sound other than those of sea and wind—minutes? Hours? He was suddenly alert, every muscle taut, ready. Ready for what? He waited. The new sound seemed not to come to him from outside, but rather from within himself, and he'd heard or felt it before.

Not at all sure he wanted to, he got cautiously out of bed and tiptoed across to his bureau. The Key lay warm and hard where he had left it among his shirts, and he took it in his hand, looking at it intently. It was no more than a dark shape against his white fingers.

The humming spread around him, growing deeper, fuller, and again he felt the room slide out from under him. The darkness wavered and faded and the sun was warm and gold, afternoon sun. Woodsmoke spiced the air and somewhere among the reeds on the lakeshore a moorhen called "curruc, curruc" in alarm. Peter recognized the island and the group of boys, all about his own age. But this time they stood in an orderly semicircle on top of a small hill, facing a round wooden hut. They were bareheaded, barefoot, wearing loose, bright-colored tunics that reached to their knees and were caught at the waist with belts of tanned leather. They were quiet, their faces expectant and a little apprehensive. All around, the waters of the lake lay still, reflecting the autumn sky, the forests beyond flushed faintly with color.

Near the doorway of the hut stood a tall, bearded man, his lined, timeless face quiet, his eyes dark and unseeing, quite blind.

Although Peter saw everything as if he were standing on the hill himself, he had no place there. He could only watch unseen without taking part.

There was movement in the hut, and the deerskin that hung across the opening was pushed back. Into the light and air stepped a tall, black-haired woman. Taller even than the blind man, she was slim and proud, her head high. She wore a long, loose-fitting robe of fine woven stuff that shimmered first blue, like the dome of sky, then the green of new grass, then the firey gold of gorsebloom. But it wasn't the gown that held Peter's eyes, it was her face. Such a face that it made him unable to look away, even had he wanted. It was perfect and complete; she was the most beautiful woman he had ever seen, beautiful in a way that frightened him even as he was drawn to her. Without taking his eyes from the woman, Peter knew that all the boys were staring as he was. If none of them saw her again, ever, they would not forget. Without hearing her name, Peter knew it. She was Caridwen.

At her side stood a sturdy, fair-skinned young man whose quizzical blue eyes studied each boy in turn, looking for something. A faint smile touched his mouth. He did not see Peter.

The blind man spoke without moving from his place by the door.

"This is the hour at which one of you will be chosen to go from here with the Bard, Aneirin. He who is chosen is he who has learned from this place all it can teach; but his learning will only have begun. With Aneirin as companion and guide, his thoughts will be shaped by wandering the world until he, too, can be called 'Bard.' From among you there is one who is ready for such a beginning."

Only one of the handful. They would have cast sidelong glances at each other if they could have looked away from the eyes of Caridwen, eyes that seemed to see them all without looking at any one of them.

Slowly the old man called each boy's name, pausing after each.

"Gwyn."

Silence.

"Elvan."

Silence.

"Huw."

Silence.

"Owain."

Silence.

"Gwion."

At this name Caridwen smiled a distant, triumphant smile and held out her hand. The boy who must be Gwion could not but step forward. That it was he whom she had chosen, there could be no question. The blind man called no more names, he too knew.

In Caridwen's outstretched hand was a silver tuning key, a harp key that shone in the light, and she said, "You are Gwion no longer. Henceforth you shall be Taliesin." Her voice filled the waiting air. It reached the listeners from within, it was felt rather than heard.

The island, lake, and sky spun together in a dizzying spiral, the wind rose over the song of the Key in Peter's ears, and he was a perfectly ordinary boy standing shivering in his flannel pajamas in his dark bedroom with a curious tarnished object in his hand. Even after he'd gotten back into bed under the covers he lay ice-cold, eyes as blind as the old man's, sure he had learned something important, but not yet able to grasp what.

3

Storm and Flood

PETER WOKE to hear someone banging around in the kitchen. Through his window he could see a rag of the same gray sky that had hung over them all day Monday. His mouth tasted even worse this morning. He got up and dressed and went out to find his father rummaging for breakfast. David looked rumpled and sleepy, as if he'd spent a restless night.

"Morning," said Peter noncommittally.

"Good morning. You're up early, aren't you? For vacation? No one else is stirring yet."

"Felt like getting up."

"Good enough reason. Have you got anything special planned for today?"

"No."

"I thought maybe you and the girls would like to come in to Aberystwyth and meet me for lunch somewhere." He glanced at his son, but Peter's face was carefully blank.

"All right," he said without enthusiasm. David sighed.

Often, when he was alone, Peter imagined sitting down and really talking to his father. He would tell him why he was unhappy and explain why he had to go home. David would listen to him sympathetically and reasonably and would offer help. They would be friends and they would understand each other. But somehow, whenever he was with his father, it didn't happen. Peter couldn't make himself say the right words and David wouldn't listen properly, and they'd end by getting furious with each other.

Jen and Becky arrived after the gas for the grill was safely lit and the kettle boiling, Jen still shivering from her stint in the bathroom.

"I never would have thought you could take a bath in steaming hot water and still get goose-pimples while doing it! The bathroom is unquestionably the coldest room in this house," she declared.

David smiled at her. "That's to keep you from staying in it too long. Do you all want toast? I was suggesting to Peter before you came down that you might come into town this morning and I'll take you to lunch."

"Good," said Becky. "We need money for Christmas decorations. We don't have any at all."

"Money," asked David, "or decorations?"

"Either one."

"All right. You can show Jen the sights and shop while I'm working."

"That should take about five minutes," muttered Peter, out of his father's hearing.

They caught the bus at ten past ten. There was a stop outside Mr. Williams's store. Jen was beginning to think Mr. Williams's store was the hub of Borth. Hugh-the-Bus was driving, cap tilted to the back of his head, whistling through his teeth. He was a big, gentle-faced man with snow-white hair, a wide, amused smile, and very blue eyes. "Morning," he said to Jen when Becky introduced them. "Going to town, is it? Good day for that."

"I'd like to see them all together," Jen whispered as they sat down. "Gwilym and Mrs. Davies and Hugh-the-Bus, I mean."

"And Susan and Sheila," added Becky with a giggle. "I know. It's too bad Gwilym doesn't look like Hugh-the-Bus." She voiced Jen's own thought. "Hugh-the-Bus is real Welsh, but Gwilym's only half Welsh because his mother's English."

"So?" said Peter.

"It makes a difference," Becky informed them. "He doesn't quite belong, and she doesn't at all. Oh, she fits in, but she doesn't belong."

Under the low sky the air was clear and the feet of the mountains stood out in sharp detail though their shoulders and tops were shrouded in thick rolls of cloud. Jen hardly glanced at the little bungalows that lined the road out of Borth. Her eyes went instinctively to those dark, wild slopes, scattered with sheep and boulders. She listened with half her mind to Becky, who was listing all the decorations they needed, and said, "Yes" and "I don't see why not" at the right moments, but she was watching the hills.

In twenty minutes they reached the top of Penglais Hill in Aberystwyth. The hills were gone, and Jen paid attention to Becky who was pointing out the landmarks.

"All the buildings on the left are the new University buildings where Dad teaches. His office is down in the old building, though. You'll see it later."

"Inspiring, aren't they?" commented Peter.

Jen had to admit they weren't really handsome. They were gray concrete and still raw and new looking. Below the University was a big, fortresslike building that, Becky told her, was the National Library of Wales. Very grand. No, they'd never been inside, but their father had. But what really fascinated Jen, as the bus paused, shuddering, at the top of the hill for passengers to get on and off, was the town of Aberystwyth below them: a cluster of buildings, spread across the mouth of the River Rheidol, like flotsam carried down to the sea by the river and left stranded on the fan-shaped estuary. Thousands of years the Rheidol had worn its way among the hills, weaving back and forth across its valley, and now it was invisible, lost among the tumble of slate roofs and steeples, channeled away among the railway sidings and bridges and stone walls of the harbor.

"And that?" asked Jen, pointing across the town. "What's that tower?"

"Pen Dinas," Becky answered. "It's a monument of some sort. Dad says there're the traces of an ancient hill fort near it."

Pen Dinas stood like a sentinel guarding the southern side of Aberystwyth, a dark, straight finger pointing at the sky on the crest of a rounded hill.

Jen shook her head wonderingly. "It sure isn't like home."

"No," agreed Peter.

They got out at the Aberystwyth railway station. "You can go and do what you want. I have an errand," Peter announced.

"What kind?" Becky wanted to know.

"Private."

"Well, I only asked. Anyhow, I have private shopping to do, too. We'll meet you at Woolworth's in an hour for the decorations."

Peter was about to say he didn't care about the decorations, then changed his mind and walked quickly away.

Jen and Becky spent a happy hour poking about in the little shops that lined the narrow streets. Aberystwyth was much livelier than Borth; none of the buildings seemed to be closed for the winter and the sidewalks were full of people. Jen had a great deal to see for the first time and Becky was quite content to wander.

The main street was very broad, with shops at the top and guest houses and flats at the bottom. A sign on the corner pointed down a side street and said simply, "To The Sea."

"But not now," said Becky. "It's time to meet Peter. We can go out on the Prom after lunch."

Peter was already at Woolworth's, looking impatient. "I've been waiting ages. What took you so long?"

"We said an hour and that's what it's been," Jen declared. "It's not our fault you got here early."

It was after twelve when they'd settled the problem of decorations to Becky's satisfaction. They had to decide whether to buy inexpensive lights or the ones that blinked and whether to have a star or an angel for the top of the tree. In the end they got blinking lights and a star and colored balls and icicles and red plastic bells.

When it was all paid for, it was nearly time to meet David, so Becky struck out at a brisk trot for the old University building with the other two following close behind. David was leaning against a pillar at the entrance when they got there.

"Sorry we're late," said Jen breathlessly.

"You're not—I'm early."

He took them to a little cafe nearby where he said he often had his lunch. It was dark and crowded with tables and there were artificial flowers in the windows.

Peter dared Jen to order oxtail soup, and she accepted his challenge. When it came, it was thick and dark brown like gravy and steaming hot. Peter and Becky and David all had plates of savory mince, which looked like spaghetti sauce, and baked potatoes.

"Well?" asked Peter, when Jen had tasted her soup.

"It's good. What's it made of?"

"Oxtails."

When Jen looked at him blankly, David laughed. "He's quite right, it is."

Jen swallowed another spoonful carefully. "I guess so long as I don't have to see them it's all right," she conceded.

"Hello, Mr. Morgan. I had not expected to see you at College this vacation." A thin little man in a well-worn suit had come to stand by their table. He wore wire-framed spectacles, pushed down on his nose.

David got hastily to his feet. "Dr. Rhys! I thought actually that with the students away I could get some of my own research done."

"Ah, yes." Dr. Rhys gave a thin, quick smile. "Welsh language, isn't it? Yes, indeed, it's blessedly quiet now without them cluttering up the libraries and interrupting with questions every time one settles down to work. I quite agree. It is so difficult to do research in term time." He spoke quickly, but Jen could detect the cadences she was beginning to identify as Welsh. He seemed to notice the three younger Morgans for the first time. "And this must be your family, is it?"

"Yes, of course. Forgive me. Peter, Jennifer, and Becky."

Dr. Rhys shook hands with each of them gravely. His grip was light and dry.

"But you should not let me keep you from your lunch now, please."

"Won't you join us?" David invited him, and the three children held their breath. But Dr. Rhys shook his head. "Oh, no, no, thank you very much. I, too, have much to do this vacation, you see. I shall read this report"—he indicated a massive sheaf of paper tucked under his left arm—"while I have my lunch. I really must. So nice to meet you."

He left them and settled at a narrow table at the back of the room. There he bent to his report like a thin crow roosting on it.

"Should think he'd get indigestion," muttered Peter rudely. Luckily David didn't hear him, but Becky giggled.

David looked at her severely. "Dr. Rhys is a well-respected member of the University faculty and he's been very helpful to me these past months. If you ever know one-half as much as he does, I'll be very proud of you," he said, carefully pitching his voice so it wouldn't carry beyond their table.

"What's his subject?" asked Jen.

"He's the head of the Welsh Studies Department, and he's written several very good books on language and folklore."

"He doesn't look like the sort of person who'd know fairy tales," observed Jen, looking at Dr. Rhys with more interest.

"Fairy tales isn't the right term, really. I think he'd quarrel with you on that. It's more mythology."

"Greeks and Romans," said Becky. "We have to read that stuff at school."

"Too bad they never teach you the Norse myths—the Celtic ones, which include the Welsh, are much closer to those. Very exciting, some of them."

"Have you read them?" Peter asked, interested in spite of himself.

"Some," David admitted. "Trouble is, there's too much to read. Now, what do you want for dessert."

"Something very sweet," said Becky at once.

After lunch, David went back to his office, and Jen, Becky, and Peter walked out to the Prom, as Becky had promised. It was a long, curving walk that ran from one end of Aberystwyth to the other along the sea. Only a few mothers with prams and small children were out on it in the watery sun, and here and there a clump of older boys or girls—always one or the other, never both together—stood talking by the rail, eyeing each other. Some of the boys smoked cigarettes, their hands cupped expertly around the butts, ready to flourish them or hide them depending on who approached.

Jen couldn't help feeling foreign, but Peter was lost in his own thoughts and not talking, and Becky was humming to herself unselfconsciously. Somehow Jen had pictured winter by the sea as stretches of deserted white sands under a cold sun and dunes scattered with fishermen's shacks, boats upturned beside them like giant turtles, men mending nets and smoking pipes. She smiled ruefully to herself. Whatever she'd imagined hadn't been this. And yet in its own way, she supposed it wasn't bad, just rather a shock.

Beyond the University, a point jutted out from the town, green grass sloping down to a war memorial and back from it the ruins of Aberystwyth Castle.

"Not much there," said Peter, but Jen had to see it when she was told what it was. "I've never seen a real castle before."

It had been landscaped into a park, with sand paths and benches supported by crouched, wrought-iron dragons. All that were left were ragged chunks of wall and one tower that they couldn't go into.

"Well, it does look old anyway," said Jen, when they'd seen all there was to see.

"Thirteenth century."

"Peter, how on earth do you know?"

"Well, don't believe me then!" He sounded annoyed.

"I didn't say I don't believe you. I only asked how you knew."

"I read it. I told you I had a lot of time for reading." Peter glared at her meaningfully.

"Sorry," said Jen with a trace of sarcasm; then to Becky, "Had you ever met Dr. Rhys before?"

"We haven't met anyone to do with the University except for an American family that lives in Aberystwyth."

"Thank heaven," said Peter. "They're awful. Twin girls four. Even Dad doesn't like them much."

"Has he talked about Dr. Rhys?" Jen persisted.

"Some. Dad seems to like him."

"He sounds as if he might be interesting."

The next few days were dry and almost sunny. There were always clouds moving across the vast expanse of sky, but there were gaps between them where the sun burned through, sweeping over the hills and moors and sea in brilliant shifting patterns. Under the gunmetal sky and the fire of the sun the dead bracken on the slopes beyond the Bog smoldered a deep bronze. Jen was dazzled by the richness of the colors and how quickly they changed. You had only to look away for a minute and when you looked back they had altered mysteriously. It was impossible to ignore the country. It was ever-present, not as a backdrop, but as an active part in everything that went on.

Jen and Becky spent much of their time outside, walking on the beach or climbing about on the rocks under their cliff. Jen was a little disappointed that there weren't more shells to find, but Becky informed her that Gwilym said you could pick up fossils and bits of agate and jasper on the sands, particularly at low tide, if you were sharp enough and lucky.

Sometimes Peter went with the two girls, more often he would disappear on his own without an excuse. He had a pre-occupied air, but he didn't seem to be brooding over the argument he and Jen had had, as she at first guessed. She didn't want to bring it up again, so she left him alone.

He had a great deal to think about, not least, of course, was the Key which he now kept with him, wearing it on a silver chain around his neck, safely hidden under his shirt. He'd bought the chain in Aberystwyth, convinced that whatever it was, the Key was too precious to be separated from. The other matter was Jen. Once his anger at her had cooled, he realized he'd made a serious mistake. It wasn't that she couldn't be an ally, it was that he'd been much too hasty with her. He saw now that he'd been counting so heavily on her for support that he hadn't stopped to think, to give her a chance to really look around, before he'd rushed her with his problem. He had to let her see how impossible life was here for herself before he tried again. He had to wait, and waiting had never been easy for Peter. So he held back and stifled his impatience, turning more and more of his attention to the Key.

Thursday, on their way back up the beach in the early afternoon dusk, Jen and Becky met Gwilym striding purposefully toward Ynyslas at the mouth of the river. He had a heavy pair of binoculars around his neck, which he held protectively against his chest. He'd been reluctant to stop for more than a moment—he said he didn't want to lose the light altogether, but Jen wondered if that were the only reason. He didn't appear really comfortable with them, more because of Jen herself than because of Becky, she suspected. There was no mention made of the promised excursion on the Bog.

She remarked on that to Becky as they walked on back to Bryn Celyn.

"I'm sure he hasn't forgotten."

"Maybe he'd like to," Jen suggested. "Not that I care if he'd rather go out on his own than be friendly. He's misanthropic." She relished the sound of the word.

"Misanthropic?" Becky peered at her. "What's that?"

"Means he doesn't like people."

"Do you really think so? I don't. He's a little strange and he isn't used to you yet, but he's not really misanthropic."

Jen woke with a headache next morning. The clouds had closed ranks across the sky and lay low over the sea. The hills across the River Dovey were hidden completely, and the layer of air between land and cloud felt compressed and heavy, stirred only sluggishly by an uneasy wind. Breakfast was a silent meal.

"Change in weather," Mrs. Davies informed them when she came in to clean and do the laundry, which she did twice a week. "Chill in me bones. Nothing good, I'd say." She hung up her coat carefully. "Get out of me kitchen now, and I'll get at the floor."

"Change to what?" Becky asked. "The weather, I mean."

"Storm coming," replied Mrs. Davies shortly. "Go on and let a body do some work." She pushed her sweater sleeves up over knobby elbows and began whisking chairs out of the way. "Or make yourselves useful, you could," she added over her shoulder, but Peter had miraculously vanished and Becky said she had to go make her bed, so Jen was left to help move the kitchen table.

"You got out quickly." She accused her brother a few minutes later.

Peter was settled by the gas fire in David's study. "Practice. She's really good at trapping you if you aren't careful."

"But there's no reason why you couldn't do a few useful things, really," Jen objected.

"Why should I?" replied Peter reasonably. "Look at it this way—she's getting paid and I'm not. Besides, you wouldn't want to give her the idea we could manage on our own, would you?"

"Very unlikely," said Jen, smiling in spite of herself. This was a Peter she knew, expert at dodging chores. "Where's Becky?"

"Dunno," said Peter. "She said something about meeting a friend of hers this morning, but I don't think she's gone out yet."

"What sort of friend?" Becky had quite an assortment.

"A girl from school, I think. Jen, I've got to talk to you."

Jen made a face. "Not about Dad and going home again, is it?"

"Partly."

"No," she said firmly. "I've already told you there isn't anything I can do for you. I'll mention it to Dad if I get a chance, but I'm not going to get him cross with me, too. There just isn't any point, it wouldn't do any good. Let's not argue about it again."

"Okay," said Peter sulkily. "It wasn't really about that anyway, but I'm not sure I want to tell you now."

"Well, it's up to you," Jen replied. "If you want to act like a baby—"

"I am *not* acting like a baby!" Peter blazed at her. "You

don't know what you're talking about. You're no better than Dad—I thought you'd at least listen, but you don't care how I feel, none of you do. You won't even try to understand. I won't tell you *any*thing!"

"Oh, for heaven's sake, Peter, don't be so dramatic," Jen snapped.

Peter's mouth was open to retort when Becky came in wearing a yellow macintosh. "Mrs. Davies says it's going to rain; have you seen my hat?" She looked from Jen to Peter and gave her head a small shake. "Rhian's coming to Borth when her mother does the shopping and I said I'd meet her. Is it all right if she comes to lunch, Jen, and stays the afternoon?" She went on as if she hadn't noticed how furious Peter looked or how cross Jen's face was.

"It's all right if she doesn't mind sandwiches and soup."

"She won't." A minute later the front door closed behind Becky. She'd issued no invitations to either of them to go along with her—she had seen the signs of a family argument and retreated.

With a great show of carelessness, Peter opened the book in his lap and pointedly ignored Jen. Whatever he'd been hinting at, he wouldn't tell her now, that was certain. With a sigh, Jen went up to make her own bed.

At half-past twelve, Rhian, with Becky in tow, burst through the front door. From the kitchen, where she was trying to decide between chicken and tomato soup, Jen heard the door bang and excited voices in the hall.

". . . jacket there."

"I am perishing with hunger! Thought Mam would *never* be done gossiping with Mrs. Williams-the-Shop! When they begin, there's no stopping them until they have run out of breath, I am saying. Will we see what's for lunch, now? Hullo! You'll be Jen, is it? I am Rhian Evans." She was small and dark, her black hair in a long braid. She was obviously not afflicted with shyness like Gwilym. Her movements were quick and decisive. She made a frank but not unfriendly examination of Jen. In spite of having been Becky's sister for ten years, Jen was still frequently surprised at the people her younger sister brought home.

She collected herself enough to ask, "Now you're here, chicken soup or tomato?"

"Tomato," said Rhian without hesitation. "Mam's always making chicken."

"Well, this is a can," Jen informed her. But it didn't matter to Rhian.

She and Becky were soon busy spreading sandwiches with butter and pickle and slapping cheese into them. Rhian seemed right at home in the Bryn Celyn kitchen, businesslike and capable. In fact, she made Jen rather nervous. When lunch was ready, she told Becky to get Peter.

He was still curled over his book in the study, pretending to read the same page he'd been pretending to read an hour ago.

"Lunch."

"Not hungry," Peter responded without looking up.

"You're kidding!" Becky stared at him in disbelief. "You?"

"No," he said firmly. "I'll get something later."

"*I* don't know what's wrong with him—if he wants to be difficult, we'll just leave him alone," Jen declared when Becky reported back. "Let's have ours anyway."

"Maybe it's the weather, like your headache," suggested Becky. "It feels funny today; even *my* bones think so."

"Are we saving him any?" Rhian asked practically. She held the soup pan poised over the fourth bowl.

"I don't see why we should—it's his own lookout if he won't eat with us."

"Right-o," agreed Rhian, and divided Peter's portion among the other three.

She must indeed have been famished. She had no trouble finishing a huge sandwich and emptying her soup bowl. Jen and Becky could only manage half of their sandwiches each.

"You are quite sure you're not wanting that extra?" Rhian asked, eyeing the other halves. "It'll go stale if you leave it."

"Go ahead," Becky urged. "Eat it."

"I suppose it's my brothers and all. You have to be quick at our table or you will miss out. They are great big and eat ever so much more than me."

"How many brothers?" Jen inquired.

"Three."

"Older," Becky explained, as Rhian had her mouth full. "They work with Mr. Evans on the farm. They're out of school."

"And wishing I was, too!" exclaimed Rhian, swallowing hard. "*And* a boy, see. Then I'd not be troubled with it now and learning all that useless stuff. I would be a hill farmer like Da and Dai and Aled and Evan. I am sure I don't know what school's good for anyway."

"You and Peter would get along," remarked Jen. "Only with him it's mostly learning Welsh."

"The Welsh is not so bad; it's the other stuff I don't see the use in. French!" snorted Rhian. "Now *there's* a waste of time for you!"

"Oh, I don't think that's so bad." Becky disagreed. "I can't see why I need to know all about the Wars of the Roses and the Spanish Armada."

"I'm glad Dad can't hear you," Jen observed with a grin.

"As soon as I'm old enough, I'll leave school, too, see if I don't," Rhian declared. "Then I'll be some real use to Da."

"What kind of farm?" asked Jen.

"Sheep, ours. Da has a few heifers and a bull, of course, and Mam keeps chickens, so we have enough eggs and some over to sell."

"Does your father grow crops at all, like corn or wheat?" Jen wondered, thinking of the farms around Amherst.

"Not up by yere, the land's not good for that. Mind you, there is some growing hay, but not on the hills. There it's just sheep. My brother Aled was working down to Swansea once, on the docks, and he says in Pembroke they grow potatoes and like that, but soil's different. It's red, he says."

"What about the Plant Breeding Station, then?" Becky asked. "Gwilym says they grow crops there."

"That's the valley," explained Rhian. "Can't plow the side of a mountain very well even say it weren't full of rocks. You can come up and see if you like. I'll tell Mam."

"Oh, we would!" said Becky eagerly. "Can't we, Jen? I've never been—it's too far for me to go alone, but if you came Dad wouldn't mind."

"Sure," agreed Jen, hoping this was more definite than Gwilym's invitation.

"If that brother of yours isn't going to eat now, we might as well wash up," stated Rhian.

Outside, the wind had begun in earnest. It came in hard gusts up the coast from the southwest, flinging itself at the houses on the top of Borth cliff, hurtling over miles of churning sea. Waves drove across the wide beach to the very foot of the sea wall, making the thin string of houses look terribly vulnerable.

Something was coming, Peter knew it, and he was pretty sure he was going to be involved in it. Against his skin the Key felt hot. There was no vibration as yet, but . . . Peter was afraid and yet he couldn't take it off, he couldn't get rid of it. He was drawn to the Key even as it frightened him. He wished someone else knew. Jen was the only person he could imagine telling, but he had sense enough to see she was in no mood to believe such an outrageous story. He heard the girls talking in the kitchen and felt very much alone, but he'd refused them.

Instead of joining them, he pulled his jacket down from

its peg and went out, down the cliff path to the monument. There was no shelter from the wind there. If anything, it was even more exposed than Bryn Celyn. When Peter turned to look south, the wind blew his eyelashes together so he could only see a blur of gray. It roared in his ears, full of the pounding of surf and stone flung upon stone. He tossed the hair back from his forehead, and shielding his eyes with his hand, he faced the coming storm. He looked out, not on roiling, foaming sea, but the tossing crowns of trees and wind-flattened grassland. When he turned, bewildered, to look at Borth he saw instead of the cement sea wall, a huge dyke built of earth and stone, against which the waves flung themselves and broke, throwing up white claws of spray. The rain had not yet begun, but the great clouds of salt-spume fell drenching, like rain. The dyke had been built to withstand just such storms as this, to protect the low-lying country from the greedy seas. It stood firm.

Peter was overcome; he wanted no part of this. He shook his head desperately, and the rough granite of the War Memorial's shaft bit comfortingly into his hands. He found himself clutching it so hard his knuckles were white; he was hugging it for dear life. But the bay had come back the way he knew it, Borth was there again and the patchwork of the Bog. He breathed a sigh of relief. The calm, sun-flecked island was one thing—this wild, storm-battered headland was altogether another matter.

Hunching his shoulders against the wind and bending his head, Peter walked along the path that led south, the path he was beginning to think of as his. He tried unsuccessfully to ignore the soft, insistent humming of the Key.

He was gone a long time, chilling himself thoroughly, struggling with his fears. He wanted company very much but didn't know how to find it.

In the Bryn Celyn study, Becky turned the lights on and closed the curtains against the storm.

"I suppose Peter's all right." She sighed. "I wish he hadn't gone out in it."

"He ought to be able to look after himself," said Jen with more conviction than she truly felt. Storms didn't bother her particularly, but she could hear the window panes rattling in their frames and feel the house shudder under the tremendous buffeting. It would have been rather exciting if she weren't actually worried about where Peter was and about being the eldest of them and therefore responsible. Becky had already tried his room, but it was cold and dark; he hadn't slipped in unnoticed. Jen hoped her father wouldn't suddenly come home and demand to know why they'd let Peter go off on his own with a storm coming.

Rhian was unperturbed by the gale. "Me Da says you've to expect the worst storms from the southwest, but up by us we don't get much blow. We're in a valley, see, and the hills keeps us sheltered. Not to worry, he says, town's been yere longer than us and hasn't blown away yet."

"I've been in a hurricane," volunteered Becky. "It blew down the telephone lines and we didn't have lights for a whole evening. It was like this."

"Our electric goes off a lot," said Rhian.

For something to do while the storm rose, the three of them sat on the floor in front of the gas fire and played Hearts. Rhian won consistently. Jen's mind wasn't on the game; she kept listening for someone at the door. Halfway into the third hand, she heard the sudden heavy splatter of rain against the window as it was driven sideways by the wind, and at the same moment they all heard the front door blow open.

"I hope that's Peter," said Jen fervently.

"Who else would it be, then?" demanded Rhian.

"Dad," said Becky, following Jen's thoughts. "He might be home early."

Jen scrambled up and went into the front hall. It was Peter, his wet hair plastered flat to his skull, his nose red and running. She bit her tongue on the furious question she wanted to ask. With unaccustomed good sense she realized it would do no one any good to start a fight, even though Peter was eyeing her defiantly, daring her to. It was a long-standing family rule that none of them ever went anywhere without telling someone else first, and he had obviously broken it.

"Your jacket will never dry if you hang it up like that," said Jen at last. "Put it in by the fire."

A sudden frantic gust of wind hurled itself at the front door. The latch hadn't caught and it flew open. Jen and Peter both moved to close it at the same moment and swung it shut together.

"What's it like out there?"

Peter shivered involuntarily. "I could see the line of rain come across the bay—one minute it was dry and the next minute it was pouring. The waves go right up to the sea wall." Was it the sea wall? Or was it the dyke? He couldn't remember and shivered again.

"You ought to change your clothes before you catch cold."

He nodded and disappeared. In a few minutes he joined the others in the study.

"Hullo," said Rhian. "Want to play Hearts with us? I shouldn't half have fun getting home this afternoon."

"Maybe it'll clear after a bit," suggested Jen.

"Not likely. Sounds as if it's setting in proper. There is someone at your door." Over the noise of the wind and rain it was just possible to hear a muffled thumping.

It was Gwilym this time, mac streaming with water, drops running down his nose, chin, and spectacles. "Mum sent me round to see if you were all right," he shouted, standing on the doorstep.

"Yes, I think so!" Jen shouted back. "Do come in so we can close the door."

"Have you checked all the doors and windows? And chimney?"

Becky shook her head. "Should we?"

A puddle grew around Gwilym's wellingtons as he stood in the hall. He nodded, as if to say I thought as much—no idea how to look after themselves. "Good job Mum took in your towels before lunch or they'd be halfway to Snowdon." He went into the lounge, Jen, Becky, Peter and Rhian trailing behind him. To Jen's horror she could see a dark stain spreading across the carpet from the fireplace.

"It *leaks?*"

Gwilym shook his head with exaggerated patience. "Flue's open. You ought to keep it closed when there's not a fire. You'd best get a pan to put under the drip till it's dried out."

Room by room, he checked the house, with the rest of them following like a small parade. Most of the window frames were all right, but the ones in the empty rooms on the second floor, where the rain and wind hit hardest were already very wet. Gwilym showed them how to put towels around the cracks.

"It's very simple," he said—unnecessarily, Jen thought. As if we're a bunch of half-wits.

Water was also coming in under the kitchen door. Rhian mopped it up, and they improvised a dam around the sill.

"That's it," said Gwilym, when it was complete to his satisfaction. "If you've more trouble, come round and get me."

"Thank you," said Jen primly.

Instead of slackening, the rain came down harder as the afternoon wore on. It sounded as if it were being emptied out of the sky in bucketfuls. From the upstairs window they couldn't even see as far as the cliff edge.

"It *can't* keep on this hard for much longer," Jen exclaimed, but an hour later it still hadn't slackened. They had all retreated again to the study. Rhian was teaching Becky a very complicated kind of solitaire she said her brother Aled had learned in Swansea. Jen was beginning to wonder how on earth they would get Rhian home again if the storm kept on. There was no telephone in Bryn Celyn. When Jen had asked why not, David had told her there was no point: phones were installed by the Post Office, and there was a waiting list of more than a year for installations. But it would have made no difference now in any case, because Rhian had informed them that her family had no phone either. Rhian was surprised Jen thought that strange. Jen felt unfairly burdened with responsibility.

Peter sat in the rocking chair by the window, rocking himself slowly back and forth. At first he watched the game progressing by fits and starts and with much good-humored bickering, but gradually he became aware that he was losing sight of it. The cards were blank squares of white, the voices faded. Frightened, he tried to shut out the singing, but it grew relentlessly inside him. He had thought he'd be safe with other people around—it had always come when he was alone before—but he was helpless to stop it. His hands gripped the arms of the chair and he went on rocking, back and forth, back and forth, automatically. The study vanished.

In its place, Peter saw the country called the Low Hundred lying flat under the hammering rain. Wind tore through the bare limbs of the rowans and birches, bending them double, causing the heavy oaks to creak and groan in anguish. Great branches were ripped from them and hurled crashing to the ground. People crouched shivering in their frail wood huts, waiting for their roofs to be blown away or trees to fall, smashing them to bits. The Key sang a wild and ominous song that wove through the gale inexorably, showing Peter a series of painfully vivid images.

Above the flat land of the Hundred, near the coast, rose a long, low mound, around its slopes a jumble of huts within the shelter of an earthen dyke. And beyond loomed the bulk of the great sea dyke. Atop the mound, on the highest part, stood the Great Hall, Caer Gwyddno, built of the best and strongest timber. Within the Hall, in the warmth and firelight, there were people feasting at a long, cluttered table, swarthy, dark-haired men who drank and laughed and called up and down the table to one another, feeding the hounds that circled them, alert for handouts. At the end of the table, on a platform, Peter saw a big golden man, the yellow hair of his mane and beard and the down on his great, muscular arms shining in the flickering light. His head was inclined toward the stocky, fair young man on his left, who was gently fingering a small harp. And sitting on the edge of the platform was a boy of about thirteen, whose gaze never left the harp strings. Peter knew him as the boy whom Caridwen had named "Taliesin." The three might have been alone for all the notice they appeared to take of everyone else. With the abruptness of a candle being blown out the picture was gone.

Peter blinked at Becky and Rhian, still absorbed in their cards and at Jen on the hearthrug, her hands clasped around her knees, watching them with a worried frown. The clock on the desk said ten past four.

"Jen! Peter! Where are you?" David was home at last, drenched and anxious.

Jen sighed with relief. She could let him worry about Rhian now. "In the study," she called. "I'm so glad you're back!"

"What's wrong? Are you all here? Becky, Peter—hullo, there's an extra one of you. Who's this?"

"Rhian Evans," said Becky. "We're all right. Gwilym's been and helped us stop the leaks. But we're not sure how we're going to get Rhian home again."

"Where do you live? In Borth?" David struggled out of his soaking overcoat.

Rhian shook her head. "Farm above Tre'r-ddôl."

"Good lord, where's that? What a storm. Two of the buses have broken down or I'd have been here sooner—I had to wait almost an hour at the station. I've never seen it rain so hard!"

"I don't mind," said Rhian. "Gotten wet before, me."

"You'd be washed away," David declared. "Have to walk all the way—out toward Machynlleth, isn't it? No buses going that way until it lets up. Can someone come and get you?"

"No phone," said Jen.

"They'll be too busy getting the sheep out of the *cwm* in case it floods. It won't matter to me, honest, Mr. Morgan."

"Well, it will to me," David declared, pulling off his wet shoes. "Becky, move away from the fire a bit, will you? I'm wet through. Good, that's fine. Look, I can't take responsibility for letting you go out in this, Rhian, and heaven knows when there'll be another bus to Machynlleth. I doubt I could find anyone to drive you for love or money tonight. Jen, what about putting the kettle on? I need something hot. Has Mrs. Davies been in today?"

"This morning, but not since," said Jen.

Over cups of steaming tea and chocolate biscuits—Peter suddenly remembered he'd missed lunch and Becky caught him helping himself to four at once—they discussed what to do about Rhian.

"You're bothering too much," she maintained.

David shook his head. "It's practically dark now and the storm's as bad as ever. You can't go alone, and if I went down with you, I probably wouldn't get back again tonight. I can't leave the rest of you. There must be some way of getting through to your family."

"You mean she'll have to spend the night?" Becky looked hopeful.

"Mam will have fits if I'm not home."

"Isn't there some way to send a message?" asked Jen.

"There's the Forestry Commission. They have a telephone in their house up by us in the valley. They might take a message down," said Rhian. "They have done before when our Aunt Gwen was ill, see. Of course, they may not be there."

"It's worth trying, certainly." David sounded relieved.

"I'll go down to the call box at the corner when I've finished my tea and see if I can get through. You can all figure out where Rhian's to sleep."

Mrs. Davies came in as usual at half-past five, dressed in Gwilym's long yellow mac and oilskin hat. She had a little trouble with the barricade at the back door, which had gotten quite soggy.

"It was good of Gwilym to look in this afternoon, Mrs. Davies. Thank him for me, please." David was just off to try the Forestry Commission number.

"I thought it best to see everything was all right, Mr. Morgan. Children don't think of things, you know, and them being here alone and all."

"Yes," said David, beating a hasty retreat before she went further.

"What have we got for supper?" Peter wanted to know.

"Boiled beef and cabbage, I'm afraid." Jen prodded a lump in the inevitable steaming pot. "I should think you'd be starved by now."

"I am," he agreed, patting his stomach.

"You ate almost a whole package of biscuits at tea," observed Becky. "Let's put one of the spare beds in our room for tonight, Jen."

"I suppose we could."

"Much better than not being together. Come on, Rhian, let's try moving one." The two of them disappeared, pounding up the stairs.

"It's a good thing the lights haven't gone off," remarked Peter. "I haven't seen a single candle in the house."

"Oh, cripes! I hadn't even thought of that!"

"Well, we've got the stove and heat anyway if the power lines go down."

"Great."

"Better than nothing," Peter countered.

"What were you doing outside this afternoon?"

"Walking. I went down the cliff path a bit and the rain came faster than I could get back." He watched his sister warily. "Are you going to tell?"

"I suppose not." She knew perfectly well she would have told already if she'd been going to. "What were you going to tell me this morning? You said it was only partly about going home."

He hesitated only a second, then said, "It wasn't important. I don't feel like arguing again." He had a momentary vision of himself pulling the Key out and trying to explain it to Jen as she stood with her fork in a kitchen smelling of boiled beef and cabbage, and he knew it was impossible. She gave him an exasperated look. "You can't say I didn't ask," said Jen.

Overhead, a loud crash followed by a shriek made them both jump.

"Oh, lord!" exclaimed Jen. "There goes the bed!"

"I'll go and see," Peter offered, glad of the excuse to leave her. "I just hope it isn't bloody."

In spite of the thoroughly boiled supper, everyone had an appetite. David was damp but triumphant, Becky very pink in the face, and Rhian had lost the elastic off her braid. It was a much livelier meal than usual. Even Peter was particularly talkative, and discussion ranged from the problems of moving furniture to the difficulties of using Welsh telephones, to hurricanes, gales, floods, tornadoes, and other natural catastrophes.

Just as Becky and Rhian were dishing up the sponge pudding—also steamed—all the lights went out.

"Well," said Peter addressing the darkness where he'd last seen Jen, "I did warn you."

"I forgot. Does anyone know where there are candles?"

"No, but there's a flashlight on the mantlepiece in the study." That was David. "Sit tight and I'll find it."

"What should I do with the pudding?" Becky wanted to know.

"Just hang on to it, of course. We'll have some light in a minute."

"There *must* be candles somewhere in this house."

They all heard a loud, indistinct curse from the direction of the hall. A couple of minutes later David returned with a dim spot of light. "Not much left in it, I'm afraid, but let's see what else we can find with it."

"What happened to you?" Becky demanded.

"Nothing," he said shortly.

"If you were a candle, where would you live?" asked Peter whimsically.

Rhian was the one to find them, in the back of one of the kitchen drawers bundled together—an odd assortment of ends of various colors, including two deep purple ones.

Supper resumed by candlelight.

"You know," said Peter, scraping up the last of his sponge, "it tastes better when you can't see it."

Jen glanced anxiously at David, but even he was grinning in agreement and made no remark about disrespect to Mrs. Davies.

The decision not to do dishes in the dark was unanimous, but David did make them clear the table and stack everything in the sink. "It'll be awful to come down to breakfast tomorrow and find leftover dinner sitting here stone cold," he said firmly.

The electricity showed not the slightest flicker of life, reading by candles proved unsatisfactory, and it was impossible to play cards, so they went to bed in the dark house early, with a stern warning from David about making sure the candles were out.

"Thank heaven you got the bed moved before the lights went out," said Jen, as she and Becky and Rhian undressed in their room. The third bed had been wedged in at the foot of the other two, and there was very little room to move around. In the dark, on the second floor, they seemed very close to the storm.

"I don't mind the lights going out"—Becky yawned—"but I hope that's all that happens."

Only Peter had been reluctant to go to bed. David wouldn't mind being alone and the other three had each other for company, but Peter had to go by himself and he didn't much want to. It wasn't that he minded the storm; he really rather relished it. He was apprehensive about what he might see in the darkness once he was alone. There was no pattern in the pictures the Key showed him, or if there was, he couldn't see it; but he did know from the warmth of it as it lay against him that it was gathering strength again, and it was only a matter of time until it began to sing.

He took a candle with him to his room and set it on his bureau where it flickered uneasily in the draughts and made weird shapes on the ceiling. In the dim light he got the Key out without taking it off his neck and peered at it. Despite the layers of tarnish and the scratches, he could see the intricate, woven design of it. He had passed the chain through the center hole—that seemed to be what the hole was for. Each shaft had been patterned to look as if it were braided. The Key had obviously been worked by a craftsman of great skill, for, though simple, it was perfect.

Nothing could have induced Peter to part with it, no matter what it showed him. He couldn't get over the peculiar feeling that he'd been meant to find it. And how on earth was he going to explain that to Jen? Or anyone else, for that matter. But he'd come closest to trying with Jen.

He sighed and thrust the Key back under his pajamas. Ordinarily Peter wasn't a coward; there had in fact been many times when his parents had wished he were or would at least show a little more sense. At home in Amherst, Peter could always be counted on to be the force behind the least responsible plans he and his army of friends carried out. He'd gotten a number of good stiff lectures on the subject, and sometimes worse.

But that was quite different. Then *he'd* been in control —the ideas, even when they got out of hand—were still his. Now all that had changed. He'd been robbed of his independence and all feeling of control, first by his father who'd landed him here, and now by the object he'd snatched from the sea.

He blew out the candle and climbed into bed, glancing uneasily around at the dark, waiting for it to dissolve, but it didn't and he fell asleep thankfully.

It was midnight when the Key began to sing. It woke Peter without warning, and as soon as he opened his eyes, he saw the same storm-ravaged landscape he'd seen earlier: tossing trees and the great, flat plain. There, too, was the dyke and near it a low circular building that had been made of thick logs, driven upright into the ground in a closed circle, the cracks between them plastered with a mixture of hard river clay and straw. It had a thatched roof that ran to a point in the middle. From the hut came the sound of coarse, slurred singing, loud and ragged. The Key took Peter inside and he saw that the hut was lit by a single, central fire. The smoke from it hung in the air. Five men lounged around it, each with a huge pot of ale. Their faces were blurred and indistinct with drinking, their mouths wide, their chins wet. A stout, red-faced young man led them all in song, his voice loudest. He half lay on a heavy, brown cloak, the leather belt unbuckled from his waist, a long-bladed knife driven point first into the hard-packed floor of the hut.

The song of the Key shifted up a tone, and the picture flickered. Instead, it became the great sea dyke. Down all its length tremendous waves burst like fireworks—they advanced with a sizzling hiss, exploded with a hollow thundering boom, and burst into showers of luminous white sparks, flinging up into the darkness higher than a man could reach, hesitating, suspended for a moment in the air, before dropping back to join the next onslaught. The whole dyke shuddered as though it were being dynamited. The sea clawed ruthlessly for a hold. Men should have been patrolling it, but the watchmen were drunk and foolish and kept to their hut.

The song was a high, keening wail, steadily building in intensity. In the northern corner of the Low Hundred was a place where a wide, swift-running river came down from the hills to meet the sea. There the dyke had been fortified with special care from water on two sides, and there it should have been guarded most closely tonight of all nights. Through the billowing smoke of the sea spray, two figures were barely visible; they moved with great effort along the dyke, clinging to one another to keep from being washed over it, for the waves already topped it in several places. They came closer—the young bard and the boy from the Great Hall, their faces pale in the gloom, their hair and cloaks running with water. And behind them, the piece of dyke they had just come over crumbled under the pressure of the sea, a jagged hole opened, the wall had been breached! The level of the water on the far side of the dyke was higher by several feet than the land within.

Again the picture changed, and it was dawn. In gray light the wind dropped, but rain continued to fall in long silver threads, making circles on the waves that rose and fell where the day before there had been forest and garden-patch, grass-plain and wattled hut. The waters were still rising, lapping higher on the mound where the Great Hall stood, but it was men now, and not the storm, who were taking it apart. They were feverishly pulling down the huge timbers and lashing them together with thongs. They were building a raft. In the midst of the activity stood the golden man, his face dead in the cold light of morning, his eyes full of tears. Near him were the bard and his boy, crouched on the muddy ground, watching the raft-builders.

Here and there on the gray, uneven surface of the new

sea floated dark things: bits of wreckage, farmers' carts, up-
rooted trees, terrified animals swimming without direction, out
of their element and drowning, pieces of huts with wet and
wretched people clinging to them, coracles and other rafts
laden with women, children, and men, too stunned and cold to
weep for all that had been lost. In a coracle that drifted close
to the mound were three of the five men who had been drinking, and the loud one was among them, now stone-sober, his
red face gone pasty, his eyes lost and wandering.

From the mouth of the golden one came words, echoing
with grief and fury, and in his coracle the other shrank with
fear.

> *Stand forth, Seithenin,*
> *And behold the dwelling-place of heroes,*
> *The Plain of Gwyddno which the ocean covers!*
> *Cursed be the sea guard*
> *Who in his drinking*
> *Allowed in the destroying waters of the raging sea!*
> *A cry from the sea arises above the dykes!*
> *A cry from the sea arises above the winds!*
> *A cry from the sea . . .*

Rhian slept curled in a tight little ball like an animal, face
hidden in her pillow. Becky was sleeping restlessly, but Jen
wasn't sleeping at all. Her eyes simply wouldn't close no
matter what she tried. She lay staring crossly at nothing for
what seemed like ages, then finally, when she could stand it no
longer, she sat up in the cold room. No point in disturbing the
others, she thought, feeling frantically for her slippers. The
floor was so cold it stung the bottoms of her feet. She dragged
on her pullover. Perhaps if she could make some cocoa or at
least warm some milk, it would put her to sleep. The squeak of
the door and the creak of the stairs were covered by the noise
of the wind. Downstairs in the hall, she groped among the

coats for her own. "Damn!" she muttered crossly as one fell. At last she settled for David's tweed overcoat and pulled it on thankfully.

She'd forgotten the kitchen lights wouldn't work and almost gave up and went back to bed, but it was silly to have got this far and admit defeat. The candles from supper were still on the table and she found matches by the stove. By the time she'd lit a burner and put a pan of milk on it, she was feeling quite pleased with herself.

A sudden blast of chilly air made the candle flame gutter dangerously and Jen looked up to see the door of Peter's room gaping black. He appeared in the middle, moving like a person sleepwalking.

"Peter! You startled me! Did I wake you up?"

He didn't answer, and for an instant she wondered if he were really awake. She went over to him and his left hand shot out and caught her wrist, his fingers were like ice and clamped tight.

"Peter!" Jen was a little frightened. "Are you all right? What's the matter?"

"Jen?" His voice was hoarse.

"What's the matter? Were you dreaming?"

He let out his breath in a long hiss. "Yes—I—no. I don't know."

"I just came down to make some cocoa—do you want some?"

"What?"

"Cocoa," she repeated impatiently. In the light of the candle his eyes had a dazed, faraway look.

"Yes." He nodded vigorously as if trying to shake something out of his head.

"You'd better put something on over your pajamas. Aren't you frozen?"

He released her and dove back into his room, reappearing in a moment with his bathrobe. Jen mixed the cocoa and gave him a mugful, then they sat down across the table from each other.

"*Was* it a dream?"

"Oh, cripes! *I* don't know, but it was awful! I went to sleep right off, you know, after we all went to bed, and then . . . and then I think I woke up again. Anyhow, it was dark and there was a storm—"

"There still is," Jen interrupted dryly. "Or hadn't you noticed."

He paid no attention to her. "I don't know where I was. I mean the place seemed kind of familiar but I didn't recognize it. There were people in it, but they really looked foreign—old —wearing strange clothes like they might have thousands of years ago. They were all sitting in a big hall and eating, and there were some others who were drunk—"

"What book have you been reading?" Jen inquired skeptically.

"*Treasure Island,*" said Peter reproachfully. "Don't interrupt. There was an awful flood. There was a dyke, like the sea wall only made of dirt and boulders, and the sea broke it down and flooded this whole country. People and animals got drowned in it. Trees came up by the roots and whole houses just got washed away, and no one could do anything to stop it."

"Peter!" Jen exclaimed sharply. "Don't!"

"It happened. I saw it."

"You dreamed it. It was a nightmare."

Peter stared at her. "I don't think it was. I'm sure I wasn't asleep."

"What else could it have been?" Jen sounded angry. He'd frightened her with his wild story and the way he'd just appeared in the middle of the night. He obviously believed what he was telling her and she didn't like it. "Well?" she demanded.

Now was the time to tell her, if only he could think of the right words, words that would convince her, words that would make her believe in the Key. With hands that shook slightly, he dragged out the chain and held up the Key.

"What on earth is that?"

"I'm not sure. I found it on the beach near here about three weeks ago. I kind of liked it, so I brought it back with me."

"So? It looks like a peculiar sort of a key. Why on earth do you wear it?"

"Why shouldn't I?" Peter demanded. "I can do what I like with it. It's mine."

Jen shrugged. "Suit yourself. But what has that got to do with your dream?"

Peter was beginning to regret having shown the Key. It wasn't going to work, but he had to try now he'd started. "I told you it wasn't a dream. It came from this."

Jen stared at him in complete disbelief.

"It's happened before, several times when I wasn't even in bed. I've seen things and I don't know why."

"Oh, boy," said Jen. "You've got a good story this time, Peter."

He was angry. "You asked and I've tried to tell you. If you won't believe me, I can't help it, but you could try."

"Do you know how fantastic it sounds? Like you've been having hallucinations. I don't know what you found, but whatever it is you ought to get rid of it."

"You don't know what you're—" Just then their eyes were overwhelmed with light, blinding and stark. It filled the kitchen without warning. Jen's heart seemed to stop for a moment before she realized what had happened. The electricity had come back on, and they had forgotten to turn the switch off when they left the kitchen after supper. Peter looked dazed and miserable. They both heard footsteps on the stairs, and Peter thrust the Key back inside his robe.

"What in God's name are you doing up at half-past two?" David demanded, his voice thick with sleep.

"I couldn't fall asleep, so I came down to make some cocoa and Peter heard me." Jen was very much aware of Peter's eyes on her, but she wouldn't look at him. "It's the storm," she said deliberately. "It gave us both bad dreams."

Peter slumped back in his chair overcome with relief. At least she wasn't going to tell David about the Key. That much was all right.

"In my overcoat yet! What about Becky and Rhian?"

"Out cold."

"Which is what you two idiots will be tomorrow if you don't go back to bed right now."

"The electricity came on," said Jen unnecessarily.

"I know. I left the lamp on in my room so it would get me up and I could turn the other lights off. Come on now, both of you. Go!"

4

To Llechwedd Melyn

THE FARM WHERE RHIAN LIVED, Llech-
wedd Melyn, was set in a cleft on the northern side of the valley, a collection of buildings huddled together: farmhouse,
cowbarn, sheds, with the hill rising steep behind it, and stands
of wiry, wind-twisted fir on either side. It was built of stone,
whitewashed recently, and it seemed rooted, low and solid in
the raw winter ground. Two great chimneys rose at either end
of the farmhouse's slate roof.

About a mile below the farm, the valley turned a corner,
shutting off the view out over the Bog and estuary and protecting the farm from the worst of winds and storms. The land
was, as Rhian had said, not much good for crop-growing; the
hillsides were steep and rocky and disappeared into a narrow, tree-filled *cwm*. The sound of the river at the bottom of it
filled the valley with noise.

There was an awful lot of mud everywhere. Although
the rough lane was paved, the asphalt was invisible under great
welts of glutinous brown sludge. It sucked hungrily at wellingtons and made walking that much more difficult. Both Jen and
Becky were panting by the time they came in sight of the farm,
but the stiff climb didn't seem to bother Rhian in the slightest.

She walked with long quick strides like a boy, impervious to the steady drenching rain. Normally, Jen reflected, the rain alone would have kept her indoors. Thank heavens she'd thought to borrow Peter's boots.

"I am soaked," announced Becky between puffs. "There hardly seems to be any point in wearing a raincoat!"

"What does it matter?" called Rhian over her shoulder. "You'll dry right enough and we're almost there."

There was water everywhere. The lane ran with it, it came in gouts off the hillside above them, the turf along the track was sodden, and still rain poured out of the sky. In the early hours of morning the wind had dropped—the sudden silence had woken Becky who in turn had woken Jen, so the day had begun at the first gray light in spite of a restless night. Jen's eyes still felt gritty. But the rain showed no signs of stopping. Even Rhian remarked that it seemed heavier than usual.

David had been a bit reluctant to let Jen, Becky, and Rhian go up to Llechwedd Melyn by themselves, but as Becky pointed out the only real danger was that of drowning, and both she and Jen could swim.

Peter went off by himself after breakfast, so they hadn't even asked him to go along. Becky, for once irritated with her brother's unsociability, had declared, "He's no great loss, really. I don't see why he's *always* in a bad mood!" Jen had said nothing. The picture of herself and Peter drinking cocoa in the candlelit kitchen, the story he had told her, had assumed an unreal, dreamlike quality. She wondered if it had really happened at all, as she thought about it now and tried to pull her hands further up the sleeves of her raincoat with a shiver. She'd begun by putting them in her pockets but had found that the rain simply ran down her sleeves like gutters and had collected in the pockets half-an-inch deep. She was wet with perspiration inside and rain outside and wishing she'd never left Bryn Celyn, when she looked up and saw the tail of

Rhian's mac disappearing around the corner of the farmhouse.

"No wellies in the house, Mam's rule," she informed them. "She says there's more than enough without mopping up all the time."

They pulled off their boots in a kind of rough porch that had been tacked onto the back of the house. "Da and the boys'll all be out, then, checking sheep."

"How can you tell?" asked Becky, glancing around.

"No boots, see?" She pulled open the heavy door and they stepped right into the kitchen, which was warm and dim and smelled of baking. It was a shock after the cold, fresh air.

"Come in then, come in with you, and close door. You'll have all the heat outside, indeed to goodness!" Rhian's mother, small and dark like her daughter, stood at the kitchen table, hands covered in flour, a smudge of it white on her cheek. She looked up from the lump of dough she was kneading and smiled at them. "And no need to slam it, Rhian, you've woke Gram!"

"Sorry, Mam. It's Jen and Becky Morgan with me, from where I stayed last night. They've come up to see the farm."

"Picked a grand day for it, you did," said Mrs. Evans with a laugh. "We're like to lose ourselves in mud this day!"

"I hope you got my father's message last night," began Jen anxiously. "He wasn't sure they'd get it to you. But there weren't any buses this way last night."

"Oh, aye. Mr. Robb from the Forestry came down with it. There is good you were to keep her. She was no trouble, I hope?"

"Oh, Mam!" exclaimed Rhian.

"Wondering how she'd get back, Gram and me, weren't we, Gram?"

Now that her eyes were used to the dim light, Jen could see a little old woman sitting in a straight-backed chair by a cavernous fireplace. She was so tiny her feet didn't reach the floor, but rested instead on a carved footstool. She smiled at them toothlessly.

"Our Gram Jones," Rhian explained. "You must say hello to her, she loves a bit of company now and then, don't you, Gram? She'll not answer, she don't speak English, Gram don't."

"Really?" asked Becky fascinated.

"Never been the need," declared Mrs. Evans. "Nor did I speak it then until I were sixteen and working at the inn in Machynlleth."

Jen and Becky both said hello to little Mrs. Jones, Jen feeling rather selfconscious, but the old lady smiled harder and nodded, her eyes bright with interest as she peered at them.

Mrs. Evans went on with her kneading, her hands quick and deft at the thump, push, and fold over. "Sit down by fire and dry out, you should."

They were glad to. The scrubbed stone hearth had a small iron grate on it, heaped with glowing coals that gave off a comforting heat. And while she sat on the edge of an old wooden settle, close to the warmth, Jen had a chance to look around her at the farm kitchen. She'd never in her life been in one before and she was curious. In Llechwedd Melyn, the kitchen obviously did the service of several rooms. It was good-sized and furnished with an assortment of chairs, the settle Jen sat on, and a low wooden bench along one wall. Six plain wood chairs stood around the huge, scarred table at which Mrs. Evans worked. On the wall next to the door they'd come through was a high Welsh dresser on which a set of blue and white china was carefully arranged, and a big, coal-burning stove sat back in one corner next to an enamel sink and drain board. A little door opened off to the right, and a larger one on the left, both closed to hold the heat in the kitchen. The ceiling and walls were whitewashed plaster with dark, heavy beams. Very little light came through the two small windows that faced the valley; the wall they were cut into was almost a foot thick.

Mrs. Evans gave the dough a final smack, rolled it over, and cut it neatly in half. "Rhian, your Da and the boys are down by the *cwm* hunting out strays. They'll be in to dinner in a bit, you can peel potatoes."

"We really ought to start back in a few minutes," Jen began.

"Indeed not!" declared Mrs. Evans. "You'll have your dinner first. There's plenty to go round and I'll not be having you leave wet and hungry!"

"Thank you very much," Jen responded meekly, glad to sit back and steam by the fire. A sleek marmalade cat appeared suddenly beside Becky and began to give itself a good wash. In her chair, across the hearth from Jen, Gram Jones sat and nodded, a smile still on her seamed old face. How odd not to understand things that were said in your own house, Jen thought, meeting her bright gaze for a second.

Mrs. Evans talked on cheerfully about the storm as she set her bread to rise on the back of the stove and began laying the table for lunch. Jen offered to help but was firmly turned down. "You sit." She felt pleasantly drowsy, with Mrs. Evans's voice drifting further away, and rested her head against the back of the settle, watching the coals flicker with heat.

She came back to herself with a jump at the sound of heavy feet on the porch outside and the rumble of men's voices.

"There is Dai's stomach for you!" said Rhian with a grin, glancing at the black iron clock on the mantle. "It remembers meals on time without a clock."

Mrs. Evans snorted. "You're not often late yourself, I am thinking, Rhian Evans! We're needing three chairs more."

Mr. Evans and his sons Dai, Evan, and Aled filled the kitchen, bringing in with them a damp, rich earth smell, chilly air falling from their clothing. It was a little overwhelming to be suddenly faced with four large hungry men Jen had never laid eyes on before. And for their part, as soon as they saw there was company at Llechwedd Melyn, they fell silent, looking at Jen and Becky not quite straight on.

Two of Mr. Evans's sons were the image of himself: strongly built, fair-haired, with pleasant, open faces, and big red hands. They were introduced as Evan and Dai. The third —Aled—was dark and slight and clever-looking like Rhian. He didn't look much like a farmer, Jen decided.

"There is cold the shepherd's pie will be if you don't wash up now, you," scolded Mrs. Evans comfortably. "Don't keep company waiting, isn't it polite, is it, Gram?"

The old lady smiled and nodded.

"These are the girls from Borth, where our Rhian stopped last night," explained Mrs. Evans.

"Oh, aye? Morgan, Mr. Robb said your name would be?" Mr. Evans's voice was oddly high-pitched for such a big man, and it had the same musical rise and fall Jen found in most Welsh voices.

"I'm in school with Rhian," Becky volunteered. "I'm Becky and that's Jen."

"From Ameryca, you are then? Rhian has told us about you." He beamed at both girls warmly. "And what are you thinking of Wales?"

Jen was devoutly glad Peter hadn't come at that moment.

"I like it," Becky answered, grinning back at him.

"Not like what you're used to, I'm thinking," put in Aled unexpectedly. His brothers were very busy washing their hands. "I've heard lots of stories about America, then. Knew an American sailor when I was in Swansea."

"From where?" Becky asked.

Aled shrugged vaguely. "Seattle, could it be?"

"Oh, well," said Becky. "That's all the way across the country from us."

"Long way, is it?"

"As far away from where we live as Wales is," said Jen. "Three thousand miles anyway."

Aled was silent, contemplating the size of America.

"Rhian, Dai, Aled, come and sit!" commanded Mrs. Evans, putting a vast, steaming pie on the table. "Evan, you bring Gram, there is good of you." The Evanses came at once. Mrs. Evans obviously ruled the kitchen and was used to being obeyed. Jen and Becky were put with their backs to the fire between Mr. Evans and Dai, then everyone joined hands and Mr. Evans said grace in Welsh. Mrs. Evans dished up mounds of shepherd's pie on each plate, together with brussels sprouts and boiled potatoes. It looked like an immense amount of food to Jen, who was wondering how she'd get through it all.

But she was hungrier than she'd realized, and for a while all conversation stopped as everyone attended to eating. The pie was minced lamb with a crust of mashed potato browned with butter, and it tasted marvelous.

"Well," said Aled finally. "What is your part of America like then?" His eyes were fixed on Jen.

"How?" she asked, at a loss.

"That it's different from Wales," replied Aled unhelpfully.

"It's not nearly so wild," said Becky rescuing her. "And we don't have mountains like you. We've got bigger towns and highways and lots of woods."

"You said it was farming where you live," objected Rhian.

"Well, there are farms, too, but not like yours," Jen said.

"Like what, then?" asked Mr. Evans.

"They grow things like corn and tomatoes and tobacco. And lots of apple orchards."

"Our houses look different, too. They're mostly made of wood or brick. You hardly ever see stone ones."

"No sheep?" asked Dai, surprised.

"Not really," said Becky. "Cows, though."

"Dairy cows," Jen added.

"And what about the ones that aren't farmers, then?" Aled wanted to know. "What do they do?"

"Well, in Amherst, the town we come from, there are two big universities—"

"*Two* is it?" exclaimed Mr. Evans.

"Yes, and three more very near. So there are lots of professors living in the town, and other people work in offices and libraries and banks and hotels."

"Like Aberystwyth, you mean," said Rhian.

"Well, no, not really," hedged Jen, jolted by the comparison. Amherst was so different, but she didn't think she could begin to tell them why. She was afraid she might say something they would interpret as an insult.

"More money," said Aled, saving her the trouble. "In America everyone has lots of cars and color telly and dishwashers and that."

"Not everyone," Becky contradicted. "We only ever had one car and a black and white television."

"What about gangsters?" asked Dai eagerly. "Do you have them in Amherst?"

Becky giggled. "Only in movies. That's Chicago."

Jen wanted to give her a kick under the table, but hit the table leg by mistake.

"Oh," said Dai, evidently disappointed.

"And there are lots of cowboys and Indians out west," continued Becky.

"Becky!" said Jen.

"Well, there are."

Mr. Evans nodded knowingly. "I've seen them on telly. We know about that." Jen let it go, her sense telling her it was pointless to argue that Becky was exaggerating. "What about Wales?" she changed the subject. "Does it ever snow here in the winter?"

"It snows in Ameryca," Mr. Evans stated.

"Lots," Becky agreed.

"Not by yere," said Dai. "We don't get snow much yere."

"North in Snowdonia they do. Blizzards they have. And further east away from the sea," Aled told Jen. "It won't be cold enough yere, see."

"It snows up by Arwell Jones past Bont Goch," offered Evan.

"Aye, he's east then, isn't he?" said Aled impatiently.

"No snow this weather you can be sure," said Mr. Evans. "River's way up the *cwm* after last night, and still there's rain." He leaned back in his chair and lit a tiny cigar. "Should think Cors Fochno'd be under water this time."

Mrs. Evans whisked the empty plates off into the sink and put another huge, hot dish on the table, this one full of rice pudding, with a pitcher of thick yellow cream and a stack of brown bowls.

"Gram, it was, saying the last storm this bad was all of six years past when the dam up by the Electric broke and John-the-Hill lost his cow byre. Weren't you, Gram? Pass cream, Dai, don't sit like a lump looking at it!"

"Aye, a night that was," said Mr. Evans remembering. "The Electric just new up there and half swept down the valley it was. Of course, they had no business putting the dam there in first place. I said that then."

Aled gave his father a scornful look. "We've heard that before, Da."

"And no one to prove me wrong, either," returned Mr. Evans warmly. "None to say there weren't something in the hills tried to stop them."

"And that something John-the-Hill himself! Never wanted the dam there, he didn't."

"Weren't John-the-Hill."

"What *was* it?" asked Becky intrigued.

"Now, Evan," warned Mrs. Evans.

"Things as can't be explained by the likes of him," indicating Aled, "things best not talked of too much. There are creatures back there it's best we have nowt to do with, my little one," he said gravely.

Aled snorted, Mrs. Evans shot him a quelling look, and he kept his mouth shut.

But, "The Old Ones," said Rhian.

"If you're through pudding, Rhian, you can clear table," said her mother.

This time Jen and Becky helped, and before long were drying dishes, trying to keep up with Rhian who was washing. The little door in the right wall opened into a stone larder, Jen discovered when Mrs. Evans opened it to put the leftover food away.

Evan settled Gram again by the fire where she took up a ball of red yarn and a crochet hook, and the four men stretched themselves in chairs around the hearth. The marmalade cat sprang into Aled's lap and made itself comfortable, closing its yellow eyes, and he hunched over it, tickling the fur behind its ears.

"Will it rain much more then, Da?" asked Rhian, scowling as she scoured the pudding pot.

"Be steady through till morning, shouldn't wonder."

"There'll be a high tide at Borth tonight," said Aled.

"The waves were right over the sea wall yesterday," Rhian told him.

"Aye. Some smashed windows, I'd guess. Sea heaves fair big stones up in storms like this. But wind's dropped anyway." Mr. Evans breathed a cloud of blue smoke. "This'll be a storm like the one flooded the country yere about thousands of years ago."

"A flood," said Becky. "Does it happen often?"

Mrs. Evans was putting away the crockery. "Nay, it were thousands of years, if you can believe the story."

"Like the Electric," said Aled darkly.

"It's true enough, the flood," Mr. Evans said severely.

"Even your scientists have been finding traces of it, see. And if you know where to look, happen you can find bits of the old land when the tide's right."

"The flood never went down?" asked Jen in a curious, choking voice.

"Not all of it did. It were out by Borth where it flooded according to the legend. A land called the Low Hundred, in Welsh *Cantrev y Gwaelod,* it being so flat. The sea just came over the sea wall in a storm like this and the land vanished, see. I've heard some say you can hear bells ring under the water out by the river mouth—sixteen towns were lost."

"What can you still see?" Becky demanded. "Can I see any of it?"

"That you can, if you know the spot. There's a great piece of the sea wall comes up out of the bay between Borth and Aberystwyth. Goes straight as an arrow from by the cliff, it does."

"And it is a very good story, Da," said Aled. "But there are other explanations for that heap of stones."

"Aye, and I've heard them," declared Mr. Evans, pitching the last scant quarter inch of his cigar into the fire. "You can believe what you like, Aled, lad. And I'll be believing what I like. You're not changing my mind."

Mrs. Evans noticed Jen's white face. "Enough talk of floods and all, I should think," she said briskly.

"Time we were back to work," said Mr. Evans. He got up reluctantly.

"And we should be getting back to Borth, I think," said Jen, pulling herself together. "It was very nice of you to let us stay, Mrs. Evans."

"Not a bit," replied Mrs. Evans warmly. "You're welcome here when you can come, you both. Does Gram and me a world of good seeing new faces, don't it, Gram? Here, you Aled, you can walk down the hill with them, just to see them on their way. They won't be familiar with the track."

Aled made no protest, just shrugged his narrow shoulders in assent. They waited until Mr. Evans, Dai, and Evan had pulled on their boots and macs in the little porch and gone before they went out.

It was raining just as hard. Jen thought it would go on forever. The sky was swollen and heavy with it.

Aled looked at it and nodded. "Rain till morning easy," he predicted gloomily.

"Do you lose any sheep when it's like this?" Jen asked out of politeness.

"Sometimes. They get mired, and some get caught in the *cwm* when the water rises."

"Why don't you think it's true about the flood and the sixteen towns?" asked Becky, matching Aled's long strides with trouble. He was small, but he walked like Rhian with quick, swinging steps.

"Superstition, that is," he said scornfully. "There is lots of people believing superstitions around here. They'll tell you the most wonderful stories, they will, and when you're asking for proof, it's then you find they can't give it. Nothing to show. Long as they believe that stuff they won't get ahead any. Like the Electric. They think that's special country up there, magic, and they'd have kept it out. But we'd not have lights at the farm without, see."

"But what about the walls your father said he could see?" Becky persisted.

"If believing makes them walls." Aled shook his head. "More likely the sea made them, not men at all. Bloke at the University says they're natural, and he's the one can show you proof, not Da."

They walked on in silence. In what seemed a very short time, they reached the bottom of the hill and the tiny cluster of houses and pub called Tre'r-ddôl. Here Aled left Jen and Becky and, without a backward glance, strode back up the hill toward Llechwedd Melyn. The two girls found shelter from the rain in the entry of the pub until the bus came and they could climb into its dry, lighted warmth and be carried back to Borth.

5

A Not So Very Merry Christmas

THE VISIT TO LLECHWEDD MELYN had not been entirely successful. It disturbed Jen more than she liked to admit to think of Mr. Evans's story about the flooding of the land called the Low Hundred. She sifted it vainly for some word or phrase that would prove he did not really believe it himself, just considered it a good story. And she drew back from making the inevitable connection between that story and Peter's.

Mr. Evans was a kind of person entirely new to Jen. She found him unsettling. He was an adult who still believed in magic and superstition and in the power of creatures Rhian had called "the Old Ones." They were things for children, things you outgrew like Santa Claus and fairy tales. Mr. Evans ought to know better—his son Aled certainly did.

And Becky was no help at all, Jen thought crossly. She liked the story of the flood. She said she could see no reason why it couldn't be true. "After all, look at the Bog, Jen. If the Low Hundred was land like that, it's no wonder it flooded."

It was a relief to concentrate instead on Christmas, which was practically on top of them, and Jen plunged into it almost fiercely. There hadn't really been any Christmas last year, because Anne Morgan had been killed only two weeks before and they had all been in a state of shock, too numb and unbelieving to celebrate anything.

Whatever could be salvaged of the holiday, Aunt Beth and Uncle Ted had valiantly pieced together for the children, especially Becky. David was beyond reach. He had shut himself off from them all like someone in a dream. He was unwilling or unable to respond, unconscious of all that went on around him. It had been a nightmare time of Santa Clauses and Christmas cards, and notes of sympathy and flowers. People had tried so hard to help, but they didn't seem to understand that there was nothing they could do.

A great aching hole had been gouged in the family that no one could fill, and, like a vacuum, it sucked them all into a void. There were presents, a few very good friends, snow on the ground, the College carol service. Jen could still feel the horror that had overcome her at seeing her father cry during that carol service. It had frozen her, made her unable to think or to move. She had not soon forgiven him for it because she couldn't bring herself to reach out and say or do something that would comfort him. *He* should have been comforting her.

And Becky and Peter? Jen didn't know what they felt. She was struggling too hard with her own feelings to be aware of theirs.

Looking back on that Christmas, Jen discovered little of it was clear. It had become a disordered muddle of isolated moments, the sight of the family car hideously flattened, the heavy, waxen lilies in the chapel, shaking hands endlessly and listening to people say "I'm so sorry . . ." Bewilderment, hurt. But it was odd that the details were not all sharp in her mind.

The hole where Anne had been was still there, its edges a little less jagged now, but Christmas had to be Christmas again for the rest of them. Jen was determined and there was a great deal to be done first.

"You're making lists just like Aunt Beth," Becky observed across a pile of breakfast dishes the day after Llech-wedd Melyn. "I thought she was the only one of us who did it."

David lifted his head from the essay he was marking. "So she always has been. Must be a latent family characteristic passed obliquely through the females."

"Go ahead and make fun," Jen retorted. "You don't realize how much there is to do!"

"Does it all have to be done?" inquired Peter.

"Not if you don't mind going without Christmas dinner and presents and all the rest," said Jen tartly.

Peter shrugged and didn't answer. He was uncomfortable with Jen. She thought he still harbored a grudge for the night of the storm, but it wasn't so much that. He hated to think of all he had blurted out that night; he hadn't done it well at all.

"What about a Christmas tree?" Becky demanded. "Is that on your lists?"

"Mmm. But I don't know where we get one in Borth. Or do we have to go to Aberystwyth? And how do we get it back then?"

"In the bus, of course," said David. "Half-fare for trees."

Becky laughed. "That's silly! Mrs. Davies told me they sell them behind the chapel. They've started already so we can go any time." She looked around hopefully.

David groaned. "I suppose we have to go through with all of that!" he teased. "Well, I can't do it now—I'm too far behind with these. I'll give you the money, though, if the three of you want to go buy one."

"We might as well go today," said Jen.

Peter said, "I don't care."

"No good," declared Becky. "We all have to go, even Dad."

For a minute David looked as if he was going to refuse. It was family tradition that everyone helped to pick the Christmas tree, which meant several hours of hopping up and down on frostbitten feet in snowy lots arguing over the choice.

"All right," said David at last, watching Becky's face. "I'll come back from town at noon and we can go after lunch. You'll be sorry, though. You'd do it much faster without an extra opinion!"

It hadn't rained at all since the storm and the roads were dry. Beyond the River Dovey the hills reappeared, mottled with sun patches and distance, looking like a painted backdrop. Borth was crowded with cars and bicycles up and down the street and people jamming the sidewalks. Two boys and a man were doing a brisk business in Christmas trees on the asphalt infant schoolyard behind the Wesleyan Chapel.

"But they've all got roots!" exclaimed Becky. "I've never seen ones like that!"

"Very sensible," said David. "You can plant them afterward instead of throwing them out covered with tinsel. Much nicer, don't you think? Look, what about that one?"

"Too easy!" Jen laughed. "We have to look at them all first."

Around the enclosure they went, examining and pointing and arguing with each other. Even Peter joined in. Every tree had an untidy, earth-covered ball of roots under it.

"We can't possibly have that one, it's got a huge hole in the other side!"

"Well, yours has a crooked top."

"That one looks much too dry, Peter."

"No branches on the bottom of that!"

At last Becky found one they could all compromise on, with a little traditional grumbling. It was as tall as she was, and very full, though a bit sparse at the top, as Peter pointed out.

David paid for it, and they all took turns lugging it up the hill to Bryn Celyn. "Thank goodness you didn't pick a bigger one!" David panted as he and Peter set it down on the doorstep.

"What do we do about the roots?" Becky asked.

"What do we do about the *tree?*" Jen asked. "We don't have a stand, do we?"

"Wait." Peter was back in a moment with a bucket. "There's that."

"Mrs. Davies's floor-scrubbing bucket," warned Jen.

"It's a Christmas tree stand," said David with an unexpected grin. "Good idea! Go ahead, Peter, we'll fill it with dirt to prop the tree up."

Once they'd installed the tree in the lounge on the coffee table, David disappeared into his study. "Don't forget to water it," he called from the hall.

The next item on Jen's list was food. But Mrs. Davies had already decided the menu for them. "Since I'll be getting it, I'll have me own say about what it is I'm getting!" she declared. "None of your fancy American food, thank you—a good plain Christmas dinner."

"What do you suppose she means by that?" Becky asked, when Jen reported this to David. "Hamburgers?"

"It'll be traditionally Welsh, I suppose," said David.

"English," corrected Becky. "She isn't Welsh."

"Only by a few miles," objected Jen. "It isn't that far."

"Doesn't matter. Ask anyone."

"She's ordered a turkey, so that's all right," resumed Jen, "but she didn't mention desert."

"Oh!" David clapped a hand to his forehead. "You've just reminded me—Mrs. Rhys is sending us a Christmas pudding and her special family recipe for hard sauce. Tell Mrs. Davies, will you?"

Jen nodded and put a check mark beside "Dinner" on her list.

"I expect we ought to give Mrs. Davies a Christmas present," said Becky.

David sighed. "I hadn't thought of that, but you're right. Jen, can you find one somewhere?"

"Cross one off, add another," said Jen, writing "Mrs. Davies" at the bottom. "Anyone else? You'd better think fast because there isn't much time."

"No. If you need extra money, let me know—within reason, of course. No sterling silver for Mrs. D., just something small!"

Becky wanted to make Christmas cookies, but Jen wouldn't. She told Becky she hadn't any idea how to begin, they had no recipes, no equipment, and no practice. That family tradition would just have to wait for another year before she'd attempt it. The memory of the Amherst kitchen full of the warm spicy smell of gingerbread and honey cakes, and of their mother, long brown hair tied back, humming carols and slapping lumps of dough out on the counter, was still too sharp to touch. Jen shook it away and Becky stopped coaxing.

Instead, they climbed the hill to Llechwedd Melyn with Rhian one afternoon and spent hours helping Mrs. Evans make mince pies and jam tarts. She taught them to make pastry dough and sent them home full of tea with a huge warm mince pie to share with David and Peter. And before Jen and Becky started back, Mr. Evans took them down into the wooded *cwm* to cut fresh holly and mistletoe. He did not mention the Old Ones.

Peter didn't go. He spent the afternoon curled in the armchair in the lounge, with a supply of chocolate biscuits and a book that he pretended to read. But his eyes rested on the bay, not his book. It was hazy and distant through the white net curtains; the light made patterns on the water so that he almost fancied he could see villages and trees among the waves. He turned the patterns over and over in his mind, wondering if there really were villages and forests under the water.

It was possible to remember the song of the flood now without sickening panic sweeping over him. The hard knot that had twisted in Peter's stomach during the storm was beginning to come undone. He had lost his fear.

But *why* had it happened? And where? And why had he seen it? Throngs of questions without any answers crowded his head. Why did the Key sing only to him? But whatever the answers might be, the Key continued to sing.

The song had changed since the night of the flood: it was no longer dark and full of violence, but teasing and cheerful. It came in snatches—quick, bright phrases that showed Peter glimpses of the other world. The Key sang often, and he saw the man, Aneirin, with his heavy, dark-colored harp slung across his back, and Taliesin, the boy, carrying his smaller one. And he saw, too, the shining silver harp key hung about Taliesin's neck—the key the woman Caridwen had given him when she had given him his name.

Aneirin and Taliesin were good companions. Peter was glad to see them and disappointed that the song never lasted more than a minute or two. They had left the flooded country behind and traveled through land that was peaceful. There were untidy clumps of huts by the road, villages where the two stopped to spend a night. Children and dogs tumbled around them in the dust, men and women made them welcome with what little food and shelter they had. In return, Aneirin would unsling his harp and sing to them: strange songs of wild places and battles, of heroes and kings and great deeds. Sometimes Taliesin, too, would sing, his voice still unpracticed, but true and clear. And the people listening would see pictures in the songs.

As well as rough villages, the Key sang glimpses of the great halls of kings, like that of the golden king, long and full of firelight, men, and hounds. No matter where the travelers stopped to ask lodging, they were granted it gladly and admitted to whatever company was there. All men's dwellings, rich or humble, were open to the bard and his boy, and always the two paid in songs and tales.

Peter's own time meant nothing to the Key. In the space of a few days he saw the changing seasons in the colors of the country and changing weather. While it rained in Borth, sun fell in drifts of gold between the trees Taliesin and Aneirin walked under. The sky was a clear, uncomplicated blue, high and full of skylarks. When a watery sun turned the bay beneath Bryn Celyn green-blue, a cold northeast wind would drive sheets of rain across the country of the Key, causing the two companions to draw their heavy cloaks tight, muffling their faces and protecting their harps.

Taliesin grew older. His face changed, understanding deepened in his eyes and voice, and his hands became sure on his harp strings. He would never be as tall a man as Aneirin, but the weeks, months, years they spent wandering together toughened his body and weathered his skin so that he resembled Aneirin. When Aneirin spoke, Taliesin listened to him, and always his eyes and ears were greedy for the world around .him.

But for Peter nothing changed. He was still twelve, still in Borth, and it remained December. He discovered it was awkward having to straddle two times as he did. He wished the Key would be a little more careful about picking its moments to sing, especially when other people were around. He wasn't quite sure what happened to him at such times and it made him rather anxious.

One moment he'd be with his family, quite normal, and then the next he wouldn't, and when he came back again, he'd find David or Jen or Becky looking at him impatiently, demanding to know why he didn't pay attention when he was being spoken to. If he hadn't been so enchanted by the Key, it would have worried him more.

As it was, Becky was the first to worry. She kept well out of his arguments with David and Jen, so it was she who first concluded that there might be more to Peter's odd behavior than just being difficult. She broached it to Jen when they were alone, doing their last-minute shopping in Borth.

"Jen—" she began, twisting a long strand of brown hair through her fingers.

"Mmm?" Jen was working out how much money she had. The coins still baffled her.

"It's about Peter."

Jen sighed. "Why is it that, whenever anyone has a problem, it always begins, 'It's about Peter—' What's the matter now?"

"It isn't that he's done anything," said Becky. "It's more the way he's been acting. Don't you think it's peculiar?"

"Not specially. As a matter of fact he's much pleasanter than he's been for days. I haven't even heard him complain lately."

"That's kind of what I mean. Don't you think that's funny?"

"I think it's a real relief. He's finally decided to grow up." Jen gave up and dumped the change back in her pocket. "Let's get some Welsh cakes for tea."

But Becky was persistent. "No, wait a minute. Haven't you noticed that sometimes, when you're talking to Peter, he goes blank? He's never done that before. It's as if he didn't see you or hear you or even remember you're there, and you have to repeat everything. He's done it to all of us."

"So?" Jen stopped and looked at Becky.

"He's never done it before," she repeated.

"Maybe it's a new plan of attack," Jen suggested.

"Can't be," said Becky. "He's not that dumb—all it does is make people mad at him without getting him anywhere. And what about the toast yesterday? That was the same sort of thing—what good did it do him to just sit there and watch it burn? He never even tried to pull it out, and he was really surprised when Dad yelled at him."

"All right, that was peculiar," Jen conceded. "Maybe he isn't feeling well."

"No good. He'd tell everyone if he was sick."

Jen knew Becky was right. Peter hated being ill, and he

was always quick to complain whenever he was. "What do you think it is then?"

"I don't know. I thought maybe you would. You know, it's just since the storm that he's been funny."

Jen didn't like being reminded. The whole business of the storm had left her with an odd and unpleasant sensation and she only wanted to forget it, but Becky's words brought back the dark kitchen and Peter's pale, urgent face in the candlelight. "If you're so worried about Peter, you ought to talk to Dad, not me," she said irritably.

Becky grimaced. "What good would that do? Dad and Peter have been arguing ever since we got here. Dad hasn't got any patience with Peter, and he's not going to listen to me if I try to tell him what I've told you. Peter won't talk to him."

"Oh, for heaven's sake," said Jen, exasperated. "Peter wants me to get Dad to take us all home. Dad wants me to make Peter more reasonable. *You* want me to find out what's wrong with Peter. Well, I can't do any of it! I thought I was here for a vacation, not to straighten out everybody's messes!"

Becky looked glum. "I only thought you'd help. I don't know what to do."

Jen was about to ask, "why do anything?" when she felt suddenly guilty. Becky was only ten, after all, and she had to struggle with the same problems the rest of them did. They all thought she adjusted so well—was that the truth or was it an excuse for them not to worry about her? Jen was ashamed to realize that she hadn't any idea what Becky was really making of all this, or if her younger sister was ever lonely or homesick. She said, "What do you think I can do, then?"

"I'm not sure. I guess I thought Peter might have talked to you."

"He's tried," Jen admitted. "About going home mostly. But I really don't want to get mixed up in that argument. It's between him and Dad. It'd be so much easier if he'd just give in for the year."

"He won't," Becky said.

"No. If it'll make you happier, I can try to find out what's wrong with him, but he may not tell me. I don't see what else I can do."

"Maybe if he thinks we want to help . . ." Becky brightened visibly.

The day before Christmas was dismal. David stayed in Borth with his children, clearly because he felt it was expected, but he was obviously not sure what he should do with them. The weather was awful: high winds drove patches of fierce sun, drenching rain, sleet and snow across the bay in rapid succession, making it impossible to go for a walk. The tree had been decorated already, presents were wrapped, the dinner prepared for. Jen's lists were covered with checkmarks, and she'd run out of made-up things for them to do.

The night before David had taken them to a carol service in the little old church at Llanbadarn Fawr, a village a few miles inland. The service couldn't help but remind each of them of other carol services, and yet it hadn't made them sad. The service was simple, a mixture of English and Welsh, carols and prayers, many of them unfamiliar, but telling a familiar story. The solid, stone church had smelled of dampness and musty books and candles. And for the space of an hour or two Jen remembered how it felt to be part of a family.

That was the way Christmas Eve Day should have been but wasn't. The closeness wasn't there. David prowled up and down, looking irritably out windows as if hoping the sun would be shining into one of them if he could only find it. Peter buried himself in a book in the lounge and ignored everyone. Becky nearly drove Jen wild by asking repeatedly if there weren't something she could do to help, and Jen was feeling irritable anyway because the day was going so badly and she couldn't find any way to change it.

Finally, David gave up and went back to work on his article for the *Amherst Quarterly,* and Becky settled in front of the television to watch mindless Christmas specials. By supper, everyone was dismal and homesick.

Mrs. Davies only made it worse by talking briskly about how much she still had to do and how hard it was, after all, with the whole family home and two babies in the house. Both her daughters were visiting with their husbands and children, and there was that much to be done, she was sure she didn't know how she'd manage.

"Not like us," said Becky glumly, when Mrs. Davies had departed. "We can't think of enough to do. Maybe we should offer to help?"

Peter looked horrified. "You're kidding!"

"Well, why not?" Becky defended herself. "It'd be better than sitting around. The Christmas programs on television are just as bad here as at home. Some are even worse!"

"Well, cheer up," said Jen. "The day's almost over."

"I always used to want it to last, so Christmas wouldn't be gone so quickly," mourned Becky.

"You all look festive and happy," remarked David, coming out to supper. "Can't you at least pretend to be jolly?"

"Why?" demanded Peter. Jen glared at him, but he refused to look at her.

"Tomorrow's Christmas, for one reason," said David, "and we're all together, for another."

"It doesn't seem like Christmas somehow," said Becky.

"That's nonsense!" There was a trace of sharpness in David's voice that made Jen wary. "Christmas is Christmas no matter where you are."

"I wish we were home," said Peter, daring his father's anger.

"You've made that plain over and over," retorted David. "There is no point in saying it again."

"You never seem to pay any attention."

Jen caught her breath. Peter was deliberately provoking an argument.

"Peter—" began Becky, her face pinched-looking.

"I don't care where we are—it's no good if it isn't home!" Peter burst out across her. "It isn't *fair!* You never asked if we wanted to come here, you just brought us. You never even bothered to say why we came. How can you expect me to understand when you won't try to understand *me?* I don't believe you care one bit what we think, and it's not fair!"

Becky's hand, holding a forkful of green beans, was paralyzed, her eyes alarmed. Jen was afraid to look at David. She could feel his anger like electricity in the air.

"Peter," he said, his voice dangerously quiet, "I don't think you know what you're talking about. If you think I came to Wales and brought you with me without the most careful and painful consideration first, you're very mistaken. I didn't just pack a few things in a trunk and buy some plane tickets. It may interest you to know that your mother and I had planned this trip—for this very year—long ago. We wanted to wait until you were all old enough, *mature* enough, to appreciate living in a foreign country and until I got the right offer. This was the year. And after a lot of hard thinking, I decided I should go ahead with those plans we'd already made."

"But you never asked us!" cried Peter passionately. "It was different before!"

"Before your mother died? You might as well say it, if that's what you mean. Of course, it was different, I'd never pretend it wasn't. But your mother wanted us to come here very much. We were waiting until I'd heard from the University before we told you. But that was—after. Peter, you have no monopoly on being lonely or homesick. You aren't the only one to miss your mother; you're being selfish if you think you are. Jen and Becky lost as much as you did."

"But they don't *mind* being here. You took away everything I had, everything I wanted. You brought me to this awful place where there's nothing at all, and then you ignore me and you expect me to be happy. You don't care what happens to us anyway, you just shut yourself up in your study or go off to the University all day. It doesn't matter to *you* how we manage." All the bitterness and anger came pouring out of Peter. His face was white and intense, his eyes blazing.

"Of course it matters!" David raised his voice. "But I expect you to be old enough to take some responsibility for yourselves. I expect you to make an effort to get along, and I don't think you have, Peter. You've never given Wales a chance—your school, this house, the town, any of it. You made up your mind not to like it before we even came and you refuse to try. You're behaving like a baby instead of a twelve-year-old boy and I'm ashamed of you! We've all listened to your complaints, God knows, and I can tell you I'm getting fed up with them. Now, unless you can buck up and try to make the best of things, I think you'd better excuse yourself from the table."

Without a word Peter got up and left the kitchen, and they all heard the lounge door slam a moment later. No one felt like finishing supper after that. Jen, glancing at her father, saw him look at Peter's empty chair with a bleak expression in his eyes, and she looked away quickly. It was a terrible end to the day. David said nothing more, but left without dessert, presumably to shut himself in the study again.

"I don't see how it can get much worse," said Becky in a small voice.

Jen could think of no comfort for her. This kind of trouble frightened her. Family quarrels were one thing, but this was much more serious and it had never happened before.

The answer to her own problems, she had been sure, was to be with her father and Becky and Peter again. Well, here they all were together and yet further apart than they'd ever been.

"It'll be better in the morning," she said finally.

"I hope so," said Becky.

An overwhelming sense of injustice filled Peter. He had finally come out and told his father exactly what he thought, and his father had sent him away from the dinner table. He hadn't listened, he hadn't *tried* to understand. He'd closed his mind. What chance did he, Peter, possibly have? And Jen and Becky had just sat there and listened to their father shout at him and made no move to help. He was alone, terribly, terribly alone, and no one cared. He felt martyred and bitter and very unhappy.

He was, in fact, very close to tears, which made him even more resentful because he hated crying. He hadn't cried since his mother had been killed, and only once then, days after, when it had begun to hurt, when he'd realized what had happened. *She* would have understood, he told himself fiercely. *She* wouldn't have made him stay; she'd admit she'd been wrong. But deep down he felt a little betrayed knowing that his mother had helped plan this trip. He hadn't known that before.

The lounge was dark. No one came to try and make peace or to cheer him up. No one came to turn on the lights and apologize, so Peter sat on in the darkness, biting his lip and feeling wretched.

And the Key began to sing to him. At first he fought against it, wanting to hold his grief like a bed of nails, not wanting to be distracted from it, but the Key disregarded him and its song grew, teasing, insinuating itself into Peter's head, ignoring the black thoughts.

It sang of summer and a pretty breeze, the dizzying shout of skylarks lost in an endless blue sky. Insects chanted in the long grass that shimmered in the sun beside a river.

Taliesin, now a grown man, sat on the bank, his head cocked to one side, eyes narrowed against the reflected dazzle of sun, his bare feet turned to gold in the peaty water. He was trying words to himself, singing without sound, listening, searching for the right ones. The neck of his coarse blue tunic was open, the sleeves pushed above his elbows, and his face and arms and throat were the weathered brown of a peasant laborer. But where his coppery hair had lain across his broad forehead, the skin was pale and seemed almost to shine when the breeze brushed it clear.

His companion this time was not Aneirin, but a gangly, near-grown boy, as brown and careless as he, flung on his stomach near Taliesin, watching fish flick in the shallows. Aneirin was nowhere to be seen. He was gone.

"Can you catch them in your hand?"

"Fish?" asked Taliesin without moving.

"Mmm." The boy nodded. "Without traps or lines or weirs, I mean."

Taliesin smiled. "When I am hungry."

"Would you teach me?" the boy asked eagerly.

"Are you hungry?"

The boy rolled onto his back. "No. But if I never learn I may be one day."

"A good answer. Reason enough for a king's son to learn to fish!"

"Then you will?"

Taliesin got to his feet and the boy scrambled up. Though younger, he topped Taliesin by several inches. "A good half," said Taliesin, "is knowing where to find what you look for. Remember that, Elphin Rheged."

The spot he chose was further upstream, among the trees, where a noisy beck joined the river, sun-speckled as a trout's belly. Taliesin stretched himself on the edge of the stream beside a wide, slow-moving pool, and Elphin Rheged squatted near him peering into the water.

"Do you see?" asked Taliesin. He sank his arm up to the elbow, his hand moving slowly toward a large fat fish that hung almost motionless in the clear stream. Elphin watched intently as the hand worked closer, slow and patient, its fingers moving gently with the same motion as the fish's gills. They touched the underside of the creature, they stroked it, they scratched it, and the fish responded like a kitten being rubbed. Elphin Rheged could almost imagine it purred. Taliesin's eyes were half closed and there was a smile touching his mouth. For a long moment they stopped thus, almost frozen: boy, man, and fish totally absorbed in one another. Then, with reluctance, Taliesin moved and moved so quickly the boy saw only a sudden flash of light and a glittering rainbow of drops in the air above the pool, and Taliesin held the great fish helpless in his hand, watching it gulp, its eyes bulging.

"You are too foolish and trusting," Taliesin told it softly. "Another time you will not be so fortunate." And he released the trout again to its own element. It rested, stunned, for several seconds, then with a thrust of its tail, it vanished into the muddy safety of the pool's depths.

"But why?" demanded Elphin Rheged. "He was so big and you caught him fairly."

"I had no need of his life," replied the man. "Hunting that has no point is worse than going hungry. That, too, you should remember." His words were grave, but he laughed at Elphin's disappointment. "Come! You shall try it yourself further upstream where the fish will not have wind of us yet. But keep in mind the dinner Urien Rheged, your father, will set before us tonight."

The sun slanted gold through the trees and the shadows were stretching when at last Taliesin and Elphin Rheged left the beck, Elphin with a new skill in his fingers and new thoughts in his mind, but nothing to show for his afternoon's fishing. He still struggled to understand what Taliesin had been teaching him and his head was full. Taliesin, for himself, was pleased with the day and sang softly.

But on the riverbank they were met, unaware, by a party

of rough, wild-looking men with salt-tangled hair and beards, and before man or boy knew what had happened they found themselves seized and bound. Their captors spoke a language that was unfamiliar to Elphin Rheged. He struggled blindly, kicking with his bare feet when they secured his arms, but they were much stronger than he and laughed crudely at his efforts. Taliesin stood still, offering no resistance, and when Elphin saw him, he too stopped fighting; he saw what Taliesin had immediately seen: that to struggle was useless. And he saw also Taliesin's slight nod to him.

The men began a heated discussion, with many gestures and shakings of fists in one another's faces, their voices colliding in the startled air. That Elphin Rheged and Taliesin were the subject of the discussion there could be no doubt. At last they seemed to reach some kind of agreement, and the prisoners found themselves caught up among them and moved quickly off, along the river toward the coast. They were marched shoulder to shoulder with men tight on all sides around them, rough and disagreeably unwashed.

"Who are they?" whispered Elphin furiously. "Do they know who *I* am? My father will not stand for this!"

"They are Irish. I know a little of their speech, enough to gather that they are sea raiders and we are being taken to their ships. As to your father, I do not believe they will have advised Urien Rheged of their plans." The man at Taliesin's right said something and gave him a shove forward. Obviously the prisoners were not meant to communicate.

"Wait," murmured Taliesin. And Elphin was forced to bide.

More men waited on the shore, and among them was one who was evidently their chief. Though wild and unkempt like the others, his clothing was incongruously fine, and he wore a heavy gold chain around his hairy neck. When he spoke, he silenced those with whom he stood. Taliesin guessed that their fate lay in this man's hands. His small eyes gleamed shrewdly

under a tangle of hair and great black eyebrows. He listened to
the raiders and squinted at the captives. Elphin Rheged looked
away from him in discomfort, but Taliesin returned his gaze
calmly.

At length the chief raised a huge, ring-studded hand, and
the explanations ceased.

"You are natives?" The words were so strongly accented
that Elphin did not realize at once that he understood them.

"Yes," replied Taliesin.

"Laborers?"

"No. I am a bard from the land of Cymru."

"He, too?" indicating Elphin Rheged.

"My companion," said Taliesin simply.

"A bard." The man was silent, stroking his wiry beard.
"You are not much of a prize," he said at last.

"We are what we are," replied Taliesin evenly.

"Not much of a prize is better than none at all, eh?"
Around them the Irish nodded, quick to agree, though they
had not understood what he had said.

"You are Irish slaves now," said the chief.

It was a miscellaneous cargo the raiders stowed aboard
their broad, high-sided sailing ships: small livestock such as
sheep and poultry, and even a young bull calf, shields, swords
and daggers taken from some chief's store, odd pieces of silver and gold work, a heap of good woolen material, and a
handful of miserable looking Britons—two men, four girls,
and a boy younger than Elphin. These were divided among
the six ships. Taliesin was put aboard the first, that of the
chief, and Elphin Rheged in another.

"Have faith, Elphin, and do not despair," were the last
words Taliesin ever spoke to him. And that night, with the
turning of the tide, the raiders made sail for their own
land.

6

Beside the Dovey

PARENTS WERE SUPPOSED to *cope,* Jen thought resentfully, sitting in the kitchen after Becky went up to bed. They were supposed to be able to handle crises like this one, but David wasn't. She had never before seen her father and her brother so totally opposed, so irreconcilable. They were strangers, people she didn't know at all, and worse, people she didn't want anything to do with.

She'd been cheated out of her vacation. Instead of being welcomed and fussed over, she'd been set down in the middle of a bitter quarrel that seemed to have no possible resolution, but hurt everyone it touched. Why on earth had she wanted to come, she wondered bleakly. Depression like this was new to her: it was cold and faceless, rising from the pit of her stomach and paralyzing her mind.

"Jennifer?" David stood, oddly hesitant, in the doorway. "I was afraid you'd gone to bed."

"I was just going." She got to her feet without looking at him. When he called her Jennifer, she always wondered what was coming next.

"Would you come into the study for a few minutes? Would you come and talk?" He was asking, not telling. She followed him down the hall, wary. David sat heavily in the easy chair, his hands restless on his knees. His eyes were tired and sad. Jen, looking at his face, thought again of a stranger and waited.

"I'm sorry I lost my temper at supper," he said at last. "I shouldn't have. I suppose Peter was just trying to provoke me."

Jen wasn't at all sure of that. She wondered if her father saw Peter's misery, but she was silent and he went on.

"I know it hasn't been particularly easy for him here. I don't think it's been easy for any of us, even Becky, though she seems to have come off best. But I get so tired of hearing Peter complain. He's a problem, Jen. I can't think what's gotten into him. I wondered if he'd talked to you at all, told you why he's so dead set against being here?"

"He's homesick," said Jen, because he expected her to say something.

David sighed. "Everyone is at first. But Peter—I thought he'd like it here. I thought he'd find it exciting."

"He wants to go home."

David gave a little snort. "Even I can tell that, Jen. I hoped you could tell me a bit more."

Jen bit her lip. He wasn't angry with her, but he was talking to her as if she were an adult and it made her uncomfortable. "I was just telling you what he'd said to me," she answered defensively.

"I came here," said David slowly, "because I couldn't think what else to do. It wouldn't have been any good to stay in Amherst this year. All I could see was your mother. I thought by getting right away to a place that was new to all of us, I could clear my head again. We could straighten ourselves out." He spoke softly, almost to himself. "I wanted life to be as different as I could make it. To break off and start again."

"But you *can't* forget Mother!" Jen protested, shocked.

"I didn't say that." David met her eyes gravely. "But we've got to live without her, we have to get used to it. Memories are important and we've all got them, but they don't help much with the practical side of things. You're old enough to understand that, even if Peter and Becky aren't. Though I'm disappointed at Peter. I think I could make it work if it weren't for him. Sometimes I wonder—" He broke off and gave his head a shake. "Maybe Beth was right after all, and I never should have done it. But human beings are capable of making adjustments."

"Maybe it's just harder for Peter," suggested Jen tentatively.

"Harder?" David leaned back in his chair. "My God, do you think it's been easy for me? Suddenly, I've got the three of you to cope with on my own as well as losing Anne." His eyes rested on Jen's face and he smiled a little. "Not that I'd rather I didn't have you; I'm just not used to being responsible for the whole show. I keep thinking if we can only hang on long enough it will all work out."

A stranger. Jen felt hopelessly confused. Her father had given her a sudden glimpse of himself she'd never seen before and a glimpse of what it was like to be an adult. She was bewildered to see it wasn't so very different from where she was now: you didn't know all the answers, you just had bigger responsibilities.

All the while she'd been insulated in her own cocoon of unhappiness, she'd missed her father's grief. And he in turn missed Peter's. It was as if they'd all built separate little rooms to live in instead of one big one. Peter's misery was no more unique than hers. Jen could see it was going to be hard to sort this one out, and in spite of her blinding flash of truth, she didn't know what to say to David.

"Anyway, if you can help at all with Peter, I'd be grateful," he was saying. He didn't sound as tense. "I still hope he'll come around."

"I don't know . . ." she began doubtfully, remembering her own problems with Peter.

"Well, do what you can, will you? And don't look so

worried—I'm through. Go on up to bed, why don't you? I've still got one or two things to do here."

Jen undressed in the dark, not wanting to wake Becky, who was snoring ever so slightly. She fell asleep, aware of an unaccustomed sympathy for her father, and woke what seemed like only moments later to find Becky bouncing excitedly on the foot of her bed.

"Merry Christmas!"

"Already?" asked Jen sleepily.

"It's eight o'clock," Becky informed her. "*And* it's a beautiful day!"

"I don't believe it."

But it was. All the clouds of the day before had been swept off the sky by a boisterous westerly wind. It brushed the sea with white horses and sang in the electric wires. The air felt light and sharp.

The morning slid by pleasantly, with a sort of endless breakfast: oranges, cocoa, coffee, eggs, sausage, bacon, toast, as much as anyone wanted, interrupted by unwrapping presents.

The argument of the night before wasn't mentioned, and though Peter didn't speak to his father more than absolutely necessary, neither did he make any remarks that would annoy David.

Mrs. Davies and her plump, cheerful daughter, Susan, came in to organize dinner. Mrs. Davies raised her eyebrows at the chaos in the kitchen, but for once she didn't say anything. And before anyone quite knew what was happening, she'd passed out jobs. Jen peeled potatoes, while Becky and David did the dishes, and Peter found himself chopping up stale bread for stuffing.

They set up the table in the lounge with a white tablecloth and two of the longer candle-ends, because, as Becky said, you couldn't just eat a turkey dinner like boiled beef and cabbage in the kitchen. It had to be special.

The smells, thought Jen, closing her eyes for a moment,

are just like the smells of any Christmas dinner: roast turkey and gravy, beets, steaming pudding, hot and rich.

Once dinner was over, they piled everything in the sink and left it while all four of them went for a walk on the bright, windy beach. The broad, hard sands were covered with people out walking, muffled against the wind in best coats and scarves and gloves, tiny children wrapped so they looked almost spherical, dogs racing ecstatically from figure to figure.

Gulls dipped and screamed raucously on the air currents, slicing through the sky on sharp wings, and Becky sent a small party of black and white birds with long red bills crying out low over the water.

"Oystercatchers," she told the others. "Aren't they beautiful? Gwilym showed me."

"Isn't that Gwilym?" asked David. "Up there?"

"He's watching something," said Becky. "Come on."

The long, thin figure stood still, looking out to sea through binoculars.

"Hullo," said David, as they joined him. He jumped and turned around. He seemed a little overwhelmed at the sight of all the Morgans together.

"What are you watching?" Becky demanded.

"Oh, um, not much. Some fishing boats, I think." He glanced around. "Too many people for birds."

Peter gave Jen a nudge, which she ignored.

"Just out walking?" David asked pleasantly.

"Up to Ynyslas, I thought, sir."

"That's the bit of beach where the Dovey joins the sea, isn't it?"

Gwilym nodded. "Good place for birds at low tide."

"Isn't there supposed to be a drowned forest somewhere down that way?"

"Yes, sir," said Gwilym.

"You mean *underwater?*" said Becky.

Peter and Jen avoided each other's eyes.

"You can see it at dead low tide, but the water has to be right out, which doesn't happen that often," explained Gwilym.

"But the trees aren't still alive, are they?" Becky asked.

"Of course not," said Jen.

"What does it look like then?"

"Nothing much, I should think," said David.

"You can find tree stumps and a peat bed like in the Bog," Gwilym said.

"When did it happen?" asked Peter.

"Some say when the Low Hundred was flooded, which'd be sixth century," replied Gwilym.

Peter looked speculative.

"You sound well up in archaeology," remarked David, and Gwilym's eyes lit with pleasure.

"I know some," he admitted. "There's a lot to find around here, sir."

They had begun walking again, all of them moving down the beach toward Ynyslas.

"Yes," David said, "I'd hoped to have more time for exploring, but the University's kept me pretty well occupied so far. Maybe when the weather gets warmer in the spring."

"It's a grand place for it, sir." Gwilym sounded approving.

"But the forest," Becky persisted. "Why did it drown?"

"I would guess the sea rose. Perhaps it's still rising."

"It could cover Borth?"

"Not right away." David smiled. He turned back to Gwilym. "This whole area used to be forested once, didn't it?"

"Hundreds of years ago, that was. Most of Wales. But it was stripped for timber and farming then. Forestry Commmission's replanting parts of it now."

"So it'll look the way it used to?" Becky wanted to know.

"Not likely. To make money lumbering. Never mind how it looks and what it does to the wildlife. There." Gwilym pointed back, toward the hills behind the Bog. "See the patches there? That's Forestry land."

Regular dark green squares stood out boldly against the rust and silver of the bare slopes.

"All the same kind of tree planted together and so close there's no light between, just so they'll grow straight."

"I see what you mean," said David.

Peter stared without seeing at the rough edges of the waves on the sand. He pretended indifference to the conversation, but he was listening hard, his mind working furiously over the new information: the drowned forest, which meant a flood, the hills covered with trees once upon a time. There must have been forests at the time of the flood.

They'd passed most of the other people, and the last houses of Borth lay behind them. The sun broke and scattered on the restless bay and high over the Bog Gwilym spotted a buzzard sailing the wind on broad, ragged wings. "All around," he said. "Cardigan's thick with buzzards." After a moment, he offered David his binoculars for a closer look. Doesn't trust the rest of us, Jen thought.

"Can you see the white patches on the undersides of his wings?" asked Gwilym.

"Mmm. Very well."

"Buzzards are the ones that hang around waiting for people to die, aren't they?" asked Becky.

"You're thinking of vultures," David told her, watching the bird lift higher and higher until it was only a dot in the towering sky.

"Vultures have bald heads," Jen added.

"No," David disagreed, "those are eagles."

"Bald eagles!" shouted Becky, laughing.

Gwilym smiled politely but without comprehension, and David handed back the binoculars.

"Those are good ones," he remarked. "What power?"

"Ten by fifty." Gwilym was back on his own territory.

"Bit big for some, but I can manage them. Dad gave them to me, got them special from Cardiff." There was pride in his voice. "Best present I ever got." He hung them carefully around his neck again.

David nodded. "Hard to beat good ones."

They went on, David and Gwilym talking together, Jen and Becky joining in now and then, and Peter coming thoughtfully behind.

After all, how long ago was hundreds of years? Gwilym had said sixth century, but that would have been 500. Imagination couldn't stretch that far, and yet vast pieces of time lay all around: in the sand underfoot, the shaping of the sea, the burnished hills, the Bog. They changed, but so gradually it was seldom noticed in a lifetime. They must all have been here fourteen hundred years ago. Suppose you could see other people's footprints in the sand—not just the ones from this time that the tide hadn't washed away, but the footprints every person had ever made on this beach. . . . Peter thought his head would burst.

David was saying, "We came from here, my family. My grandfather was twenty-seven when he emigrated to New England. I remember he used to speak Welsh sometimes. He came from the coal valleys in the south near Tredegar and he settled in Massachusetts."

"And he met Great-grandmother," Becky prompted. They all knew the story and she always loved to hear it.

David smiled at her. "Yes, he met Great-grandmother. She'd emigrated with her own family from Machynlleth when she was seventeen. I think she was always sorry she'd left Wales, she told us such stories. We always swore we'd come back one day and see it, but none of us ever did till now." His eyes were on the mountains across the river as he spoke.

"She saw them, too, didn't she?" Jen asked softly. "She grew up with them. It's hard to imagine."

"But why?" asked Becky. "Why did they leave Wales?"

"Money. A better life. It was a bad time for many people in the nineteenth century. Lots of them left. Huw Morgan's brothers all went to Pennsylvania from Tredegar to work in the coal fields because it was what they knew, but Grandfather tried farming instead in the Connecticut Valley."

Becky nodded, satisfied.

Gwilym had been keeping pace with David, listening in silence, but he stopped abruptly and lifted his binoculars.

"Birds?" asked David, stopping, too.

"No," said Gwilym, "some kind of boats."

They all looked in the direction he pointed, and on the horizon they could make out four—no, five—little black specks.

"Out by Towyn that is," said Gwilym after a minute. "Sailing boats."

"Good wind for it," remarked David, shading his eyes with his hand.

"Odd shape they've got. Not fishing boats on Christmas Day, but too big for pleasure boats." He passed David the binoculars. "What do you think, sir?"

"They certainly do look peculiar. Double-ended and one square sail each. Maybe something special for Christmas? A race of some kind?"

"They're Irish," said Peter, who'd been silent till now.

"How in blazes do *you* know?" asked his father, surprised. "You can hardly see them without the glasses!"

"They just are."

"Let me see," Jen demanded, and David gave her the binoculars. He frowned at Peter.

There were six boats visible through the glasses, sailing close together. Their sails were well filled with wind, they were broad and high-sided, rather like barges, with two pointed ends, so it was hard to tell at a glance which way they were going, but in a minute Jen saw they were tacking away from the coast—toward Ireland.

"My turn," cried Becky impatiently. "I want to see!"

Reluctantly Jen passed the binoculars.

"They are sailing toward the Irish coast," said Gwilym slowly, "but—"

"They look like replicas of the war ships used by the ancient Celts," David said. "It must be some sort of pageant. An old Welsh custom, like burning a Viking ship the way they still do in the Shetlands every year."

"They're neat," said Becky. "I wish I could see one close."

"There'll probably be a picture in the *Cambrian News* next week," David replied.

Peter was too overwhelmed by what was happening to speak. He'd seen the ships once before, when Taliesin and the boy had been taken aboard them as prisoners. He knew they were Irish. He knew they weren't replicas. But—everyone was straining to watch as the ships disappeared over the horizon—they had *all* seen them this time, not he alone! Of course, the others understood even less than he did, but they all had seen them.

Somehow, when the ships had gone, no one wanted to walk any further up the beach. Above the hills to the northeast, clouds were beginning to pile and the wind had a bite to it they hadn't noticed while they were moving. Gwilym alone went on toward Ynyslas, reluctant to lose the light. He turned when he'd gone a dozen yards or so.

"If you want to go out along the Dovey tomorrow, I'll be going," he called. "Early, mind."

"Of course, we do," Becky declared. "When?"

"Half-past six. We can get a ride up to Ynyslas with my Dad if we're sharp."

"Why not the Bog?" Jen asked.

Gwilym shook his head. "Too wet since that storm. Not safe."

"Well!" said Jen, when they were well out of earshot. "I thought he'd forgotten all about promising."

"Not Gwilym. It was Dad being interested that did it,

though. You could tell. I bet he'd like it if you came, too."

David shook his head, smiling. "We'll see, but I doubt I can spare the time, much as I'd like to."

To everyone's surprise, Peter allowed that he might like to go, even though it meant getting up at six.

It was still dark when Jen and Becky fell out of bed next morning—dark and bone-chilling. But Becky declared it wasn't nearly as hard to get ready for a special expedition at six as it was to get up for school at seven-thirty. She thumped on Peter's door, and he came out of his room fully dressed, as if he'd been waiting for her.

David had given all three of them small knapsacks for Christmas, and they began rummaging for food to pack in them.

"I have no idea how long we'll be out," said Peter, "but I have no intention of going hungry."

Becky sliced bread for sandwiches and Peter cut chunks off the cold turkey, while Jen made toast and cocoa for breakfast. They all got in each other's way, scalded their mouths on the hot cocoa and dripped butter on the table quite amicably.

"I tell you, though," Peter stated, shifting his knapsack to find the most comfortable spot, "I hope we don't have to go too far before we can eat this stuff. It's heavy."

"*You* shouldn't complain. You put most of it in," Becky observed.

"Come on," said Jen, "we'll miss Gwilym."

He was waiting outside Bryn Celyn. Jen thought she saw a flicker of surprise in his eyes when he saw them emerge on time—in fact, five minutes early. She grinned to herself.

"We're in time for the bus if we nip down to Williams's smartish," he greeted them and was off before anyone could respond. They could only gallop after him.

East, beyond the Bog and over the hills of Montgomery-shire, the sky was stained with first light. It moved across the sky like water spreading across a blotter, drawing mist up from the country. A few windows on the hill were lighted, but not many people were up at half-past six the day after Christmas.

Hugh-the-Bus was. He sat leaning over the steering wheel of his bus, reading a two-day-old newspaper. He grinned at the Morgans as they stumbled on behind Gwilym. "Up early, is it? You'll have a grand morning for it. Wind's up, but sun'll be out in two shakes, look you. Down to Ynyslas is it, Gwilym?"

"Don't you mind having to work today?" asked Becky. "I thought it was a holiday." The bus was empty but for the five of them.

"Aye, Boxing Day. But it's not so bad, and twice the money, see. Someone has to."

"It's the babies," said Gwilym darkly.

"And for you!" said his father with a laugh.

The Morgans looked puzzled.

"My sisters," Gwilym explained. "Susan and Sheila and both with babies in the house."

"Two mums and a gram and the bath full of nappies and the sink full of bottles." Hugh-the-Bus chuckled. "More than a man can stand, and for three days. Better it is to leave them fussing and go."

"Worse than with summer visitors," added Gwilym. "At least with visitors you aren't expected to take an interest. But babies—"

"You're an uncle!" exclaimed Becky, delighted.

"Aye, he is that," agreed Hugh-the-Bus solemnly. "Twice over."

"Ahh," protested Gwilym, disgusted.

The only soul to be seen down the length of Borth was the paper boy on his cycle. Hugh-the Bus saluted him as he drove majestically down the middle of the long straight road to the Ynyslas Turn by the golf links.

"Right you are! Have a good day then, and mind you

don't let Gwilym drag you too many miles!" With a wave of his hand, Hugh-the-Bus left them and turned inland along the river.

"Well, come on then," said Gwilym, striking out across the dunes.

The hard, bright air filled their lungs and scoured their faces as they tramped down to the sea. Gwilym took them out to the sand spit at the mouth of the Dovey where fresh met salt water. It must have been a mile or so, but they covered it quickly. To Jen the world appeared unusually sharp, in perfect focus, every detail clear, from the pebbles and strings of seaweed at her feet to the distant windy horizon.

"You can see so far!" she shouted against the wind. "What's the land out there?"

"That's up in Caernarvon," Gwilym told her. "It's the Lleyn Peninsula and beyond it, further to the west, you can just see a bump, can you?"

"Wait." Jen peered in the direction of his hand, northwest. "Yes, just barely. What is it?"

"Bardsey Island. Supposed to be a grand place for birds," he said longingly.

"Have you never been there?" asked Becky. "It doesn't look far."

"Might as well be the other side of Ireland. I've no one to go with me, and no money to get there. Mum doesn't approve of hitching and she'll not hear of me taking my motorbike."

"I didn't know you had a motorbike," said Peter.

"Aye. Bought it last year off the student Mum had living in. It needed a lot of work, but I got it running. Don't have a proper license yet, only 'L' plates, but I'm going for it next year. Mum doesn't approve, but it's my own money and Dad said I could do what I liked with it."

Peter looked at Gwilym with new eyes. Here at last was something he understood. "Can I see it sometime?"

"Tisn't much. Not fancy, you know."

"Just the same?"

"Aye."

Becky prodded him. "What's that the other direction?"

"Pembroke. Strumble Head, that'd be. You can see both ends of Wales from here when it's clear like this."

"Not very much to it," remarked Peter.

"Enough," said Gwilym. "There's a lot to Wales, you know."

"You sound like Mr. Evans. Do you believe in magic?" Becky asked suddenly.

Gwilym's face stiffened, and Jen looked warily at her sister. Peter alone was unconscious. He whistled softly as he gazed down the coast at Strumble Head. "Why Strumble Head?" he wondered aloud.

"Why should I?" asked Gwilym suspiciously.

"Other people around here do. Mr. Evans up at Llechwedd Melyn was telling us about it."

"Do people in America?"

"Not like that. At least not people *we* know. They believe in things like witches and exorcism."

"That's just because they think it's fashionable," Jen broke in irritably. "But it's not, it's silly! And the other's just superstition, not really magic at all, Becky, it's just in your mind."

"How do you know?" inquired Peter. "You sound like an expert."

"Anyone with any sense would say just what I have," snapped Jen. "Magic is for fairy tales, like Aled said."

Gwilym looked uncomfortable. "We'll not see anything if we stand here all morning." He changed the subject. "We'll just head up the estuary."

Peter walked along beside Gwilym agreeably, his thumbs tucked in the straps of his knapsack. He appeared quite unperturbed by Jen's irritation, which irritated her still further. His moods seemed to change as quickly as the Welsh weather; she wondered what he was up to.

"There," said Gwilym after a bit. Becky yelped as Jen trod on her toes. "You can't shout or you'll scare them," admonished Gwilym.

"Sorry," apologized Jen. "What is it?"

"Goldeneye. They're sea duck. Pretty common, but better than nothing." Jen could just distinguish a clutch of small white ducks with dark heads on the far side of the river. Behind them the cottages of Aberdovey tumbled down the hillside looking like a toy village.

"And pochard," reported Gwilym, sweeping the estuary with his glasses. "Whitish with brown heads and dark breasts."

"What are the big ducks?" asked Becky, pointing.

"Shelduck. Red bills. There are lots of them."

The names meant nothing to Jen. Gradually they worked their way along the inside of the sandy spit built by the river, gazing dutifully in the direction Gwilym's binoculars pointed, trying to pick out the tiny specks he had no trouble identifying. All around stretched the hard, ripple-marked tide flats, still puddled with water from the last high tide, which reflected splinters of the morning sky. The wind smelled strongly of salt and wet sand. Jen was surprised to find she was quite happy just ambling behind Gwilym and Becky, her mind empty. Becky chattered on to Gwilym, asking questions, learning birds.

Peter was content, too. It was hard, but he was beginning to learn patience and the day was far from over. The Key lay comfortably warm against him. It, too, was waiting.

It was nine when they stopped beside the river and shared round the turkey sandwiches. Gwilym took out a small notebook and wrote down what they'd seen so far. They sat on an abandoned railroad sleeper, idly watching a boy upstream from them who was puttering about in a little round boat, too far away to be more than just part of the view. Until Gwilym said, pocketing the notebook, "Hullo. He's got a coracle. You don't often see them, specially this far north."

Then, of course, he had to pass around his binoculars again and explain what a coracle was. "A traditional Welsh boat. Used to use them for fishing, made of tanned skins years and years ago. Now they use tarred canvas. Just made to show tourists now mostly. Down to Newquay I've seen them, but this is the first I've seen on the Dovey."

The boat was almost bowl-shaped, and the boy in it, roughly dressed with a thatch of curly gold hair, was working intently on something in the water close to the riverbank.

"We can find out what it is when we get up there," said Becky. None of them could guess what he was doing.

"If we decide to go on up the river," said Gwilym. "We can do that or start back from here."

"Follow the river," said Peter promptly.

Jen was more cautious. She remembered what Hugh-the-Bus had said about Gwilym dragging them too many miles. "How far is it that way?"

"Too far to Machynlleth, but we'll join up with the road in about six miles and catch a bus back to town if you like. Makes no difference to me whichever, though I'd like a closer look at the coracle myself."

"Then let's go on." Becky agreed with Peter.

"Six miles—" began Jen dubiously.

"But flat," coaxed Becky. Jen gave in.

However, when they reached the place they'd seen the coracle, the boy had disappeared.

"I did want to see how it worked," said Becky, disappointed.

"Well, it's still here," said Peter. He'd gotten ahead of the others when Gwilym had stopped to look at a flock of knots feeding on the mud. At this information, Jen gave up trying to make anything out of the little dun-colored dots and hurried on with Becky. Peter was standing beside the coracle, which had been left upside down above the high tide line. It looked like a huge black turtle, legs and head drawn into its shell, lying there. It was the same boat they'd seen on the river, and its stiff dark skin was still wet.

"It's leather," Peter remarked, touching it. Jen and Becky both felt the coracle. The hide was stretched tight over a basketlike frame: the whole boat couldn't possibly have held more than one person. Becky lifted an end a few inches off the ground experimentally.

"It's light. I bet I could carry it. Wouldn't it be neat to have a boat like this?"

"Put it down," Jen said quickly. "It isn't ours and we don't even know who it belongs to." The coracle made her distinctly uneasy; it was such an unlikely-looking object to find on an ordinary riverbank.

"I wonder what he was doing with it." Becky went down to the river's edge.

"It's an old one, that," said Gwilym, joining them. "Made of animal skins, like the ones I told you about." He inspected it curiously. "It's in awfully good shape." It made a hollow sound like a drum when he thumped it gently with his knuckles.

"Hey, Gwilym!" called Becky. "What are those things in the water? Those stick things?" A row of saplings had been cut and carefully stuck upright in the mud of the riverbed. They were set close to each other and woven with brush, and they stretched in a shallow crescent half across the Dovey, horns pointing upstream. Only a foot of the construction showed above the water. "He was working on it."

Gwilym frowned. "I don't remember that being here when I was along a fortnight ago."

"Doesn't look new," observed Peter. "What do you think it is?"

"*Looks* like a fishing weir," hazarded Gwilym. "Works like a sieve, see. Fish swim against it and can't get through, then you catch them. I've not seen one in this river before."

"You said that about the coracle," Peter pointed out. "Do you suppose they used to have them along here?"

"No doubt sometime, but why now? I'll ask Dad about it. He'd be likeliest to know whose they are. Funny, him not mentioning any such."

Jen was only too happy to leave the coracle and the weir behind and to concentrate with renewed attention on Gwilym's birds, flattering him with her interest.

But Becky dropped behind with Peter, still curious about what they'd seen.

"Why would people use a weir instead of nets, Peter? Do you know? It doesn't seem very practical, does it?"

"Maybe they didn't have nets when they started using fishing weirs," suggested Peter.

"But they do now, so why do they need them?"

"Gwilym said the coracle was old," said Peter carefully. "Maybe the weir was, too."

"*How* old do you mean?"

"Just old," said Peter.

"I wonder if *we* could make a boat like that. Wouldn't it be fun? I bet you and Dad could. Jen didn't like it much, though, you could tell by her face."

All the way along the river, Peter kept wondering what had become of the boy from the coracle, half afraid, half hoping they'd see him as they walked. But they didn't. Peter hadn't gotten much of a look at him, but enough to see he was about Gwilym's age and wore a tunic belted with a leather thong. He was confused; somehow his two worlds, some fourteen-hundred years apart, had touched each other, for there was no question in his mind that the boy, the coracle, the weir belonged to the Key.

But the rest of the morning was quite uneventful. By the time they reached the head of the estuary, all four of them were ravenous and a little giddy with the wind and sun and with walking. It was lovely to be tired and to sit and rest against a rough old stone wall beside the road while waiting for the bus.

"Not bad for a morning," said Gwilym, counting up the list in his notebook. "Would have been better without the wind. It's too strong for small birds."

"We saw all those?" exclaimed Becky, peering over his shoulder.

"Well, one of us did," amended Jen.

"Will you take us again?" Becky wanted to know.

Gwilym looked surprised. "I suppose so, if you're interested."

Jen considered him for a moment. Perhaps he wasn't solitary from choice; it was an interesting thought.

"We could go back in the hills behind Rhian's farm," Becky was saying enthusiastically. "Mrs. Evans invited us back any time."

"Best time for that's spring," said Gwilym. "The birds are back and starting to breed then. But there'll be some up there now, the ones that winter here."

The bus was as empty on its way back from Machynlleth as it had been starting out that morning.

"Terrible slow day." Hugh-the-Bus greeted them cheerfully. "If it weren't for you lot I might as well have stayed in!"

But he could tell them nothing about the weir. He was surprised to hear about it himself. "They'd not have been using them things along the Dovey since before my dada's time. Our side of the river, you're saying? No, there is no one in Borth I have heard of building one. Some joke, I am thinking."

"A lot of work for a joke," Peter commented.

"Whoever it was built it has a coracle, too, Dad. A proper one made of skins."

Hugh-the-Bus scratched his head with long, knotted fingers. "That's a good one, that is. You wouldn't be making it up now?"

They all assured him they weren't—they'd all seen the

boat and the weir. And Hugh-the-Bus could tell them nothing about either.

After lunch and a period of contented collapse, Peter grew restless; he felt the need to be out in the blustery afternoon and walking again. He left Jen absorbed in working out the stitches for a crewel-embroidery pillowcase. It was one of Aunt Beth's Christmas presents to her. She kept twisting her French knots the wrong way and scowling as she undid them.

But Becky caught her brother at the front door.

"Hey," she said as he turned the knob. "Where are you going and can I come?"

She wasn't in Peter's plans and he was on the verge of saying no when David came downstairs. Peter saw he was trapped. If he refused Becky, there'd be a hassle with his father, and for once he didn't feel equal to it. Becky was already pulling on her windbreaker. So they walked in silence down to the War Memorial.

"I don't suppose you really wanted me along," said Becky bluntly, "but I wanted to talk to you and I can't inside."

"Oh? What about?" Peter was only half listening. The Key was humming very quietly under his shirt.

"The things we've been seeing. That stuff this morning and the boats yesterday."

Abruptly, his attention shifted back to her.

"You know more about them than you've said," Becky stated flatly. "They're connected some way, aren't they?"

Peter had obviously underestimated Becky. "How do you mean?" he asked guardedly.

"Those boats, for example. They aren't as simple as Dad claimed. I felt something funny when I looked at them. I think Jen did, too, but she wouldn't admit it. And again today. Gwilym, too."

"I don't think I want to talk about this now," Peter hedged.

Becky shrugged. "I didn't think you would, but I want to know."

They were sitting side by side on the granite base of the monument. Peter took a deep breath. "Do you remember when you asked Gwilym if he believed in magic?"

"Mmm." Becky waited for him to go on. When he didn't, she turned to look at him. "What kind of magic do *you* mean?"

"Not rabbits out of a hat or fairies or saying spells," said Peter quickly. "I don't believe in that kind. An older kind than that—things that happen that can't really be explained. Things you just have to believe in, without knowing why."

Becky's eyes narrowed. "That's like Mr. Evans—Rhian's father. He believes in that sort—he said so in front of everybody. But the coracle was real, we all touched it. It's easy to believe in."

"But how did it get there? Where did it come from? Nobody knows, you heard Hugh-the-Bus say so. And do you think it would still be there if you went back now?"

"Wouldn't it?"

"I don't know." The Key was growing louder; in a minute it would take him. "But I don't think we'll find it again."

Becky stared at him. "Peter—"

He shook his head fiercely. "Not now! I can't!"

The six Irish boats were not quite a day out to sea. They beat along the Cymric coast against a gale wind. Once around the great northwest point of the Kingdom of Gwynedd, the wind grew even wilder, tearing at the square sails, hurling storms of spray over the men crouched in the boats. Even the Irish, seasoned seamen, felt uneasy, rolling uncontrolled in the heavy seas. In Taliesin's ship they had made the cargo fast and clung wherever they could find handholds. They were much too preoccupied to notice that the captive had worked his arms free.

Night. And in the darkness, with the wind screaming like

the hounds of Arawn, the Dark Lord, they failed to notice the captive had disappeared and with him one of their coracles. . . .

The wind was from the west, blowing up the Dyfi, sweeping the tiny boat over gray seas that had once been dry land, a kingdom surrounded by sea walls. Taliesin lay low, clutching the wicker frame of the craft, drenched and cold, afraid but calm. In his heart was deep sorrow for the son of Urien Rheged, still prisoner of the Irish. He knew he would not see Elphin Rheged again. There was nothing to be done but wait for the coracle to touch land wherever it would and trust he would not be broken on the rocky coast of Cymru.

In the first light of May Day, Taliesin saw his trust upheld, for he had been blown up a wide river and his boat had caught against someone's fishing weir. The wind dropped with dawn and left him there.

Becky sat absolutely still beside Peter, staring out at the blank windy sea, trying to see whatever it was he saw out there, but the bay was empty to her eyes.

He'd forgotten she was there, until he moved and brushed against her. Then he came to with a start and met her frank, curious gaze. Neither of them spoke, but after a while Peter got up and walked away by himself, down the path toward the beach, a small, lonely figure.

7

A Harp Key

FOR THE THURSDAY after Christmas, Dr. and Mrs. Rhys had invited all the Morgans to dinner at their house in Aberystwyth. They had six tickets to a harp concert in the church next to the Castle, and David was excited at the chance to hear Howell Roberts.

"One of the best harpists in Wales! And his father before him. Your great-grandfather used to talk of seeing him when he was about Peter's age. He came to Tredegar," he told his family.

"I just wonder what dinner at the Rhyses' will be like," muttered Peter to Jen.

She hoped desperately that he would behave and not go into one of his peculiar moods. She felt she couldn't bear another Christmas Eve, especially not in front of strangers. But she needn't have worried. Peter was quiet but cooperative, excited himself at the idea of the harp concert, though he carefully hid it.

Scrubbed and brushed with great care on the Thursday evening, they followed Dr. Rhys's directions through the maze of little streets behind the Aberystwyth railway station, up the hill to the house called Pen-y-Garth. Its name was spelled out in the wrought iron of its front gate.

Dr. Rhys answered the bell, small and serious in a dark suit and shirt with a high starched collar. "Ah, David! Yes, right on time, you are indeed. Do come in." He took their coats and passed them on to Mrs. Rhys in the front room. She was not at all what Jen had expected from seeing him. She was large and smiling, with wild gray hair and very blue eyes.

"I'm *so* glad Gwyn managed to get you all here! I've been after him for weeks, you know, but he's terrible at remembering things like that, I'm afraid. Wonderful on dates several hundred years ago, but quite hopeless about the present! You'll want to sit close to the fire, I shouldn't wonder. It's sharpish out. No trouble finding us? Shall I call you David, shall I? Gwyn couldn't tell me any other names, so I must ask for myself. Becky, that would be Rebecca, wouldn't it? And your brother? Peter, and Jennifer. And I'm Marjorie. There."

Jen and Peter exchanged rather startled glances as Mrs. Rhys swept them all into the sitting room on a flood of words, but Becky was right beside her, grinning happily.

"Now, will you have something to start? Gwyn, do ask what everyone wants to drink whilst I see to the dinner. No, Jennifer, you can't do a thing, yet. I'll let you know when I need you, not to worry! I've only to check on it now." When Mrs. Rhys left the room, the silence was overwhelming. It wasn't that she spoke fast, but she seemed to build up great momentum as she went. Her voice had a lilt to it that was not Welsh.

There were bowls of nuts on the coffee table, and Peter and Becky were soon sipping large glasses of orange squash, but Dr. Rhys won Jen's heart without even knowing by offering her sherry. She didn't like it much, but she did like the idea.

The Rhyses' front room was very like the lounge at Bryn Celyn, a jumble of colors and patterns, but full of paintings and books, large comfortable furniture, a clutter of photo-graphs on the mantle, and a cheerful coal fire in the grate. It was a used, personal room.

"Well, then," said Dr. Rhys, when everyone was settled. "Well, then. Did you have a nice Christmas?"

David nodded. "Yes, we did. Quiet, but nice. And you?"

"Oh, indeed. Not so quiet, though. We went to my wife's family in Yorkshire near the city of York, they are. Do you know it?"

"No."

"Ah, well. You must get to York, it's a lovely city. Lovely. Very old, with a marvelous medieval church and four-teenth-century city walls and the Minster, of course. Worth the uproar of visiting relatives to see it. I'm sure I don't know what would happen if they lived in Leeds!"

Mrs. Rhys filled the room again. "There you are!" she ex-claimed, beaming. "Food in fifteen minutes, and we will be just in time for the concert. Have you all got whatever it is you want? Good! I'll just have a drop of sherry, love. And how are you finding Borth? Gwyn and I had our first flat out there, did he tell you? On the cold side during the winters, don't you think, with the wind right off the sea. But the hills are lovely there, and all that beach to walk on. We've only got stones in Aberystwyth, though why a few miles should make such a dif-ference, I don't know! But there, you can't have everything." Dr. Rhys handed her a glass with more than a drop of sherry in it.

"How long have you lived in Wales, Mrs.—er, Mar-jorie?" asked David.

"That's right, then!" She smiled at him warmly. "Much more comfortable, I always think. I've been here since Gwyn and I were married, thirty-two years next August, that will be. We met at university in Hull when he was teaching there. Such foolishness to go to university, especially for a girl, my father thought. He wouldn't hear of me going further than Hull! We were in Cardiff for almost five years then, but Gwyn had family still in Aberystwyth, so when we could we came up here to stay."

"You must be a native by this time," remarked David.

"Bless you! Indeed I am not! I shall be a foreigner here no matter how many years I have! It's not England, you know, quite another country, and unless you've been born and raised this side of the border, you're never a native. Isn't that so, Gwyn? Why down in Cardiff, mind, Gwyn himself wasn't native! South Wales is a different place entirely! Of course, people are nice enough and you don't mind, but it's a fact."

"But Wales is so small," objected Jen. "I would think people would all be the same, at least within it."

Dr. Rhys was shaking his head. "Not a bit of it. They are not. South Wales is not like this at all. You must see it, too, before you can say you've seen Wales. We are almost in the mountains here, and the land is used for animals, mainly sheep. But around by Cardiff are the industries and the shipping and above it the coal valleys. Further to the west is Pembroke where the land is good for crops, and that is different too."

"My own family came from near Cardiff," commented David.

"Did they then? Miners?"

He nodded. "My grandfather emigrated when the trouble began over unions. He was from Tredegar."

"Indeed. A bloody time that was, too. We lost many men to Canada and America, the conditions in the mines were so bad and the owners mostly English and wanting money more than anything."

"Lucky we were farmers in my family," put in Mrs. Rhys. "Yorkshire's coal country, too, and I wouldn't fancy seeing my men going down the pits, I can tell you. But I suppose we are fortunate men will still do it. Now, Cardiff—there's another matter. Nice shops and a lovely park along the river. I quite enjoyed Cardiff while we were there. I still like a trip down now and then to see friends and do the shops. Gwyn thinks a lot of the University, don't you, Gwyn? Well. And there's our roast, I can smell it done. Will you come?"

By the time they'd sorted themselves out around the dinner table, Dr. Rhys and David were deep in a discussion of Welsh nationalism.

"Oh, aye," said Mrs. Rhys to Jen, Becky, and Peter. "I could tell you a thing or two about nationalism myself." She dished up carrots while Dr. Rhys chipped away at the beef. "They're that strong on it hereabout with their newspapers and telly programs and news in Welsh on the wireless. *And* spelling all the names of towns the old way. Mind you, I don't object to a bit of patriotic feeling now and again, but they do go on so."

"And all the people speaking Welsh," Becky added. "Do you?"

"Lord bless you, no! It's the very devil of a language, though all very well for Gwyn who was raised with it."

Peter gave his father a meaningful look.

"Ah," said Dr. Rhys at once, "but my dear, so much would be lost if it weren't for the Nationalists. They're bringing back the language and traditions and folklore. So much is already forgotten—there is so much one doesn't understand, so many gaps one cannot fill. We must hold on to whatever we can." His eyes were keen in his narrow face. He was so intent on what he was saying he quite ignored his dinner.

"But hasn't it all been written down?" asked Peter. "Can't you just look it up in histories?"

"Oh, no! No, no. And that is the tragedy, do you see. When people first spoke Welsh, they hadn't yet begun to write. It was an oral language, nothing written down at all. The stories and songs were in the heads of the bards who passed them to each other from memory and wandered the country gathering news and singing their songs. When people learned to write, they began to copy out the stories, but so much must never have been recorded. We have only fragments. Only fragments."

"That's what you're working on, isn't it?" said David. "Translating the fragments."

"Yes." Dr. Rhys removed his spectacles and polished them on his tie. "Some of the oldest we have—*The Black Book of Caernarvon, The Red Book of Hergest, The Mabinogion,* and the books called after the greatest bards: Llywarch Hen, Aneirin, Taliesin."

Peter had forgotten his dinner now, too.

"The difficulty," Dr. Rhys continued, "is in sorting out the oldest poetry from that of the writer's own time. You see, in the beginning, none of it was written down, it was simply told. Then, hundreds of years later, people who'd learned to write put it in books, but they often added bits or changed the stories round to suit themselves. In *The Mabinogion,* for instance, there are a number of tales—Mabinogi—but only the first four are considered truly ancient. They are mythic tales, hero tales, one might call them, concerning the great King Math, who could know whatever anyone was thinking if he chose, and his nephew Gwydion, who stole the pigs of Prince Pryderi of Dyfyd by conjuring and made a woman of flowers for the son of his sister Arianrhod: and the head of the warrior Bran, which lived for eighty days after his slaying. These stories have been faithfully retold. But in the same collection are tales that concern King Arthur and the Bard, Taliesin, which were made up much later."

"Well, now," Mrs. Rhys interrupted from across the table. "He'll go on for hours with the slightest encouragement, and if we don't hurry we'll not get seats for Howell Roberts. Come now, Gwyn, finish up and go and get coats, will you."

Doors had burst open in Peter's head. He was quite dizzy and he could only sit and watch while Dr. Rhys methodically finished his cold dinner. No good trying to ask him anything now, with the others around—but there was so much to know! Taliesin! Aneirin! How could he ever have guessed that small, dry Dr. Rhys knew so much about them? When at last Dr. Rhys went out to collect the coats, Peter followed him, unable to hold back his questions.

"Excuse me," he began, in a voice that trembled slightly, "those bards you were telling about—Aneirin and Taliesin. Were they real men?"

Dr. Rhys looked at him with surprise. "Indeed they were. Important men, both of them, Taliesin the more famous of the two, you know. Much of the poetry we have recovered from the sixth and seventh centuries was theirs. And have you an interest in the bards, then?" His eyes were very bright behind their spectacles.

"Well, yes," said Peter cautiously, "I suppose I have."

"If you want to know more, I can loan you a couple of my books, if you are careful with them, of course. Here. In my study." He disappeared and in a moment returned with two small, old-looking volumes. Peter took them eagerly, *The Mabinogion* and *The Four Ancient Books of Wales.* They were well-worn, both of them, inscribed with Dr. Rhys's name on their fly-leaves in a thin, careful hand, and Peter could hardly stifle the surge of excitement as he took them. "Thank you," he managed to say.

"You are entirely welcome," said Dr. Rhys gravely. "I hope you will find them of interest. Perhaps you will come and discuss them with me later?"

Before Peter could answer, Mrs. Rhys burst out of the kitchen, driving Jen, Becky, and David ahead of her like a flock of sheep.

"Good plain cooking, that's all it is, and I'm glad you enjoyed it!" she was saying.

"That's what Mrs. Davies's is, too," observed Becky, "but it doesn't come out the same at all."

"Aye, well. Mine's from being brought up on a Yorkshire farm, feeding five hungry brothers."

Peter just had time to slip the little books in his coat pockets before the others saw. He didn't want to have to explain them.

St. Michael's Church was neither old nor specially noteworthy, but it was warm with light and rapidly filling with people. As Mrs. Rhys said, the Welsh did love a bit of music and that was certainly in their favor, though she couldn't see much in choral concerts sung all in Welsh. "They've grand voices, but you don't just know what they're singing about, do you?"

There was a great harp set before the altar, a stool beside it, and punctually at eight Mr. Roberts appeared. The church vicar gave him a rambling introduction full of Welsh names and glowing praise, then Howell Roberts took his seat. He was a thin, wiry man, with a sharp-cut face, great tangled eyebrows half hiding piercing blue eyes. He took in his audience at a glance and turned to his harp, settling it against him with infinite care and an odd gentleness, stroking it lightly with long, fine fingers, his head to one side, listening.

Everyone in the church was silent, all eyes were on him. The Morgans and Rhyses had seats in a pew near the front, for the church had filled back to front as most public places do, so they had a clear view of Howell Roberts, and they all saw him take a small metal object from his pocket. With it, he began to tighten and tune the strings of his harp, fitting one shaft of the object over each peg in turn.

Jen, sitting beside Peter, heard her brother catch his breath sharply. His gaze was riveted on Howell Roberts's hands. She looked more closely and something in her mind clicked: a strange, tarnished shape in candlelight. The tuning key of a harp.

"But Peter, it doesn't make any sense! Who on earth would lose the tuning key for a harp on the beach?"

"If you're not going to believe what I tell you, there's no point in talking about it anymore, is there?" Peter faced his elder sister with calm stubbornness. "I don't know how it got there, I only found it."

"Maybe it isn't a harp key at all."

"Jen!" exclaimed Peter, exasperated. "You saw the one Howell Roberts had last night, and look"—he pulled out the object he wore—"it *can't* be anything else. See for yourself."

Jen glared at him across her half-made bed. "Even if you're right, what difference does it make? Pull that blanket over, will you? You don't have a harp, so what good is it?"

"I'm supposed to be the difficult one, not you," Peter remarked, stuffing the covers under the mattress. The Key hung, dull and black, against his jersey. "There's no reason why it has to be useful. I found it and I'm going to keep it because I like it. I thought you might be interested, that's all."

"What about that story you told me in the middle of the night?"

Peter felt himself turn pink, but bluffed. "What about it?"

"You said it made you see things. I hope you don't still believe that."

"You sound just like a grown-up this morning," he complained. "For your information, I do still believe it, but I guess you aren't ready yet."

"What do you mean 'ready'?" demanded Jen. "If you want to play games, Peter, that's all well and good, but I don't like this one, so leave me out. I suppose you know that you've got Becky worried? She thinks there's something the matter with you because of the way you've been acting lately."

"Becky?"

"She notices a lot more than we think."

Peter nodded thoughtfully. He walked to the door of the bedroom and paused. "But it isn't a game you know, Jen," he said seriously, and was gone, leaving her to stare after him, disturbed.

If Saturday was dry, Gwilym, Rhian, and the three young Mor-

gans planned to carry their lunch into the hills behind Llechwedd Melyn. Rhian was to meet the others at the foot of her
valley where the early bus would leave them. The morning was
gray but not wet. David was up to see his family off. "No falling off cliffs, pushing each other into rivers, or falling into
mine shafts, and I expect you home for supper," he warned
lightly. "See that the Evanses know where you're going."

Jen was not quite sure how the three of them would manage to keep up with Gwilym and Rhian who were used to all-
day walking trips, but Peter and Becky weren't worried. They
were both in unusually good spirits and greeted Rhian loudly
as they climbed off the bus in Tre'r-ddôl.

"Hullo! Hullo!" She grinned. "There's luck for you! Da
says it won't be raining more than a shower or two the day and
yesterday so wet. He says why not go along Cwm Einion and
could we be keeping an eye out for Llechwedd sheep then.
Practical, my da!"

Gwilym nodded in agreement. "It's nice up the valley
without the trippers." He took his binoculars out of their
leather case and hung them round his neck.

"Do let's start!" urged Becky. "It'll be lunchtime before
we get past the farm."

The little road up to Llechwedd Melyn was every bit as
steep as Jen had remembered. She and Becky and Peter were
panting when Gwilym stopped conveniently to look at a pair
of wagtails and they could catch their breath. Jen began to see
a useful side to birdwatching.

They passed the farm without stopping. Mrs. Evans had
promised them tea on the way back. Beyond the byre, they
turned north along a dirt track. Gwilym had half a dozen birds
on his list by then, and the others had even seen one or two.
They could hardly miss the big flashy black and white magpie
that shot across in front of them.

"Best to your missus," Rhian called after it cheerfully.

"Why?" asked Peter.

"Bad luck seeing one," she explained. " 'One for sorrow, two for joy . . .' Mam taught me ages ago, that. So you always call after when you see one."

"Superstition," accused Gwilym. "There's almost always a pair around anyway. See?" A second magpie flew up after the first as if to prove him right.

"But there's no harm," said Rhian, "and it's better being safe."

Overhead the clouds stretched thin and broke in places letting scraps of blue sky through. The track to Cwm Einion sloped up gradually between solidly built drystone walls, past a couple of farms with mucky, hen-scattered yards and pens of square, shaggy black cattle. Welsh Blacks, Rhian informed the others. "Best cattle there is, my da says, but not so common now. There is a pity to see the old breeds go, he says."

At the top of a small rise they stopped and rested their elbows on the top of the wall and munched sausage rolls Gwilym handed around. Below lay a breathless sweep of silver-green hillside, tumbling down to the great mottled Bog and, beyond, Cardigan Bay lost in haze. Spots of burning sun chased across the country, and in the sky above three buzzards wheeled in great, slow arcs. Gwilym pointed out a sparrowhawk hunting the rough grass on the brow of the hill.

"Do you know," said Jen after a bit, "this is the first time I've been out in the country since I came. There's so much of it all around."

"We went out along the Dovey," Becky reminded her.

"But that's not the same. It isn't as"—she groped for the right word—"as wild as this."

"Do you like it, then?" Rhian wanted to know.

"I'm not sure," Jen answered honestly. "It's not very *comfortable* country somehow. It's beautiful, but it's a bit frightening really."

"It watches you," said Becky.

They had lunch in Cwm Einion. Rhian picked the spot,

among water-worn boulders beside the river. Each of them contributed something different to the picnic. Gwilym had more sausage rolls and a huge lump of yellow cheese; Rhian took three fat meat pies and a bottle of fizzy lemonade out of her knapsack; and Jen unpacked oranges, chocolate biscuits, and salt and vinegar potato crisps from the Morgans.

"If we eat all that lot," said Gwilym, eyeing the collection, "we'll be sorry in a couple of hours when we're hungry again."

"Or doubled with cramp more likely," Rhian said with a grin.

In the end they saved the biscuits, sausage rolls, and three oranges for later, Peter grumbling a little over the biscuits.

To Gwilym's chagrin, Becky was the first to spot the dipper. She poked him hard in the ribs and pointed to the neat dark bird with its white bib, bobbing up and down on a rock across the stream. Everyone sat up to see what Becky and Gwilym were peering at. As they watched, the dipper flew out over the water and dove in, disappearing altogether. Gwilym explained that it was able to walk underwater along the stream bed, finding insect larvae to eat.

"There it is up again," called Rhian. It perched on a rock near them, shook itself briskly, then flew off downstream, low over the water, giving an odd metalic "clink" as it flew.

Gwilym nodded with satisfaction and wrote "dipper" on his list.

They packed the remains of lunch back into the knapsacks and set off again before anyone was tempted to go to sleep on the springy turf. Further up the *cwm,* the track crossed the river on a narrow bridge, then climbed to a farmyard gate.

"Where do we go now?" Peter asked, looking around.

Rhian unlatched the gate and pulled it open. "Through here."

"But it's somebody's front yard," Jen objected. "We can't just walk through."

"It's a public path," said Rhian. "There isn't any other way unless you fancy plowing through the gorse and mud. They don't mind so long as you close gate again after and aren't bothering the dogs, see. Go on."

Not at all convinced, Jen followed Gwilym and Becky. Furious barking erupted from the cow byre as they passed it, but no one came out to challenge them and the dogs seemed safely shut up.

"Only trouble is"—Rhian slipped the catch off the far gate—"some people are leaving the gates open and the animals get loose. Happens sometimes at Llechwedd in the fields up on top and we must all go fetch them back again. It doesn't half make Da cross."

Above the farm the track became overgrown with coarse grass and bracken; it didn't seem well-traveled. The country was all around them here, wild and desolate. Traces of men were insignificant, the merest scratches on the surface of the hills. Given years enough they would disappear without a sign.

"I can't imagine living up here," said Jen at length. "It's so lonely. There's nothing."

"Depends," said Gwilym, "on what you call nothing, doesn't it? For some, there's no need of more. They'd rather have done with shops and cars and people."

"Aye," agreed Rhian. "Da says there is no better place than a valley without people. Ours was like that until the Forestry built up by there and the Electric came. You get used to it."

Jen shook her head. "I'm not at all sure I could."

"It would really depend," said Peter thoughtfully, "on how you felt about the hills, wouldn't it? I mean, whether they were friendly or not. If you made a sort of peace with them you could be quite happy and not need anyone else. But if they didn't like you—if they didn't want you here—it wouldn't work at all."

"You make the hills sound alive!" exclaimed Jen with a shiver.

"Maybe they are," suggested Peter, looking at her oddly.

"You sound like Rhian's father," said Becky. "Which do you believe?" she asked Rhian. "Your father or Aled?"

She grinned. "Whichever! I'll not say either is wrong till I've made up my own mind. If Aled's right that's one thing, but if he isn't, I'll not chance making them mad, see!"

Gwilym was skeptical. "All it really is is whether you'd rather live in a town or the country. If it's town, then country will make you uneasy and the other way round. Me, I'd rather have the country. I wouldn't mind living up here."

"Hadn't we better think about getting back?" Jen interrupted, looking at her watch. "It feels as if we've come miles."

"We'll fetch up at the Forestry track this way in a bit," said Rhian. "If we follow it round Foel Goch, we'll come in over the top by Llechwedd and not have to go back the way we came. It's no further that way, and Mam'll be waiting tea when we get in."

"Good! I'm starving again," declared Becky.

In a few minutes they reached a forest with a track cut straight through it, like a part through hair. The trees were all pine and all the same age, planted tight against one another, so their branches were tangled together and all the lower ones had died from lack of light. It was dark and silent and oppressive beneath the trees. Nothing grew on the ground under them, nothing stirred. It was one of the Forestry Commission's plantations that Gwilym had complained about. They were all relieved to reach the bare, windy hillside beyond.

Rhian led them along an almost invisible path once they left the Forestry track. She knew it well and didn't hesitate; an old sheep track, she told the others. All trace of the sun was gone now and an ominous layer of cloud was blowing up from the south. Jen was glad she'd brought an extra sweater. The air had turned raw. They went in single file, strung out behind Rhian: Becky, Peter, Jen, then Gwilym. The path was full of roots and rocks and holes and needed to be watched constantly.

As they rounded the shoulder of the hill, Foel Goch, a sudden spattering of rain hit them, but it blew past before Jen could say anything about getting to cover. In a few minutes it came again, harder.

Rhian scowled when Jen shouted up the line about shelter. She would just have ignored the rain and gone on, not minding a bit of wet. But the Morgans weren't hill people.

"There is an old *hafod* up a bit. Some of the roof'll be standing yet. It'll do."

It was the remains of a stone hut, cupped in a hollow on Foel Goch. To get to it they had to wade through bracken waist-deep, trying to avoid the gorse, which Peter discovered was covered with thorns. They reached the empty doorway damp and out of breath, just in time to see a sheet of rain close on them from the hill opposite. Jen brushed the wet hair from her eyes and looked around. Most of the far side of the roof and walls had fallen in and the dirt floor was matted with weeds. There were only two small windows cut in the thick front wall, so that the corners under the roof were deep in shadow.

Rhian explained that *hafod* meant a hut, used by shepherds up on the hills during summer when the flock was out on the hills. This one had belonged to a farm near Tre'r-ddôl that was now deserted, and, like the *hafod,* falling to ruin. The last of the farmer's sons had been lured away to Birmingham with the promise of an easier life than tending sheep on a cold Welsh mountain, and the old man hadn't been able to manage by himself. He'd found no buyer for his farm.

"That's sad," said Becky.

"Aye, but more are leaving. Da is lucky, he is. Dai and

Evan have never wanted to leave and even Aled came back. And if they didn't want Llechwedd, *I* would be having it." Rhian's small face was determined.

"What did they do all summer up here, with no one but sheep to talk to?" Jen wondered.

"There'd be the dogs," said Rhian. "They're grand company, sheepdogs, that smart and they don't talk back." She began to peel an orange.

"I'd like a dog," observed Becky. "Where are those biscuits, Jen?"

"We have the two—Bran and Bryn. Grand workers, they are. Da has won prizes at the Agricultural Show for working sheep with them."

Jen listened hard to Rhian and Becky chattering on about dogs and sheep. She watched Gwilym leaning against the old stones just inside the doorway, wiping the lens of his binoculars with thin sheets of paper, saw him mutter to himself. She struggled desperately to keep the little cold voice out of her mind that told her she'd made a mistake by asking Rhian to bring them up here. It whispered icily that they did not belong here, but she was helpless. The rain pelted down around them and they were trapped.

Peter was sitting by himself on a fallen stone, watching Becky and Rhian divide the uneaten lunch into five more or less equal portions. His face was inscrutable in the half-light. He was concentrating on the feeling Jen was fighting so hard against, trying to understand it. The *hafod* was waiting, the air was full of tension, and the Key began to hum, very softly.

"What are you doing?" Jen hissed. She came and sat beside him, her face tight.

"Nothing."

"Yes, you are. I can feel it."

"It isn't me," insisted Peter. "I tried to tell you before and you wouldn't listen."

"That's rubbish!" said Jen in a furious whisper. She was uneasy.

But Peter didn't rise to the fight as she'd hoped he would. Instead, he said after a moment, "Did you notice the fireplace?"

Jen hadn't, but she saw it now: a round, blackened patch in the middle of the hut where no weeds grew and, stacked beside it, a neat pile of firewood. She must have almost walked through it. The ashes looked fresh and dry.

"Where do you suppose the wood came from?" said Peter softly.

"The Forestry plantation, of course. It's the only place," she answered crossly. "So what?"

"This wood isn't pine."

Jen stared at it in disbelief. He was right, it was largely birch; she recognized the white bark.

"Hey!" called Becky at that moment, "Come and look! There's a perfect rainbow!"

Jen went at once to the doorway, thankful for the distraction. Peter followed slowly. The view through the rough stone frame was spectacular. Rain sifted across the hills in uneven showers, lit by moments of dazzling sun, which turned the cloud banks the color of old pewter. Through the veils of rain came glimpses of the broad sweep of valley and a corner of Cors Fochno. Above it all, to the southwest, arched the rainbow, flickering with the change of light, a vivid bar of colors. They stood watching it, transfixed, awed by the wild glory of it.

Then Gwilym said, "Hullo. That looks like the chap we saw on the river the other day. The one in the coracle, only he's got friends this time."

Reluctantly, Jen focused her eyes on the near hillside and saw a group of tiny figures climbing toward them. They were still a long way off, but Gwilym had his binoculars on them.

"Who is that then?" Rhian wanted to know. Becky explained hastily and Rhian shrugged. "There's lots stranger goes on," she said.

"Where do you suppose they're going?" Gwilym said.

"I think we're in their hut," said Peter quietly.

"Wasn't I telling you no one owns this *hafod* now?" Rhian demanded.

"But it did belong to someone."

"So?" said Gwilym. "not much good to anyone, falling in this way."

"It doesn't matter anyway," said Becky, watching her brother curiously. "It's stopped raining, so we can go."

"Good!" exclaimed Jen. "We're late now." She only wanted to get away from the *hafod* as fast as possible. It threatened her. She fought against looking one last time at the fireplace.

They were wet to the waist by the time they found the path again, but once on it, Rhian set off at a trot, sure of her way. The rainbow had vanished, the light was fading rapidly, and the setting sun made an angry red stain behind the clouds to the west. Sheltering at the *hafod* had cost them half an hour.

And as the five of them hurried down Foel Goch, the little party of men below climbed toward them. Peter took his eyes off the path as often as he dared, and it was he who first saw that their path and that of the strangers were not going to meet or even to cross. Rhian saw it, too.

"They are on a path I don't know," she said, stopping abruptly and causing the others to bump together behind her like cars on a train. "And they are odd-looking, too. Foreign. I have not seen them before." She frowned. "Where are they going then?"

"Wherever it is, they seem to know the way," remarked Becky. "They can't be that foreign."

"No," agreed Peter. His heart was pounding fiercely and he felt hot, as if he'd been racing flat out.

The men were still at a distance, but they could be distinguished clearly now. They were all dressed similarly in long dark cloaks; they were bareheaded, and all but two had black hair. The leader did indeed look like the boy from the coracle on the Dovey. He had the same thick gold hair and a strong, square face. And the man in the middle of the group was shorter than the others. His hair shone copper in the sunset. None of them seemed aware they were being watched; their path took them below and to the left of the children. Yet when they came even with the children, the slight figure turned his face and looked up—at Peter. If he actually saw Peter, he gave no sign but kept walking. Against Peter's skin the Key burnt with icy heat and the song shouted in his head, blotting everything else out for an instant. Then it was gone. The group hurried past, following their path that twisted around up the Goch toward the *hafod*. And Rhian had started downhill again, practically running.

Peter stumbled at the end of the line, half-blind. Instead of the path, he saw the shoulder of Foel Goch humping dark against the sky and a man standing astride it, a big man with a great rough beard and white hair. He was watching his son climb the Goch with the day's catch from the fishweir on the river.

Peter's foot caught a root, and he only just saved himself from falling into Gwilym. The *hafod* was gone; in its place in the hollow was a low, round hut. The hillside was dark with trees, birch mostly. But the lookout rock on which the man stood gave a view down across Cors Fochno to the estuary, and beside the rock was built a great pile of brush and wood ready to be lit as a signal beacon when needed. Other huts were scattered among the trees, small fires glowing at their doorways.

The tall man waited, his eyes calm, his face seamed with age and unfathomable grief. As the fishing party came to a halt before him, his eyes sought out those of the red-haired stranger, and for an instant a smile touched his mouth.

"So, you have come back."

Taliesin nodded. "I have. But I am alone now, and I have lost much."

"You speak to me of loss?" demanded the man.

"To you of all people," was the reply. "You have lost a kingdom; I have lost a friend and the son of a friend, the boy whose care I was charged with."

Gwyddno Garanhir nodded. "Tell me," he said, and Taliesin told him of the time he had spent in the Kingdom of Urien Rheged, as teacher to the king's son Elphin, and of the Irish sea raiders who had taken Elphin and Taliesin prisoner, of his escape and of washing ashore in Gwyddno's fish weir. The old king listened in silence, his eyes lost on the distant sea horizon where once had been his kingdom, the drowned Low Hundred.

And when Taliesin had done, he too fell silent. Then Gwyddno called the fair-headed young man from the group of fishermen.

"You," he said to Taliesin, "are welcome here. You have, I think, been sent to me. I, too, have a son and his name also is Elphin. We live here in the hills and make our living from the fish weirs on the Dyfi. I ask you to live among us and to be teacher to my son, Elphin, son of Gwyddno."

Taliesin looked from the old man to the young man. "If I have been sent, I do not yet know for what purpose. But I will stay."

"He looked right at you," said Becky. "I saw him."

It was after dinner. Jen, Becky, and Peter were cleaning up. It was the first chance they'd had to talk alone since coming down Foel Goch.

"But he didn't see me," said Peter. "He went right on, didn't you see that, too?"

"That doesn't mean he didn't see you," Becky persisted. "It just means he didn't show it."

"Well, why shouldn't he have seen Peter?" asked Jen with a trace of impatience. "He was there, after all."

But Becky paid no attention to her. "And that was the boy from the coracle, wasn't it? There's something funny about him—do you know what it is?"

Becky's face was intent, eager; Jen's was closed. Peter looked from one to the other with a frown. This wasn't the way he'd thought things would work out. He'd picked Jen for his ally and he'd been wrong. It was Becky who was willing to listen and to believe. Jen was afraid. He'd been afraid, too, when he'd first learned what the Key did, but he wasn't any more; he was too involved in it.

There was a purpose in what the Key was doing. He didn't know what it was yet, but the pattern was growing; it was catching other people besides Peter himself.

"Do you remember," Peter began, "that night we were at the Rhyses' and Dr. Rhys was talking about the Welsh bards?"

Becky nodded.

"One of the bards was a man called Taliesin. Dr. Rhys said he was the most famous of all of them."

"What's this got to do with anything?" demanded Jen.

"Do be quiet, Jen, and let him finish. I want to hear. Go on, Peter," cut in Becky. Jen was too surprised to answer back.

"Well, Taliesin spent quite a lot of his life around here. I've got a book from Dr. Rhys that tells about him—the story's a fairy tale, really, but there are some notes about him in the back of the book. He was a real man and he did live here, near Borth for a while. There used to be a kingdom that belonged to a man named Gwyddno, only it was flooded and sixteen towns were drowned."

Jen's hands were clasped tight on the dishrag. "You and Mr. Evans would make a good pair," she exclaimed. "You could tell each other stories. Next you're going to say that man on the hillside was Taliesin!"

Peter and Becky both looked at her in silence.

"Well?" she said hotly. "For heaven's sake, Peter, it's bad enough your making up things like that without your getting Becky to believe them!"

"Was it?" asked Becky softly.

Peter shrugged slightly. "A lot of it fits together if it was."

"I suppose you're going to say it's all because of that thing you picked up off the beach, Peter." Jen's voice held scorn. "I think I liked it better when you complained all the time. Making up stories is all right, but not when you start *believing* them."

"What did you find?" asked Becky.

Peter made up his mind. He took out the chain and the Key and held it for her to see. "It's the tuning key of a harp," he said. "Howell Roberts had one at the concert. Taliesin had one, too."

8

Jen Argues

SCHOOL STARTED again Monday, and Jen was left on her own. She hadn't really thought about being alone until she watched Peter and Becky go off down the hill a few minutes behind David. The house was suddenly very empty.

David had said, "I hope you won't find it too dull by yourself," sounding faintly concerned.

"Of course not," Jen assured him. "I have dozens of things to do before I go back."

But, now she had the time, she couldn't settle. It was pointless to write the letters she'd neglected—she'd get home before they did now. Her handful of school books lay unopened. American history and French were somehow irrelevant in Borth. And the Sunday crossword was much too difficult to hold Jen's attention.

She made her own bed, then Becky's, then slowly straightened their room. It was a relief to see Becky trudging up the walk at 12:30 for lunch.

"It's so quiet with everyone gone," Jen exclaimed, as they made sandwiches.

"Do you mean you really missed us?" asked Becky with a grin.

"Well, we've been together so much for the past two weeks, the silence is unnatural!" Jen answered lightly.

Becky's grin vanished. "You won't be here much longer, though. Are you glad you're leaving Friday?"

"It'll be nice to get home and see Aunt Beth and Uncle Ted and everyone at school. Yes, I suppose I am glad."

"Home," echoed Becky. "Not sorry to leave us? I wish you weren't going."

"Of course, I'm sorry to be leaving you," said Jen hastily, annoyed with herself for having blundered. "I'll miss you very much."

"Then *stay!* Oh, please, Jen!"

"But—" The fierce intensity in Becky's voice and face caught Jen unprepared. She groped for the right words, startled. "But it's all arranged. My ticket and the Sullivans to meet me in London."

"I know. It's just—I thought once you were here you'd want to stay. I thought you'd understand."

"Understand what?" asked Jen more gently.

"That we need to be together."

"Becky—"

"We do. I can't explain it, but it's important. Don't you feel it at all?" Becky's eyes searched her face.

"But it's just not possible!" Jen protested, uncomfortable. "Even if I did want to stay, you know Dad wouldn't hear of it. I've got to go back to school next week."

"Talk to him," urged Becky. "I don't think he wants you to go either, but he won't say it unless you do."

"How do you know?" Jen demanded. Becky's words upset her, and she was angry with herself for allowing them to. What business was it of theirs to question their father's arrangements? *He* was responsible for making the decisions and for taking care of them all. They could protest, but they shouldn't try to take responsibility on themselves. "I'd miss half a year of school—he'd never agree to that. And Aunt Beth would raise the roof."

"But she couldn't do anything, if Dad told her he wanted you here."

"I don't see why you think he does. It isn't as if I could keep house for you. What difference does my being here really make?"

"A lot to me," said Becky in a low voice.

Oh, damn, thought Jen. She really did care about Becky. Jen knew there must be times when her sister was lonely and unhappy and needed a family. At the moment, there wasn't much of one for her.

"Anyway." Becky looked up defiantly. "Why *couldn't* you keep house? You could learn and I'd help. I'm sure Mrs. Davies could teach you, and it wouldn't be that hard."

"Scrubbing floors and doing laundry and cleaning up after you? Instead of going back to school?" Jen sounded incredulous. "And what about cooking? I don't know how to cook!"

"You'll have to learn sometime. Couldn't you just talk to Dad? I don't think it would be so awful and we could all be together."

After Becky had gone back to school, Jen pulled on her jacket and walked down into Borth, ignoring the spits of rain. What was Becky doing to her, she asked herself furiously. What made Becky think she, Jen, had the power to change what was already decided? Why would she want to anyway? She would climb on the train Friday on schedule, and fly home from London the next day. She'd go back to being an ordinary high school student, with nothing more important to worry about than what to wear tomorrow and an exam on Thursday. It wasn't her job to worry about the family, it was their father's. Becky wasn't fair to push her into a corner and ask her to do things she couldn't.

But when Jen thought of her father she rememberd Christmas Eve. He had said, "I'm just not used to being responsible for the whole show." For the first time, she wondered uncomfortably if that weren't too much responsibility for one person alone to have to take. She saw them all locked into their private miseries: Peter, Becky, herself—and their father, too. They needed someone to pull them back into shape, make them part of each other again.

"I can't do it!" she said aloud, desperately, and was startled at the sound of her own voice. The gulls drifting along the beach paid no attention. Jen sighed. How could she blame Becky? It was she herself who wanted to escape, to go back to Amherst and pretend life hadn't changed, when she knew perfectly well it had.

She longed for her mother to talk to. She walked along the sea wall, her eyes fixed on the distant mountains, trying to imagine what she would say. It was Becky she heard, her mother's voice speaking Becky's words: "We should all be together." Whether in Wales or Amherst, being together was the most important thing.

"What do you mean, you don't think you want to go home Saturday?" David looked blankly at his daughter across the untidy desk. "I don't understand."

Jen cleared her throat nervously. "I just think it would be better for all of us if I stayed here with you."

David frowned. "It's all set for Friday—the Sullivans expect you, Beth and Ted are waiting in Amherst, your plane ticket's been confirmed. Why on earth would you want to stay longer anyway? There isn't anything for you to do, with Peter and Becky in school all day."

"Well, actually," Jen began, "I've been thinking. There's a lot I could do. I could look after the house for you and I could learn to cook. I could even do some independent studying."

"Mrs. Davies does the housekeeping," said David impatiently. Then the full import of Jen's words hit him. "Wait a minute, do I understand you, Jennifer? Are you proposing to stay on, not for just another week or two, but the rest of the year? Is that right?" He stared at his eldest daughter in genuine astonishment.

"Umm, I guess I am. Yes."

"Good God in heaven! *Why?* What's possessed you? You don't honestly expect me to—what's to become of your schooling, may I ask? And all of Beth's careful plans?"

"May I sit down?"

"You might as well." David sighed. "It sounds like a long evening." He pushed aside his papers and leaned his elbows on the desk. "You've got my undivided attention."

Jen took a deep breath. "I think it's more important for me to be here with the rest of you than to go back to school. I think we need to be together. It sounded all right last year when you said I could stay in school at home and live with Aunt Beth and Uncle Ted. I thought it would work. But it didn't. Last semester wasn't very good. I did pretty badly."

"Maybe you weren't trying hard enough, Jen." David sounded tired. "It isn't easy adjusting, believe me I know. But we have to adjust, we haven't been given a choice. If it's bleak sometimes, we just have to stick with it and be willing to accept new responsibilities. The three of you have got to grow up a little faster than your mother and I would have liked."

"But that's just it. I want to stay so I can help, so I *can* take responsibility, Dad. Let me prove it. I can learn a lot, just from being here, that I wouldn't get at all in school."

"What? Housekeeping?" David was unbelieving. "Do you know what that amounts to, Jen? Your mother used to say it would drive her wild if she hadn't had other things to do as well. It's dull and repetitive and it has to be done. You can't stop because it bores you. You may think it would be fun now, but in a couple of weeks, when you'd had enough—what happens then?"

"I'm not offering because I think housework sounds like fun!" Jen protested hotly. "I'm offering because I want to *help*."

David pushed his hand back through his hair. "I'm sorry, Jen. I didn't say it very well. What I mean is that it's serious, hard work, and I have too much else to worry about right now. I appreciate your offer, I do, believe me, but it's not practical."

"You don't think I can do it, do you?" Jen said, looking her father in the eye. "Well, I can and I'll show you. Becky'll help and I asked Mrs. Davies if she'd teach me about shopping and show me what has to be done in the house."

There was a long, brittle silence. "And what," said David at last, "will Mrs. Davies say when she finds out you're after her job?"

Jen's heart began to slam against her ribs. "Her daughter Susan is having a baby next month," she said cautiously. "Mrs. Davies will be busy helping her. She'd be glad of the time off."

David's eyes rested on Jen's face, troubled and thoughtful. "I only wish I knew," he said softly. "Do you really want to stay? Or do you feel you ought to. If your mother—"

"Mother would have wanted us all in one place." Jen interrupted with all the conviction she could muster.

"Would she? Your school bothers me most. I don't know anything about schools for you here, and I don't know that it makes sense for you to start one now anyway. You'd have to repeat a year."

"You could tutor me," Jen suggested tentatively.

"In all my spare time!" David shook his head. "It's not the same as proper school."

"No, but I'd have the experience of learning about another country by living in it. You told Becky and Peter that last summer, before you came."

"Did I?" David allowed himself the merest hint of a smile. "And who's going to explain to your aunt, Jennifer? She will not be pleased, I can tell you. I was irresponsible enough to have brought Becky and Peter here. I can just hear her, if I write to say you're staying, too."

"I could write and say it was my idea to stay."

"You'd have to! I'm not going to take the blame!" He rubbed his chin. "And I'm not going to decide this now, either. We'll talk about it in the morning when I've had a chance to think. If you want to change your mind you're free to say so then."

Jen could hardly believe he meant he was actually going to consider the idea. She had expected him to dismiss it altogether as nonsense.

"Have you got any other bombshells, or is that it for the evening?" David asked.

There was a tentative knock on the study door.

"Yes?"

"Me." Becky stuck her head around it. She was in pajamas and bathrobe. "I just came to say good-night."

David looked from Becky to Jen and back. "Did you?"

"What have you been talking about?"

"As if you didn't know," said Jen tartly.

"Were you really? And?"

"This sounds like a conspiracy," declared David. "I should have known. And nothing. Nothing's been decided and nothing will be tonight. It's long past your bedtime, Becky."

"Are you cross?"

David suddenly grinned. "No. Not yet, anyway. But if you don't go to bed and let me think, I will be! Go on." He pulled the papers across in front of him again. "Good night."

"Good night!"

"What did I tell you?" whispered Becky, once the study door was closed. "He wants you to stay!"

"Shhh," warned Jen sternly. "He didn't say yes. Not yet. I can't believe he'll really let me do it, Becky. Don't count on it."

"No," said Becky, "but you asked. I'm glad. Let's go tell Peter."

"There isn't anything to tell," objected Jen.

"No, but . . ."

Peter was in the kitchen, chin on hands, absorbed in a little brown book propped open on the table in front of him. He only dragged himself out of it reluctantly when Becky insisted and listened with annoying indifference to the news that Jen might be staying in Borth the rest of the year.

"I don't see why you'd want to," he said bluntly. "If you don't even go to school, what is there? But it's your funeral."

"Thanks." Jen glared at him. Peter didn't rise; he went back to his reading.

Jen spent a restless night going over and over the day's events, wondering how she could be so sure of herself one minute and so scared the next. She ought to have waited and given the matter more thought before going to David. She shouldn't have let Becky push her so fast.

By morning Jen was convinced that her father would have decided to send her home. The whole idea was impossible. She could afford to feel regret now: too bad she wasn't going to be allowed to help. After all she was fifteen and quite sensible, and her father ought to treat her as an adult. She was especially nice to Becky, especially confident with the stove, especially efficient with breakfast.

When they'd all finished, with nothing more said than, "Looks like rain, Peter, take your mac," and, "Don't be late after school, Becky," Jen and David were left alone. Becky reluctantly followed Peter out the front door, hoping in vain for some sort of sign from her father.

"Well," said David at last. "I don't have to guess your Aunt Beth's reaction to all this—we ought to be able to hear it in Borth with no trouble."

Jen's stomach gave an unpleasant lurch. He couldn't . . .

David went on. "I spent most of last night thinking over what you said. I can't agree with all of it, Jen, but you were quite right about one thing: your mother would have made us stay together. She would have thought that was more important than all the rest of it. I'm not certain that's right, but if you've honestly made up your mind to stay, we'll make the arrangements."

Jen had no words. She couldn't turn around and tell him she'd thought about it too and come to just the opposite conclusion. She felt panic.

"You understand that this has got to be a working agreement, Jen. It's not going to be easy. I have a hunch there's more to housekeeping than you think, but we all have to learn. And I don't expect you to take over the whole business, of course. We'll work out a plan with Mrs. Davies. And if you're going to miss half a year of school, you can at least keep up with your reading. I'll give you a list." He hesitated. "Jen, I never did like leaving you in Amherst last fall, but Beth persuaded me it was right, and this may be all wrong. I'd like to have you here, but are you quite sure you want to stay?"

He was giving her a last chance. He was being honest with her, she knew he was, he did want her to stay. And she heard herself saying, "It's only six months. Lots of kids miss school because they move or get sick or travel."

David nodded. He seemed to be thinking hard. "We've had problems this year I'd never expected, all of us. I'm afraid I've gotten pretty wound up in my own, and I don't know as much as I should about yours and Becky's and Peter's, that's obvious." He searched carefully for the right words. "I've hedged myself in with work, and I think I seem to you too busy to listen when you need me. But I'm not—I don't want to be. If you've got something to say, just come and shout at me until I hear you. I don't have lots of answers, Jen, but I'll do my best for you. Please don't count me out."

"No," said Jen in a strange, tight voice.

"I suppose the thing to remember is that if we're together then none of us has to be alone. Pretty heavy stuff!" He smiled at her. "Cheer up—I almost think the worst part'll be telling

Beth and Ted. Beth's opinion of me can't get much lower! I'll cable them and phone the Sullivans in London, and your first chore can be writing that letter."

Jen was still at it when Becky burst in at noon. Rejected beginnings littered the kitchen table.

"I *knew* he'd agree! I knew he would! I told you he wants you to stay." Becky beamed at her in delight.

"He's going to expect a lot," said Jen.

"That's all right. I'll help, I promised. I'm *so* glad!"

Jen had to smile at Becky's enthusiasm.

After lunch they went down the hill together, Becky back to school, Jen to post the letter she'd finally finished to Aunt Beth. She hoped it sounded properly grateful, apologetic, and reasonable, but she was afraid it mainly sounded awkward. She stuck it quickly through the slot in the post office, and it was gone. There was no way to get it back again.

Mrs. Davies's reaction was down to earth and practical. "It'll make a difference to me schedule, of course," she said. "I shall have me hands full between you and Susan, shouldn't wonder. Good thing it isn't summer, too."

Jen had enough sense to realize that she must stay on the better side of Mrs. Davies; she needed her help if she was going to succeed. More than once she only just saved herself from making an unfortunate remark, when Mrs. Davies criticized or pointed out jobs that had to be done.

It was agreed that Mrs. Davies would continue to supervise Bryn Celyn until Jen and David both decided it wasn't necessary. Jen would learn shopping and the fundamentals of cooking, and Jen vowed to herself she'd learn as fast as she possibly could.

Mrs. Davies wanted no nonsense. Housekeeping was her vocation and she was a tyrant about square corners on beds and dust on mantels and sand on the kitchen floor. She made a tidy income from bed and breakfast at Ty Gwyn, and this was her business. It didn't take Jen long to learn that the depressing part of housework was that it never stayed done. You never finished a job and then forgot it. You washed breakfast dishes, made beds, straightened the bathroom, swept the floors. Then the sink was full of lunch dishes, and someone had tracked mud in from the back garden or had taken a bath and left puddles of water on the floor. Work came undone almost as fast as you did it, and people only noticed what wasn't done, not what was.

Jen's nervousness wore off quickly. She suffered a morning of real homesickness the first Monday, when she suddenly realized she ought to be in Amherst, starting school again that very day, instead of changing beds and sorting laundry. Becky was as good as her promises, though. She could be counted on for help with anything, and her delight in having Jen still in Borth was flattering.

But Becky's enthusiasm couldn't quite make up for Peter's aloofness. Jen was cross with herself because she let it bother her, but she couldn't help it. Peter made it clear he didn't care what she did, so long, he stated flatly, as she didn't try to give him orders. She didn't have the right to do that. She must leave him alone.

"He is the most uncooperative—!" she exploded frequently to Becky.

"Och," said Rhian with a shake of her head. "They're all like that—men."

"Peter's hardly a man," contradicted Jen irritably. "He's behaving like a little boy!"

Rhian shrugged. She often came up to Bryn Celyn for lunch with Becky. The smoky Welsh dusk crept into the afternoons so early that it was dark by the time school was out. She had to get home, and there were farm chores at Llechwedd Melyn. But she took a lively interest in Jen's domestic struggles.

"Why you should be *wanting* to do all that, I can't see. Me, I am never wanting to learn!"

Jen gave up trying to answer Rhian. Secretly, she wondered herself sometimes. There were days when it rained and she forgot the laundry on the line in the backyard, and the Washeteria was full of squalling babies and mums gossiping about whose daughter was seeing whose son, and why Mrs. Thomas had left her husband *this* time. She had even burst into tears one gloomy afternoon when she couldn't get the clean socks to match.

It was so easy to forget that the toothpaste was almost gone or that they were out of cornflakes until it was too late. And she hated lugging groceries up the hill. But she had her own share of pride and stubbornness. She gritted her teeth and kept at it. Admitting she was wrong to her father was bad enough, but admitting defeat in front of Mrs. Davies was unthinkable!

Gwilym Davies began coming round in time for tea two or three times a week. Jen was too preoccupied with supper to think much about it at first, but after a while she grew curious. He never said much, just sat with the three of them, content with a cup of tea. His ears turned quite pink whenever anyone took notice of him.

"But why does he come?" Jen asked Becky one evening.

"He likes being over here, he told me," Becky replied. "He thinks we're peculiar."

Jen snorted. "I suppose we are."

"Besides," Becky added shrewdly, "it keeps his mother quiet."

"Oh?"

"Mmm. She thinks he ought to have friends his own age."

"But he never opens his mouth except to swallow tea, unless he's excited about some bird," Jen exclaimed.

"*She* doesn't know that, does she? Haven't you noticed that she's always in a better mood when she finds him here? Not that it matters anyway. I like him, and even Peter's interested in that motorbike of his."

9

The Battle of Cors Jochno

THAT SATURDAY, on the wet shoulder of Foel Goch, the shape of Peter's life had begun to alter rapidly. It had been shifting ever since he'd found the Key among the rocks of Sarn Cynfelin, the ancient sea wall—*if* you chose to believe it was a sea wall—but after seeing Taliesin, and incomprehensibly *being seen by him* across thousands of years, the sensible part of Peter's mind had gotten lost in the other, darker part. The Key consumed him, it demanded his whole attention, and he awaited its songs impatiently, absorbing their images like the great, gaunt hills absorbed the endless winter rain.

Jen's stubborn refusal to accept the Key no longer bothered Peter. Becky's willingness to be persuaded didn't matter. His father's preoccupation with the University didn't irritate him. Bryn Celyn, school, Borth—all became a flat, remote background, unimportant behind the rich patterns of light and dark that the Key wove him into.

For the first time since he'd arrived in Wales, Peter opened his eyes and his heart to the ancient country of the Cymraeg around him. He felt its quickness and strength and knew, without having to learn, the mysteries of its buried past.

The *hafod* on Foel Goch, the vast, checkered expanse of Cors Fochno, the Dyfi emptying into the sea: these were suddenly more familiar to him than his own backyard in Amherst had ever been.

It was so much easier to be left to himself—he need not bother about what people thought. Jen had her hands full, learning the routines of Bryn Celyn and satisfying Mrs. Davies's rigid standards; Becky divided her time between school and helping Jen; and David was kept busy with university work and his own study of the Welsh language in the twentieth century. What little spare time he had he spent with Jen, planning her studies. Even Gwilym was lost in schoolwork.

So Peter was free to wander with the Key. Taliesin had taken upon himself the education of this other Elphin, the son of Gwyddno Garanhir. The Bard was older, more thoughtful now than he had been with Elphin Rheged. He taught Elphin the secrets of the high russet hills and the shadowed *cwms*. Together they tended the fish weir on the river and walked the long, silver beach. Life was not so easy here; everyone, even Gwyddno himself, king of what was left of his drowned land, worked hard for food and shelter. But there was a satisfaction in it Taliesin seemed not to have known before.

Whenever the Key called Peter, no matter where he was —at Bryn Celyn, at school—he went with it. And he thought, when he bothered to, that no one noticed he was gone. After all, the outer part of Peter Morgan stayed wherever it was. He was wrong.

One gloomy Thursday, not long after the beginning of the new term, Mr. Griffith, Peter's schoolmaster, kept him back after school. Mr. Griffith only did it with the greatest reluctance. He wanted to give Peter every chance, but at last he'd had to admit to himself that he could get no response from Morgan.

"I have no essay from you this week, Morgan," Mr. Griffith said carefully, reading through the next day's lesson plan. "Have you been working on it, then?"

"Not really, sir," Peter answered honestly.

"Why not? Have you an excuse?" The teacher kept his voice reasonable, his eyes still fixed on the papers in front of him.

"No."

"Do you intend to do it?"

Peter was silent, and Mr. Griffith had to look up at last. He was a young teacher, only two or three years out of university, serious about his work. He tried hard to strike a spark of interest among his students that might catch and spread. He had grown up, the son of a coal miner in south Wales, and he knew the difficulties he was facing: boys without money, without interest in learning more than they had to, boys who would go to work as soon as they could. But if he could convince only a handful to go on in school past leaving age, some even perhaps to university, he could feel he had achieved something.

Peter Morgan puzzled him. Mr. Griffith knew Peter was not stupid. He knew Peter did only as much work in school as he could scrape by on and not attract attention. That in itself was a sign of cleverness. But, since the start of this term, Peter had stopped doing even that much. Except for the fact that he was physically present in the classroom, he might as well have dropped out of school altogether. And Mr. Griffith couldn't understand why.

"I will be forced to give you an incomplete for the week unless you can produce that essay, Morgan," said Mr. Griffith quietly. "I don't want to do that, mind, and I should not be having to. It was not a very difficult one, you know. I am sure you could have written something."

"I didn't have time, I guess."

"Oh? Has there been a problem at home? If you have a reason . . ." He knew a little about Peter and could see the boy was unhappy and rebellious. He was willing to be patient for the slightest reason.

But it didn't seem important to Peter to make up an excuse even though Mr. Griffith was inviting him to. It just didn't matter. "I don't have a reason."

Mr. Griffith sighed and stacked the papers in a precise pile. "Then I have no choice. If there is something I can do to help you, Morgan, I would like to."

Peter shook his head. "May I go, sir?"

"Yes."

Peter felt vaguely irritated as he stood at the top of Penglais Hill waiting for the bus to Borth. What difference did it make to Mr. Griffith what he did and didn't do? He would only be going to school here for a few more months and then he'd never set eyes on the teacher again. He didn't make trouble, he wasn't fresh, he came to school every day. If he chose not to do any work that should be his own business. He dismissed the entire matter from his mind then, expecting that was the end of it.

"Peter's teacher wants to come and see me," said David to Jen after dinner Friday. They were alone in the study going over a reading list. "I wonder why." He frowned at *David Copperfield*.

"Mmm?" said Jen, absorbed. "Why does he want to come?"

"That's what I just said—why? I hope it isn't trouble. We seem to be on a fairly even keel right now and it's very restful. Has Peter said anything to you about school lately?"

"No. He hasn't said much about anything lately. When's his teacher coming?"

"Tuesday afternoon after school. Didn't say what he wanted, but said it was important. Oh, lord, and I thought Peter was sorting himself out at last!"

"Maybe he is and that's why his teacher's coming." Even

in her own ears Jen knew it didn't sound convincing. She realized with a start that she and Peter had lost contact recently; they'd hardly seen each other except at breakfast and dinner. And no mention at all had been made of harp keys, magic, or superstition.

Peter's mind was full of the sense of unrest among Gwyddno's people. Uneasiness hung like a mist from the Bog over their villages. Men coming out of the north brought word of violence and fighting. The warriors of Maelgwn, Lord of the large and powerful Kingdom of Gwynedd above the Dyfi, were gathering at his court. There had been successful raids on the country to the east, outside Gwynedd. The raiders had come from Maelgwn's fortress, Dyganwy.

Gwyddno's melancholy face grew graver daily as he listened to reports brought out of Gwynedd by weary, travel-stained men. Not without cause had the monk Gildas called Maelgwn "The Dragon." Now he was beginning to itch for activity after one of his periods of peace and contemplation. He was talking of battles and conquests and new lands again, talk that could only be dangerous, and the young men of Gwynedd were listening. Between Maelgwn and Gwyddno's precarious kingdom lay only the Dyfi, all the defense Gwyddno could count on. His people were too busy with the tasks of keeping alive to build fortresses and earthworks. But Gwyddno had no choice; he began preparing his people for battle.

The singing of the Key shifted subtly; a thunderhead grew between the sun and the earth, darkening the summer sky. The days Taliesin and Elphin shared were lent an urgency. There was so much to speak of, to seek for, and to learn.

"Will there be war? If anyone knows, it must be you."

"No, I do not know. I know no more than you of what *will* be, Elphin."

"My father expects a war, and I shall fight beside him if

there is one." The young man's eyes flashed even as Gwyddno's must once have.

"So shall I," replied Taliesin. "But only because there is no choice. I would not choose to fight if there were one. Life is too precious."

Elphin regarded his friend thoughtfully. "You are not a coward, I know. Do you believe fighting is wrong, then."

Taliesin smiled a little and gave his head a shake. "Some men fight, some do not. Of those who do, some have to, and some want to. Maelgwn is the latter, your father the former. But look at me, Elphin. I am a bard and it is in the calling of a bard to sing of kings and battles, to record great courage and glory in war. That is my work, even as a king's is to lead his men and a *taeog* must work all his life plowing fields and growing vegetables."

"That doesn't answer my question."

"Let us say then"—Taliesin's smile deepened—"that if there were no fighting I would not have difficulty finding things to sing of."

Peter was out all day Saturday, not telling anyone where he was going or when he'd be back. He ranged the high, windy cliffs south of Borth as far as Sarn Cynfelin, eating a lunch of chocolate biscuits and ginger beer. He managed to get back to Bryn Celyn a bare fifteen minutes before his father came in from Aberystwyth for supper. There were no awkward questions to answer; Jen and Becky were used to Peter's absences and David was unaware.

But Sunday Peter was not so fortunate. He slipped out after breakfast. However, David stayed at Bryn Celyn, reading the newspapers and working on the article he was writing for publication: "Celtic Languages—The Revival of Welsh in Wales."

Dinner was at one as usual. At one-fifteen Peter was still missing. He was not in the house; Jen tried his room, but it was empty. Becky said she remembered hearing him go out just before she went down for the papers, but no one had seen him since.

"He *knows* what time we eat dinner on Sunday," said David, looking at his watch again. Jen watched helplessly as all the vegetables turned to mush in their pots.

"It's all going to be horrible in a few minutes," she stated.

"Well." Irritation frayed David's voice. "We'll just go ahead without him and he can take his chances on what's left over. Becky, are you sure he didn't say where he was going?"

"No. He didn't."

So they sat down to eat without Peter, his empty place painfully obvious. Becky ate as slowly as she could. Jen knew she was hoping Peter would come in before they'd finished the main course. But he didn't. Before dessert, Becky asked to be excused, saying she wasn't very hungry. It was all too evident what David was thinking from his face. Jen's own mind was full of wild thoughts. Peter was in for a good row when he did get back, but of course he was asking for it; and Jen found she was dreading the confrontation between her father and her brother.

At five there was still no sign of Peter, and Jen had begun to realize how truly worried her father was under his irritation. It was dark enough for lights in the house, and Jen made a pot of tea. When she took David a cup, she found him sitting in the study at his desk, not even pretending to work, just staring out through the curtains. She guessed what he was wondering and shivered involuntarily.

"I'm sure he's all right, Dad," she ventured. "He probably went for a walk and got further away than he'd realized."

David sighed heavily. "I don't know. Honestly I don't. I thought he'd gotten over all this. He's got me baffled. This is such a silly thing to do."

"He can't have done anything like run away," said Jen, and immediately wished she hadn't.

"For God's sake, Jennifer, I'm sure he's got more sense than that!" David exploded. "Where on earth could he *go?* He doesn't know anyone very well and there aren't any trains or buses from Borth on Sunday. No, I don't think he's run away, but I'd like to know what he *is* playing at. If he isn't back by six, I'm going to have to call the police and begin looking for him—heaven knows where!"

Then, miraculously, they both heard the front door open and close. David was up like a shot and out into the hall, Jen close behind him. Becky had heard, too, and was in the lounge doorway.

Peter looked around at them with an expression of surprise, apparently quite unconcerned. Jen held her breath.

"Well, where the hell have you been?" demanded David, hiding his worry in anger.

"For a walk," said Peter. Then he added as an afterthought, "Sorry I'm late."

"*Late?* Have you any idea how long you've been gone? Why on earth didn't you tell anyone when you left?"

Jen couldn't remember seeing her father so furious, but she and Becky, who stood pale and wide-eyed across the hall, were more afraid than Peter seemed to be.

"I forgot," he said.

"Did it never enter your head that what you were doing was dangerous? Where's your sense, Peter! I had absolutely no idea where you'd gone."

"I just went for a walk, I told you." At last David's anger was beginning to penetrate.

"Where?"

"Along the cliffs."

"And suppose something had happened to you out there. Suppose you'd gotten lost or fallen and broken a leg? I wouldn't have had the faintest idea where to begin looking for you! For all I knew you might have been wandering on the Bog or down at Ynyslas. If you'd needed help, what would you have done—would you have known where to go? There are hundreds of sane, sensible reasons why you should never, never go off like that without telling anyone! Stop and think!"

Peter was silent, his face closed. He looked at none of them. Jen wondered if he did indeed know how long he'd been away. He didn't seem to.

"With everything I have to worry about," David went on, "I thought at least I didn't have to worry about you three. You're intelligent enough not to get yourselves into senseless trouble, or so I thought. Now I find I'm wrong. I didn't think that by this time I'd have to spell it all out for you and make all kinds of rules, but I see I do have to. After this, Peter, you will not go anywhere outside this house without telling *me* first. Not Jen, or Becky, but *me*. Do you understand?"

Peter nodded sullenly.

"If you behave like a baby, I have no choice but to treat you like one. Now you'd better go to your room and do some thinking."

"Yes, sir." Peter's voice was icy.

He really isn't scared, thought Jen in amazement, as she watched him walk, unhurried, down the hall to his room. The anger went out of David as if he'd turned a switch. He just looked tired and unhappy. It was Becky who broke the immobilizing silence, her voice husky. "Could we have some more tea?"

"I'll put it on," said Jen, thankful for action.

"Yes," said David. "All right."

Whatever Peter's teacher, Mr. Griffith, came to talk to David about on Tuesday, Jen knew from her brief glimpse of him on his way into the study, it wasn't an improvement in Peter's attitude. He smiled gravely and shook hands with Jen when David introduced her, then the two men retired behind the study door, and she was left wanting and not wanting to know what was going on.

She was torn so dreadfully by Peter. Their father really ought to be told the whole wild story, no matter how far-fetched it sounded, about the Key and Taliesin and Peter's own explanation for them. Even while the sensible Jen argued for it, the emotional one warned her that trying to tell David would most likely only make the situation worse. If she didn't understand Peter, she didn't see that David would.

Then, too, Becky would never agree to telling David unless Peter agreed first, and there was no hope of that. Thinking about Becky only upset Jen further because Becky was willing to believe Peter's wild story.

Mechanically, she helped Mrs. Davies put supper together, her mind far from brussels sprouts and mutton chops. It got later and later. Becky came and set the table, chattering on to Mrs. Davies about Susan and Susan's soon-expected baby. Peter stayed in his room with the door shut, ignoring them all.

"Jennifer?" David called her from the hall. "Jen, would you please come in here for a minute?"

Mrs. Davies gave her an interested look but said nothing.

There was a worried frown on David's face, but he wasn't cross. Mr. Griffith looked apologetic.

"Come in and close the door, will you? Mr. Griffith has been telling me about Peter's work at school and the peculiar way he's acting right now. Jen, if you've got any idea why, please tell me. I'm at a loss."

"Well, now," began Mr. Griffith. His gray eyes were anxious.

"What's he done?" Jen feared the worst without knowing what it was.

"Nothing wrong," said Mr. Griffith quickly. Jen decided he didn't look like the kind of person to make trouble. "No, you couldn't say he's done anything wrong, you know. It is more that he is not doing anything at all."

"Peter's evidently decided not to do *any* schoolwork now," David explained. "And he won't say why, I gather. Do you know?"

Jen shook her head. "No."

"Has he said much to you about school?"

"Not since I first came and he complained about learning Welsh. He never mentions it, but he seems to do quite a lot of reading. Could it be," she hesitated, "too hard?"

"Nonsense," said David roundly. "He's not stupid, though he sometimes *acts* it."

"Excuse me, Mr. Morgan, but I do agree with you. I am sure he can do the work that I assign without trouble, though he has never been exactly eager. It is just that since the holidays he has stopped doing any. If it weren't that I could see him at his desk each day, I would say he wasn't even in class. I had wondered if perhaps something at Christmas had upset him?"

"Jen?"

"I don't know." Jen felt resentful; she was being put on the spot by both David *and* Peter and it wasn't fair. "*I* didn't do anything."

"Of course not," said David. "But you mustn't be reluctant to tell me if you know what has happened. I really would like to understand Peter better. I might be of some help to him if I did. I suppose a lot of this is my fault. I've lost my temper with him so often, I know he won't come to me by himself now. We're both much too stubborn."

Mr. Griffith coughed gently. "I think perhaps I should get on home, Mr. Morgan. I am sorry to have come on such an errand, but I thought it was my place to. And if I can help in any way, please do call on me and I will do what I can."

"Yes. Thank you, Mr. Griffith, I'm grateful to you for coming." David saw the teacher out, then turned to Jen. "I like him."

"He seems nice," she said cautiously.

"He's the kind of teacher who really cares about teaching. They're lucky to have him here."

"I ought to get back to the kitchen." Jen escaped.

At dinner Jen and Becky did valiantly at providing conversation. Becky went cheerfully on about Rhian's family and Mrs. Davies's daughter.

"Mrs. Davies says she's gotten simply huge."

"Why?" asked David absently.

"She's pregnant, of course," Becky told him impatiently. "Only Mrs. Davies says it must be twins. She's having a terrible time with varicose veins, you know."

"Oh." David looked as if he wished he hadn't asked.

Jen plunged into a description of grocery shopping and how different it was from shopping in Amherst where you just went to a supermarket. Here you had to go from shop to shop to shop. And a week from tonight Mrs. Davies had told her she'd be away, so Jen would have to cook her first supper alone.

"Peter," said David at last, "I suppose you know I had a talk with Mr. Griffith this afternoon."

Peter was carefully cleaning his plate.

"He's concerned about you," David went on quietly. "He said he spoke to you last Thursday."

Peter nodded. He was trying to decide how he should react. His father was being too calm.

"I'm concerned, too, Peter. I know you're capable of doing your work, so does Mr. Griffith, so it's not that. There has to be another reason, but Mr. Griffith said you wouldn't give him one. And to be perfectly honest with you"—they all three waited—"I don't know what to do next. It's obvious you feel you can't talk to me, and I don't seem to get through to you either. You can miss a bit of school, just as Jen can, that isn't what bothers me."

There was a peculiar expression on Peter's face. "What are you going to do?"

"What would you suggest? I'm not going to stand over you every time you have an essay to write. It wouldn't do either of us any good, would it? Just make it worse. I won't threaten or bargain with you. I guess what it comes down to is that I'm not going to do anything right away." His eyes were on his puzzled son, and there was just the hint of a smile around his mouth. "But I *did* mean what I said yesterday about not going out without telling me."

And he got up and left the table while his three children looked at each other.

"Well," said Becky in wonder. "I thought he'd yell at you at least. I wish he'd tell me *my* homework doesn't matter!"

"He was so furious Sunday," said Jen, "perhaps he used it up?"

"It's psychological warfare," Peter said thoughtfully. "I wonder if . . ." But his voice trailed away and he never finished the sentence. "I'm going to take a bath," he announced.

Becky shook her head at Jen when he'd gone. "Why can't people behave the way you expect them to? It's so confusing. They don't either one of them seem upset."

"Well, *I* am," Jen declared. "It sounds as if Dad's given up, and I don't like it. This is serious."

"Maybe he's just decided shouting doesn't help," suggested Becky.

Jen wondered. She didn't see that ignoring Peter's behavior was going to make him change it. He just seemed to be getting further away from them. And it was worse now because outside people, like Mr. Griffith, were beginning to notice.

"Becky," she said firmly, "has Peter been talking to you?"

"About what?" Becky was sorting knives and forks noisily.

"You know about what."

"The Key." Becky met Jen's eyes steadily. "Why don't you say so?"

"Because it's nonsense. I don't believe in it and you shouldn't either."

"But," Becky pointed out, "it doesn't matter whether we believe in it or not—*Peter* does. And he has the Key and you won't convince him it's nonsense no matter how hard you try."

"You're quite sure he does believe in it?" Jen challenged.

"Positive."

"Doesn't it bother you?"

"No. It only bothers me because it's making such a lot of problems. I don't see why Peter can't believe what he wants to. You can't stop him, can you?"

"What if I could?" said Jen. "Suppose I could convince him it isn't true."

"How?"

"I'll talk to Dr. Rhys."

"Would you really?" asked Becky. "Would you dare?"

"Of course, I would. Don't be silly. He's a friend of Dad's, isn't he? And he knows a lot about legends and history." The idea of going to Dr. Rhys had been at the back of Jen's mind for several days. Becky had pushed it into the open. It did make her a little nervous, but she wasn't going to let Becky see that. Instead, she said, "You can come, too. I think you ought to. We'll do it tomorrow, right away. I even know where his office is." With Becky along, Jen knew she'd have to go through with it and that would help.

With the coming of dusk, the weather had begun to change, but no one noticed until after supper when they all sat in the lounge busy with books and writing paper. Outside Bryn Celyn the wind was up, rushing around the corners of the house, doubling on itself, twisting backwards. Puffs of it kept coming down the chimney making the coal fire flicker and smoke and blowing clouds of soot into the room. The windows rattled in their frames and the curtains danced eerily.

Jen read the same scene of *King Lear* twice without understanding a sentence, and Becky kept looking up from the vocabulary list she was writing.

"This is hopeless!" exclaimed Jen at last. She put down her book and turned on the television, hoping to drown the wind. But it didn't work; the wind drowned the television instead and made Jen and Becky even more aware of the restless dark outside. Several times they heard David come out of his study and check the front door and the kitchen. The air was full of a waiting violence barely restrained, the tension that builds just before a storm.

"I think we're all tired," Jen said after a bit. "It wouldn't do any of us harm to go to bed early tonight."

"Not me," said Becky quickly. "I'll stay down here until you're ready."

Jen looked at her in surprise. "You don't mind going to bed alone—you never have."

"I'd mind tonight. I don't like the wind."

At half-past eight Peter came and joined them, curling himself into the window chair without a word. He had brought nothing with him but sat looking into the fire, his hands on his knees. And the wind tore at itself in fury, howling like a great pack of wild beasts. There was no rain.

Everyone jumped when David came in. "Quite a night," he commented. "Radio said nothing about a storm this evening."

"They're often wrong," said Jen, remembering washlines full of wet laundry. "Unless you wait long enough."

"It's from the north," Peter said in his chair. "They've come from the north."

"*They?*" Jen gave him a queer look.

"I mean the wind. It sounds like 'they'."

"It does a bit," David agreed. "We get the full force of it here. Right down from the mountains of Snowdonia like a battering ram. Nothing to protect us."

Peter curled himself tighter.

"Well," said David after a minute, "I'm going to bed pretty sharp. Can't do any useful work with this racket."

"Let's all go," Becky suggested.

David had just checked the kitchen door a last time and Peter was brushing his teeth, when Jen called out from the front bedroom, her voice urgent.

"Come and see what's happening, will you?"

She and Becky stood by the window in the dark room, Jen holding the curtain back. David came to stand beside them, and Peter a moment later.

"What do you suppose they're doing out there?"

There was no mistaking what Jen meant: below the bluff, the narrow string of lights that marked the town ran straight up to the river as usual, and to the left lay the great empty bay. But to the right the blackness of the Bog was pierced with lights, a great many of them moving about rapidly in no particular pattern. They looked like flaming torches, leaping and dancing in the wind, flaring white-orange. On the far side of the Bog, along what must be both banks of the river, were bonfires. Every now and then a small black figure would pass in front of one.

Jen could feel Becky shivering beside her. David put a hand on Becky's shoulder, reassuring.

"What are they?" Jen asked again.

"I really don't know," said David.

"But they're walking all over the Bog!" said Becky. "How can they?"

As she spoke a sudden burst of flame erupted into the night sky from the dark hillside to the east, high up the slope. Someone must have touched off a huge pile of dry wood that had been set ready. It blazed like a signal beacon above the Bog. And the wind roared with new fury.

"I don't like it one bit," declared Becky. "I don't care what it is."

"That fire must be right near . . ." Jen stopped abruptly, remembering the ruined *hafod*. She felt cold.

"Foel Goch," supplied Peter.

"You know the place?" asked David.

Becky answered, "Rhian took us up there with Gwilym during vacation."

There was a moment's silence, which David broke. "All right," he said briskly, "there's bound to be a perfectly simple reason for all of that. It could be farmers getting a cow out of the Bog or some peculiar kind of celebration."

"Really?" Becky sounded hopeful.

"Really. The English celebrate Guy Fawkes Day with bonfires and fireworks, we celebrate the Fourth of July, the Welsh must celebrate something like that. Britain's full of obscure folk customs and rites. We just weren't told. Now"—he pulled the curtain out of Jen's hand and drew it firmly across the window—"there's a terrific draft here and, Jen, you haven't even got slippers on. Into bed, all of you, before we catch pneumonia standing here! Someone'll tell us what we missed in the morning and we'll be sorry we didn't see it properly. Go! Everyone!"

The Key throbbed with excitement. It sang a fierce, joyous battle song, drowning Peter in its frenzy. The wind from the north was Maelgwn, sweeping out of Gwynedd, leaping the Dyfi as if it were no more than a trickle, challenging Gwyddno's hastily formed army to do battle on Cors Fochno. There was no modern ritual out there, no celebration—there was war. Peter knew it but could tell no one. Who would believe him if he said that in the sixth century two armies had fought each other on Borth Bog and that was what they were seeing now?

Taliesin's voice rose above the uproar, chanting strange Cymric words that pounded and sang in Peter's head. Taliesin was urging the men of the Cors to hold their ground, to do their utmost against the odds.

All night the wind continued to scream unabated. The curtains in the front bedroom stayed shut, but neither Jen nor Becky slept well. Lying awake in the seething dark, Jen heard Becky turn restlessly, and once she heard David come to their door and pause, then go downstairs. To Peter, she supposed. She clung grimly to what her father had said about the lights on the Bog—that they were real and could be explained away sensibly. She had to believe that . . .

"Are you all right?"

The darkness in Peter's room was complete. "Yes," said Peter.

"Can you sleep?" asked David.

"I think so."

"Good night then." The door shut, and Peter heard his father go back down the hall. The stairs creaked as he went up to his room.

For one desperate moment Peter longed to call David back again, to tell him, no, he couldn't sleep, to ask him to stay for a while. The hugeness of the battle seemed unbearable. He remembered the flood, the great sheets of black water, the dyke crumbling into the sea, trees and huts torn away, and the wretched feeling of utter helplessness. He could only watch: he, Peter could do nothing to prevent any of it. And it was happening again. The pattern was set by the past and could not be altered. He was only a spectator, not of that time, and therefore powerless.

Gwyddno's ragged troops fought valiantly for him and for what was left of their country, but they could only hope to hold Cors Fochno against the men of Gwynedd and tire them if they could. These were country men: farmers, fishermen, herdsmen—not trained warriors; they could not defeat Maelgwn's army with force.

The Dragon's attack at night had been unexpected. He had chosen the weapon of surprise against Gwyddno, but once that surprise wore off, Gwyddno had the advantage, for he knew the country they fought on: the hills, the Bog, the river. And he had lit the great signal fire on Foel Goch, which would call men to Cors Fochno from miles east and south. They came on foot or horseback with all speed to reinforce those already fighting.

All night the battle shook Cors Fochno, the air rang with the sound of sword on shield, the cries of men fighting and dying. And the red of dawn staining the sky over the hills seemed to be reflected on the levels below as if in water. The Cors was red with blood. Men from both sides of the river lay scattered and broken on it. Gwyddno's army had suffered heavily, and in the light they could see their own losses and they despaired. Whatever slim hope they had was gone, and the day belonged to Maelgwn.

But, unbelievably, there came a shout, and another, and another! And the men of Gwynedd drew back from the battle. They turned and recrossed the Dyfi on their rough-built rafts. They retreated. The weary defenders stood and watched them go, too dazed and weary to understand. It was incredible that the enemy, so close to winning, should withdraw!

But Maelgwn, The Dragon, did not retreat. He went with his honor unscathed, for he carried with him the greatest prize Gwyddno could lose. He had satisfied his lust for violence.

In the sudden quiet that fell across Cors Fochno, the white-haired King raised his fists to the morning sun, his eyes hard and dead as chips of granite in his ravaged face. "He has taken my son!" The wail of anguish was borne across the Dyfi on the dawn wind; it brought a cold smile to the lips of Maelgwn.

Gwyddno's men stood about him, stricken. They were too few and it was too late. Elphin was Maelgwn's captive.

"Do not grieve, Lord." Taliesin, battle-wearied but steady, was at Gwyddno's side. "Elphin has not been harmed and shall be returned to you. I promise."

The old King's face was a mask of bitterness. "And how

shall he be returned? Maelgwn releases no prisoners. I have lost my kingdom, now I have lost my son. Neither can be recovered. I have nothing."

But Taliesin stood firm, his eyes blazing. "Not so! It is for me to bring Elphin, son of Gwyddno, safely out of Gwynedd. I, too, have lost much. I have lost one king's son, I will not lose yours!

> *A journey will I undertake,*
> *To Maelgwn's gates I will come;*
> *His hall I will enter,*
> *And my song I shall sing.*
> *A riddle I will pose*
> *To silence the Royal Bards*
> *In the presence of their Chief.*
> *A contest I will win*
> *And Elphin I will free*
> *From haughty tyrant's bonds.*
> *To his fell and chilling cry,*
> *By the act of a surprising beast*
> *From the far distant North,*
> *There shall soon be an end.*
> *Let neither grace nor health*
> *Be to Maelgwn Gwynedd,*
> *For this force and this wrong!"*

IO

Dr. Rhys

THE NEXT MORNING, when Jen opened the curtains, she and Becky looked out on a perfectly ordinary world. The wind had dropped with the coming of light, and the sea and Bog were empty, beaten flat by cold, streaming rain. There was no movement on either, no traces of the night before.

"They *were* there, weren't they?" said Becky, echoing Jen's own thoughts. *Had* they actually seen lights and fires on the Bog last night or had they dreamed it?

Gwilym appeared while the Morgans were still at breakfast. He came to the back door, his yellow mac shining with rain. He would only come inside far enough to allow the door to close behind him, and he dripped carefully on the door mat.

"Morning," he said, glancing quickly around at them. "Mum told me to stop in to say we won't be going to the shops this afternoon, and she'll do your cleaning tomorrow, if that's all right. Our Susan's to go to hospital."

"The baby?" Becky wanted to know at once.

"Not yet. She's going for tests and that and she wants Mum with her."

"What about supper?" asked Jen apprehensively.

"Not to worry. Mum'll be back in time for that easy."

"Nothing wrong with your sister, I hope?" said David, looking up from his scrambled eggs.

"No, sir. Mum says it's just her being so tired and all, but what can you expect with Simon not yet two and a house and husband to see to as well." Gwilym shifted awkwardly on the damp mat. "I'll be off now."

"Hang on, Gwilym," said David. "I want to ask you about last night. It must have been after nine, I'd guess, we noticed lights out on the Bog. It looked as though there were torches and fires all over it and all along the river. Do you know what was going on?"

"It's odd, that," replied Gwilym slowly. "We saw them, too. I wanted to go down, but Mum wouldn't have it. She said it was only trouble, and too late and dark, and best to leave well enough. Dad was out on shift and didn't get in till late, but this morning he said like as not it was someone lost out there."

"Mmm," David said. "I thought so, too, but there were so many of them. I wondered if it were a celebration of some kind?"

"Not that I know of, sir. Now you mention it, it did look a bit like Guy Fawkes."

"Well, I'm sure someone from town will know."

"Ah," said Gwilym.

Jen wasn't especially pleased to see Rhian arrive for lunch with Becky later that day. It complicated her plans. She had made up her mind to go and see Dr. Rhys that afternoon and to take Becky, which meant Becky would miss school. Jen was uncomfortable about that and hoped David wouldn't find out, but it was necessary that Becky be convinced once and for all that Peter's stories were just that—stories, and nothing more. If anyone could help, it had to be Dr. Rhys. Jen needed his reassurances, too, though she hated to admit it.

But now Rhian would have to be told Becky wasn't going back to school, which was a nuisance. Jen scolded the two younger girls for leaving puddles in the hall and not hanging up their wet macs properly. But Rhian didn't seem to notice Jen's bad humor: she was as cheerful and full of energy as ever.

"You know, Jen"—Becky trailed her sister into the kitchen—"Rhian says that up her way they could see the lights last night, too."

"How could they? The hills are in the way," said Jen brusquely.

"We did, though," Rhian informed her. "Not from the farm, it wasn't, but Da and our Aled were seeing them when they came up from the pub at Tre'r-ddôl. And wasn't there an argument about that, then! Still at it when they got in, they were!" She grinned.

"About the lights?" In spite of herself Jen was interested.

"Mmm. Aled was all for going to find out what was up, see, and Da would have none of it. Aled said it would be someone lost or a cow mired and shouldn't they help, but Da said to leave it. Wasn't natural, he said, and they'd only have trouble for going. Didn't Aled shout about that!"

"Did he go? Aled, I mean," asked Becky.

Rhian snorted. "Not him! Great for talking, that one, but he knows better than to get across Da, especially and he's had a few pints."

"So what *did* happen on the Bog?" Jen demanded.

"No one knows," said Becky. "Lots of people saw the lights, but no one knows what they were for."

"Happen Da was right," said Rhian.

"You mean ghosts, I suppose," said Jen scornfully.

But Rhian shook her head impatiently. "And you're meaning sheets and chains and skulls and that! Baby stuff, that is. My Da doesn't believe in that any more than you. I suppose you didn't mind the wind last night? That wasn't bothering you at all?"

"I didn't like it much, but that doesn't mean I thought it was supernatural," Jen retorted.

"I did," said Becky softly. "It didn't feel right, somehow. Is that what your father means about the hills, Rhian?"

"It is."

Jen slapped together a cheese and pickle sandwich crossly. "For heaven's sake, you two! Someone in Borth must know what that was last night. Didn't anyone see?"

"Not likely. You can believe what you want, but my Da is right, I think. It's best not messing around with that you don't understand."

"You won't ever understand if you don't try to find out," objected Jen.

"Did you go?" asked Rhian, fixing Jen with a sharp stare.

"No, I didn't. We were getting ready for bed when we saw the lights and Dad would never have let me go out. Even so—"

"But it doesn't matter now anyway," interrupted Becky, sensing Jen was on the defensive. "It's over."

"Aye," Rhian agreed. "The wind and the feeling both. Ach, look, will you? It's time to get back already. We'll be late if we don't go sharp."

"Becky's not going back," said Jen.

"I'm not?" and "She isn't?" said Becky and Rhian together.

"No, you aren't. You're going with me to Aberystwyth, remember?"

"I didn't think that was today—"

"I meant what I said. I'm going and I think you've got to come too."

"Lucky," said Rhian enviously, pulling on her wellingtons.

The dull, heavy rain made Aberystwyth look dismal and shabby: a jumble of stucco houses, cracked sidewalks, a few anonymous people with overcoat collars turned up and hats or umbrellas. It was early closing day and all the shops were shut, which added to the derelict feeling of the town. Jen and Becky got off the bus at North Parade, the main street, and hurried up it under the uncomfortable, contorted monkey puzzle trees, then around corners until they reached the old University building. Without pausing, Jen pulled Becky with her between the pillars at the entrance and past the porter, drinking tea and reading a magazine in his little lighted cell inside the door. He didn't even look up.

Jen had given a good deal of thought to this trip. She'd chosen a time when Hugh-the-Bus was off the Aberystwyth route and when her father would be up at the new University, not here in his office. She didn't want to see anyone but Dr. Rhys.

The main hall was dim and empty; their footsteps shattered its gloomy silence.

"Shh," hissed Jen, and Becky obediently tiptoed. It took them some time to find the right office—it was up several flights of stairs and down a little passageway: Dr. G. H. Rhys, Director, Welsh Studies, on a brass plate on the door.

Jen hesitated for the first time; her hands were damp.

"Suppose he's not there?" whispered Becky.

"We'll have to come back." Jen knocked lightly.

"He'll never hear that."

"All right then." She rapped hard.

And from the other side of the door they heard, "Come?"

"At least we don't have to come back."

"Shhh!" said Jen.

The office was small and very full of books. They lined the walls, floor to ceiling, filled the narrow windowsill, stood in neat stacks on the floor. The only furniture was a desk, also piled with books, two chairs, a small stepladder, and a little file cabinet. Over the books on the desk Jen and Becky could just see Dr. Rhys's head looking oddly disembodied. He was evidently absorbed in something in his hands, for he didn't look up right away. A cold trickle of water from the collar of her mac found its way down Jen's neck. Panic rose in her throat; she'd forgotten what she was going to say.

After what seemed like ages, Dr. Rhys raised his head, peering at his visitors nearsightedly. "Yes?" He obviously didn't place them immediately.

"Dr. Rhys"—Jen cleared her throat—"I'm Jennifer Morgan and this is my sister Becky."

She saw recognition then, and he actually smiled at them. "Of course, David's children, aren't you? Ah, yes. Have you come to find your father? His office is on the first floor, you know, but I believe he is up at Penglais this afternoon."

"I know. We came to see you actually."

"Oh?" He sounded surprised.

"Do you mind? Are you busy?"

"No more than usual. It can wait, it can wait. Take off your coats, why don't you, and I'll just find another chair."

When they'd all sat down, Dr. Rhys and Becky both looked expectantly at Jen.

Where did she begin? Jen tried to find a logical place. "It's our brother Peter we came about."

"Yes, yes. I remember Peter. He's interested in Welsh folklore—he asked me about it when you visited."

"He did?" It was Jen's turn to be surprised.

"Indeed, yes. If I am right, it was the Bard Taliesin he wanted information on. Gratifying to find such an interest, especially in a boy his age."

"What did you tell him?"

"Only a little. But I did loan him two of my books to read."

Jen turned to Becky triumphantly. "There. You see? That's where he's gotten it from—he read it in a book."

"Well, I'm not sure," said Becky frowning.

"*I* am." Jen turned back to Dr. Rhys. "You see, Peter's

been acting very strangely for quite a while. He's been a real problem to everyone. His teacher's even complained."

"Are you sure you've come to the right person? I don't really know your brother, do you see." Dr. Rhys removed his spectacles and polished them carefully on his necktie.

"I know," said Jen. "The trouble is that he's been telling stories, the kind you were talking about when we came to dinner. Only he tells them as if they weren't stories at all, but things that had really happened and he'd seen them."

"Oh?" Dr. Rhys seemed genuinely interested.

"Back before Christmas, Peter found this thing on the beach and it's very complicated and it sounds silly, but he claims it's got some sort of"—Jen fumbled uncomfortably with the words—"some sort of magic power."

Dr. Rhys didn't laugh; he didn't even smile. He pressed the tips of his fingers together and nodded. "What is this 'thing,' do you know?"

"I'm not sure. It looks a bit like a key. He says it's the tuning key of a harp, and it does look sort of like the one Mr. Roberts used at his concert."

"You have seen it?"

Jen nodded. "It's tarnished and scratched, but Peter says it's silver. I don't see how it could be, but he wears it on a chain around his neck."

"You don't believe it has magic power?"

She examined the man's face to see if he were making fun of her, but she saw nothing to make her suspicious. "Of course, I don't. It's curious-looking and it may be old—it may even be worth something, I suppose, but that's all. He's playing a game with it, Dr. Rhys, but the trouble is he's forgotten it's a game now and he thinks it's serious. He won't admit he's just pretending."

"What has he said about this key? Will you tell me?"

"Not much. He says it makes him see things—the stories."

Becky had been silent, listening to Dr. Rhys's questions and Jen's answers, but now she said, "No, that's not all, Jen. He knows who it belonged to. It was Taliesin's."

"Taliesin?" Dr. Rhys's voice was suddenly sharp. He looked hard at Becky. "You are sure he said Taliesin? Did he say why?"

Becky gave Jen an apprehensive glance. "The pictures he sees all have to do with Taliesin, and Peter's seen him with the same key."

"This is quite a story indeed," remarked Dr. Rhys, sitting back in his chair. "Either your brother is playing a very clever game, or . . ." He let the sentence hang.

"Or?" Jen caught him up.

"Or he isn't. You told me he found the key before Christmas—we'll call it a key for convenience, shall we? I had not met your brother before Christmas, of course. I had not lent him any books then."

Jen stared at him, bewildered. He seemed to be arguing *against* her. "But you don't *know*," she burst out. "Peter's been miserable ever since Dad brought him here. Peter never wanted to leave home. He's sulked and been unhappy and refused to try to like it. I think he's made all of this up because he hasn't got anything else to do and he feels more important. But he's got Becky half-convinced, too."

"Are you?" Dr. Rhys asked Becky gravely.

"I'm not sure," said Becky, looking troubled. "I know Peter's acting funny, but it isn't just him any more. What about the other things, Jen? Like last night. No one's explained it."

"Tell me," said Dr. Rhys calmly. "You have begun, you may as well finish. Perhaps we can put some of it together then."

Reluctantly Jen began. She told Dr. Rhys about the night of the rainstorm and Peter's first story: the flood. Then about the strange boats they'd seen on Christmas Day and the coracle and fishing weir along the Dovey, the *hafod* and the men on Foel Goch, and finally the lights on the Bog. Becky refused to let her leave anything out, but Jen tried to sound as flat and matter-of-fact as she could, adding the explanations that seemed to her to make the best sense. "But Peter's used all of these things, don't you see? They're peculiar, but they must all have reasons," she finished, appealing to Dr. Rhys to agree with her.

"Other people don't think so," challenged Becky. "The people who live here, like Rhian's father. And even Gwilym wasn't sure about the fires."

Dr. Rhys was watching Jen shrewdly. "You came to me, Jennifer, because you believed I would agree with you that your brother has made up these stories, didn't you?"

"Y-yes." Jen was startled at how easily he'd seen it.

"What do they teach in your American schools?"

"The same as they teach here, I suppose," said Jen, not seeing the sense of his question. "What has that got to do with Peter?"

Dr. Rhys sighed. "They teach you that reason can answer everything, and that there is a scientific explanation for even the most unscientific events. People do not like *not* understanding, do you see. Because as long as we understand, we feel we have control. You are really here"—he leaned across the desk toward Jen—"because you are not quite sure of yourself. You would like me to say that you are right and Peter is wrong."

"I'm afraid I don't know what you mean," said Jen stiffly.

"I do not wish to offend you, truly I don't, but that is what I hear in your words, underneath them. And you see, I cannot offer you that support, because I am not at all sure you *are* right."

Jen stared at him, open-mouthed. She had never expected this, never. "But how can you say that? That means you *believe* Peter!"

"And I believe in magic and superstition? I have shocked

you, I'm sorry." His voice was mild. "I am educated. I have studied history and folklore and mythology for many years—some might say too long—and you thought I would have the answers you want. But, my dear, the more I learn the less it is I know. If we think a thing is impossible, does that truly make it so? Who are we, after all? Why should there not be forces we do not understand?"

"Then it's true?" asked Becky. Jen sat in numb silence.

Dr. Rhys smiled a little sadly. "You flatter me greatly if you think I can tell you that. I *can* tell you that the things you have seen and explained with reason could fit the story of Taliesin, though your sister would rather not hear it. This is his country, do you know, Cardiganshire. He became the friend of the king Gwyddno Garanhir whose lands were flooded, the legends say, through carelessness. The man set to guard the sea wall did not attend to his job and the wall broke during a storm. Much later Taliesin, who had been bard to a king in the north called Urien Rheged, was captured by Irish pirates. He escaped and washed ashore in a fish weir on the Dovey, tended by Gwyddno Garanhir's son. Elphin. During the time Taliesin stayed with Gwyddno, another king called Maelgwn invaded the country at Cors Fochno, your Bog, and captured Elphin. It was Taliesin who won Elphin's freedom in a contest with Maelgwn's bards. He composed a riddle in the form of a poem that none could either answer or match. The answer was 'the wind' and, according to legend, it came to Taliesin when he called it. This frightened Maelgwn, so he released Elphin as he had agreed.

"But that is all in the story of Taliesin, and it is very difficult to say how much of it is legend and how much true. That Taliesin himself, Maelgwn, Gwyddno, and Elphin were real men, that *is* known."

Quietly, effectively, Dr. Rhys destroyed Jen's hopes. She had come looking for an ally and had found none. Becky was listening raptly to the story he told, but Jen scarcely heard it, she was too shaken. She had put trust in adults and they had failed her—they didn't know the answers, they simply didn't. Dr. Rhys was saying what Mr. Evans had said at Llechwedd Melyn, in different words, of course, and Jen was utterly confused.

She got Becky away from Dr. Rhys as soon as she could, without being downright rude, and they rode back to Borth together in silence. Becky took one look at Jen's withdrawn face and didn't try to make conversation.

"No one can have gotten enough sleep last night," remarked David, looking at his family that evening. "You all look dismal. Bed early again, I'd say."

But before she went up, Jen finally broke her silence. "Peter?"

He didn't look at her. "Yes?"

The question was terribly hard to ask, but she had to ask it. "Do you know what happened on the Bog last night?"

"Yes," he said. And that was all.

The Key grew distant now, its song became a whisper that Peter found sometimes hard to hear. He felt as if he were all pins and needles, just coming back to life after being asleep when he oughtn't to have been. It was a very odd sensation. There seemed to be a lot he couldn't remember very well and he wondered if anyone had noticed him. It was a relief not to be pulled back and forth through time quite so much; it had been rather exhausting.

Taliesin had left Gwyddno's lands. Harp slung across his shoulders, he crossed the Dyfi and struck into the wild, mountainous country of Gwynedd. As a bard, he was welcomed in hut or hall, wherever he stopped for the night, but he always went on the next day at first light. He found, as if by instinct, the secret ways through the mountains of Eryri.

Taliesin went away, and Peter came back.

II

Roast Chicken and
Mashed Potatoes

"WELL, THEN, I'm just going," said Mrs. Davies, sticking her head around the kitchen door. "I'll be in tomorrow morning same as usual."

"Yes," Jen answered absently. "That's fine." She was trying to make up her mind between peas and corn for dinner. Her father and Becky really liked corn, but it was the same color as chicken and Jen had read somewhere that you oughtn't to cook meals that were all the same color. So it should be peas. And some other vegetable—there ought to be two anyway.

"Do you think—" Jen began, looking up, but Mrs. Davies was gone. She was off to houseclean for Susan in Bow Street, and Jen was truly on her own. She wrote "Chicken" and "Peas" on her shopping list and thoughtfully chewed her pencil. Surely it didn't take Mrs. Davies this long to plan each meal? It *had* to get easier with experience, and the nervous feeling must go away. But, Jen supposed, she was entitled to feel nervous the first time she cooked a whole meal by herself for her family. This was really a test; it would prove whether or not she was capable of managing Bryn Celyn for her father. She wrote "Mashed potatoes."

She had grand dreams of exotic casseroles or a roast of beef or leg of lamb, but commonsense won and she chose broiled chicken, quite plain, to begin on. The morning passed quickly and satisfactorily as Jen made a chocolate cake— from a package. Her conscience had given her a little trouble on that, but she put it to rest by making her own butter cream frosting. And it looked beautiful when she'd done: high and smooth and shiny.

After lunch she walked down to the shops, with her grocery bag, in very good spirits. In the business of planning her first meal she'd managed to put Dr. Rhys and his disturbing conversation right out of her thoughts. She'd made a point of not discussing it with Becky after their visit. Instead she'd bottled her confusion and frustration inside herself, trying to find her own way out of the maze Peter had unknowingly created for her.

The queue at the butcher shop was quite long when Jen joined it: older women, Jen observed, studying them out of the corners of her eyes. They'd all had years of experience and knew precisely what they wanted. Her spirits fell a little. There was a bewildering variety of meat and poultry at the counter to choose from. Jen glanced at it and chewed her lip.

"Next? Miss?"

She started when she realized the butcher was talking to her and she had to make up her mind. He was brusque and businesslike, anxious not to keep his customers waiting too long.

"I'd like a chicken, please."

"What kind of chicken, then?"

Jen looked at the man blankly. "Kind?"

"What do you want it for?" he asked as if she were dim.

"Just eating," she ventured.

"Roaster? Boiler? For stewing?"

"Boiler." She clutched at a straw. Why on earth wasn't chicken just chicken?

"Head and feet taken off, do you?"

Jen felt herself going scarlet. She thought everyone must be watching her and wondering why she'd been sent to do the shopping. "No," she managed, "I'll just take it!" Thankfully, she grabbed the brown paper parcel he handed her, paid, and escaped from the shop.

The peas and potatoes were simple enough to buy, at least.

But she knew she'd made a mistake the moment she unwrapped the chicken. It lay in front of her, quite dead and plucked—not a chicken at all. It was a corpse. The sight of it, with its scrawny neck and funny little head, its feet stiff, made Jen feel queasy. She stared at it for several minutes wondering what in the name of heaven she ought to do with it. She couldn't broil it whole, obviously. Finally, in desperation, she grabbed the bread knife and without stopping to consider, she somehow hacked off the head and feet rather untidily, then stuffed them quickly back into the paper and pushed them into the garbage. She couldn't bring herself to chop any more, so she decided to roast the thing instead.

When Becky and Peter came in after school, they found Jen red-faced and cross, pounding potatoes in a large pot. Exchanging a glance, they left her to it and vanished quietly. It looked like a good idea not to interfere.

But they both came racing back to the kitchen half an hour later when they heard a horrified shriek. They collided in the doorway. The kitchen was full of the smell of burning, and smoke and flames were coming out of the open oven.

"What is it?" cried Becky.

"It's caught fire, can't you see?" wailed Jen.

"*Do* something!" Becky advised, dancing up and down.

"What?" said Jen furiously.

"Close the oven door first." Peter took command.

"But my chicken—"

"Just *close* it or your chicken will be a crisp! Oh, here!"
He ran over and slammed the door. "It'll stop burning if it
can't get air, see?" He fiddled with the oven knobs. "What did
you do to make it catch fire?"

"I didn't do anything! I turned it on to warm up and I put
the chicken in, then I smelled it burning and when I opened
the oven, there were flames." The outside of the oven was
smoked black.

"Well, no wonder," said Peter in a tone that made Jen
bristle. "You had the grill on. The oven should have been
turned to bake."

"But how did you know to close the door?" Becky asked,
interested.

"You smother a fire. You stamp on people or wrap them
in blankets when they're burning because the flames need
oxygen. I learned that in Boy Scouts *years* ago."

Hesitantly Jen opened the oven again. The flames had
indeed died, but a cloud of bitter smoke rolled out making her
eyes smart. She looked at the charred object with helpless
rage.

"Stopped burning anyway," said Becky encouragingly.

"What does *that* matter?" cried Jen. "It's *ruined!* It's a
cinder! Oh, damn, damn, damn!"—

Becky looked at Jen in amazement. Peter matter-of-factly
pulled the roasting pan out and set it on the edge of the sink.
"Don't swear," he told his sister maddeningly. "All you need to
do is scrape off the black part, and under the skin there's
nothing wrong with it. See? It didn't have time to burn
through. Just cook it the rest of the way and no one'll know."

"*You* will," said Becky.

"I'm not sure—" began Jen.

"Oh, it'll be all right. I'm sure Peter's right."

Jen relit the oven, making sure it was set at bake. Peter
suggested she lower the rack inside two notches so the chicken

wouldn't touch the heating coil this time. He handed her the pan without further comment.

"Thank you," said Jen a little stiffly.

Peter shrugged. "Not at all."

They'd got rid of the smoke and set the table by the time David got in. The chicken smelled as if it were properly roasting.

"How are things going?" David asked his elder daughter.

"All right," she answered, crossing her fingers.

"Good. It smells fine," he said encouragingly.

It would serve no useful purpose, as far as Jen could see, to tell him about the earlier crisis. At six-fifteen she announced supper in what she hoped was a normal voice. The chicken lay dark brown and crisp on its platter in front of David's place. He looked at it with interest but made no comment, just began carving. It appeared to offer some resistance, but David still said nothing, just bore down harder. Jen winced a bit. He sliced down firmly and the knife hesitated.

"Stuffing?" he inquired.

"Oh," said Jen, stricken. "I forgot."

"Doesn't matter," said David quickly. "We don't need it with potatoes—I just thought—" He probed gently. "What's this?" He'd uncovered a smallish bundle wrapped in what seemed to be paper and stuck in the middle of the bird.

"I don't know." In horrified fascination, Jen watched him pull it out.

"Like a message in a bottle," observed Peter, and was instantly quelled with a frown from his father.

"Did you take out the liver and gizzard?" David asked. Jen shook her head unhappily. "Oh, well. As they say in these parts, not to worry! It won't make any difference." He went on carving.

Jen dished out the peas and potatoes when David finished and watched closely as her family started to eat. For a long moment there was silence while everyone chewed.

Then: "It's good," exclaimed Becky with too much conviction. David nodded in agreement. Peter continued to chew.

"What's wrong with it?" asked Jen accusingly. "You might as well say."

"Nothing," David said. "Chicken's a little tough, but that's not your fault."

And in spite of the pounding Jen had given them, the potatoes were lumpy. And the peas were lukewarm and hard as beebees—Jen had been so careful not to cook them too long, she hadn't cooked them long enough. Any one of these problems by itself wouldn't have been awful, but all together they amounted to a disaster. The first bite she took stuck in Jen's throat and choked her. A flood of self-pity drowned her. "It's awful! All of it!" she cried, slamming down her knife and fork. "Don't sit there eating it! The chicken tastes burnt and it's tough and the potatoes are terrible and the peas are *raw!* It's all my fault!" For the first time in months—since her mother had died—Jen felt tears, and instead of trying bravely to hold them in, she gave in almost gratefully. The effect was electrifying. Becky froze, mouth open, fork in the air, staring. Peter's face registered shock. And David watched her helplessly, as if he wasn't at all sure what he should do. Jen wept harder.

"Go ahead and say it! You should have sent me home when I was supposed to go—I've ruined a perfectly good dinner. I can't do it, I promised I would, but I just *can't!* I'm hopeless!"

"Oh—" cried Becky in distress.

"It's not that bad," muttered Peter. "We can eat it." He took another bite to show her. It alarmed him unexpectedly to see his sensible older sister go to pieces over a chicken. She wasn't supposed to act this way.

"Of course, you're not hopeless," said David briskly, cutting across them all. His face was calm and sympathetic now; he had made up his mind about the situation. "It's silly to say you're hopeless, when you know it's not true. You just got nervous and tried too hard, that's all! Everyone does it one time or another. Good heavens, I remember vividly some of the dinners your mother ruined just after we got married—of course, you didn't know her then!" He grinned. "She was much older than you when she started learning, cheer up!"

"B-but I promised . . ."

"So you did, and you can try again. Whoever said you only got one chance?" David stood up. "Come on, all of you, I've got an idea."

"W-what?" Jen raised her face to him, damp with tears.

"Here. My napkin's clean. Dry your face and get your coat. We're going out!"

"In *Borth?*" Peter was incredulous. "Nothing's open!"

"Shows how little you know," David retorted cheerfully. *"Quick!"*

Becky caught hold of one of Jen's hands and pulled her out of her chair.

"But what about all of this?" she protested weakly.

"Leave it. It'll be here when we get back," David said.

The night was very dark, the sky like the inside of a bucket full of holes, without a moon. Below the cliff, the sea crunched up and down the beach, and overhead the wind sang in the electric wires. David put Jen's arm firmly through his and Becky clutched her other hand. Peter was right beside Becky. It struck Jen that it had been a long time since they'd all been that close to each other. She began to relax; no one seemed to mind about the disastrous supper. David was even whistling softly, as if pleased with himself. It was a minute or two before Jen recognized the tune and smiled in spite of herself; it was *Lord Jeffrey Amherst*.

David piloted them along the Borth street at a quick, purposeful pace, down to a shop across from the bakery. Glaring white light spilled out onto the pavement through its open door and the thick, hot smell of deep-fat-frying. David pulled them into the queue of University students, hunched laughing and talking outside.

"I've always wanted to try this," David remarked.

"Fish and chips," exclaimed Becky. "Rhian calls it the chippy."

"Isn't it awfully fried?" hazarded Jen.

"Terribly, by the smell of it. Hundreds of satisfied customers, though," said David. "It'll make your hair shiny."

The queue moved fast and in a very short time the Morgans were through the door. Ahead was a glass-fronted counter and a man and two girls in tired white aprons, laughing and talking as hard as the customers, scooping up mounds of French fried potatoes and great slabs of crusty fish and bundling them into brown paper. The windows ran with steam.

When they emerged, they were each clutching a hot package.

"We can take them home and eat them with our fingers," David said.

"I did make a cake that turned out." Jen brightened. "Dessert anyway."

"Good!" Peter exclaimed through a mouthful of fish.

"You're supposed to wait," objected Becky, opening her own bundle.

"Who cares?" asked David. "I'm hungry!" So they walked back along the street and up the hill, swapping bits of fish and munching chips happily.

In the kitchen at Bryn Celyn, David and Peter simply heaped the remains of the dinner by the sink while Jen and Becky put out clean plates and napkins and the cake; and the meal that had begun more than an hour before in disaster finished in triumph, with them all chattering and grinning and stuffing themselves.

There was no trace of the unfortunate chicken for Mrs. Davies to find the next morning; the potatoes and peas had disappeared with it, and there was only one very small piece of cake left under a bowl on the shelf. No other clue. And none of the family offered any.

Finally Mrs. Davis had to ask, "And did your meal go all right, then?"

David looked up from his coffee and paper. "Oh, yes indeed. Very good. A bit more practice and there'll be no holding her, Mrs. Davies. Hmm?" He looked around at Becky and Peter, who exchanged glances, grinned and nodded. A sudden rush of affection filled Jen, affection for all three of them.

"Well." Mrs. Davies was obviously curious to hear more, but had no intention of saying so. "Well, I'm that glad to hear it, Mr. Morgan."

After dinner Sunday Peter announced loudly to everyone that he was going for a walk along the cliffs if no one minded. David shook his head and said mildly he saw no reason why not if Peter were home at a reasonable hour.

Becky waited until she heard the front door close, then said, "Me, too!" flung on her jacket and was gone after her brother before Jen or David could speak.

"She's in a hurry," remarked David. Jen nodded and turned back to the letter she was struggling to write to Aunt Beth. It never seemed to get easier, but it had to be done every week and she was resigned. Aunt Beth's letters back had bristled with disapproval ever since she'd been told Jen was staying in Wales. David took the brunt of it, and Jen felt guilty every time one of the letters came.

Outside, it was one of those sharp, gray afternoons when the clouds hung low, but the air was clear between the sea and the sky, so you could see for miles along the coast. Peter had got as far as the War Memorial when he realized he was being followed by someone going faster than he was. The path beyond the point was narrow, worn deep into the cliff top and wide enough for only one person at a time, so Peter stood back and waited for the other person to go by. It was Becky, steaming along, head down, watching for roots and rocks. She was almost on top of him before she discovered he'd stopped.

"Whew," she panted thankfully.

"What are you doing?"

"Coming after you."

"Why?" Peter made no attempt to sound welcoming.

"I wanted to talk to you. And," she added frankly, "I wanted to know where you go off to."

"That's really my business, though, isn't it." He started out along the path.

"I suppose so." Becky followed undiscouraged.

"What about?" asked Peter after a moment.

"Hmmm?"

"What do you want to talk to me *about?*"

"Well, it's kind of hard to tell you to your back. It would be much easier if we could sit down somewhere. Do you mind?"

Peter said nothing, but in another five minutes he turned off the path and climbed over the scrub into a little hollow almost at the cliff's edge. The two of them sat down side by side on a flat boulder out of the wind. Peter waited.

Becky sighed. "It's just that I thought you should know Jen went to see Dr. Rhys last week."

"So?"

"About your Key."

Peter went very still. "She told him?"

"Yes."

"But she had no right to! It's nothing to do with her—she doesn't want it to be."

"That's just it. She doesn't like it, it bothers her."

"How can it? She doesn't believe in it."

Becky shook her head.

"And Dr. Rhys told her I was crazy or making up a story." Peter's hand clenched around a bracken stem.

"But that's the strange part," said Becky. "That's what I really wanted to tell you—he didn't say that at all. He said it might be true."

Peter looked at his sister coldly. "I *know* it's true. You didn't have to come out here to tell. I don't care about Dr. Rhys."

"Well, you should," retorted Becky. "This is important. It isn't like *me* saying I believe you, or even Jen. This is Dr. Rhys. He's old and he's a professor and people listen to him, Peter. He's studied Welsh history and he knows all about your Taliesin. He was interested."

"Were you there?"

"Mmm. Jen made me go, too. Dr. Rhys told us the story of Taliesin, how he washed ashore near here, and saved the King's son—what was his name?"

"Elphin." Peter was listening now, his eyes wary but with a glint of excitement.

"Taliesin rescued Elphin from the king of the north by asking a riddle that no one could answer."

The bracken stem broke in Peter's fingers and he twisted it thoughtlessly. In a strange, distant voice he said,

> *Guess who it is.*
> *Created before the flood.*
> *A creature strong,*
> *Without flesh, without bone,*
> *Without veins, without blood,*
> *Without head, and without feet.*
> *It will not be older, it will not be younger*
> *Than it was in the beginning.*
>
> . . . .
>
> *And it is as wide*
> *As the face of the earth,*
> *And it was not born,*

And it has not been seen.
It, on sea, it, on land,
It sees not, it is not seen.

"I know!" cried Becky suddenly. "The wind, Dr. Rhys said it was the wind! But how do you know the riddle?"

Peter shook his head. "I just do. Taliesin called it and the wind came into Maelgwn's great hall and blew out all the torches." The distance left him abruptly. "It's in the book, you know."

"If Jen really thought you were making all of this up," said Becky slowly, "I don't think it would bother her nearly so much. It's not being sure that upsets her and that's why she had to go to Dr. Rhys."

Peter looked skeptical, but Becky continued. "She hasn't said a word about it since we saw him, and before that she kept trying to convince me the story wasn't true."

"What did Dr. Rhys say then?"

"That it wasn't impossible. He was very nice you know, Peter."

All round were the great, endless sounds of wind and ocean. Peter stared out at the gray restlessness beyond their hollow. "What about Dad?" he said at last. "Did she tell him, too?"

"No, he doesn't know about any of this, not even about our going to see Dr. Rhys. Jen won't say anything and neither will I." She read Peter's thoughts with disturbing ease. "Jen didn't send me after you."

"At first I thought she'd help," said Peter with a sigh.

"She's afraid."

"Aren't you?"

"Are you?"

"Sometimes," he admitted with sudden relief. "It gets so strong—and it isn't always very easy."

"Tell me," Becky demanded, her eyes steady on his face. "Tell me."

And haltingly, Peter began. Words weren't much good for describing the Key and its singing, he discovered. It was difficult to explain what happened when the songs came; how it felt to be pulled out of his own time and plunged into another, but as he talked he relaxed. By telling Becky, he found he could put the pieces together better himself, he saw the way they fit. And Becky listened raptly, working to follow him.

"Sometimes the song is very strong, and then it fades away. It's been strong lately, and the other night . . ."

"But you don't really *go* anywhere."

Peter shook his head. "Only inside myself. But I see these things so clearly. The night of the storm when I saw the flood —well, it was pretty awful."

"But the storm really happened," said Becky. "I mean, it happened to us at the same time. And *we* saw the coracle, too, and the men on Foel Goch, and the lights on the Bog. How could we? I didn't hear any singing."

"I'm not sure," Peter replied, frowning. "It's almost as if the time we're in and that other time get crossed. But Dr. Rhys said this is Taliesin's country, and the things you've all seen really did happen here—that *must* be the connection, Becky. The Key is strongest when it shows me things that happened here, and maybe it's so strong it affects you, too. Everybody."

"Do you think it really could do that?"

Peter drew the Key out from around his neck, and they looked at it.

"I don't suppose it would work for me," Becky said with a trace of envy.

"Here." Peter took the chain off and handed it to her. "What does it feel like to you?"

She took it in her cupped hands and sat still as though listening. "It's warm," she said after a moment.

"From being inside my shirt."

"Mmmm."

"Well?"

"It feels—it feels as if it's about to move, as if it's alive almost. But I don't hear anything." Reluctantly she handed it back. "Dr. Rhys would know about it, he could tell you what it is."

But Peter said impatiently, "I don't need him to tell me, *it's* telling me. I didn't see at first, but the songs fit together in order. The first time I saw Taliesin he was my age and now he's more Dad's. He's getting older—it's his life. Do you believe that?"

"I think I do. At least I don't *not* believe it."

The air was cold and they were cold sitting still, though they hadn't noticed until now. Becky got up and stamped her feet to get the blood running again.

"Are you going back?" asked Peter, pulling his hands up his jacket sleeves. "It isn't late."

"You mean Dad won't get mad for another hour or two." Becky grinned.

But instead of retorting, Peter grinned, too, a bit sheepishly. "I just thought that if you wanted—well—I could show you where I found the Key. The tide's out and you could see the wall."

"Really? The drowned cities? Oh, yes!"

Peter set off south along the path. He knew it well and could go fast and Becky had to trot to keep up. To their right was the plunge of the cliffs down to a slate-colored sea; to the left were open wild-grown moors, seamed with stone walls and dotted with sheep and boulders. Now and again they had to climb a stile to cross one of the walls.

At last Peter paused at the edge of the little valley he had first found in December, and Becky came up beside him. She looked down in delight. "How beautiful! Wouldn't it be neat to have a little house like that with your own beach?"

"And hundreds of tourists walking through your front yard in the summer," said Peter dryly. "But over there's the wall. See?"

Straight out from the sand it ran, a tumble of huge granite blocks, straight out into the waves.

"This is Cantrev y Gwaelod," said Peter, "the Low Hundred."

12

Cardiff

DAVID HAD NEWS for his family on Monday. He was going to Cardiff Thursday to do some business at the University there that he'd been putting off too long, and he was taking all three of them with him. He slapped the four bus tickets down on the kitchen table at tea.

"A *city!*" Becky's eyes lit up. "*And* a day off from school!"

"Shops!" breathed Jen rapturously. "Real department stores."

"We'll all go into shock," declared Peter. "After months and months of Aber, we won't know how to behave!"

"Well," said David with a grin, "if you think it's too dangerous . . ."

"Not a chance!" Becky shook her head emphatically.

"Watch it!" exclaimed Jen. "You got your hair in the milk, idiot. It'll be wonderful. Is Cardiff nice?"

David laughed outright. "Do you care? From the sound of you, I'd guess it doesn't much matter what the place is like. But Gwyn Rhys says we'll like it. There's a park and a castle and a terrific museum."

"And stores."

"So Mrs. Rhys says. Good ones."

Thursday couldn't come fast enough. Cardiff was a real adventure, unknown and exciting; there was a feeling of holiday at Bryn Celyn all week. Even Peter was eager for the trip, though he tried to hide it when he remembered to.

Hugh-the-Bus had the first run to Aberystwyth Thursday morning, and he greeted the Morgans cheerfully when he stopped for them in the early grayness.

"You're early, aren't you? Off on a toot, is it?"

"Cardiff," Becky announced.

"Oh, aye. All of you, then. That *is* a toot! Happen you'll have fine weather south of yere. I was to Cardiff once my own self—what was it? Three years come October, it was."

"Did you like it?" Becky wanted to know.

Hugh-the-Bus shrugged. "Glad to be home, me. Mind you, there's many can't get enough of it, and it is a fine city. You'll like it, I shouldn't wonder." He winked encouragingly. "Saw a football match there, I did."

The day-excursion coach was waiting at the station when they got to Aberystwyth; it was already half full: women dressed in sober best for shopping with gloves and hats, a few weathered old men in overcoats and cloth caps, and a handful of rather scruffy students.

It was the first time any of the Morgans had gone south out of Aberystwyth, the road was new and they all looked avidly at the unimaginative, raw, new, row houses of Penparcau and the open farm country beyond. Once around the brooding bulk of Pen Dinas with its tower, the land rolled comfortably past the bus windows in long, swelling humps: green and stitched with hedgerows and lines of wind-bent trees. Sheep and cattle filled the fields. For the first fifteen miles or so the road followed the coast and often there were sweeping views out over the blunt cliffs to the sea.

In Aberaeron it was drizzling; a few people got off, a few

got on, then the bus swung out of the harbor town, starting inland.

"It flattens right out," said Jen in surprise. "All the mountains are gone."

"There are a few in the south, but not like the ones above the Dovey," David told them. "There are mountains in the coal country. But it certainly looks different."

In what seemed a very short time, they reached the sprawl of the industrial suburbs of Swansea and Cardiff: rows and rows of houses with tiny front gardens, then factories. The country vanished. Peter pointed out that they had just driven down half of Wales in about two hours.

The bus terminal in Cardiff was overwhelming. After weeks in Borth and Aberystwyth, the sudden explosion of people, traffic, and noise was alarming.

"I feel like a real country girl!" Jen exclaimed.

"Well, if you'd close your mouth and stop staring—" said Peter and sidestepped neatly as her elbow shot out.

"Hey," said David. He was frowning at a map of the city he'd taken out of one of his pockets. "Stop slanging each other and be useful. I have to figure out where we are."

They clustered around the unwieldy sheet, searching for the terminal. David was notoriously bad at map-reading. Anne had always been navigator for her husband, shaking her head sadly over his attempts.

"There!" said Becky after a moment. "You are here." She pointed in triumph.

"Where?"

"There. That pie-shaped thing that says Bus Sta."

"Ah." David nodded. "Okay, we want to get there—to the green part. That's the park, and the Castle and University are right near it. Can you find them?"

"That way," said Peter. "See? Down that street and up St. Mary's Street."

David nodded. "Mmm. I see."

In the end he asked an obliging bus conductor, who sent them off through the right exit with a grin, pleased that he had correctly identified them as Americans. "Not from Florida, are you? My wife's cousins moved to Florida."

A watery sun shone on the streets of Cardiff. Choked with people, taxis, cars, and buses, they were beautiful. The air smelled of damp cement and diesel exhaust, and the shop windows were full of fascinating things to look at: shoes, clothes, books, candy, toys. They made very erratic progress along the sidewalk, dodging crowds and peering in shops.

At a street corner, David caught them together. "Just don't come all apart on me! If I lose one of you along here, I'll probably never find you again, and I don't want to spend the rest of the day in the Cardiff police station waiting for you to turn up!"

"There's so much to see!" exclaimed Becky.

"Light's changed," said Peter, and they were off again.

David gave them each money to spend, and there were practical things like clothes and shoes to buy, so it was noon before they finally reached the top of High Street and saw the walls of Cardiff Castle across the traffic. They all clutched bundles and were ravenous for lunch. David found a Golden Egg restaurant and ordered everyone an omelet and chips.

"Indigestible no doubt," he remarked, shaking vinegar on his chips. "I don't know why we never thought of vinegar on French fries in the U.S."

"And omelets for lunch," said Jen.

"What do we do after this?" asked Peter, finishing his orange soda.

"My money's gone." Becky looked fondly at her pile of paper bags. She'd bought a jigsaw puzzle and three Famous Five mysteries as well as a practical thick blue cardigan.

"I'm going to steer you over to the Castle and leave you to look around, I think," said David, glancing at his watch.

"I've got to do my business at the University, and I don't think you want to sit in a stuffy office somewhere. Then I'll meet you at the museum, which is—" He spread out the map.

"National Museum," Peter read off. "Right there. We can find that easily."

"Gwyn gave me the name of a man there—hang on— here it is, Dr. John Owen. Gwyn's written to him, and he'll show us around and tell us about the best exhibits. They were at University together, I think. I'll meet you on the steps at three."

Cardiff Castle was in much better repair than the castle in Aberystwyth. It had a moat around its walls, full of grass now instead of water, but you had to cross on a drawbridge just the same. A man sitting inside the gate sold tickets; beyond him was a wide grassy courtyard, scattered with canvas deck chairs. A few determined figures, well-wrapped in coats and scarves, sat in the sun. David left Jen, Becky, and Peter to explore and strode off toward the University buildings.

"What a neat place to live," said Becky, looking around in delight. "It looks just the way a castle ought to."

"Right out of King Arthur," Jen agreed.

"Except that King Arthur never lived in a castle like this," said Peter.

"How do you know?" demanded Becky.

"He was dead hundreds and hundreds of years before this was built."

"You knew him personally, I suppose," said Jen dryly.

Instead of getting cross as she expected, Peter just shook his head patiently. "The real King Arthur was a Welsh chieftain probably."

"How do you know?" repeated Becky.

"Dr. Rhys's books," was the answer. "There's quite a lot about King Arthur in one of them. I'll show you when we get back to Borth, if you want."

"Thanks," said Jen. "I like my illusions."

"Let's not just stand here talking," suggested Becky. "Let's go inside."

"You go," said Peter. "The old part's out here—the walls. I want to look at it."

Jen gave her brother a hard look. She was faintly irritated by his unexpected fund of information. He knew too much.

"Stay out here, then. Becky and I are going inside; we'll meet you later."

Peter nodded agreeably and went wandering off across the smooth lawn toward the steep green mound in the far corner. It had a small fortress on top. He was well-content to be left to himself for a while. The Castle was familiar, he recognized the lie of it—oh, not as it looked now, peaceful and civilized—but as an earthwork fort, a network of dykes and ridges and rough timber huts. Taliesin had passed through it on his way southeast to the great Court of Caerleon. Then it was alive with cattle and dogs and chickens, inhabited by the fierce, strong people of Cymru, who had here mixed their blood with the last of the Romans, producing handsome, dark children.

Time lay thick between the Castle walls, thousands of years of it enclosed in such a narrow space, so difficult to grasp. How did you ever really understand centuries and the layers of people who had all lived and walked in the same place? But Peter had made contact with those people; he couldn't touch them, of course, nor they him, but those people were as real as the ones sitting in their deck chairs on this February afternoon in the twentieth century. Peter didn't have to imagine Taliesin's face—he knew it.

David was waiting for them on the steps of the National Museum of Wales as he had promised. Jen and Becky were deep in a discussion of castle architecture and domestic problems and Peter was looking thoughtful.

"Did you like it?"

"Weird, but nice," said Becky. "It really looks as if you could move right in."

"Yes, it's been painted and restored and furnished with stained glass windows and paintings on the walls and ceilings. It looks like a giant toy, not so much a castle."

"I suppose you want dripping walls and damp tapestries," said David. "All right to visit, but no fun to live in. The Marquis of Bute restored it in the nineteenth century—he had a lot of money and a good imagination, Gwyn says. We'd better scout up Dr. Owen before it gets any later. Come on."

The National Museum was a solid, gray stone building, simple and impressive, and as soon as he set foot across the marble threshold, Peter knew he didn't want to go any further. It was as if an alarm went off in his head, unmistakable, a warning. It was odd because he could think of no reason. In fact, he'd been looking forward to this visit ever since his father had told him what was in the museum: Welsh folk artifacts of all kinds—pottery, ancient brooches, Roman coins, glass, metal work. And Dr. Owen was a friend of Dr. Rhys, just the person to answer questions.

"You'll get left behind, Peter, if you don't hurry," said Jen, and Peter couldn't bring himself to say that he wouldn't mind being left, so he took a deep breath and tried to ignore the warning.

In the main hall, David found a guard to ask about Dr. John Owen. The man nodded gravely and led them off rapidly, like a small parade, down corridors, around corners, up stairs and through exhibit halls. The museum smelled of dust and floor polish.

They came to a halt at the door of an office. "This will be Dr. Owen, then," the guard informed them and left, touching his cap to David's thanks.

David knocked and a preoccupied voice said, "Come?" Behind the door lay a small, tidy office, furnished with a rug and several comfortable chairs and lined with shelves full of small objects in neat arrangement. The man at the desk was deeply absorbed in the typescript he was reading and for several moments, while the Morgans stood uncertainly in the doorway, he didn't look up.

"Yes?" he said at last, looking inquiringly at David. "Can I help you?"

"Dr. Owen?" The man nodded and David introduced himself and Jen, Becky, and Peter.

"Indeed yes." Dr. Owen smiled in recognition. "Gwyn Rhys told me you were coming." He rose and came around the desk to shake hands with them all, disregarding Peter's obvious reluctance. He was a slim, sandy-colored man with a sharp, clever face, obviously younger then Dr. Rhys, and dressed in a brown corduroy jacket with leather elbow patches and a dark green turtleneck sweater, very cool and polished.

"From America, Gwyn said, didn't he? Ah, yes. He said you were spending a year at the University. Like it, do you? It's quite a decent school, all things considered, though Aberystwyth is *rather* a dismal hole, don't you find? Why on *earth* they put the National Library there, I cannot fathom—so damned inconvenient to get to. Sit down, do. Have we enough chairs for you? Yes, good." He spoke in a smooth, precise way, giving various words particular emphasis, which made everything he said sound significant. He had only the faintest trace of Welsh inflection. "Now then, what can I do for you? Have you been round the Museum?"

"Not yet," said David. "We were hoping you would be able to tell us what we ought to see, so we came here first." He added, with a glance at his subdued children, "We don't have a great deal of time, I'm afraid."

"That is too bad." Dr. Owen knit his long fingers together and rested his chin on them, regarding his visitors with pale green eyes. "We have quite a *lot* of very fine stuff here. I don't know what Gwyn has told you, of course, nor what *precisely* you're interested in."

"We're open to whatever you'd recommend," said David. "Just point us in the right direction."

Dr. Owen looked thoughtful. "Well *actually,* as it is, I can spare you an hour myself. Show you a few of the *highlights* as it were. Not terribly satisfactory, I know, but better than nothing, and it wouldn't do to tire your—to tire *you.*"

Jen and Becky exchanged an apprehensive glance. Something about Dr. Owen made them acutely uncomfortable. Peter had sunk down in his chair, his face expressionless, and seemed to be pretending he wasn't there. The office felt very small and close. David must have noticed it, too, for he said quickly, "That would be very good of you, Dr. Owen, but we don't want to disrupt your schedule. I'm afraid you must be very busy."

Their hopes were short-lived. "Oh, goodness, I can *certainly* take an *hour* or so to pilot you about. After all, Gwyn's friends. I can't have you thinking us inhospitable," he said firmly. "But I do think we'd better get right to it if you don't mind. We've an enormous amount of *ground* to cover. It's David, isn't it? Do call me John." And he led the way out of his office without waiting for a reaction. David shrugged apologetically at his children—it couldn't be helped, they'd have to make the best of it for an hour.

Once set in motion, Dr. Owen was evidently difficult to stop, and the Morgans could only trail behind him, looking attentively at the objects he pointed out and pretending to absorb with interest everything he told them.

Much to Jen's relief, Dr. Owen addressed his remarks almost without exception to David. She and Becky were glad to let their father cope, for they were both somewhat in awe of the sharp, confident Welshman. Peter simply shut everyone out completely. He stayed as far from Dr. Owen as he could manage and looked at anything but what he was supposed to. This man was a threat; in what way Peter wasn't sure, but he knew he wanted no part of Dr. John Owen.

Archaeology was Dr. Owen's special field of study; he

could apparently talk with authority on it for hours. He took his captive audience through halls lined with cases displaying shards of pottery and glass, ancient weapons, rows of black and pitted iron objects, silver jewelry wrought in curious knots and woven patterns. All the while a battle raged in Peter's head: on one side the power and magnetic attraction of these objects, and on the other the disturbing negative presence of Dr. Owen. He longed for freedom to wander through the rooms on his own, submerged in time. The layers were here, just as they had been in the Castle. Unobtrusively, Peter began to edge away from the others.

"One of the fascinating things," said Dr. Owen, "is that new objects are *constantly turning up,* often in the most unexpected places. The countryside is full of them, but the real trick is in *unearthing* them once someone's made the discovery. There are scandalously few people with the training and experience to tell really valuable stuff from the junk, do you see. But it's rather *exciting* to go into a farmhouse at the back of *beyond*—the hills of Brecon or up some valley in Carmarthen —and see something like *this.*" He indicated a large silver bowl that stood by itself in a glass case. Jen and Becky had been admiring its shape and intricate design.

"Yes," said David, "it must be."

"That was on the mantlepiece in a farmer's cottage in Merioneth. The man had not the *slightest idea* what he had, of course, no idea at all. He couldn't begin to tell me its age or value, only that he'd found it behind his cowbarn and he *rather liked it.* He kept fruit in it." Dr. Owen shook his head in amusement. "An eighth century chalice full of apples and bananas tarnishing in a two-room farmhouse. If I hadn't seen it there, it would conceivably have been lost to historians forever."

"But if he found it," objected Becky, "shouldn't he have been able to keep it if he wanted? I mean, if it was behind his cowbarn?"

"Keep it?" repeated Dr. Owen, looking at Becky as if

he hadn't quite heard right. "Good heavens, something like this doesn't belong to any one person, you know, it belongs to *Wales*. It's an important piece of history to be preserved and studied. It would be selfish to withold an object like the chalice."

"But what about the farmer?" Becky persisted in spite of a frown from David. "Did he get anything?"

Dr. Owen gave a short, unamused laugh. "Oh, I see. Yes, he was *compensated,* of course, and that's his name on the card: Ivor Davies, Abergynolwyn. And he has the satisfaction of knowing that he's made a unique contribution to his country, which is no small reward in itself. This" —he looked fondly at the chalice—"is where it belongs, and he has something quite *adequate* but slightly less *exotic* to put his oranges in."

Becky opened her mouth and David said quickly, "What about these brooches over here? They look old."

"Indeed yes." A nod of approval. "Exceptionally fine examples of late twelfth-century work. But you evidently know something about metalwork? It's rather a pet subject of mine. I located three of those myself eight years ago on a working holiday in Cardigan."

"What if the farmer didn't want a reward," Becky whispered indignantly to Jen. "Suppose he just wanted the bowl?"

"Shhhh," hissed Jen. "He'll hear you."

"No, he won't. He's much too busy talking to Dad. I wish we could get away from him before he ruins the whole day. I think we make him uncomfortable."

"He seems to like Dad," said Jen, "and there's nothing we can do. It's nice of him to spend time with us when he's probably got hundreds of other things he'd much rather be doing this afternoon. You've got to pretend to be interested even if you aren't." Jen felt strangely raw, irritated, herself, at the way the trip was turning out, aware they couldn't change it, but cross. Becky always put her feelings into words before Jen could and that irritated her, too.

And Peter. Jen glanced around for him and saw that he had wandered off to the other side of the gallery and was ignoring them. David was too busy listening to Dr. Owen to notice, and Becky was looking glum. It was unfair of Peter to escape.

"Go tell him to come back here," she ordered Becky.

"What?" Becky followed her stare. "He's being smart."

"He's being rude. Tell him to come back before Dr. Owen misses him."

"But—" Becky was going to argue, but one look at Jen's face and she went. Jen watched the two of them talking earnestly together. Peter glanced in her direction, then quickly away when he saw her looking. She felt left out. A brown head and a coppery one bent together in front of jagged chunks of rock, carved with strange symbols, and she, Jen, didn't know what they were saying. For heaven's sake, all Becky had to do was bring Peter back with her, thought Jen resentfully. But at last they came, Peter with reluctance, looking over his shoulder, then at his feet, never at Dr. Owen. Becky was composed.

"What took you so long?" demanded Jen in a furious whisper. "What were you doing?"

They weren't going to tell her, and her resentment increased. Dr. Owen's voice went on and on, quiet, self-assured, explaining the process of dating silver, and the day that had begun so beautifully was ending horribly. Jen didn't want to let Peter and Becky off; she didn't like herself much and she felt very isolated. They trailed behind the two men, from room to room.

"And these are examples of early musical instruments. Some of the best in the British Isles. It's rather a superb collection, don't you think?"

Jen sighed and glanced resignedly at the cases of crude

flutelike instruments and small drums. Then a click in her mind; beyond the cases was a low platform on which were mounted harps of different sizes and shapes, the very simplest to the most elaborate.

David noticed them, too, and remarked.

"Ah, yes. But the earliest instruments are in the cases. Nothing among the harps earlier than seventeenth century, and precious little that old. They're *wretchedly* perishable, of course. So far we've had to be content with descriptions and stone carvings, nothing more substantial. But, of course, that's part of the game, isn't it? There is always a chance something will turn up. Bit by bit, we're completing our picture."

"I thought harps were Irish," said David. "I mean originally."

"In derivation perhaps, David, but they've been used in Wales since the third and fourth centuries. At a conservative guess. Welsh harp music is quite famous, I'd have thought. And the bardic tradition is *very strong* here."

"Of course." David nodded as if he should have known.

"Not much of interest here actually," said Dr. Owen, moving quickly down the row of harps. "Those on the end are *quite* modern. One needn't look hard to find any number of them."

"What are these?" David paused in front of a case that displayed some small miscellaneous-looking objects.

Jen's heart gave a sickening lurch when she saw he was looking at half a dozen metal keylike things. Peter and Becky came close, as if drawn by a magnet. Becky bit her lip nervously, and Jen could feel the tension in Peter like a sudden charge of electricity.

None was exactly like Peter's, but the three children knew before Dr. Owen answered David's question that they were looking at harp-tuning keys.

"Modern tuning keys," said Dr. Owen, without much interest. "For tuning harp strings. We have them here *simply* as illustration. It's unlikely that they've changed a great deal through the centuries, but somehow we've never been able to locate a truly old one. God knows they should be relatively *indestructible,* but whether because they're so *small* or because they were important enough to be buried with their owners, we haven't turned any up."

"Perhaps they didn't have them?" suggested David.

"Oh, indeed they did, David. They appear in one of the earliest codes of Welsh laws. It was criminal to steal the tools of a man's trade, do you see, and harp and tuning key were the tools of a bard's trade. We *know* they existed."

Jen stared at the keys with unwilling fascination. Dr. Owen was right—they had changed very little. None of these were as elaborate as Peter's, but the size and shape were right: three hollow metal arms joined in the middle to form a Y.

How on earth had Peter found one? Where had it come from? Was it really old? Jen had to concede he knew what he had now, the proof was irrefutable.

"Jen?" David was calling her from a great distance. "Dr. Owen has to get back to work. We all appreciate the time he's taken with us, and I'm sure you want to thank him."

A hard, cold knot tied itself in her stomach. If she could just bring herself to do it, Jen could solve the problem of Peter's key once and for all, right here, right now, with Dr. Owen. Very quickly, without turning around, she said, "What if someone found an early harp key? Could you tell how old it was?"

"Jennifer—" began David.

"Well, of course, we could tell how old it was. We have very sophisticated dating methods for pinpointing such things *exactly*. I ought to be able to tell within say *fifty years* myself merely by looking. It would be quite a find, but so far nothing."

"If there were an earlier one though, it would belong here, wouldn't it? In the Museum." Jen dared not look at Becky or Peter.

"Without question. It would provide us with an invaluable link to a part of the past we still know sadly little *about*. It would be terribly important to historians and music scholars. But look here, I'm dreadfully *sorry* to have to leave you like this, but I really must get back to my office. So nice to have met all of you and I do *hope* you'll enjoy the rest of your visit. Do give Gwyn my regards, David, will you?"

Jen faced Dr. Owen with a kind of desperation. She had to catch him now or lose her chance. "Suppose someone found something really old. It might be possible to find one of those keys, mightn't it? I mean you might come across one lying around outside somewhere?" She couldn't let herself think about what she was saying, she had to say it quickly. "Suppose I found it, or my brother, for instance. We ought to bring it to you, oughtn't we? It wouldn't belong to us, really. Any more than the chalice belonged to that farmer. It would be our *duty* to give it to you."

David was frowning at her in perplexity. Peter, behind him, had gone absolutely rigid, his face white, his left hand clenched in his pocket, his right clasped protectively to his chest.

Dr. Owen, who had been rather absently answering Jen's questions, his mind already gone ahead to the work in his office, brought his attention back sharply to her. His eyes narrowed speculatively; her desperation had reached him. "Now, what's this? *Have* you actually found something? There's a chance it might be important—worth a look anyway." He glanced at David. "Naturally there are a lot of *nonessential* artifacts—spearheads, bits of pottery, now and then a coin—but we've got to check every possibility. Sometimes even *children* —"

"It's so hot in here!" said Becky suddenly, and burst into tears. Jen's moment was gone, the focus shifted to her sister. Other people in the hall looked at them, then quickly away. David went down on one knee beside Becky, his hand to her forehead.

"Don't you feel well, love?" he asked anxiously. Becky shook her head, gulping with sobs.

Dr. Owen was clearly not prepared for anything of this kind, but kept his composure. "Hadn't she better go outside? Perhaps some air—?"

"I'm sorry," said David brusquely. "I'm sure she doesn't want to upset anyone, she's obviously not feeling well. I think fresh air would be a very good idea." He turned back to Becky with concern. "Do you want a cold drink? Or something hot?"

"No," she said, her voice blurred with tears. "I'd like to go outside, please."

David thanked Dr. Owen again, formally and briefly, took Becky's hand and headed toward the main entrance. Jen's last glimpse of Dr. Owen was as he walked quickly in the opposite direction without glancing back; there was nothing she could do but follow her family. Becky was all right, Jen knew that. It had been the tension, the awfulness of what was about to happen. Becky had stopped it and saved Peter's secret, and Jen felt strangely relieved. It had gone out of her hands, but at least she'd tried.

Outside on the front steps of the museum, Becky was mopping her eyes and blowing her nose on David's handkerchief and assuring him that she was fine. "I don't know what happened," she said, taking deep breaths. "It got very hot and I didn't think I could breathe. I thought I might be sick. I'm much better now."

"Thank heaven for that!" David exclaimed.

"We don't have to go back in, do we?"

"No. I think Dr. Owen is feeling well quit of us by now. At least we can say we saw him."

"And escaped," added Becky, much recovered.

"It was good of him to spend so much time on us." But David was only mildly reproving.

"I didn't like him much," said Becky candidly.

"Neither did your brother. It's a good thing Dr. Owen

wasn't particularly sensitive to you lot! Jen looked miserable most of the time, and I don't think you opened your mouth at all while we were with him, Peter. Not an unqualified success, I'd say." He shook his head. "Still, you never can tell ahead of time, and the museum, what we saw of it, is fascinating. We ought to come back later and spend a day with*out* a guide. And where, may I ask, Jen, did you find your sudden interest in harp keys?"

Peter, who had been sitting hunched over on a step, staring at his hands between his knees, seemed to stop breathing.

"I just wondered, that's all," said Jen lamely. "They were curious looking, and I suppose you might find something small like that. It might not occur to you it was important."

"What shall we do now?" asked Becky, folding up the handkerchief and giving it back. "Is it time to go?"

David consulted his watch. "Very nearly. We should get back to the bus station, I suppose." He looked from Becky to Jen to Peter with a slight frown, as if to say, "I don't know all that's going on here, do I?" then got up. "Come on, Peter, let's see if we can find a taxi. I'm tired."

They walked off together and irrelevantly Jen noticed that Peter was almost as tall as David now; his wrists stuck awkwardly out of his jacket sleeves and his stride matched his father's. Aunt Beth would have taken him shopping for clothes that fit. There was so much Jen didn't know how to do.

"You were going to tell, weren't you?"

She turned on Becky defensively. "What if I was?"

"You mustn't."

"What if that thing of Peter's is valuable? He can't just hide it."

"But he has to decide what to do, not you, Jen. It isn't yours."

"It isn't Peter's either. It doesn't really belong to him—I agree with Dr. Owen, it belongs to Wales." She knew she was sounding stuffy. If only Peter's key didn't upset her so much, she could be much more objective about it.

Becky said gravely, "Maybe that's true, but Peter found it, so it's up to him. It's to do with him, Jen, not you."

"And you pretended to be sick to keep me from telling."

"No, I didn't. All of a sudden everything felt awful and I did feel hot. I couldn't help it. I didn't want you to tell, though, not Dr. Owen. And what about Dad? Will you tell him now?"

"I don't know," said Jen helplessly. She didn't feel like telling anyone anything at the moment.

"Don't. It won't help."

"I'll make up my own mind," she said stiffly.

Becky sighed. "We'd better go after them or we'll lose them." She started down the steps. "Jen?"

"What?"

"Please don't be cross with Peter. Or me either. I know you don't feel the same way about the Key, but it's all worse if you're mad."

Jen didn't answer. She wasn't sure how she felt any more. She'd been so close to telling—what would have happened if she had? Would it really have been the end of the Key? And she knew it wouldn't have been.

In the terminal David bought them all orange drinks in the crowded cafe, and they sat on stools along a sticky counter sipping and watching people until bus time. They were quiet on the trip back to Aberystwyth, sunk in various thoughts. Becky took a nap, though she indignantly denied it later. The day had been exhausting.

13

Wolf!

THE WELSH WINTER was not like a New England one. Through December, January, and February, the country lay cold and damp, the trees bare, the hills behind the Bog muted with frost. But there was no snow; there were no hard freezes. Inland, two or three miles, the country was often dusted with snow and it lay deep among the mountains of Snowdonia in the north. But along the coast there were only long days of rain. Sometimes the rain came in fierce, sudden showers; usually it lay as a gray curtain across sea and land for hours at a time.

The hooks in Bryn Celyn's front hall seemed always to be full of dripping macintoshes. Umbrellas dried open beside the stairs, and there was a jumble of wellingtons inside the front door.

Gwilym had looked genuinely surprised when, one extremely wet afternoon on the bus to Aber, Jen had complained loudly about being shut in the house all day by the weather.

"Why should you be?" he asked.

"Because it rains all the time," Jen answered crossly.

Gwilym's forehead wrinkled thoughtfully. "I suppose I don't really notice. I have things to do outside whether it's raining or no, and a bit of water doesn't hurt. I just wear my boots and a mac."

"Well, yours must be better than mine because I get wet even when I wear them," retorted Jen.

"Ah, see now," Hugh-the-Bus put in, smiling at Jen in his rearview mirror, "there is a wise man said either you wear a mac and get wet, or you don't wear a mac and get *very* wet, you see?"

Even Jen, sitting there dripping, couldn't keep herself from laughing.

But as the winter blustered by, the Morgans adjusted to it. The damp air was fresh and smelled good—it cleared the head of too much thinking and stuffy rooms. There were always dry clothes to change into after being in the rain: wool socks and warm sweaters; and the heat of the stove in the kitchen or the coal fire in the lounge could be counted on to take the chill out of fingers and feet.

At Mrs. Rhys's suggestion, Jen bought four hot water bottles, and filling them each night, then sliding them between cold sheets half an hour before bed, became a ritual like brushing teeth. Grumbles and complaints grew less frequent and more good-humored, as the Morgans got used to a different kind of living.

Routine settled in again after the trip to Cardiff: school, university, housework, meals. And gradually the days began to spin themselves out so that it was no longer necessary to go off in the morning and come back in the afternoon in darkness. No one mentioned Dr. Owen or harp keys; David asked no questions, Jen made no explanations. But without apologizing to him, she made a kind of peace with Peter, leaving him alone, but not ignoring him.

Jen found plenty to keep her busy during the week. The formidable routines of housework came easier with practice and she no longer had to think so much about the chores she did. She discovered she had not the least compulsion to clean corners and scrub the front doorstep like Mrs. Davies, but she could manage to keep Bryn Celyn in pretty good order and still have time to herself.

Rather to her surprise and pleasure, Mrs. Rhys took a lively interest in Jen's domestic progress and invited her to stop in for coffee any morning Jen was coming to Aberystwyth on errands. Over sweet, milky coffee and delicious homemade scones, Mrs. Rhys taught Jen to knit, listened to problems, and gave all kinds of advice on scores of subjects; she was very good company indeed.

And one afternoon Jen discovered the tiny Borth library, stuck away in a shabby building by the station—just one room lined with books, open apparently according to the librarian's whim rather than regular hours. Some days Jen would be lucky and others she would find it locked and dark. The librarian was a tiny, white-haired man, bent over with age. He sat in a corner reading—always the same huge book, moving slowly through it, then starting again. She wished she knew what it was, but it was in Welsh. He smiled at her when she came, and she at him, but she couldn't understand a word he said, and she hunted through the books on her own. Many of them were in Welsh, all of them were old and well-worn, but she unearthed an endless series of identical romances, which caused David to raise his eyebrows when he found her reading them, and an ancient copy of Mrs. Beeton's *Cookery and Household Management,* which caused Mrs. Davies to snort, and dark little volumes with the titles worn off: the history of Cardiganshire, Welsh folklore and customs, poetry, biographies of Owain Glendwr. Jen had a lovely time exploring them.

On weekends she and Becky, sometimes even Peter, usually climbed back up the valley to Llechwedd Melyn. There, in the comfortable farm kitchen, Mrs. Evans showed Jen how to make Bara Brith—speckled bread full of currants and raisins—and flat spicy Welsh cakes in an iron skillet.

These were eaten hot with cinnamon sugar or butter and honey. Mr. Evans and his sons got used to finding two or three Morgans at their table for Saturday tea.

A little nervously, Jen tried making her own Bara Brith at Bryn Celyn one Wednesday afternoon. She did everything Mrs. Evans had told her, and the dough did everything it was supposed to. The loaves came out of the oven miraculously rounded and golden, filling the house with their rich smell, and Jen felt like crowing. From flour and sugar and yeast she had made her *own* bread instead of buying it in a shop.

David, when he came in tired and damp as usual, found his three children sitting companionably around the kitchen table, devouring new bread, strawberry jam, and tea. Peter, with a book open in front of him, and Jen, cutting more Bara Brith, were listening to Becky relate the latest Borth scandal about a young English professor at the University and the respectable widow, ten years his senior, with whom he'd been keeping company.

"Where on earth did you get that from?" inquired David.

"Mrs. Davies," said Becky promptly.

"I've never thought of her as a gossip. Jen, could I have a piece of that—and is there another cup of tea in the pot?"

"Oh, she's better than anyone else. She knows *every*-thing."

"And so do you now."

"I was helping to fold sheets this afternoon. She wasn't really telling me, she was telling Hugh-the-Bus, but I don't think he was listening."

"I'm not at all sure you should have been!" They all watched David take his first bite; he looked up and found their eyes on him.

"Is it all right?" asked Jen, struggling to sound casual.

"Mmm. Very good. Why?"

"Jen made it!" said Becky. "This afternoon."

"You did? From scratch?"

Jen nodded.

"Wherever did you learn that?"

"From Mrs. Evans."

"Congratulations to both of you—it's delicious!"

Jen grinned triumphantly. "And *that* cancels out the chicken!"

"What chicken?" said Peter, taking another piece of bread.

Toward the end of February the days began to swell with spring; the wind was full of impatience and sent clouds racing across the sky, making sun shadows on the sea and hills. New plants pushed up along the roadsides, and Jen ferreted out a plant guide in the library. When she went walking, she paused to examine the uncurling ferns and strange little leaves she found. Daily Gwilym reported fresh migratory birds on the estuary or singing in the bog grass.

But to Jen and Becky at least, most wonderful of all were the lambs.

The second Saturday in March the sun rose out of the morning mist, catching rainbows in the new grass and leaves, dazzling Jen and Becky on their way up the lane to Llechwedd Melyn. They paused for breath, leaning against the lichen-covered stone wall that bounded the field descending into the *cwm*. Jen was content to stand in the sun, her face turned up toward it, but Becky stood watching the ewes. Mr. Evans had brought them down from the hills to be near the farm where he could keep an eye on them during lambing.

Becky suddenly caught Jen's sleeve. "Look!"

Jen turned to see a fat, woolly ewe nibbling grass close to the wall.

"Wait till she moves," said Becky, staring fascinated. In a moment the ewe took a few steps ahead and Jen saw it too— a tiny, wobbly white lamb, left standing splay-legged. Both ewe and lamb were marked with the daub of red dye Mr.

Evans used to identify his sheep: a splash on the left shoulder.

"New this morning," said Rhian, who had come down to meet them. She was dressed as usual in gumboots, jeans, and a heavy brown pullover. "There'll be a flood of them now. Once one starts, they all go!"

"You mean it was just born *today?*" Becky was incredulous.

Rhian nodded. "Four more further down the *cwm,* too."

Becky shook back her tousled hair and gazed around at the sun and the green valley, full of the sounds of running water and the overhead cry of gulls, the smell of damp earth and grass. "What a day to be born!"

"There's lucky, that one is," Rhian agreed. "They do get born in storms or at night, down the *cwm* or up on the hills where we aren't always finding them quick enough."

"But not this one," said Becky, and laughed aloud, delighted. "Think of it seeing all of this for the first time!" She stretched out her arms. "Imagine, can't you?"

Rhian looked around her thoughtfully, then her face lit with a wide smile. "I am seeing this every day of my life. Don't suppose I pay more attention to it than that old ewe there! But you are right!"

Then they were all three of them laughing for no reason except that it felt good, and they ran up the rest of the lane to the farmhouse, arriving out of breath and noisy at the kitchen door.

"What's this then?" said Aled, who was pulling on his boots in the doorway. "If you've so much energy, why not turn it to mucking out the byre?"

"It's the lambs," said Becky.

Aled grinned and shook his head. "Mad you all are!"

Rhian stuck out her tongue. "And Da, too, if you don't get on up to the *ffridd!*"

"Ah, now that's a different kind of mad entirely. And far more dangerous, that."

"What's a *ffridd?*" asked Jen, when he'd gone.

"Field we keep most of the ewes in above the farm. Do you want to see?"

"Go on with you," said Mrs. Evans from the sink. "You're not wanted indoors on a day like this. Too good for that, says Gram."

The old lady smiled and nodded.

So they spent the day on the hills. Up first to the *ffridd* where the men were working, going through the flock with the dogs, checking the ewes for signs of trouble, marking new lambs. For a while Jen, Becky, and Rhian hung on the gate watching, then they went on up the cart track. The highness and vastness of the windy hills brought Jen to a new sense of freedom. The world stretched endlessly away in every direction, and the energy of life filled her to bursting. Becky and Rhian shared her exhilaration; they walked miles, not returning to the farm until late afternoon, weary but content.

It was lovely to wake up Monday morning and remember it was spring vacation, no need to get up and rush for school, not for another two weeks. Breakfast was late and long. Even David paid no attention to the clock for a change, but sat comfortably drinking coffee and eating toast.

"What will you do with yourselves? Any plans?" he asked.

"Lots," said Becky at once.

Jen said, "Gwilym's talked about going to Ponterwyd to the reservoir hunting for red kites. And we've only begun to explore the hills behind Rhian's farm."

A loud knock at the back door interrupted them. Without waiting for anyone to answer, Gwilym burst in, looking excited, his hair on end. "D'you know what?" he said, "they're organizing a hunt down at the post office!"

"A hunt? What sort of hunt?" David asked. "Isn't it the wrong time of year?"

"It's Jones-the-Top, the farmer above Llechwedd. He says some beast has been after his sheep. Killed two lambs last night, it did."

"Lambs!" Becky sounded shocked. "But Rhian said the only animal that kills sheep around here would be a dog that's gone wild."

"Yes," said Gwilym. "That's right enough, but Jones-the-Top swears it isn't an outlaw dog. Says he's not seen the likes of it round here before—big and gray, it is. No one has a dog like that."

"A stray then," said David.

Gwilym hesitated a moment. "Not a dog at all, says Jones-the-Top."

"What then?"

"More like a wolf, he says."

"Impossible, isn't it?" exclaimed David. "There aren't any wolves left in Wales these days. They've been extinct for years."

Gwilym nodded vigorously. "Yes, I know that, sir, but it's being said. The beast came down last night while Jones-the-Top was watching. He claims his Bett wouldn't go near it and when he'd got his shotgun loaded it was gone."

"But there did used to be wolves," said Peter.

"Makes a good story," David said, "but there isn't any way there could be wolves in the area now without people knowing. Just can't be."

"Well," said Gwilym, "I'm going to join up with them. I want to see this beast myself."

"They'll only kill it, won't they?" asked Jen.

"If they catch it."

"I'm going too," said Peter, getting up.

"Hurry then and I'll wait," Gwilym offered.

"We could go down to the post office," Becky suggested. "We wouldn't have to go on the hunt, Jen. Just to see what's happening."

David set down his coffee mug. "I think I'll go with you, Gwilym."

So in the end they all went trudging down to join the sizable crowd outside Williams-the-Shop's. It was mostly men in earth-colored overcoats, cloth caps, and gumboots. Some of them carried shotguns tucked in the crooks of their arms, most of them had dogs beside them, who were sitting patiently trying to ignore one another. Sometimes it was just too much, though, and a couple of them would have to be dragged apart, complaining. Children of various sizes wove in and out of the group.

The Morgans and Gwilym stood on the edge waiting for someone to take charge. A sheep-killer was nothing to be taken lightly here where hard-pressed farmers could ill afford to lose ewes and lambs. No dog that could not be taught to leave the beasts alone could be tolerated. These men lived precariously close to the edge of subsistence, sheep were their livelihood, and there was a serious feeling to the crowd—faces were grim. What happened to Jones-the-Top last night could happen to anyone else today or tomorrow unless the killer were stopped.

The Evanses were there; Jen saw them clustered to one side: Mr. Evans, Aled, Evan, and Dai. Rhian dodged across to the Morgans.

"You've heard, then."

"What's happening?" asked Jen.

"They're waiting on John Hughes Machynlleth to come with his dogs. Big ones, his. Jones-the-Top says they'll be needed. The hunt'll go over Foel Goch, me Da says. Like as not it's gone into the Forestry along the Einion—can get water from the river."

"Has anyone else seen him?" Gwilym wanted to know.

"Not good. Mind you, there's a man at Blaeneinion thinks he's seen him two nights gone, but that's the first there's any report." Rhian was pleased to know so much.

While they stood there, a light rain began to fall, though no one took any notice. In fact, Jen got quite wet before she realized it. After fifteen minutes or so a battered green van pulled up and a man got out with two enormous cross-bred black-and-white dogs.

"That'll be him, John Hughes Machynlleth. I'm off to see what Da says."

But Mr. Evans was coming over to his daughter. He nodded gravely to David Morgan.

"Day, Mr. Morgan."

"Hullo, Mr. Evans. I understand you've got a sheep-killer in the hills."

"Seems like. Bad business this."

"Will you go out with the hunters, Mr. Evans?" asked Gwilym.

"Aye. My sheep too, up there, see. Me and my lads are going."

"And me," put in Rhian quickly.

"That'll be what I've come to ask, Mr. Morgan. Would you mind keeping your eye on Rhian while we're gone?"

"Oh, Da!" Rhian protested. "I can keep up with you!"

"Your mam would not be happy at all should I take you, and well you know it."

"But I'm already yere."

"Aye and you'll stop yere and that's an end."

"You can come home with us," Jen offered. "Becky and I'll wait at Bryn Celyn till they get back."

"I'm going," said Peter for the second time that morning.

"Don't see why I can't," Rhian grumbled.

"Rhian—" Mr. Evans gave her a stern look.

"Well, it's not fair, see."

"Never said it was, but you'll be staying yere, girl."

Rhian scowled but held her tongue.

David was studying his son whose attention appeared to

be absorbed by the two Machynlleth dogs lying side by side near the van. The men were beginning to organize into groups. Dai, Evan, and Aled came up behind Mr. Evans.

"We're to start from by the farm, Da," said Dai. "Work back from our *ffridd*."

Mr. Evans nodded. "Best go then."

"Mr. Evans?" David spoke. "Would we be in the way if we came with you? Peter and I?"

"And me, sir," Gwilym added hastily.

"Nay. It'll be more eyes."

"Well, then!" exclaimed Rhian. "Couldn't we go with you to the farm just, Da? Only that far? We'll stay there."

"Mr. Morgan?"

"As far as I'm concerned, they'd be as well off at the farm as here in Borth. If your wife won't mind."

"She'll not mind. Into the Land-Rover sharp then!"

Rhian needed no urging. She scrambled into the back, pulling Jen and Becky with her. Somehow everyone crammed in: Mr. Evans, his three sons, Gwilym, Peter, and David. As they drove off toward Llechwedd Melyn, only a few onlookers and a handful of children were left in front of the post office.

"Why do you want to go so much?" Jen whispered to Peter, who was sitting sideways hard against her on the back seat.

"To see if it really is a wolf."

"But you know it can't be—you heard Dad and Gwilym."

"They haven't seen it yet." Peter's expression was intense. "I think it is."

"Peter? Are you going to pre—is it that business again?" Jen wanted suddenly to get out of the car—get out and go back to Bryn Celyn and not know about any of this. But she was thoroughly wedged in with Becky on her lap and Rhian beside her and without making an awkward scene, there was nothing she could do but sit tight.

Peter read her thoughts. "Whatever the animal is, Jen, it's real. I didn't make it up, and you can't possibly say I did. If it's not a wolf, you're safe, but if it is . . ." He left the sentence hanging.

Mrs. Evans made them all troop into the farmhouse kitchen when they arrived and gave them steaming mugs of thick brown tea and chunks of bread. The rain was steady now, not hard but settled. Rhian knew better than to ask again about going, though it was obvious she wanted to as she watched the men pull their collars up and caps down. Mr. Evans whistled up the two sheep dogs, Bran and Bryn, who were lying alert by the stove. "Won't go for the beast, but they'll tell us if they smell un," he said.

"Damn!" said Rhian under her breath as the door closed. A dull afternoon stretched ahead, full of the usual chores: feeding the animals, cleaning the byre, gathering eggs, checking the ewes in the pen by the house. And all the while who knew what kind of drama was out on the hills!

"I think Jen's right," Becky said at last. "I don't think I'd like seeing an animal hunted even if it did kill sheep."

"There, nor should I," agreed Mrs. Evans. "Mind you, we'll be hearing enough about it all to have been there ourselves, I shouldn't wonder. There's been no sheep-killer yere since the bitch from Talybont, and that were eight years back."

"Still—"

"You go along and gather the eggs then. They'll be hatching if it isn't done soon. Go on, all of you."

The hens laid in one side of the long narrow shed where the extra hay was kept, opposite the back door of the house. Their roost was partitioned off from the rest of the shed, but they often got loose, and finding the eggs meant searching the hay with care. Jen took special pleasure in collecting the new-laid eggs; she supposed it was like baking her own bread. She was seeing things at their source instead of boxed and wrapped in plastic; she knew they were fresh. Mrs. Evans could always be counted on to send a few eggs or some fresh butter home with the Morgans when they visited, so David began giving Jen money enough to pay for a regular order. He must have realized the money would be useful.

Today, with the rain dripping off the low, slate eaves and no other sounds but the shuffle of feet in the hay and the quiet mutter of hens talking to themselves, Jen began to regain her sense of balance. There was no point in upsetting herself yet, she couldn't keep the hunt from happening. She was as sure as Peter that the sheep-killer was a wolf; as soon as Gwilym and David had said it wasn't possible, she'd felt it. And Peter had said if it wasn't a wolf she was safe, but if it was . . . She had to wait and see.

The eggs were still warm. When they'd been gathered, the three girls slogged out in the rain and found the ewes and lambs huddled against the overhanging hedgerow: the lambs wet and miserable, the ewes patient and long-suffering. At least the rain couldn't penetrate the thick oiled fleeces of the ewes. The lambs butted up under their mothers for shelter and milk.

"When they're bigger, they'll lift their mams' hind legs right clear off the ground with butting," said Rhian. She counted the beasts. "No trouble yere. I'm wondering what they've found on top."

After tea there were the orphaned lambs to be fed and a cow with a sore foot to be seen to—no end of things to keep busy with. Mrs. Evans was making a vast stew that could simmer for hours on the back of the stove until the men got back, tired and hungry. And Gram, whose hands were gnarled with work and arthritis, crocheted endlessly on a blue and gold afghan. Over her head, on the mantle, the black iron clock kept track of the minutes and hours of the afternoon.

The hills were gray and sodden; they were a world of emptiness. Except for the small group of men, boys, and two dogs, there was no living thing to be seen—only expanses of wet bracken and here and there a wind-crippled tree. They followed the cart track up above the farm, past the *ffridd,* a double furrow of rich, dark mud. It was a long walk to the top, but when they got there and Peter could look deeper into the hills, he found that by fixing his eyes on a distant spot he became aware of movement in the scrub. He could see it best when he didn't look straight at it.

Mr. Evans was staring intently toward the southeast. He raised his arm and whistled and was answered almost at once by someone further over. "That'll be John Griffith Garthgwynion." He turned to David, who was standing with Peter and Gwilym. "The goin' will be rough now. We shall make for that line of trees there, can you see?"

David nodded. "If we can't keep up, Mr. Evans, we'll turn back. Don't worry about us; we'll mark this hill and meet you at the farm."

"Ah, well." Mr. Evans was clearly relieved.

"Should we go in a line?" asked Gwilym. "You know— to scare it up?"

"No need," said Aled. "Beast'll be too smart to be lyin' in the open. Especially in this rain. He'll have gone down the river—right, Da?"

Mr. Evans rubbed his chin. "Aye, most like. But we'll spread out the same."

There were sheep paths through the bracken, narrow mazy things, booby-trapped with roots and rocks. It was hard going, as Mr. Evans had warned, but Gwilym and David kept. moving forward, and Peter was determined not to turn back.

They came down Foel Goch without raising anything; like Aled, Peter was sure they wouldn't, but he had another reason for believing it: his ears sang with a hunting chant. In his eyes the men on either side of him, sweeping the hill, wavered in and out of time—sometimes silent, sometimes exchanging loud, good-natured banter, dressed first as sheep farmers, then in coarse, heavy tunics and dark cloaks. One minute the dogs were black-and-white Welsh sheepdogs, the next rangy, lop-eared hounds.

Peter didn't even try to sort the present from the past, they were too closely interwoven here, they were merging. His heart leaped with joy when he saw against the trees ahead the slight, familiar figure of Taliesin, his copper hair dark and rough in the misty air. So he had returned from traveling in the south and was once again hunting with his friend Gwyddno Garanhir!

"Hie, Peter! You'll break your neck if you run like that!" David was beside him. "I don't particularly want the privilege of carrying you back up the hill!"

Peter shook the damp hair out of his eyes. "Thought I saw something," he muttered. "One of the other men, I guess. I'll be careful." He met his father's glance for a moment.

"See anything? Blast these spectacles!" Gwilym dragged them off and wiped them impatiently on the bottom of his pullover.

"Not yet."

The Forestry Commission had planted larches further down the Einion, but here they'd planted hemlock close together so they'd grow straight. They were so dense that their lower branches were dead and their green tops tangled together. The soil beneath them was clogged with fallen needles that were barely damp. It was here the dogs were at their best, for the men had to keep almost entirely to the paths cut by the Commission. It was odd to walk through a wood that had been sown like a field of corn, in precise, spaced rows that ran off on either side of the path like endless dark tunnels.

At the edge of the trees several groups of men came together. Jones-the-Top was speaking rapidly in Welsh to a solid, dark-haired man with the end of a little cigar forgotten in the corner of his mouth. Every now and then, he grunted or shook his head. Then there was a pause, and in it the world was perfectly still except for the mournful, disembodied cry of a bird. Gwilym stiffened beside Peter.

"Whimbrel," he muttered under his breath, and Peter smiled for an instant.

"There's another lot that is workin' other bank of the river," Aled explained. "We've to go right on. Clear of the trees, there are old mine workin's. Blaeneinion thinks the beast may have gone to earth among them."

They set off again, watching the dogs for any sign of excitement. It was the woods, not the open hillside that gave the strongest feeling of desolation, Peter found, and yet he knew the country had once all been forested. He caught glimpses of the old forests now: birch, ash, beech, oak, and rowan, their branches bare overhead, crazing the slate-colored sky. These were the ancient trees, many of them with great, twisted trunks grown with moss.

The hounds ran as a ragged pack, casting about for the scent of their quarry. Peter saw that the men following were armed with spears and knives, but Taliesin carried none; his short dagger was sheathed at his belt. It was seldom drawn except for cutting meat at table. Although the bard walked with the same light, springing stride as always, he was older now. There was gray streaking the russet of his hair, and the weathered lines in his face had deepened. But his eyes were quick and sharp and his forehead untroubled.

Gwyddno, too, had aged, but far less gracefully. He had grown stiff in his joints and heavy, no longer able to set the pace, content to follow and let his son, Elphin, lead.

Ahead, where the path bent suddenly out of sight, the dogs had found something. Bryn and Bran were barking excitedly. A little border collie that had been trotting obediently at her master's heels whined pleadingly and was off like a shot when given the word of release. Without actually running, the men quickened pace, moving deceptively fast. Peter had to jog to keep up.

The dogs had plunged down off the path toward the river. Aled, Dai, Gwilym, and two other men pushed into the trees after them. But the Key sang with no urgency here and Peter waited. It wasn't time. There was a shout, some crashing, another shout, and the sound of the dogs coming back to them. A few minutes later Aled came panting onto the path, the others behind him.

"Yon terrier got onto a pine marten in by yere. That's all."

Disappointed, the men called their dogs back to them and the party moved on. At the edge of the trees they stopped to watch for the other group. It was good to be clear of the wood and in the open air again. Pipes and cigarettes were lit, and a thermos passed that contained very strong tea laced with something that brought tears to Peter's eyes when he swallowed. When David tasted it a moment later, he looked a little startled, then grinned at his son.

"How are you doing?"

"I'm all right," said Peter.

"Grand!" said Gwilym. "I got a jolly good look at that pine marten back there. I haven't seen but two others before."

Mr. Evans joined them. "Not much to show so far."

"Do you think we'll find the animal?" asked David.

"Shouldn't wonder. More likely from now on. They'll come in to a farm for sheep, see, but not stay close."

"Aye, he'll have gone to earth in one of them old mine holes, I'm thinking. Dogs'll take the scent if they find un. We'll know." It was the solid farmer who had been listening to Jones-the-Top earlier. "And how are your two-year-olds, Evan Evans?" he asked.

Mr. Evans nodded. "Comin'."

"It will be a good year for lambs."

"If we find that sheep-killer," put in Dai.

"We'll be finding un."

The talk turned to a discussion of Dai Pritchard, who was selling his farm at Bont Goch to an Englishman from Bristol.

Dai Pritchard had no sons and could not get help on his land.

"Aye," said one of the other men. "Hard it is to find a sheepman yere now. And you, Mr. Evans, you are the lucky one with your three lads, then. I had three girls before I got even one for help!"

There was a mutter of laughter; the men were familiar with Hywel Davies's family problems, as they were with the private business of all the farmers in the area. Their lives were hard and isolated, but they knew one another well, and word of mouth was still the best way of circulating news, just as it had been for thousands of years.

It came to Peter as he stood, part of the group, watching the men talk, that it didn't matter which faces he saw there; they were the faces of the country. He and his father and even Gwilym would always be foreigners because they weren't Welsh born and raised, but the unexpected regret he felt at knowing that was softened by the realization that it didn't matter as much as he had once thought.

At last someone spotted the second group coming out of the trees. They had nothing to report either, and after ten minutes or so they reorganized again. One lot was to follow the track between Llyn Comach and Llyn Dwfn, the second to work south through the mine area. David, Peter, and Gwilym elected to go with the Evanses in the second group. By dusk everyone would meet at the road that came in past Nant-y-moch Reservoir; it would be easier to walk back along it to Talybont than to track across the hills as they'd come.

John Hughes Machynlleth and his two dogs joined the second party this time. "Must think we have a better chance," observed David. Peter wished they'd start off again. He hadn't noticed how tired his legs were until they'd stopped. The ground was much too wet to sit on, but he found standing still very uncomfortable and wondered if his father felt it, too. Gwilym was used to walking all day over rough ground and he didn't seem bothered. Peter shifted from foot to foot.

The men called up their dogs then, and they set off along

an overgrown dirt track across the shoulder of a long, curving ridge. From the top of it more Forestry Commission plantings were visible ahead, and against the dark green wall were the remains of several derelict stone buildings grouped on the far side of a small dark pool. They were all that remained above ground of the old mine workings. The hills were full of abandoned slate quarries and lead mines. The overgrown pitheads were a hazard to unwary hikers. Centuries before, according to Dr. Rhys, the Romans had found gold in the Welsh hills, and gold was about all they got from Wales; it was a wild, inhospitable country to them.

These ruins were a desolate reminder that men were very impermanent among the ancient hills. They came and scratched away for a while, then disappeared, and the country gradually destroyed all traces of them. The roofs had gone from the huts, and the walls were falling in. An old miner's cart stood upended, two of the boards broken out of its bed and one of its wheels missing. Gorse and heather had crept in over the once bare-trodden ground.

Peter stumbled on a root coming down the slope, glanced at his feet, and when he looked up again, the huts were gone. He heard a shout from his left, and another, then the hounds gave tongue. The pack of them were off around the *llyn,* tails up, yelping joyously. Brushing the hair from his eyes, Peter stared after them and could just make out a large dark shape bounding into the trees. There were more shouts, and the men around him were running, hot in pursuit of the hounds and their quarry, spears held at the ready. Elphin was in front; Taliesin and Gwyddno followed slowly, each for his own reasons.

"They will have her now," said Gwyddno. "She will not cross the river."

Taliesin nodded.

"You will not go and see the kill?"

"Not I."

Gwyddno smiled. "You have not changed, friend, for all your wandering. If I had not grown so ancient, I would be there."

"And I would like to think you wrong, Gwyddno, and that I *have* changed. I have seen many things between here and the Great Court at Caerleon, and I have talked with many people. If after that I remained unchanged, I would feel I had done nothing with myself! But in this—no, I suppose I have not changed."

"We hunt that beast because she has killed our stock and she threatens our children. We do not hunt her for pleasure, you know." Gwyddno's voice was gently chiding.

"Indeed, I do know. And for those reasons I wish your men success. But it is not necessary for me to watch the beast killed. I will not be missed down there."

"This time *you* are wrong!" Gwyddno laughed. "They are hoping you will honor their hunt tonight by weaving the hunters into a song."

Taliesin looked at his friend with fondness. "So I shall. But between you and me alone, one hunt is very like another. There are hunters, and there is the quarry, and there are hounds. There is a chase, a moment when all seems lost, when everything hangs in the balance. And then—triumph!"

Gwyddno put his hand on Taliesin's shoulder. "I am glad you have come back. Even though I can read in your eyes that you do not mean to stay."

The sound of the hunt rolled across the heather to the two men and to Peter, exciting, enticing, and yet none of the three moved for a long moment.

"No," said Taliesin at last. "I have about done wandering, Gwyddno Garanhir. I would go home now."

"You have a home here, you know."

"I am grateful for it. It may well prove that I have need of your generosity." He frowned, gazing up at the sky. "But it is in my heart to return to Llanfair, to my beginning, and there to discover my end. I've come many years and many miles from the village where I was born, and I have not seen it since I left as a boy of twelve." He smiled, remembering. "I was called Gwion then and knew very little of the world. I think perhaps I know only a little more now."

Gwynddno nodded. "But you must take care, my friend. It is Maelgwn's Kingdom you go home to, and I shouldn't wonder if he is still put out at not guessing your riddle." Gwyddno chuckled.

"I have thought of that, but I shall see."

The sudden crack of a gunshot made Peter jump. He was standing alone, up to his thighs in wet bracken, on the empty hillside. There was a second shot. He shook himself and ran as fast as he could toward the trees. A figure emerged from them and waved to him. It was his father.

"I'm sorry. I didn't realize we'd lost you," he said, as Peter came up to him breathless. "They've found it. Dai Evans shot it."

Peter's face was pale and strained. "What? What animal?"

David gave him a strange look. "Come and see." Peter knew he had to.

The men were standing in a tight circle in a fire cut. They were oddly quiet, their faces grim. Gwilym alone looked excited, his spectacles glinted as he saw Peter.

"It *is* a wolf! It really is! A she-wolf, Peter!"

The beast lay on her side, her legs crumpled under her, blood staining the gray fur at her throat, her tongue caught between her jaws, foam-flecked, her eyes filming over with death. She was a great, rangy animal, bigger even than John Hughes Machynlleth's dogs, and unmistakably a wolf. Even someone who'd never seen a real one would have known.

But who were the men in the circle? Cardiganshire farmers? What time did they belong in? They changed—they faded in and out, but the beast on the ground was a wolf in either time. Peter felt suddenly dizzy and turned away. David's arm went around his shoulders, though David said nothing. But Peter knew it was his father who touched him and he took a deep, thankful breath. No one in that other time had ever touched him.

"They'll have to believe us when they see the hide," said Gwilym. "No one can say we imagined it."

"Aye." John Hughes Machynlleth touched the body gingerly with his boot. "Whelpin' too, that be, by the look. She's carryin' milk, see?"

"Dogs are quiet," said Aled. "Caught no scent of pups, they haven't."

"Queer, that," Mr. Evans said. "But no time for looking now, I'm thinking. It'll be dark the hour and there's a long way home. We'd best find the others."

Dai Evans and another man found a small fallen spruce and lopped the branches off it, then bound the wolf's legs together around it, so she hung belly up when they shouldered the pole.

"Pups should mean a male around, too," said David to Mr. Evans.

"Should do," he agreed, frowning. "Hasn't been wolves seen yere since before me own da's time. No one else has reported trouble that I've to hear, but it may be we have to come back. Queer business, beginning to end, this."

The hunters were subdued. They seemed to take no joy in the killing—it was a necessity not a pleasure, as Gwyddno had said, but they glanced uneasily at the wolf and walked clear of it. Peter was very tired.

14

A Birthday Expedition

THE NARROW, black-topped road took them west to
Talybont. The lights were on in the village when they got there,
shining yellow out of a gathering mist. Never had lights looked
more welcoming, thought Peter, willing himself toward
them.

From Talybont, someone suggested calling Billy-Davies-
Taxi in Borth and telling him to round up enough cars and
vans to get everyone home again. David and Peter still had
the journey back to Llechwedd Melyn ahead of them, to collect Jen and Becky, before they could think about supper and
bed, but Mr. Evans said not to worry. There'd be dinner at the
farm, then he or Aled or Dai could run all the Morgans back
to Borth, and no trouble.

It was just half-past five when the party of hunters
reached the door of the Red Goat public house on the green
in Talybont, and Mr. Roberts, the publican, was unlocking for
the evening. He found himself faced immediately with fifteen
wet, hungry, and weary men who were beginning to revive a
bit at the thought of a pint of beer in a warm pub. Mr. Roberts
greeted them all with undisguised delight and ushered them
into the bar—men, dogs, Peter, and Gwilym. He sensed a good

story and the chance to liven up an otherwise dull, damp evening, and his round face shone with pleasure. Most of the men were well acquainted with Mr. Roberts, and he greeted them by name as they stumped into the low-ceilinged, whitewashed public bar. It was plain and clean: benches set against the walls, a couple of polished wood tables and chairs, and a high dark wood bar, which opened on one side into the public bar and on the other into the more formal lounge bar. Whoever was working could tend them both from the middle, using the same collection of bottles and spigots. Hanging from the beam above the bar was a collection of pewter tankards of different shapes and designs, dull with age, battered and scratched with use. The men in the group who were regulars at the Red Goat took their own down from the hooks for Mr. Roberts to fill.

Tired as he was, Peter absorbed the scene with interest. He'd never been in a pub before. He was under age, but no one paid the slightest attention to that sort of legality tonight. Mr. Roberts bobbed back and forth behind the bar, pulling pints of beer and listening most appreciatively to the story of the hunt. He was a short, chunky man with a shock of stiff gray hair and eyes that disappeared between wrinkles when he grinned, which he did constantly. He had an endless supply of questions to ask, and Peter could hear him say, "I never!" over and over, whenever someone paused for a swallow.

David bought himself and Gwilym each a pint of bitter and Peter a gingerbeer, and they shared packets of potato crisps. It felt good to sit with the men on one of the long benches, leaning back against the rough plaster wall, while warmth crept slowly back. As more people came in for the evening, the story had to be told and retold and visits made to the shed behind the pub where the body of the wolf had been put—to keep it safe from inquisitive dogs. The second group of hunters was disappointed at having missed the climax of the day, but everyone agreed the wolf was indeed genuine. Peter heard the word "supernatural" muttered more than once, though no one said it loudly. The usual jubilance after a successful hunt was somehow missing.

It was well past six when Billy-Davies-Taxi arrived with three other drivers, one the Borth greengrocer's boy who'd brought the delivery van. Of course, they all had to have a pint while the story was told one more time. Then the carcass was carried out of the shed and exclaimed over before everyone piled into the vehicles and set off at last for home. Mr. Roberts looked very sorry to see them go.

Billy-Davies-Taxi took the Evanses and Peter and David to Tre'r-ddôl, and from there they wearily climbed the last hill to Llechwedd Melyn, but Gwilym would not be separated from the wolf. He rode to Borth in the back of the van with it to see it safely locked in one of the abandoned railway huts near the station. The Nature Conservancy Officer from Aberystwyth was coming to examine it in the morning, and Gwilym was determined to be on hand. The men had agreed the officer should be notified, but no one was very eager to do it, so finally Gwilym, his voice gruff with excitement, had rung him. He was longing to know what the authorities would say about the discovery of a real wolf in Wales after so many years of supposed extinction. On the phone, the authorities had sounded very skeptical.

By seven Rhian was pacing up and down, frantic with impatience, unable to settle anywhere. Her mother and Gram ignored her; the stew on the back of the stove filled the kitchen with a thick golden-brown smell; the fire dropped to coals on the hearth. Thomas, the kitchen cat, lay next to it, cat-fashion, paws folded under, tail wrapped around, like a large yellow tea cozy. His ears flicked occasionally at noises, but his eyes stayed fast shut. Becky had gone to sleep in Mr. Evans's arm chair, her chin propped on her hand. Jen and Mrs. Evans sat side by side on the wooden settle, knitting squares for a blanket, while Gram crocheted endlessly on her afghan. But Rhian paced, going outside to check for signs of the men every other minute.

Then, at last, "They're back! Coming up the *cwm* from Tre'r-ddôl, Mam! I'm off then, to meet them!" and she was gone, slamming the heavy door behind her, before any of the others had absorbed what she'd said. Then Thomas got up and stretched elaborately to cover the fact that he had jumped when the door banged.

"Well," said Mrs. Evans, laying aside her work, "table to be set. Becky?"

Becky rubbed the end of her nap out of her eyes and stretched like Thomas.

"Jen, you just give the fire a poke, there's good. They'll be wanting it, I shouldn't wonder."

In a very short time it seemed, all eleven of them sat down at the scrubbed kitchen table, talking, listening, asking dozens of questions, with huge plates of stew, stewed tomatoes, fresh thick slices of bread and butter, and mugs of strong tea. Rhian had to be reminded more than once that dinner was getting cold and that the men were hungry. The story they told between mouthfuls was simple and straightforward—the plain facts. An odd feeling of restraint hung in the air. Not even Aled tried to explain away the reality of the wolf and its unexpectedness. Rhian made no attempt to hide her envy of Peter, who'd gotten to go along, and he only a year older than she.

When finally the dishes were scraped clean and the last crumbs of rice pudding gone, David stood up. "If you don't mind, Mr. Evans, I think I should take my lot back down to Borth. It's been a long day for everyone."

Mr. Evans nodded. "Aye. Odd, but I am not sure at all whether it has been a good one or not so good." Aled glanced quickly at his father then away. "The hills is full of stranger things than many'd be believin'."

"Yes," said David seriously. Jen and Peter met each other's eyes for a long moment, but it wasn't until she was beside her brother in the Land-Rover, jolting down the track, that Jen spoke to him directly.

"Was it bad? The killing part?"

"No." His voice was tired. "I didn't see them shoot it. But I didn't like it, anyway. I don't think anyone did much."

"Would it have been there if you hadn't gone?" she asked.

"What do you mean?" he said guardedly.

"You know."

But Peter shook his head and didn't answer.

Next day at tea, Gwilym reported on his morning with the Nature Conservancy Officer. Mr. Lord had been clearly disconcerted to find the local men really had hunted and killed a wolf in the hills above Talybont. Gwilym watched as the man measured and photographed and took notes. Finally, Mr. Lord had gone away to call his headquarters in Bangor to explain the unusual situation and ask what he should do next.

"Did they believe him?" Becky wanted to know. "You said he didn't believe you yesterday."

Gwilym shrugged and helped himself to another slice of swiss roll. "I don't really know what they said in Bangor. But he took it off then—right on the 12:20 train with him. Put it in a baggage car and got in as well. Wish I could have gone, too, to see."

"Will they hunt for more wolves?" asked Jen.

"The Conservancy might." Gwilym was feeling extraordinarily talkative, but then it was his story now. "Not anyone here, though. They don't seem to think they'd find more. Seemed glad to see the body go."

"Of course, logically, there must be more," said David. "After all, that was a female still feeding pups. Her litter and her mate must be somewhere around."

"Does it have to be logical?" asked Peter.

"What do you think, Gwilym?"

"Well, I do agree with you, sir," said Gwilym slowly. "There should be more, but I doubt anyone will ever see them. I don't know why."

David nodded.

It had been a lazy sort of day for them all, a chance to catch up from the day before, but when tea was finished David got to his feet. "I don't know about the rest of you, but I need some fresh air. Leave the dishes, Jen, and let's go for a walk."

Gwilym included himself, and Peter came willingly; all five of them pulled on coats and tramped down to the wind-buffeted shore. The tide was out, and overhead lay the usual cloud cover, but above the sea was a narrow, shining strip of clear sky and into it slid the westering sun, glowing like one of the coals from a fire, hesitating before it sank below the horizon. The cloud bank turned the color of wet slate and the waves caught the light like broken glass. Oystercatchers, dark-bodied, wings flashing white, flew out over the sea, crying shrilly, and black-headed gulls stood one-legged along the water's edge, keeping a wary eye on the people walking toward them, waiting until the last moment to fly. The long beach was deserted except for the Morgans, Gwilym, and the birds. It was a time to be conscious only of that exact moment, to fill the mind with sunset, sea, beach, and wild things—and each other's company. They had no need of talking.

In many small ways, spring vacation was entirely different from the Christmas holidays. Of course, the weather had changed: summer lay ahead instead of a dull dripping winter; the sun, when it shone, was warmer, the days drew out, birds began to sing, and the Cardiganshire air was full of the thin, insistent bleating of new lambs. With the coming of spring, Jen discovered more and more excuses for being outdoors. In fact, they all did.

And they were spending far less time alone. Becky and Rhian were usually together, and Jen and Gwilym often joined them. The Evanses even got used to seeing Peter at Llechwedd Melyn with everyone else. They explored the beach and estuary and the hills around the farm. Gwilym showed them long-tailed tits in the Llyfnant Valley and took them out on the Bog to look for sundews— "There are *three* varieties out here, you know! People come to study them," he explained.

In a sheep field above the Dovey, Jen and Becky stood with Gwilym and heard the first spring cuckoo and shared his excitement at the strange-familiar call.

When the Morgans had first come to Borth, David bought a copy of the Aberystwyth Ordnance Survey Map, which showed the country around on a one-inch to one-mile scale. He'd tacked it up on the kitchen door and left it for his children to look at, but they hadn't paid it much attention. Now, after months, they began using it. Gwilym had been shocked to discover that none of them knew how to read it properly, and he spent an afternoon painstakingly showing Jen, Becky, and Peter.

It opened new windows for them. The map showed in detail the lanes, tracks, and footpaths, the mine workings, rivers, *cwms,* woods, and villages; it even showed individual farms and their names. Becky spotted Llechwedd Melyn immediately.

Once they had learned how to use the map and had gotten to know the land around Borth well enough, they felt the freedom of the country and began to enjoy it. David finally had to buy three more maps so they could each have one, instead of wrangling over the kitchen copy.

"Of course," he warned, as he handed them out, "this doesn't mean you have my blessing to wander off in all directions by yourselves. You've got to use sense about it and never, *never* go far alone. Never—" He looked at Peter.

Grinning, Jen and Becky chorused, "—go without telling someone!"

David laughed, then added, "This is wild country, re-member, and you aren't very experienced yet."

"But anyway," Becky remarked to Jen later, "it's much more fun to go exploring with someone else."

"Yes," said Jen, surprised that she agreed with Becky wholeheartedly. It *was* more fun to be with Becky and Rhian, or Gwilym, or even Peter, than to be alone. A couple of months earlier, she realized, she might not have thought so. But they were much more comfortable with each other now, used to being together. Even David was interested in their plans for expeditions; he didn't quite join the debates and dis-cussions, but he sat listening, instead of shutting himself into the study to work always.

And Peter was positively agreeable these days. Or per-haps, thought Jen with a sudden flash of insight, they were *all* more agreeable.

Besides the day-to-day sort of plans for picnics and hikes and shopping trips, there were two special occasions to be planned during the vacation: the first was David's birthday on the twenty-first of March, and the second was a dinner party for the Rhyses.

After a good deal of agonizing over it, Jen had finally suggested the dinner to David. Her cooking had progressed a lot—David was the first to say so—and Jen really felt they owed the Rhyses a meal for all their kindnesses. She *wanted* to do something for them.

Instead of saying, "Do you think you can?" David had said at once, "Good idea! You decide when and I'll invite them for you, if you want."

"It would be all right, you think?"

"I think they'll be delighted."

"I'll have to figure out a menu," said Jen.

"You could do shepherd's pie, like Mrs. Evans," sug-gested Becky. "I love it."

"Or perhaps chicken," said Peter solemnly.

Jen was about to retort indignantly, when she caught sight of his grin. "Monster!" she said, lobbing a dishtowel at him.

"You could never duplicate your first effort, I feel sure," said David.

"You should be grateful! I think that's enough about the chicken." But she could laugh at it herself now.

Jen chose the last Friday of vacation for the dinner party. David issued the invitation to Dr. Rhys and it was promptly accepted.

But when the subject of birthdays came up, David said he didn't see why the dinner couldn't do for that as well. "When you're my advanced age, you don't need anything special, believe me."

Becky wasn't satisfied, however. When David was out, she said so. "You can't just not celebrate a birthday, it's important. He wouldn't like it if we told the Rhyses, because they'd have to bring something, so it really won't be a birthday party at all."

"But he said—"

"I think he'd be pleased if we did something special."

"I suppose we could take him out to dinner," said Jen thoughtfully. "What do you think, Peter?"

"In Aberystwyth?" he snorted. "At the Milk Bar? Or a fish-and-chips shop?"

"There's a good restaurant in one of the pubs, I've heard Dad say so," declared Jen.

"Anyway, if we did that, we'd only be taking him to dinner on his own money."

"We've got allowances," said Becky.

"*His* money," Peter pointed out.

"But we'd be spending it on him instead of ourselves," said Jen. "Have you got a better idea?"

Peter hesitated. "Maybe."

"What?" demanded Becky.

"Well—you probably won't like it, but what about having an expedition to a place we haven't been yet? A picnic somewhere?"

"It might rain on Thursday," said Jen doubtfully.

Peter shrugged. "The world might end, too. I told you you wouldn't like it."

"I do," said Becky. "I think it sounds neat. We could go into Aber and buy all kinds of food and go out all day. Dad's never gone with us before."

"Well—"

"We could even ask Gwilym and Rhian."

Jen glanced at Peter. He said, "Why not?"

"Do you really think he wants to go hiking with us?"

"If he doesn't, he can always say so," Peter said.

"He'll want to," said Becky confidently. "'But let's keep it a surprise until the last moment."

Once his idea had been accepted, Peter began having doubts. He was nowhere near as sure as Becky that his father would indeed want to go. He thought of Cardiff, when they'd all been together for the day. At least with Gwilym and Rhian along, there couldn't very well be any sort of family disagreement, and Peter realized it was too late to stop Becky now; she had her mind made up.

So the three of them pooled their allowances and went into Aber on Wednesday morning to shop for supplies. They wandered around the little town, arguing agreeably over favorite kinds of biscuits and whether it was better to buy two large bottles of lemonade or six small ones. In the bakery, they decided on pork pies, sausage rolls, and half a dozen fat eccles cakes; in the greengrocer's, they bought tomatoes and six huge green Granny Smith apples. Becky swore their father liked best the chocolate and orange biscuits called Jaffa Cakes, which Jen and Peter knew were also her favorites, and Peter insisted on a pound of nuts and raisins from Woolworth's. In the end they got the big bottles of lemonade, and on the way to the bus stop Jen bought a lump of yellow cheese and Peter a bag of barley sugar candy.

"I'm sure I don't know how we'll carry this tomorrow," said Jen, hefting her shopping bag as they stood in the queue waiting for the bus.

"We've got knapsacks," Peter said. "So's Gwilym."

"And Rhian," Becky added.

"We'll manage."

"We still don't know where we're going," Jen pointed out.

They had each come up with a different suggestion and they discussed it off and on all afternoon. Becky had said the Llyfnant Valley, but Peter disagreed because they'd already gone. He wanted to go to Nant-y-moch.

"But you need a car for that," Jen pointed out. "It's too far to walk there and back in a day. What about following the river that goes along the Bog and over to Talybont? We've never done that, and we can start right here in Borth."

"Rhian'll think that's pretty tame," Becky predicted. "But she'll go anyway, she said she would."

"Peter?"

"I suppose that's all right. Not very exciting—I agree with Rhian, though."

"What's not very exciting?" David wanted to know putting his head around the kitchen door. "And when's supper?"

"As soon as you clear out and let me get it," said Jen. "Or better still, set the table first." She soon had them organized. Privately, she wondered what David would say tomorrow when they told him their plans. No one had mentioned his birthday, and presumably he thought they'd taken him at his word and done nothing special. Perhaps he'd say he had work and couldn't go. Becky would be dreadfully disappointed if he did. So would she, Jen admitted to herself.

Jen woke to find Becky shaking her. "Get up and see! I think it's going to be a gorgeous day!"

"What time is it?"

"Six."

Jen groaned and tried to roll over, but Becky ruthlessly stripped off her blankets. "It's still dark!" she complained, setting her feet gingerly on the cold floor. But beyond the curtains, the sky was a clear dove-gray, stained with rose over the hills to the east. Now that she was beginning to wake up properly, Jen felt a twinge of excitement. "Is anyone else up?"

"I don't think so." Becky was already dressed.

It was chilly. Jen shivered hastily into her own clothes then hurried into the bathroom.

Becky met her as she came out. "What about Dad?" she asked in an anxious whisper.

"Here goes," said Jen, and thumped loudly on her father's door twice.

"Suppose he's mad?" said Becky a little apprehensively.

"What?" came a muffled sleepy voice.

Jen gave Becky a conspirational wink—too late for second thoughts. "Time to get up!" she called.

"What on earth—?" But by the time David had struggled out of bed and opened his door, Jen and Becky had escaped, laughing and breathless, to the kitchen, where much to their surprise they found Peter dressed and making tea.

"Good morning. I heard you get Dad up."

"What if he goes back to bed?" worried Becky.

But a minute later they heard the creak of water through the pipes and soon after David appeared, looking puzzled and unshaven. "What in the name of heaven are you up to?" he demanded.

"It's an expedition," began Becky.

"We decided that if today was nice we'd go out for a picnic," Peter elaborated. "And it is, so we are."

"Why didn't you say something last night? Did you get me up just to tell me where you were going?"

"Not exactly," said Jen. "Gwilym and Rhian are coming, and—we thought you might like to come, too."

David looked slowly round at his children. "Where are you going?" he asked finally.

"Along the Leri River to Talybont, then back in the hills."

"You needn't come if you're busy," said Peter quickly.

"But we'd like you to," Becky added. "We just thought—"

"Well," said David in an oddly stiff voice. He cleared his throat, and Jen and Becky and Peter waited, their eyes on him. "Well, is there any breakfast first?"

Becky's smile was broad and relieved. "Gwilym'll be here in less than half an hour," she warned. All hands turned to at once and by the time Gwilym knocked, they were actually ready: food stowed in knapsacks, breakfast eaten, dishes soaking, and David had even managed to shave.

Rhian met them at the station in Borth where Aled had left her on his way to Machynlleth with the farm eggs. She and Gwilym accepted David without questions, and by the time they had redistributed the provisions among four knapsacks, everyone was eager to be off. David offered to carry one of the packs, but Becky protested that it wasn't proper for him to work today, so Gwilym, Rhian, Jen, and Peter ended up with them.

Gwilym took the lead across the Bog, past the tiny church of St. Matthews, isolated on its mound behind the station, ringed with rowan trees. Not many people were about yet, and it felt good to have the new day to themselves. David made no attempt to interfere with their organization, but seemed quite content with his place in line behind Becky.

At first the Leri was very civilized, idling along its canal, past backyards and within sight of the railway tracks. In Dolybont it almost met the main road to Bow Street, and here the expedition crossed it on a hump-backed stone bridge. The sun had climbed a good way up the cloudless sky by this time, and the morning was perfect.

Peter took charge now, leading up a narrow lane to the top of a hill, then to the right through a farmyard gate.

David hesitated. "Is this legal? Isn't it private property?" He eyed the cow byre from which came the sounds of a motor being coaxed to life.

"The path goes through and out the other side," explained Becky. "Come on."

"It's marked as public," Jen reassured him. "It's on the map."

David gave a shrug. "All right, but if I'm arrested on my birthday . . ."

"Is it your birthday then?" asked Rhian with interest. "How old are you?"

"Ancient."

"Not so very," Peter said, swinging the gate shut and latching it.

"Thank you. One rather back-handed compliment!"

The motor suddenly caught and a man appeared in the doorway of the byre. He paused to nod to them, his eyes narrowed against the sun.

Recklessly, Becky called, *"Bore da!"* grinning, and he grinned back, showing jagged white teeth. *"Bore da!"* he answered, and followed it with a long sentence that was unintelligible to everyone.

"Good lord," said David. "Becky, you asked for that!"

"But all I know is '*Bore da*.' It means good morning."

The man returned to his machine. On the far side of the farm they found the path, a neglected green track. It crossed a bare field and rejoined the Leri in a plantation of larch and fir. On their left, before they reached the trees, they passed a steep symmetrical hillock.

"Hill fort," Gwilym informed them, when David pointed to it.

He nodded. "I thought it might be."

"Once you know where to find them and how they look, you can spot them all over."

"And the feeling of them," put in Rhian. "They have a feel, too."

"Old, I suppose," said David, studying the hillock.

"Old as the hills," Peter said quietly.

"Too many forts and such for the archeologists to bother with," Gwilym went on. "They don't excavate unless they've found something special. Mind you, there are axes and worked flints to be found, if you look. I've some."

"I wouldn't mind finding an axe myself," David remarked.

Almost too casually, Peter asked, "What would you do with it?"

"Keep it for good luck, I suppose."

"Even if it wasn't really yours?"

"But it would be yours if you found it," Gwilym objected. "Museums don't get excited over axes and bits of pottery any more."

"They do over brooches and bowls," said Becky. "Dr. Owen does."

"Oh, well," said David. "Dr. Owen's another matter altogether. Though really he's quite right about the important stuff —it does belong in a museum."

Out of the corner of her eye, Jen fancied she saw Peter give his head a very small shake, more out of perplexity than disagreement. He didn't pursue the conversation further.

For the best part of an hour the path led them through sun-dappled, damp-smelling woods. On their right, the Leri rushed by, tumbling and swirling around debris caught along the bank. It was a cold golden color, its depths not yet touched by the spring sun; it filled its bed from bank to bank, carrying down the first of the melted snow and ground frost from higher in the hills. The rushing sound it made was so loud it seemed to fill the world, covering the sounds of wind in the evergreens and the calls of the tits and wagtails which darted ahead of the party.

It was just past nine when they reached Talybont, entering it from the back, down a cobbled alley. Although it was early, the sun had already caused lines of laundry to sprout in the backyards, flapping and cracking cheerfully in the breeze. A small white dog with very muddy feet bounced out a half-open gate to challenge the expedition as it went by.

In front of the Red Goat they stopped for a short debate; it was necessary to decide how they would go next: they could either continue along the Leri on a paved road or follow a lane north, back into the less civilized hills. Gwilym settled the matter finally by saying, "Actually, there's a very old site up the lane a bit, if you'd like to see it, sir. It's called Bedd Taliesin on the map. Just there."

Jen froze at the name; Becky, too, was suddenly alert.

"What does Bedd mean?" asked David. "Taliesin was the Welsh bard, I know that." He pronounced the word "Beth," as Gwilym had.

"It means cairn. Bedd Taliesin is a burial cairn that's been opened."

"The grave of Taliesin," Rhian said. "My Da can tell you about that, lovely great stories."

"But it isn't really," contradicted Gwilym.

"Isn't it then! You just ask my Da about it!"

"Why isn't it?" asked David.

"It's much too old—it's Bronze Age—and Taliesin didn't live until the sixth century!"

"Ych y fi," exclaimed Rhian in disgust. "Facts again! As if they prove everything anyway! My Da could convince you different before long."

"You're right, I think he could," agreed David with a grin. "Well, let's see this cairn. We can have lunch there, though I wouldn't mind eating it right now!"

"But it isn't anywhere near time," objected Becky.

Jen was last to start up the lane; she couldn't help wondering if this day would end the way the day in Cardiff had. Peter waited for her to catch up.

"Come on, we don't want to lose the sausage rolls," he urged with a grin. His face was open, his voice friendly; Jen could find no trace of withdrawal. "Gwilym's quite right about Bedd Taliesin, you know," he said conversationally. "No matter what Rhian says. I've read about it." So he knew what she'd been thinking. Together, they hurried after the others.

The lane worked its way up out of Talybont, winding deep between earth banks and blackthorn hedges that were misted green with new leaves. There were fat buds on the branches just wanting a day of sun to burst them into white flower. And climbing the banks, scattered in the grass were little yellow flowers. "Primroses," Gwilym told Jen when she asked, and she stared at them in delight.

Above them, out of sight in the fields, they could hear the frantic bleating of lambs and the equally frantic answers of their mothers.

"They've all got different voices," Becky observed. "Can you hear?"

"You'd make a very good lamb," said Peter. "You could tell which was your mother."

The sun had polished off the last of the morning's mist, and protected by the hedgerows, they could feel the warmth in it. Rhian wasted no time in shedding her windbreaker and the others soon joined her.

"Oh, it feels good not to wear a jacket!" excaimed Jen. "Like shedding a skin! Hello, what's this?"

Coming around a blind corner, they surprised a large, ragged ram with corkscrew horns. He had been grazing the side of the lane, and they'd caught him with his mouth full. He faced the intruders alert and tense. Jen was close enough to see his strange, pale eyes, with their hyphen-shaped pupils. His nostrils flared.

"What do we do? Is he dangerous?"

"Keep going," instructed Rhian.

"But what if he runs at us?"

"Not that one." She approached the ram confidently. "I've no doubt but you're wanted at home, you."

The ram bunched himself together, like a spring contracting, and waited until he judged Rhian had come too close, then he bounded backward and turned tail, running nervously up the lane in short, panicky bursts. There was no way for him to go but straight on—the banks were too steep and the hedges too dense to allow a good-sized ram to escape.

In ten minutes or so, preceded by this rather unlikely herald, the party came to a whitewashed farm: raw, new farmhouse on the left, ageless, thick-walled byre and huts on the right. A red-faced young woman was out on the front step feeding a flock of chickens with the help of a small child, who kept putting handfuls of grain in its mouth. Its hair was cut straight across and it wore an overall, so there was no way of telling whether it was a boy or a girl. Beside them lay a fat baby in a battered black pram.

The woman smiled gratefully when she saw them and unconsciously patted her wispy brown hair. "Oh, ta very much! Wondered where that one had got to. Devil he is for getting out. Saves going to look."

"Halfway to Talybont," Rhian told her cheerfully.

"Ta!" she called after them again, as they went on.

The earth banks flattened away and the primroses disappeared. The ground grew rough with wintered grass and boulders and clumps of gorse coming into bloom. The great, flat expanse of Borth Bog spread below to the left, and beyond the Dovey the mountains of Snowdonia sprang up, merging with layers of cloud so it was hard to tell which were mountains of earth and which of air.

An ancient, lichen-covered, drystone wall ran beside the lane, which was no more than a cart track here. The land was open for grazing and punctuated with sheep, intent on tearing up grass as quickly as possible.

"Oh!" cried Becky suddenly. "Isn't it *beautiful!* Let's stop right here for lunch."

"It's still early," Jen looked at her watch.

"I don't care," stated Peter, sitting down. "I'm ravenous."

"*I* was hungry in Talybont," said David.

Gwilym set down his knapsack. "Bedd Taliesin's just up there, so this is a good spot."

Jen looked uneasily over her shoulder in the direction he pointed, fully expecting to see some unpleasant apparition, but the hill was wild and empty.

"Well, if we're that close let's have a look first. We can leave the packs," suggested David.

It wasn't very impressive to look at—just a hole in the ground with great slabs of rock lying untidily around it. They stood gazing down in silence for a long moment. Jen remembered what Rhian had said earlier about places having a feel to them. This one certainly did, its appearance was unimportant. It had once been a sacred, magic place for people so far distant in time they could hardly be imagined: strange, hairy, dark little figures that appeared in history and science books. You knew perfectly well they had been real, but you couldn't actually believe in them.

But here there was contact. Here, that dim, inconceivable world touched the present for an instant. The magic hadn't all worn away. Jen shivered.

I wonder how the country looked when this was built," David said quietly.

"Forest," Gwilym answered.

"It's hard to imagine the hills forested, they look so old and wild the way they are."

"Only because you haven't seen it with trees," said Peter.

"You sound as if you have, then," said Rhian.

"I have a good imagination," said Peter smoothly. "Whoever was buried here must have been important."

"He'd not have been given such a cairn if he weren't," Gwilym agreed.

"But he wasn't Taliesin," Peter said with certainty.

They moved away from the cairn, back toward the knapsacks and lunch.

"What I cannot see," Rhian said to Gwilym, "is how you can be so scientific always. Mind you, I'm not always agreeing with Da myself, but he does say it's not right to try explaining everything. He says we're not meant to understand some things."

Gwilym frowned. "Not everything, you can't explain. But the bits you can, you've got to find out."

"Does everything have a reason, though?" persisted Peter.

"Doesn't it?" asked David. "Even when we don't know what it is? I agree we don't know all the answers, but I do believe there are answers."

"Maybe we aren't supposed to know them all," Becky said.

David nodded. "The world looks quite different to me from this side of the ocean, I have to admit," he said with a smile.

"And to me," said Peter.

The midday sun blazed overhead in blue sky, and so far above them it was invisible, a skylark spilled its song over the hillside. The sound of sheep tearing grass came down the breeze.

Looking out over the Bog, David continued thoughtfully, "I think Gwilym's right about learning as much as possible, but perhaps one of the most important lessons to learn is to accept what you can't explain. We can get too tied down by facts."

Jen's head was bent, her face hidden by dark curtains of

hair, her fingers busy knotting and unknotting the drawstrings of her knapsack.

It was Rhian who said loudly, "I'm wanting my lunch, and if we're to sit here talking about what's real and what isn't, I don't see why we can't be eating at the same time."

"I don't either," declared Becky.

They spread their jackets on the wiry turf in a circle and set about dividing up the picnic.

"Of course, I didn't bring any cups," moaned Jen, when it was all spread out.

"Who needs cups?" demanded David. "Much too civilized and we'd have to carry them with us all day." He took a long drink out of one of the bottles of lemonade.

The great mound of food Peter, Jen, and Becky had bought disappeared at astonishing speed.

"But," said Becky, through a mouthful of sausage roll, "do let's save enough for tea."

"I shall be so full I won't want to move in a minute," Peter announced, falling backward, his hands behind his head.

"This will be Bedd Peter," declared Becky with a giggle. "Twentieth century and not very important."

Peter didn't deign to answer.

"Do you really believe, sir—" Gwilym was beginning, anxious to get back to serious matters, when Jen cried suddenly, "Hey! Hey, Gwilym, what's that? Not a buzzard, is it?"

Shielding his eyes from the sun, Gwilym looked up. "Oh, I say! Look!" The excitement in his voice brought everyone to attention. Two small birds were harrassing a big one in the sky over Bedd Taliesin. They flew at it, chittering in agitation, but it seemed to ignore them, planing and gliding effortlessly, coming within a few feet of the ground, then swooping upward. Its long forked tail twisted like a rudder, its long bent wings carried it easily with spellbinding grace. After a minute or two, it swept out of sight over the crest of the hill, the two small birds with it.

Gwilym let out his breath in a long, satisfied sigh. "That's the bird to see, a red kite. Wales is the only place in Britain you'll find them, and not many here either."

"A birthday present," said Becky.

"The whole day is a birthday present," David said quietly. "The best I've had in years."

They all looked at each other and smiled, a little awkwardly at first, but the awkwardness faded. After lunch they sat about for a while, feeling comfortable, then packed up the remains of the food and the papers and bottles, leaving no trace of the picnic. "As it should be," observed Rhian. "Leave it as you find it."

15

Dinner Party

"ARE N'T YOU THROUGH in there *yet,* for heaven's sake? It's quarter to six already!" Peter gave the bathroom door a series of impatient thumps.

"Tell her something's burning on the stove—that'll get her out in a hurry," advised David on his way downstairs.

"I heard you!" cried Jen, flinging open the door and emerging in a cloud of steam. "That's dirty fighting! You could have finished in here while I was down in the kitchen, slaving over dinner. Dad, would you tell Becky to fill the kettle and put it on? I'll be there in a minute." She dove into her room to get dressed.

The house was full of the lovely warm smell of roasting lamb; it was tidy and comfortable. David and Peter had built a fire in the lounge several hours earlier to drive out the damp chill.

"In honor of our first real company," David had pronounced, heaping coal on liberally.

"But they'll think we live like this all the time," said Becky, "instead of shivering in the kitchen. You know, those poor soft Americans!"

"I'll tell them we don't," Peter promised, wiping his black hands on his jeans.

"Oh, Peter!" Jen groaned. "You just put those on! Next time *you* can go sit in the Washeteria for an hour and a half."

"It's not as if you have to carry them down to the river and bang them on stones."

Jen snorted. "All right then, you can try it. That place is truly dismal! Full of mums and diapers and little kids and never enough benches. Pink and blue washing machines, half of them out of order. Ugh—depressing!"

"You wring my heart," said David. "I had no idea you hated the laundromat so much. It sounds like cruelty to children."

"I am *sick* of the whole ungrateful lot of you!" retorted Jen with a laugh.

"Even me?" asked Becky.

"Of course. No favorites. And if you want to win back my affection, you can clear off the table in the study and move it in here. We are not going to feed company my good dinner in the kitchen, and the study is hopeless."

"And if you lay a finger on my papers, you risk a father's curse," warned David. "*I'll* clear the table."

"Who said anything about wanting to win back affection?" demanded Peter.

"You can set the table, too," added Jen, ignoring both of them.

Haphazardly, but with everyone pitching in cheerfully, it all got done: the house straightened, the dinner cooking, the table set, and when the doorbell rang just after six, they were all ready—hair brushed, dresses straight, jackets tidy. David ran a critical eye over them, then shook his head.

"Can't find a thing wrong. Nothing short of a miracle."

"Not at all," countered Jen. "It's perfect timing and organization."

"Aren't you going to let them in?" asked Becky.

"Goodness, yes! I almost forgot, I was so dazzled by you." David grinned and opened the front door.

"Hullo, hullo!" cried Mrs. Rhys cheerfully. "Fearful evening, isn't it? *So* nice of you to invite us—we've been looking forward to it. Isn't it lovely and warm in here?" Becky nudged Peter. "It's still so cold for spring, I think. I always forget how long it takes for the chill to leave." She beamed around at them.

David helped her out of her coat. "Come and sit by the fire and I'll get you a glass to warm you inside. Gwyn, good to see you."

"Yes, indeed," said Dr. Rhys quickly before his wife began again. "I just thought I'd bring a little wine for the dinner." He handed the bottle to Peter, who suddenly looked older. "It should be chilled, do you see?" Peter took it off to the kitchen at once.

"Dinner smells simply marvelous!" exclaimed Mrs. Rhys. "Jen, you've been doing more than knitting lately, I shouldn't wonder! There's ever so much more to good cooking than you think when you don't do it yourself, I always say. You must see that your family gives you credit enough!"

"Oh, they're not bad," said Jen. It was impossible to feel nervous with Mrs. Rhys, so solid and comfortable in a shapeless heather-colored knit suit, her peppery hair a bit wild, her eyes very kind.

"Not bad?" exclaimed Becky indignantly. "We do all the nasty parts like cleaning up, after all!"

"Exactly right," approved Mrs. Rhys. "Cooks should never have to wash up as well."

"I don't know about that," said David, handing around glasses of sherry. Even Becky was given a little to celebrate. "We don't want the cooks to get above themselves."

"Don't let him bully you," said Mrs. Rhys to Jen with a twinkle in her eyes. "Did I ever tell you about my first dinner party? The one I gave in Cardiff just after Gwyn and I were married? And wasn't *that* a disaster!" She burst into laughter, and Dr. Rhys looked at her and smiled. She launched into a very funny description of the meal, which they all thoroughly appreciated, Jen especially. The memory of her chicken was no longer painful.

Almost too soon, it was time to put dinner on the table. Mrs. Rhys offered to help, and she and Jen and Becky went off to the kitchen, talking gaily about burned pudding and gummy rice.

In the lounge, David and Dr. Rhys settled into a discussion of work, while Peter sat on the hearthrug, arms wrapped around knees, watching the pulsing coals. He half listened, half dreamed.

"How is your paper progressing then, David?"

"It's coming slowly. Trouble is, every time I begin to research an idea, I turn up more loose ends. I'll have to draw the line pretty soon and finish what I've got."

Dr. Rhys nodded sympathetically. "Just so. One idea leads on to another and more besides, and there is never enough time! I cannot understand people who do not find enough to do with themselves or the ones who do the same research over and over. They never get under the skin of a matter, do you know?"

"Yes, I do. But I've unearthed at least another two or three years' work, just doing my little project on Welsh language. And it's exciting, too, even though Peter doesn't share my enthusiasm."

"What?" asked Peter, catching his name.

"Your battle against learning Welsh," said David mildly.

"Oh, that." He considered a moment. "It's not so bad, I guess."

David merely raised his eyebrows without comment.

"It is good that the language is coming back," said Dr. Rhys. "If it were lost, so much would be lost with it. We cannot afford that. But speaking of things lost, David, I hear from my colleagues that there are still wolves in Wales! That is news indeed."

"I thought you'd be interested in that. Pity the wolf had to be killed, really, but she was a sheep-killer so there wasn't a choice. I rather like thinking there might still be wolves in the Welsh hills, it seems right."

"David," said Dr. Rhys, with a quiet, dry chuckle. "You are beginning to sound like a Welshman."

"Thank you," replied David. "I consider that quite a compliment."

Peter, his cheek resting on his arm, was now listening fully to the two men.

"Your wolf hunt has upset the scientists, you know," Dr. Rhys continued. "The people from the Nature Conservancy have been making inquiries at the Biology Department. They appear quite fussed."

"Have they found out more?"

"No, and I doubt they shall. They would have been much happier if your men hadn't killed the beast and brought it back. They cannot dismiss it as an illusion now that it's been put before them."

"You don't think much of scientists, do you?" remarked David with a smile.

"Oh, they do have their uses, but they are much too serious and do not accept their limitations."

"They won't find more wolves though, will they?" asked Peter. "I mean, it isn't likely, is it?"

"I think it's unlikely myself, but then you can argue that it is unlikely to find only *one* wolf."

"The sheep-killing seems to have stopped," David said. "There's been no trace of another wolf as far as I know. Very peculiar, the whole business."

"Hardly the first time a peculiar thing has happened in Wales, David, and I doubt it will be the last. But then you Americans are not comfortable with magic, are you?"

"Magic?" David sounded skeptical. "That wolf was genuine enough, Gwyn."

"But how did it get here?" asked Peter.

"Ah," said Dr. Rhys. "That is a good question, Peter. Perhaps there is room for belief."

"Now, look—" began David.

"Peter," said Becky, coming through the door with a great steaming bowl of peas and carrots, "you didn't put any hot pads on the table. Hurry, before I drop this!"

Mrs. Rhys brought the potatoes and gravy, and Jen came last with the roast leg of lamb lying in state, crackling brown and gleaming with juices on a bed of fresh parsley, provided the day before by Mrs. Evans.

"It looks wonderful," said David warmly, and Jen glowed, seeing his pride in her. "Gwyn, will you open the wine while I carve? Did anyone think of glasses?"

"I hope you know what a pleasure this is, eating someone else's dinner for a change! And not a better one to be had in Cardiganshire, if looks and smells are to be trusted," pronounced Mrs. Rhys.

When they had all sat down to full plates, Dr. Rhys lifted his glass of wine gravely. "I shall propose a toast if I may. To Jennifer."

Jen blushed hot and couldn't look at anyone.

"Then one to all of us," said Becky, "or can't you do that?"

"Of course, you can," David said. "To all of us!"

"There, it is delicious, what did I say? I shall eat until I can't move," declared Mrs. Rhys, piling her fork.

Jen was kept gratifyingly busy refilling plates for people; everyone had a good appetite. No one but she knew how much fretting and planning had gone into this dinner, which was perhaps just as well. But she caught David's eye for a moment and he smiled; he knew. The dinner meant as much to him as it did to her, and it was a success for them both.

"What were you talking about before dinner?" Becky wanted to know.

"The wolf hunt," said David, "and whether or not it was magic."

"Magic? Do you think it was?" Becky looked from her father to Dr. Rhys.

"I'm a skeptic," said David. "I need convincing. I admit the business was very odd, but I'm not sure I'd go that far."

"But what is your definition of magic, David?" inquired Dr. Rhys.

"There are different kinds, aren't there?" asked Peter.

"Oh, indeed."

"Not just card tricks and magic wands and sawing people in two," said Becky.

"All right," said David, "what do *you* mean?"

"I am afraid that is what we have done to the word, do you see," said Dr. Rhys a little sadly. "We have taken the real magic away from it. To me, it is something very old and not in the least scientific, a feeling, perhaps, most of all. I am not sure I can give you a satisfactory definition. But it is there behind all my work—the ancient beliefs of the country."

"But people still believe in magic," said Becky. "Almost everyone we know here—Mr. Evans and Rhian, my teacher, Hugh-the-Bus and Mr. Williams-the-Shop. Even Gwilym, though he won't come out and say so."

"They're superstitious," Jen corrected. "They don't necessarily believe in magic."

"But they do," objected Becky.

"Why not?" said Mrs. Rhys. "If your magic is there, you're safe because you believe. And if it's not, well, no harm done, is there?"

"That's what Rhian says."

"But one becomes extremely vulnerable when one admits a belief in magic, especially one in my position," said Dr. Rhys. "It makes people uneasy when I speak of it, perhaps because such an admission touches beliefs in them they would rather ignore."

"You mean they believe, but they would rather not," said David with a frown.

"Exactly. Some fight very hard against their own natures. Those who are sure of themselves, whether they believe in magic or do not believe, are the fortunate ones. Your Mr. Evans is comfortable with himself, it sounds. My friend John Owen at the Cardiff Museum is equally comfortable, and he is certain that magic is nonsense."

"Which are you?" asked Peter.

"I must declare myself with Mr. Evans. He is closer to the country than I, and if it stirs, he would know. John Owen and I have had many discussions on this subject and we will not alter one another's minds. Still, we keep trying. I spoke with him last week in fact, at the annual meeting of the Cambrian Archaeological Society. He told me how much he had enjoyed meeting you in Cardiff."

"He *did?*" Becky sounded disbelieving.

And David said, a little too quickly, "The museum is a fascinating place."

"Indeed it is," agreed Dr. Rhys. "I have spent much time there. It is John's life, you know. He is responsible for many of the best pieces in it."

"So I understand," said David.

"Come on, Becky, let's get the dessert," said Jen, and Becky went with her reluctantly. Peter stayed where he was.

"John has a finely developed instinct when it comes to archaeological finds of any importance. He is extremely clever at ferreting them out," Dr. Rhys went on. "And once he is on the track, he will seldom be distracted. He can be a little difficult at times, I think." He placed his wine glass exactly over a spot on the tablecloth. "John is interested in your children, David."

"Oh? Why?"

"Something one of them said while you were at the

museum, I believe. He asked me in particular about Jennifer. He said she had asked some questions?"

"Mmm. Yes, I guess she did."

"He said he never did have a chance to talk to her properly—someone was ill?"

"Tired. It was Becky."

"She is over it now?" asked Mrs. Rhys. "I was just thinking how very well you all look—as though Wales agrees with you!"

"Yes, she's fine. It was a long day, nothing serious."

"Did he ask you—about Jen?" asked Peter urgently. The scene in Cardiff in the museum came back to him with gruesome clarity. He had just begun to think of Dr. Rhys as a real ally. He had forgotten Dr. Owen.

Dr. Rhys sighed and looked at Peter. "I am afraid I may have been careless. I mentioned to John that I knew you were interested in ancient Welsh history and you might indeed have discovered something in this area. I did not think before I spoke and I did not realize how interested he already was."

"He knows," said Peter in a low, hopeless voice.

"John and I are very old friends indeed, but I do not always agree with his methods of dealing with people. He has the best of intentions and the highest principles, you must understand."

Mrs. Rhys snorted. "You and John Owen seldom agree about people, and that's a blessing! That man has no notion of tact!"

"I think," said David, regarding his son, "I don't really know what's going on, do I? It's not the first time this year I've had that feeling."

At that moment Jen and Becky returned with bowls of ice cream and chocolate sauce. "Would you like coffee, or . . ." Jen's voice trailed away as she saw their faces.

"Does everyone know? Have you told?" asked Becky at once.

Peter shook his head.

"Told what?" asked David.

"No," said Dr. Rhys.

"But it doesn't matter," said Peter miserably. "Dr. Owen knows."

"Oh, Peter!" said Becky, distressed.

"Well, David," said Mrs. Rhys calmly, "it seems as if you and I are the only ones who haven't a clue what's happening. But the ice cream is melting, and I would very much like a nice cup of coffee, Jen, love. So would Gwyn."

Jen had been standing stricken, unable to take her eyes from Peter. At Mrs. Rhys's words, she set down the bowls and slid into her chair. "The water's on," she said absently.

"But we don't ever have to see Dr. Owen again, do we?" said Becky. "We don't have to go back to Cardiff."

"I am afraid he is coming here, however," Dr. Rhys said apologetically. "He will be in Aberystwyth next month to deliver a paper at the University and to do some work at the National Library. He asked me to mention that he would like to see you again, especially Jennifer."

"Why me?" asked Jen, alarmed.

"You asked all the questions," Becky reminded her.

Peter said nothing; his hand had gone protectively to his chest in a familiar gesture.

"You need not tell him anything," said Dr. Rhys gently. "It is entirely up to you, do you see, Peter. But he is a very single-minded man, and I wanted to give you a bit of warning."

"Single-minded!" Mrs. Rhys exclaimed. "He runs on one track only, like the steam engine up the Rheidol! And I don't suppose you will tell us what it is you're talking about, Gwyn Rhys?"

"I have already said too much, and I have had no business saying anything at all."

"All right," said David. "I can't pass any kind of judgment on this when I don't know what's going on, but I will say we can't refuse to see Dr. Owen if he wants to talk to us when he comes."

"But, Dad—" began Becky.

"Talk," David repeated firmly. "Talk won't hurt."

Mrs. Rhys was the only one who did justice to the dessert. She declared it the best chocolate sauce she'd ever eaten and continued imperturbably to make pleasant, determined conversation, as if she hadn't noticed the abrupt change in atmosphere. David and Dr. Rhys did their best to help, but the enthusiasm had gone from the evening. They moved back to chairs by the fire, and Jen brought in coffee.

And all the while she sat trying to drink hers, she agonized over Peter's white, expressionless face. She wished he'd come out and say it was her fault, but he was silent. It was pointless to blame anyone now, the whole matter had gone out of their hands and there were no more choices. They would have to talk to David about it, they would have to see Dr. Owen. Peter would lose the Key.

All along, Jen had thought that was what she wanted, and now it was too late, she wasn't sure any more. The four of them: Jen, Becky, Peter, and David had only just begun to grow together, to understand they belonged to one another; they could so easily pull back and lose each other again.

Guiltily, Jen found herself wishing the Rhyses would leave. There was a great deal to be said among the four Morgans.

And the Rhyses must have guessed as much, for neither of them would have a second cup of coffee. As soon as was polite, Mrs. Rhys got up.

"We really must be getting back to Aberystwyth, I suppose. Gwyn has a Department meeting in the morning, first thing. But it was so nice of you to have us. Dinner was lovely! Jen, love, if you stop in next time you're in town, we'll have a cup of tea and I'll give you that knitting wool I mentioned. Just enough for mittens and a hat, I should think. David, where did you put my coat? There, is it? Oh, yes, thank you! We shall have you all come to us again soon. Have you got your gloves, Gwyn? Thank you all again for a delightful evening!"

On the doorstep, Dr. Rhys paused. Jen heard him say, "I am afraid I have upset your son, David. I would not have done it intentionally, please believe. If I can be of any assistance to him, please tell him to ask without hesitation."

"I will. And I'll see you at the meeting tomorrow."

"Yes, of course. Well, good night to you."

Jen, Becky, and Peter cleared away the last of the dishes from the lounge in silence. Jen ran water in the kitchen sink, Peter stacked bowls, and Becky rummaged for a clean dish towel.

"There isn't anything I can say, is there," said Jen at last.

"No," said Peter.

"It's my fault and I'm sorry, even if it doesn't help."

"I know it's your fault," Peter replied, "but it doesn't matter. I want to be mad at you"—he gave her an odd look—"but I can't be. It wouldn't do any good. I just have to figure out what happens next."

"Will you tell Dad?" asked Becky. "There isn't any reason not to now, and he might be able to help."

"How?"

"You won't know till you try me," said David, joining them. "Becky, find another towel, will you? Let's clean up while we go, it might be easier."

It was hard to know how to begin. They washed and dried the glasses before anyone spoke. Then David said, "Can you tell me why you don't want to see Dr. Owen?"

"Because he wants something Peter has," answered Becky.

"Why has he waited? Why hasn't he said so?"

"He isn't absolutely sure I have it," said Peter. "He hasn't seen it."

"Do you have it?"

Peter hesitated, unwilling to take the plunge. "Yes," he admitted at last.

Thoughtfully, David wiped a dirty plate with his towel. "And you're sure he wants this object?"

"Yes."

"Then you must be sure it's important to him; that means it's old. Who else has seen it?"

"Becky and I have," said Jen, drawing lines in the soapy water with her finger.

"Dr. Rhys?"

"Hasn't. But we told him about it," Becky said.

"*I* told him," Jen corrected her. "I wanted Peter to get rid of the thing, so I went to Dr. Rhys about it."

"But it was Peter who found it, not you?"

Jen nodded.

"So you've been minding Peter's business."

Jen swallowed her protest; David had put it bluntly but accurately. This was not the time to try to explain her fears and doubts about the Key and what it did to Peter. There was a more important matter to discuss and Becky went straight to it. "What do we do now?"

"Well, if this thing you've found, Peter, is really something important, why shouldn't you give it to Dr. Owen? I know you don't like him particularly, but this doesn't sound like a question of personal feelings. It's business, and he does know his business. You've heard Dr. Rhys say so."

"It doesn't belong to Dr. Owen."

"Neither do any of the other objects in the museum, if it comes to that. They belong to the country."

"But this one shouldn't be put in the museum. It *can't* be! I found it, not Dr. Owen."

David ran a hand through his hair making it stand on end. For an instant he looked very like Peter. "Do you want to keep it yourself? Is that it?"

"I—I'm not sure. I just know I can't give it to Dr. Owen."

"You've got to give me more than that, Peter. What about you two? What do you think?" He turned on Jen and Becky.

With reluctance Jen said, "It's up to Peter." Becky nodded.

"I thought you were the one who wanted to give the whole game away, Jen."

"I did," said Jen unhappily. "I still do, in a way, but—I was wrong," she finished lamely.

"Do we have to see Dr. Owen?" asked Becky.

"Yes," David replied. "I'm afraid we do. If he wants to talk to us, it would be terribly rude to refuse him."

"But—"

"And it wouldn't be very smart," he continued. "If we did, there'd be no question we were holding something back. Use your head. But, Peter, what I want to know is why you're so sure what you've found is valuable to Dr. Owen? Suppose he looks at it and says it's nice but not worth adding to the museum and lets you keep it? Have you thought of that? You might be worrying over nothing."

"No," said Peter. "I know it's important." Meeting his father's eyes, he saw the question. Peter suddenly longed to try to explain everything right then: all the strange, improbable songs the Key had sung, the places it had shown him, the story it was telling. But, said a small, cold voice in his head, that's exactly what it all is: improbable. And Peter knew, even if he might have been able to find the words, he couldn't risk his father's disbelief. It was too dangerous.

"You only have to see it to know," agreed Becky. "If Peter showed it to you—"

"No!" David spoke so sharply they all looked at him in surprise. "I don't *want* to see it. The less involved I am the better it is for all of us, right now. I don't begin to understand this, but I'm not sure I don't already know too much. I probably should simply confiscate this object and hold onto it until we have an official opinion on it."

Peter turned white and Jen bit her lip.

"Don't," pleaded Becky.

"I still don't understand why I shouldn't," said David quietly.

"Because——" said Becky.

"Please." Peter's voice was oddly stiff. He had just got himself under control. "Please don't take it."

"What do you think I should do?"

The kitchen was dead still, waiting. Then Peter said, "Trust me with it."

"All right," David answered. "I'll make a bargain with you. I will leave you alone until Dr. Owen calls—you have that much time. And if I possibly can, I will leave the decision to you. I can't promise more."

"That's enough," said Peter, suddenly shaky. "I need time."

"It isn't always easy to trust people you love—not because you don't love them enough, but because you don't want them to be wrong and get hurt. But getting hurt is a part of life, and so, thank God, is trust," said David. "I do trust you, all three of you."

The wind funneled up the hill behind Peter, swirling dry leaves and dust, making him sneeze. He had to blow his nose while he waited on the top step of Pen-y-Garth for someone to answer the doorbell. He had just time to stuff the handkerchief back in his jacket pocket when the door opened.

"Well, Peter Morgan! Good afternoon to you!" boomed Mrs. Rhys cheerfully. "This is a lovely surprise! Have you just come by for a visit, or is there something special I can do for you? Or Gwyn perhaps?"

"Yes," said Peter nervously. "I mean, I came to see Dr. Rhys, actually."

"Well, do come in. We can't leave you standing about on the doorstep in this wind. Beastly weather, isn't it? I sometimes doubt we shall ever see the sun again. No matter, we do manage to get through the winter somehow, and the Welsh spring when it does arrive is almost worth all the wind and rain! We certainly enjoyed ourselves last night—your sister is becoming a first-rate cook. Do take off your jacket, won't you? I'll go along and tell Gwyn you're here. Was he expecting you?"

"Oh, no. I don't know—that is—perhaps he's busy?"

Mrs. Rhys laughed. "Bless you, no more than ever! It'll do him good to take his nose out of his books for a while. Just you wait there a moment, I'll be right back."

Peter shifted uncomfortably from one foot to the other, wondering if he'd been right to come. He did have Dr. Rhys's book to return, but he could have mailed it or put it through the letter slot in the front door or asked his father to deliver it for him, instead of interrupting this way. He glanced furtively at his jacket, hung over the back of a hall chair. He could just grab it and . . .

But Mrs. Rhys was back. "He's delighted you've come and says go right in. There, just pop along to his study, won't you?"

No escape now. Clutching *The Mabinogion,* Peter walked down the hall and met Dr. Rhys at the study door.

"How good of you to come," he said formally, as if he'd been expecting Peter. "Come and sit down. What can I do for you?"

"Well, actually," began Peter, "I just came to return your book. I've had it an awfully long time I'm afraid, but I've finished it."

"Have you? Which book was that—? Ah, yes, *The Mabinogion.*" Dr. Rhys nodded. "Was it any use to you? It's rather an outdated translation, I fear, but it has a certain flavor lacking in the more recent ones. And it has excellent notes. Did you find it difficult?"

"A bit. At least until I got used to the language," Peter confessed. "But it's interesting."

"Do you think so? Or are you saying that to please me?" Dr. Rhys gave him a shrewd look. "Of course, it is interesting to me, but I am a bit surprised you find it so. Welsh mythology is a peculiar taste—unlikely in most people your age, I'd have said."

"No, I like it."

"Was there anything in particular that struck you? Anything you'd like to know more about? Perhaps I can help."

Peter gripped the arms of his chair tightly. "It's the story of Taliesin," he said. "I need to know more about it."

Dr. Rhys did not seem surprised. "It is an old story but not one of the original Branches of the Mabinogion. It must have been written down in the eleventh or twelfth century, I suppose, though Taliesin was a sixth-century bard. It's legend, of course, though many of the people in it were, like Taliesin himself, real. It is impossible to say how much of it has a basis in fact."

"But even a legend has to start somewhere."

"Indeed. And the roots of this one are here. There are places not far away that still carry his name—a village to the north . . ."

"Bedd Taliesin."

"Not really his grave, of course, but it is proof that people remember him."

"Where is his grave, do you know?"

Dr. Rhys shook his head. "It has not been found."

"The story has no end," said Peter. "What happened to Taliesin?"

"I cannot tell you. He is said to have spent time in several of the great courts as chief bard: in Urien Rheged's kingdom in the north of England; here in Cardigan with Gwyddno Garanhir, and at Caerleon, the court of King Arthur near Cardiff. He was much honored, but believed to have been turned off his own lands by Maelgwn, the powerful king of Gwynedd. Perhaps he actually does lie near Bedd Taliesin."

Peter was silent for a moment, absorbing this information. It all fit into place, but the end was still missing. "Was there really a flood here?"

"The flooding of Cantrev y Gwaelod, you mean? That is subject to much debate. My colleagues on the Geology Faculty at the University can give you impressive scientific reasons for not believing in the fortified cities. But there is Sarn Cynfelin. Have you seen it?"

"Yes," said Peter eagerly, "I have. It's a strange place."

"It is."

"I found the Key there. I know Jen's told you about it. I found it among the rocks of the dyke, but I didn't know what it was."

"Now you are sure?"

Peter studied Dr. Rhys carefully for any trace of disbelief and found none. "Yes. I know what it is and whose it was, and if I can hang onto it long enough, I think I'll know what I should do with it."

"Which is where I have put my foot wrong." Dr. Rhys sighed. "You do not want to give it up to Dr. Owen, do you?"

"No. It wouldn't matter if it were just an object, but it isn't. It's part of a pattern that isn't finished yet, and if it gets stuck away in a glass case in Cardiff, it never will be finished," said Peter passionately. "There must be a reason why I found it."

"Yes, I think you are right."

"You do?"

"When your sister came to see me, she said you believed you had found Taliesin's harp key. I could not understand how you would know that unless you had in some way been told. It is not a likely thing to believe so deeply in."

"I've seen him with it. Again and again."

"And now you must decide what to do with it."

"I found it," said Peter. "It's mine."

"But is it?"

Peter's eyes clouded for an instant. Had the Key ever really belonged to him? Could he truly say he owned it? He met Dr. Rhys's gaze and said, "No, it isn't. It still belongs to Taliesin. It was never meant to be lost."

"Then you must find a way of giving it back."

"But how?" Dr. Rhys was right, Peter knew it at once, but indeed, how?

"It has told you a great deal already. Do you not think the Key will tell you that also?"

"There isn't much time . . ."

"No, but perhaps there is enough. Harp and tuning key were a bard's chief possessions," Dr. Rhys said quietly. "He was not careless with either one. Certainly Taliesin would not have been. Had you considered that you might be part of this pattern you speak of? You are meant to carry the Key?"

"But I haven't done anything with it," Peter protested.

"You yourself say the pattern is not completed yet. Be patient. I am sure you will know what is to be done with the Key, Peter."

Their eyes met and held—an American schoolboy and a middle-aged Welsh scholar. Between them was a moment of perfect understanding.

"Do you want to see it?" Peter asked, reaching for the chain.

"Indeed, I want to very much," said Dr. Rhys shaking his head sadly, "but you must not show me. I would be able to identify it if I saw it, and then I should have no choice but to make you give it to John Owen."

"But you do believe me?"

"Yes. But a sixth-century harp key—one that may have belonged to Taliesin himself? That is a national treasure, Peter Morgan. Nothing like it has yet been found."

"I'm sorry," said Peter, "because I would like to show you, but I see what you mean."

"And I am sorry. But," Dr. Rhys brightened a little, "would you like some tea? It's time for a cup, I think. You can tell me what you made of the rest of *The Mabinogion!*"

16

A Homecoming

To the East the dawn sky was bright with the expectation of sun. It had rained hard during the night and the traveler had taken shelter in a tumbledown hut, already several miles behind him. His swinging stride carried him along a road that was little more than rutted mud with chips of puddle caught between the furrows, reflecting the April sky. He traveled light, his cloak flung back, his harp on his shoulder, a small skin pouch at his belt, his only other possession, the silver key, hung about his neck on its chain.

The road led downward, winding out of the hills toward the sea, and the man's step was quick and sure upon it. Somewhere along his way, he had been joined by a scruffy little brown dog with nothing better to do than follow, and they had become companions.

The air was sweet; rich with bird song and the smell of waking earth seasoned with the sea and the shrilling of gulls.

Taliesin passed huts where the inhabitants were just stirring, rolling out half-asleep to begin the day's chores: work in the vegetable patches, look to the beasts, cut wood. And Taliesin's eyes grew bright with remembering . . . it was so many years ago that he had been a boy in such a hut. People paid little mind to him as he walked by.

Peter knew the country, too. He felt he had dreamed it once, that it was old in his memory though the Key had never shown it to him before. There were no familiar details or landmarks, but there was a sense of home, and he caught the joy in Taliesin's heart. Taliesin himself sang a gay, infectious walking-song.

There were a great many fascinating smells for the little dog to investigate on both sides of the road. Every now and then he shook himself away from them and raced to catch up with his new man, determined not to be left behind.

Whenever he was wished good-day, Taliesin broke his song and called back in a voice that gladly affirmed the morning's goodness. The Way he traveled was old even in Taliesin's time. It had been known to the Dark Folk before the Romans, and to the Legions of the Eagle that had dared the wildness of the hills and forests and magic; most of those Legions had followed the Way into Cymru but never home again.

Taliesin left it only once, to climb a smooth, bare hill that rose on the right. From its summit the world spread out to the west: league upon league of wind-scoured sea, a vastness of fierce blue sky without a flaw in it, and a jagged scar of beach running as far as could be seen north to south. In that moment of revelation, Peter saw with Taliesin's eyes and ached for the unspoiled freedom: no roads, no bungalows or caravans, no shops or crawling lines of traffic, no footprints on the sand. The world was new and beautiful.

On the crown of the hill stood a circle of weathered gray stones, grouped around one tall standing stone, which pointed like a finger to the north, to Maelgwn's fortress, Dyganwy, built on the highest of two hills above the River Conwy. Although at the northernmost end of Gwynedd, Dyganwy was at the center of the most powerful of the Cymric kingdoms. And even it had been built years after the gaunt stone had been hauled erect on this hill. Peter's sense of time had no meaning here.

Taliesin stood next to the stone now, as straight but not as tall, and lifted his arms to the sun as it rose silently above the eastern hills, flooding the country with gold, casting shadows from the stones.

"I am home!" cried Taliesin.

"I must admit, Jen, I'm very glad your aunt and uncle are three thousand miles away," said David, "and that·I don't have to try to explain any of this to them in person. I can't see either of them swallowing it."

Jen grinned at her father. "Aunt Beth would probably declare you an unfit parent."

But David's face was grave. "I'm afraid that's not funny. There are times when I wonder myself. It's quite possible that I've made a very serious mistake with Peter, you know, and if I have, he could be in bad trouble. I'm not at all happy about his involvement with this object of his. It seems to have a terrific hold over him."

Jen nodded soberly. "I know. I was afraid of it—in fact I still am. He's absolutely serious about it, it's changed his whole attitude. When I first came, the only thing he wanted was to go back to Amherst, now I'm not sure he wants that anymore."

"I haven't done much to help, have I? I ought to have seen long ago that there was more than stubbornness in Peter's behavior, but I didn't look at him hard enough. I left you and Becky to cope, and that wasn't fair. I'm·sorry."

It was a straightforward apology, and it both embarrassed and pleased Jen. David was speaking to her without restraint, as he would to an adult.

They stood leaning against the railing at the south end of the Aberystwyth Prom, the sudden green bulk of Constitution Hill above them. Only a few students had wandered down this far; Jen and David were essentially alone. She had met him at the University after his Monday class and he'd suggested the walk.

All her life, Jen reflected now, she had truly believed that with age came wisdom; that when she finally grew up all the complexities she wrestled with would straighten themselves out for her and she would be able to deal with life confidently, with perfect assurance. She had only to wait.

But it wasn't so. Her father, who ought to know all the answers by this time, had just told her that he, too, was still groping. Oddly, Jen felt closer to him at this moment than she ever had before; he was as human as she and as much in need of reassurance and faith. Was he better at hiding it than she, or had she simply not noticed before?

"What are you thinking so hard about?" asked David with a smile.

"I was just wondering what other people worry about," Jen answered. "People like the Evanses and Dr. Rhys and Mrs. Davies."

"Lots of things, I imagine, some important, some not." He hesitated, choosing his words carefully. "Jen, will you give me an honest answer? Do you think there's something the matter with Peter? I know he's had a hard year; I expected more of him than I had any right to, and perhaps he hasn't been able to handle it. You've seen more of him than I have—he told you about this business he's gotten into long before he had to tell me. My own fault. What do you think?" It was a hard question for him to ask. Jen saw it in his face.

And it wasn't easy to answer. She needed far more time to sort out all the changes she'd come through in the past months, but her father needed an honest answer, and she had to give it as best she could.

"I wouldn't be sure," she said carefully, "if it weren't for Becky. There's nothing at all wrong with her, except what's wrong with the rest of us—we still miss Mother, we get homesick, we get cross with each other. But Becky believes Peter.

When he first told me this story about a key he'd found on the beach and the peculiar power it had, I thought he'd made it up. He was unhappy and lonely and he needed something to do with himself. Then Becky got into it and now Dr. Rhys as well. I don't know any more. But if you mean do I think Peter's sick—no."

"What about this—key, did you call it? No, I don't want to know what it is, I've told you that. I want to know what Peter claims it does. Finding it has affected him a good deal, hasn't it?"

"Well, yes," said Jen uncomfortably.

David looked at her hard. "You don't want to talk about it, do you?"

Jen sighed. "I can't, Dad. I really wouldn't know what I was talking about. Peter's story sounded so impossible when he first told me—it still does—there didn't seem to be any question of believing him. I didn't."

"But?"

"Peter's one thing, but now there're Becky and Dr. Rhys. *They* do believe him." She hesitated, then said, "If you want to know what the key does, you've got to ask one of them. They're sure, I'm not."

"Still, you think Peter ought to be left alone. You think I can trust him to be responsible?"

Jen nodded.

"Does Peter still want to go home so much?"

"I don't think so. It doesn't seem important to him right now."

"Peter has got some impressive allies, Jen: Becky, Gwyn Rhys—even Mr. Evans in a way. Now you." David sighed. "I promised I'd wait until Dr. Owen arrives and I won't break my word to Peter. I've just got to hope he can sort this out himself, I don't want to see him hurt any more than he has been. But" —he turned to Jen with a rueful smile—"come on, I'll buy you an ice cream. It's time we started back to Borth."

At the far end of the Prom, the amusement pier and the

old University building were hazy in the afternoon light. The windows of all the little guest houses and hotels that lined the bay shone gold in the west-slanting sun, above them a jumble of slate roofs and chimneys.

"I've gotten to like Aberystwyth," David remarked thoughtfully. "It's a funny place, but I'll miss it."

"What do you mean?" asked Jen.

"In another two months the University year will be over. I've got to decide what we do next. Beth expects us back, Amherst College expects me back, and you three have school. There isn't a lot of time left."

"Then you have decided we go back," said Jen flatly.

"I suppose so. The University's offered to keep me on if I want to stay, though, and I have to give them an answer in the next two weeks. I should just tell them no and be done with it, but I've been putting it off."

"*Ych y fi.*" Without thinking, Jen used one of Mrs. Evans's expressions and was startled to hear her father laugh. Then she joined him.

Becky and Gwilym met Peter walking slowly along the sea wall toward Ynyslas at the end of the afternoon. They had come from watching ducks and were hungry and cheerful; Becky saw Peter before he noticed them.

"Hey, Peter!"

"Oh. Hullo." He smiled absently. "See much?"

"The usual sea ducks," Gwilym replied. "Nothing very exciting."

"We're going home for tea—come with us?" Becky offered.

But Peter shook his head. "I'll be in later. And you needn't worry, I left a note for Dad! I'm just going to the end of the wall."

"Jen's got cream buns."

"Save me one." Peter passed them and kept walking. He

heard Becky and Gwilym start on, Becky beginning to hum *Men of Harlech* and Gwilym joining her with a recently discovered bass. Peter smiled to himself. He would have gone back with them if it hadn't seemed more important to be alone right now and ready for whatever came next. Dr. Rhys had given him the confidence he needed to hang onto the Key and trust his own judgment.

The lights were coming on in the houses across the road, the sea was merging with the twilight. There was a girl walking a dog on the sand. Then sky, sea wall, girl and dog suddenly fell to pieces before him and rearranged themselves in a new pattern, like colored glass in a kaleidoscope, catching Peter off balance for an instant. The voice of the Key came to him, cold and somber. Peter slid off the wall and leaned against it, planting his feet firmly in the sand, then gave himself up to the song.

Clouds, thick and dark, massed in the sky, and out of them came the steadily rising grumble of thunder. Shadow rolled across the sea, turning it the color of steel, and the wind knocked the tops off the waves leaving them white and jagged. The tiny village of Llanfair had been built to withstand storms. The dwellings were thick-walled and thatched double to hold out the rain and salt spray, and they claimed whatever shelter they could in hollows and against the sand hills, their backs to the sea.

As soon as a hut was deserted, the weather began to destroy it, working between the stones, tearing at the roof, driving sand through the door. It was such a hut Taliesin had returned to. When he had been a boy called Gwion he had lived here with his mother and father and eight brothers and sisters. He had been taken from them by an old blind man when he was just twelve and set upon the path he had followed ever since. The hut was long empty, the family gone: taken by disease, war, new masters, or husbands. The fireplace was neglected, the one small room quite empty.

But Taliesin knew the place as surely as the storm petrels know where to return each spring after the winter at sea. He made no attempt at first to intrude on the people of Llanfair, nor did they disturb him. They were curious, they sent speculative glances his way, but they were silent. Taliesin shared his homecoming with only the small brown dog he called Hu. They slept together at night, wrapped in the man's travel-stained cloak, and by day they scavenged the windy beach, or sat quietly among the dunes, or climbed the hills.

One day passed into another and Taliesin was at peace with his solitude, but he had not gone unnoticed. The boy Gwion had been one of many like himself, the bard Taliesin was not. And when this storm came, it brought more with it than wind and rain. It brought riders down from the north, out of Dyganwy, at their head Maelgwn himself, of whom it was written that he was "strong in arms, but stronger still in what kills the soul . . ." He was a great bear of a man with a black beard, unruly black hair and wild eyebrows above eyes that were hard as flint. The men who followed him would follow him to Arawn, Lord of Hell, if commanded and, according to many, were bound to in the end.

They rode up to the hut and Maelgwn's voice bellowed through the growl of thunder: "Taliesin! It is Maelgwn Gwynedd who summons you!"

"I am here." He appeared in the doorway, his legs slightly apart, his hands resting lightly on his hips.

Maelgwn dismounted, waving his men to keep their horses.

"Why have you come here?" he demanded.

"This is my home," replied Taliesin mildly. "I've come home."

A cold smile touched Maelgwn's mouth, twisting it oddly. "You do not belong in Gwynedd, Taliesin. I should have thought you would know that without my telling you."

"I do no harm to anyone here, Maelgwn."

"You dare say that to me? You, who came to Gwynedd as a thief years past and stole what was rightfully mine with your treachery? Do you truly believe you could return unchallenged? If so, you are more of a fool than I had thought."

"I stole nothing. Nor did I trick you. It was you who went south and stole from Gwyddno Garanhir. You agreed to the contest I proposed, Maelgwn."

The king's tangled brows drew together; he was not used to being answered back. "You!" he roared, pointing at Taliesin. "You are not welcome in Gwynedd!"

"I only want to be left to myself here in the village where I was born. I ask only this hut and the chance to make a bare living. I am old, Maelgwn, I do no harm. I want my peace."

"You shall have none here! I will not permit you to stay in my country!"

Taliesin sighed. "I can do you no injury."

"Your presence here offends me! I am not stupid, I do not forget. You wronged me, Taliesin, and I do not forgive. Ceretic!"

"Here, Sire." A long, dour-looking man dismounted and came to stand beside Maelgwn.

"Take this man and—" the King paused and looked hard, consideringly, at Taliesin. "Put him in an empty coracle as he stands there and set it loose on the sea. I will have no more to do with him, I will waste no more time here! I do not wish to set eyes on him again, do you understand?"

Ceretic inclined his head and signaled for two more men.

"I am sorry." Taliesin's voice was sad and resigned. "You have no need to wish me ill."

Maelgwn turned on his heel, leaped astride his nervous horse and cut hard with the hazel switch he carried in his belt. The horse bounded away, followed by all but the three men who had dismounted.

Taliesin raised his arms to show he had no weapon and

meant no resistance and went with them. The brown dog, Hu, stuck to him like a shadow. The men did not allow Taliesin to take either his harp or his cloak, and as he left the village this time, he did not look back.

One of Jen's "assignments" from her father during the spring and summer terms was to keep a journal. "You need practice writing," he told her. "You've got to keep at it or you get rusty. And I think you'll be glad later if you keep a journal now."

Jen began by doubting it. She found it a chore to think of things worth writing down at first, but gradually it got easier. She looked around herself and noticed details she would otherwise have missed; she thought harder about people and the country, the weather, herself, her family.

David trusted her to keep the notebook; he never asked to see it, but Jen learned to discuss parts of it with him. The distance between them dwindled and they could talk. There were still questions Jen knew her father couldn't answer for her, and she often missed her mother. But the excruciating, immediate pain of loss was gone, instead she felt a gentle ache of longing.

Suddenly Jen had grown up. She couldn't deny it whether she wanted to or not, and she needed time to herself to understand her new feelings. She hoped fervently that she would know enough to be able to help Becky when the time came. In spite of her self-sufficiency, Becky would need help.

The journal gained importance, for in it Jen could put her most private thoughts in some kind of order that made sense.

With the journal, the house, and her other schoolwork, Jen's days were comfortably busy. She didn't mind being alone while the others were off at school and University, but she was glad to see them when they came back at night. It was good to sit around the kitchen table, eating supper or doing homework with Becky, Peter, and David.

But the routine of life at Bryn Celyn was abruptly interrupted the second week of term when Peter appeared at the
breakfast table Monday in his bathrobe and slippers.

"You'll be terribly late!" exclaimed Becky. Then, "You
look *awful!*"

David glanced up from his bowl of cornflakes and saw
Peter's puffy, red face and running nose. "Good lord, what are
you coming down with? You do look awful! Come here—have
you got a fever?"

"I feel terrible. I'b dnot goig to school." Peter sneezed
violently.

David held him at arm's length, his hand on Peter's forehead. "You're hot. Are you sick to your stomach?"

"Dno. Dnot yet."

"Orange juice," said Jen automatically, reaching for the
pitcher. The Morgan family doctor had always said to drink
quarts and quarts of orange juice, no matter what was the matter with any of them. Orange juice was linked in Jen's mind
with every kind of ailment from a broken collarbone to mea-
sles and influenza.

"Dno!" cried Peter, looking almost pale. "I couldn't—
don't want anythig!"

"Back to bed," ordered David. He checked his watch.
"Jen, if you can hold the fort, I'll go and call Mr. Griffith and
tell him not to expect Peter in school for a few days. I'll check
with Dr. Pugh as well. It looks like a cold, but I want to be
sure it isn't worse."

"I guess we're lucky this is the first," said Jen, resigned.

"You could get Mrs. Davies to help," suggested Becky.
"She'd be glad to give you all kinds of advice, I'm sure."

"Thanks a lot," said Jen tartly. "It may come to that, but
not yet! Mothers get stuck with all kinds of dirty work,
don't they?"

Becky and David went. Jen put the kitchen in order and
made a second piece of toast for herself, then looked in on

Peter. She'd always hated nurse games when she was a little girl, and it was no different now. Except that Peter was really sick and she had to look after him, but she hadn't any idea what she ought to do for him.

"Peter?" She spoke to the long thin lump on his bed. The curtains were drawn across the window, making a dull gray patch on the wall. "Do you want anything?"

"Dno."

"Are you warm enough?"

"I don't want a *thig*. By head aches."

"Well, if you're sure. I'll be in the house if you change your mind." Jen withdrew thankfully and went upstairs to make her bed. But Peter stayed very much on her mind and she worried about him. He so seldom got sick.

David was home early and he brought Dr. Pugh, a small, dark Welshman with—Peter complained later—very cold hands. He poked about at Peter, made him open his mouth— "Wiyde, yess, wiyde, please"—and took his temperature. He wrote a few words on a prescription blank that might or might not have been in Welsh and handed it to David.

"Not to worry, Mr. Morgan. Keep him quiet for a few days and he will be right enough. Only a cold, it is." He added cheerfully, "Infectious, you know."

"Yes," said David. "Thank you."

"If either of you so much as sneezes, I won't be responsible," Jen warned when Dr. Pugh had gone. "One's bad enough."

"It could be you, of course," Becky pointed out reasonably.

"Becky, go on down to the chemist and get this filled, will you please?" said David.

"Ab I goig to die?" asked Peter morosely from his bedroom.

"Not likely," David replied briskly. "I wonder where you caught it?"

Peter spent an uncomfortable night. The pills Dr. Pugh prescribed did help clear his head and he could breathe more easily, but he was hot and restless. He was oppressed by an unexplained foreboding. Something was about to happen that he wouldn't like at all, and he could not go to sleep no matter how hard he tried. He was awake, staring into the darkness above his head when David came in on his way to bed.

"Can't sleep?"

"No." Peter expected his father to say good-night and go up to bed, but instead David came in and sat on the edge of the bed. The light from the kitchen cut a bright triangle on the floor.

"I have masses of germs," said Peter tentatively.

"I don't doubt it!" David gave a chuckle. "It's one of the hazards of being a parent." He sat in silence and Peter began to wonder if David expected him to say something.

"I've been thinking," said David at last. Peter waited, wary. "Thinking about next year and this year and whether it's been worth the trouble. I've been offered a contract at the University for next year. I've told Jen about it."

"Here?" asked Peter. David's words were unexpected.

"Mmm. It's too bad in a way because I'll have to turn them down, but it's nice to have been asked back."

Four months earlier Peter would have been giddy with relief—the idea of another year in Borth would have filled him with horror. But the relief wasn't there now, he was disappointed instead. "Why? I mean, why should we go back?" he said hiding it carefully.

"You of all people should ask?" In the half-light from the open door, David's face looked amused. "For all the sensible reasons, of course. My job, your school, our house, Aunt Beth and Uncle Ted. We can't just leave them over there indefinitely. I doubt Amherst will keep my position open another year, and you three cannot afford to miss any more school—your education's too important to play with."

"But we've been going to school here—Becky and I have," protested Peter.

David nodded. "And how much have you gotten out of it? Becky's managing, but I'm worried about you, Peter. Oh, I'm not blaming you for reacting to it the way you have, it just hasn't worked very well. Like Jen, you'll survive missing a year, but not two. Perhaps if I'd been more help, but it's no good rehashing that. You may have been right when you asked what good it would do you to learn Welsh! But I hate to think the year's been a complete mistake."

Peter said with difficulty, "It hasn't been. It's been hard."

"A lot harder than it needed to have been, you mean." David's smile was rueful.

"Have you made up your mind?"

"What do you think about it?"

"But have you made up your mind?" It was terribly important for Peter to know.

David got up slowly. "Almost. I don't think there's much choice. See if you can get some sleep, it's after eleven."

Peter was allowed to sleep late the next morning; the rest of his family crept carefully around the kitchen getting breakfast. It was raining and dark, and everyone felt subdued, in any event.

Jen saw Becky and David off, then sat down at the cluttered breakfast table to read *David Copperfield,* part of her reading list. She felt not the least compulsion to clear up. She simply pushed the debris off a small square of tabletop and got herself a fresh mug of cocoa. She wished Mrs. Davies would look in now and see her being deliberately negligent, then changed her mind and wished instead for Aunt Beth. A smile caught her mouth; she would say to Aunt Beth, "Look here, I'm perfectly capable of coping with all this, you know"—an airy wave of the hand—"but I don't *choose* to right now! I'll do it when I'm ready, and I'll get all of it done besides." The idea pleased her absurdly.

What, Jen wondered, did Aunt Beth really make of all this anyway? It was impossible to tell from the letters she sent, which were meant for the whole family, full of news of friends and the college, the weather and the town. Did Aunt Beth really believe her niece could manage a house for her family? Would she ever believe that undomestic Jen was actually learning to cook successfully?

There were moments when Jen herself scarcely believed it, when she would suddenly remember that Amherst was home and that home was very far away. She would see again the country as she had first seen it, strange, wild, inaccessible —unknown—and be filled with an irrational panic, incredulity that she had asked to take this on!

But at other times, just now for instance, she was aware of a deep new satisfaction. It *was* hard, but she could handle it. Her father had allowed her to learn this for herself, and she was grateful.

Jen tucked one of her feet under her and wrapped her hands around the mug for warmth. What if they hadn't come? What would it be like if they'd all stayed in Amherst instead?

There was a crash behind her that made her jump and spill the cocoa. Peter had flung open his door. "Did you *have* to—" Jen began, but he interrupted.

"It's gone! I've lost it! It isn't here anymore!"

Jen turned quickly at the grief and desperation in her brother's voice. His eyes were wide and staring, his face white. In his right hand he clutched an object—the Key—its chain dangling.

She stood up, afraid. "What's gone, Peter?" She wondered if he'd been having a nightmare and wasn't quite awake.

Slowly Peter looked from Jen to the Key and back. "It's gone," he repeated, his voice flat. "There's nothing to it anymore. It's just a piece of metal."

"What? Did you have a dream?"

He shuddered convulsively. "No! It's never been a dream,

any of it!" The knuckles of his right hand were white. "Oh, Jen!" he said suddenly, and she was horrified to see his face crumple. Tears fell soundlessly down his cheeks.

The shock of seeing her brother cry hit Jen hard. The first step toward him was almost impossible to take, but then she was there, her arm around him.

"Hey, come on," she said gently, steering him to a chair. "Don't cry—it'll only be worse. Tell me what happened." She crouched beside him, watching his face. Great wet splashes dropped onto his clenched hands and bathrobe as he struggled to calm himself. Jen waited helplessly.

At last he took a great, sobbing breath and straightened his shoulders. "I couldn't help it," he said.

Jen nodded, still at a loss.

"Can I tell you what happened? I don't think—I mean I want to tell you."

Without answering, she pulled a chair over and sat down in front of him, close enough to touch.

"I know you don't believe in this." He opened his hand. The Key had left red, angry marks on it from being held so hard. Their eyes met over it.

"Please," Jen said.

Peter gave a little nod. "I knew it had to finish," he said quite calmly. "As soon as I figured out what the Key was doing. It's been telling a story from beginning to"—he hesitated—"end. I'm still not sure what I'm meant to do about it, but there is a purpose. It scared me at first, because I didn't know what was happening to me. Everything would be perfectly normal one minute and the next I wouldn't know where I was. You know."

"Yes. You acted as if you were daydreaming. You've had all of us worried."

"But I wasn't daydreaming at all. I did when I first came here—I kept wishing I was back in Amherst and I'd imagine what I'd be doing. Then I found the Key, and I began to see

people and places and things happening that I'd never seen before. I couldn't have—they're all old, I mean centuries old. Always there was one person; the Key I found belonged to him in
that time, I've seen him with it."

"Taliesin," said Jen softly.

Peter looked up sharply to see if she were serious, then
away again, satisfied. "Taliesin. You've seen him, too, I was
sure you had that day on Foel Goch."

Jen was perfectly still, not wanting to accept this, unable
to deny it.

"Everything that you and Dad and Becky, and every
one else has seen—the coracle, the lights on the Bog, the wolf,
the *hafod*, fits into the story of Taliesin. They were all here
once." Peter's voice was urgent, he was willing her to believe
him. "I talked to Dr. Rhys about it. I went to see him, Jen, the
day after the dinner party."

"You never said."

"I couldn't."

"Did you show him the Key?"

"He wouldn't let me. He wanted to see it, but he said the
same thing Dad did—that if he saw it he'd have to make me
give it up."

"Didn't he think you should?"

"He believes me. And if I'm right, it doesn't belong in a
museum anywhere. He knows that, too."

"But what'll you do with it, Peter?"

His face clouded. "I wish I knew. I thought it would tell
me—that would be the end of the story. It has somehow to get
back to Taliesin. But it can't now—it's gone dead. It won't tell
me any more."

Jen listened to Peter. She struggled to open her mind to what
he was telling her, to believe the unbelievable. He had been
lying in bed, halfway between sleeping and being awake,
when the room had faded around him. It was replaced by

empty gray sea; ragged, restless waves and a biting wind. He saw a tiny dark spot out on the water, rising and falling without direction. It was a battered skin coracle, and in it sat Taliesin with Hu pressed hard against his legs, shivering. The wind carried a high wailing song, full of aching and sadness and loss. Endlessly it seemed, the coracle tossed about, unguided save by the wind and tide carrying it helplessly south.

From the wave crests sometimes, to the east, the dark line of shore was visible, out of reach, but within sight. Maelgwn's men had taken him far from Llanfair, out along the great peninsula that pointed west like a finger toward the Kingdom of the Irish. They took him to Trwyn y Gwyddol, and set him in the coracle and launched him on the sea. No blood was shed, no one died on the soil of Gwynedd, and indeed the King himself did not know what had become of the bard Taliesin, though his guess might be a good one.

For two days and nights Taliesin and Hu shared the little boat, and they were driven down along the wild rim of Cymru, out of Gwynedd. As the third day broke, the wind rose and the sea roiled in fury. Rain came slashing out of the low gray clouds. Thunder rolled about the hills, crashing against its own echoes, and lightning cracked the sky. In the midst of chaos the coracle was thrown violently at the shore, in amongst the rocks where it smashed on the ruined walls of Cantrev y Gwaelod, at Sarn Cynfelin. Man and dog were flung into the waves and left to swim as best they could to the edge of shingle under the cliffs.

Here Peter stopped, his eyes far away, his face taut.

At last Jen asked, "Were they—did they—drown?"

"It was like a nightmare you can't wake up from. It was *real!*"

"But what happened to them?"

"I don't know."

"It couldn't just stop there. You must have seen."

"No." Peter held the Key cupped in his two hands, like

water. "I saw them in the water, trying to stay up. I lost sight of Hu—I'm not sure what became of him. Then it was all gone. I was back in my room and the Key was dead. It doesn't even feel the same anymore. I've read the story, Jen. I know he didn't drown. He came back here to live, but that doesn't help. I just don't know what I'm supposed to do!" He sounded desperate. Jen ached for him. She knew how hard it was not to know the answers.

"But if it's dead," she said carefully, "couldn't you give it to Dr. Owen? It wouldn't really matter, would it?"

"But it *does!* It still belongs to Taliesin and he must have it back. He lost it there in the sea and I've found it thousands of years later, but it connects the two of us somehow. If I give it to Dr. Owen, then the whole thing might just as well never have happened."

Jen saw again the rows of neatly labeled brooches and coins and the beautiful silver bowl and knew in her heart Peter was right. "But how can you give it back to someone who's been dead for centuries? Unless . . ." Bedd Taliesin, a pile of stones on a bare hillside, a grave, a burial cairn.

Peter knew what she was thinking. He shook his head. "That's not the right place. It's not really his grave. I'd have known if it was, and besides Gwilym said it's much too old to be."

"So you're stuck."

"I feel awful. Sort of used up."

"You ought to be in bed," said Jen. "It won't help at all if you get sicker. Do you want some cocoa or toast or something? You're probably hungry."

Peter was about to refuse when he changed his mind. "Maybe cocoa." He got up and went to his bedroom door.

"Peter?"

He stopped with his back to Jen. "What?"

She felt awkward. "I'll bring your cocoa."

He nodded.

Then quickly before she could stop herself, "I'm not sure I can ever believe in the Key. But—but I believe *you.*"

The tension went out of him, and unbelievably, he smiled at her. "Thanks," he said simply.

17

Cannwyl Corph

AFTER THE INITIAL SHOCK of loss had worn
off, Peter accepted the end of the singing and of Taliesin with
remarkable calm. As he had told Jen, he knew it would end
eventually, and he was still sure the story wasn't finished. Jen,
of course, knew what had happened, and it didn't take Becky
long to guess. She was, as usual, sensitive to all changes in her
family. It was hard to tell what David noticed for he said
nothing more about Peter's "object."

Peter's cold settled in to run a normal, irritating course.
He was quite content to spend a week quietly convalescing at
Bryn Celyn. He had a great deal to think about now that he
was no longer caught up in the Key. For the first time since
he'd found it, he could step back from it and consider the
whole picture it had shown him.

At teatime Wednesday, Gwilym arrived—he had a
happy facility for choosing teatime for his visits, Jen noticed
—with an old wooden chess board under his arm and a macintosh pocket full of chessmen. "I thought you might like to
play," he said rather tentatively to Peter. "Have you before?"

Peter shook his head and Jen looked skeptical. "You

won't get to first base trying to teach him that, Gwilym, it isn't his sort of game."

"First base?" Gwilym repeated, puzzled.

"Baseball," said Peter helpfully. "My poor sister can't tell the difference between baseball and chess—she's quite hopeless that way. Show me what you do."

And to Jen's surprise, he and Gwilym spent the next two hours hunched over the board in fierce concentration, arguing amicably over legal and illegal moves and pawns and rooks.

It was after six when Jen reminded them it was dinnertime, the table needed to be set, and Mrs. Davies would soon be breathing fire if Gwilym didn't get home for his meal. The chessboard was retired to the top of the fridge.

"Chess?" said David, when he saw it there. "Who's been playing?"

"Gwilym's teaching Peter," explained Becky.

"I used to play chess in college. Haven't played in years, but I used to enjoy it."

"It's a pretty good game," said Peter noncommitally.

The supper dishes were dried and put away, but David seemed reluctant to leave the kitchen. He glanced at the chess board, then at Peter. "You wouldn't be interested in another game, would you?" he asked finally.

"Well," said Peter, "I wouldn't mind."

So they set up again, and Jen shook her head in quiet wonder. It was a pleasant, domestic, incongruous picture somehow. At nine she had to drag Becky out of the kitchen and push her toward bed. David and Peter played on.

In a few minutes Becky returned in pajamas and bathrobe.

"Becky—" Jen began warningly.

"I just came to say good-night," said Becky innocently.

David set down a knight he'd just claimed from Peter and smiled at her. "High time, too! Good lord, I've got a quiz to think up for my Lit. class tomorrow—I had no idea it was so late! Sorry, Peter, but I have got to go do some work. What do you say to a return match this weekend sometime? I'll play with you until you start winning!"

"It's Gwilym's set," said Peter, packing the men away in an empty biscuit tin. He didn't look at his father. "If he'll let me borrow it, all right."

"Good." David got up to leave, then stopped. "I've got to warn you," he said reluctantly. "We're almost sure to have a visitor this weekend."

"Who?" asked Becky. Jen and Peter looked at each other, already certain they knew.

"Dr. Owen."

Becky made a face.

"He's in Aber and he's talked to Gwyn Rhys about seeing us. Gwyn says he'll probably get hold of me tomorrow, and if he wants to come, I thought I'd invite him to tea to get this over with. No good scowling at me, Becky, I'm no more anxious to have Dr. Owen come than you are, but we do owe him the courtesy to hear him at least."

"The enemy in our camp," said Jen.

"We only ever met the poor man once, you know," protested David mildly. "He may not be as bad as he seemed in Cardiff. Everybody has off days."

"He'll be as bad," Becky predicted glumly. "You think so, too."

"Then I don't set you a very good example, do I?" David sighed. "Beth would be very annoyed with me. Still, the four of us ought to be able to manage being polite to one Welshman for a couple of hours over tea."

Peter was silent.

Dr. Owen did indeed want to see the Morgans. The next evening, David announced that he had invited Dr. Owen to tea at three-thirty on Saturday because the man had expressed a special interest in talking to all of David's children. There was no escape.

"Not only is he someone I'd rather not see," mourned Jen to Becky after supper, "but he'll ruin a whole day of the weekend. If it weren't for Dr. Owen, we could be up at the farm or on the beach somewhere instead."

"I know." Becky nodded soberly. "But we can use him as an excuse to buy all kinds of special stuff for tea—cream buns and tarts and rock cakes—and we can buy enough for a picnic Sunday."

"Good idea," said Jen. "We'll have an orgy. The thing *I* can't understand, though," she added frowning, "is why Dr. Rhys likes him."

Jen, Peter, and Becky were all sitting around the kitchen table doing homework. Peter had been very quiet; he was writing an essay he'd missed during the week, but now he set down his pen deliberately.

"Dr. Owen doesn't think the way we do," he said slowly. "He puts things in a different order—what's at the top of my list is at the bottom of his. Reasons and facts are much more important to him than feelings. I think he and Dr. Rhys connect because they're both involved in the same kind of work: history and Wales and Welsh language. But you can like a person without agreeing with him."

"You sound as if you're making excuses for Dr. Owen," Becky accused. "You haven't gotten soft about him, have you?"

"Not really. I just think Dr. Rhys was right when he said Dr. Owen has good intentions. I don't believe he puts all those objects in the museum for himself; he does it for the country."

"That sounds suspiciously charitable coming from you," said Jen. "After all this fuss, you aren't simply going to hand him the Key, are you?"

"I thought you wanted me to."

"Not any more," said Jen firmly. "We've all gone too far to give it up now."

Becky grinned delightedly. "Hooray!" she said softly. Then, "You can't give it to him now that it's all four of us together, Peter!"

"I don't intend to." Peter's serious face suddenly brightened. "I think it's going to be pretty awful tomorrow, you know!"

Peter was right—it was awful all day. The tension in Bryn Celyn Saturday morning was electric—everyone was nervous and irritable. Jen flung herself feverishly into housecleaning, giving Becky and Peter orders until they rebelled and went down to Borth to get out from under her. David stayed shut in his study, presumably hard at work on his paper.

Dr. Owen was punctual; at exactly three-thirty he rang the front doorbell and David went to let him in. Jen, Peter, and Becky were all in the kitchen, getting tea ready and putting off until the last possible moment the time when they had to go join the two men. Jen suppressed a suggestion that they all join hands in prayer before going down the hall.

And then Peter disappeared. One minute he was beside Becky, pinching crumbs off a cream bun, the next he had vanished.

"Where is he?" demanded Jen, looking around.

Becky shook her head, equally astonished. Out of the corner of her eye, Jen saw the outside doorknob move, but by the time she'd wrenched the door open, Peter had gone.

"How *could* he?" she exclaimed indignantly. "How could he run out like that? It's because of him we're in this mess!"

"It isn't really," Becky reminded her. "It's because of you Dr. Owen's here at all. You told him and Dr. Rhys."

"Did you know he was going to sneak out?"

"No, he didn't tell me, but I think it might be better without him."

David called them just then, and Jen snapped her mouth shut. Her thoughts were black, as she took the tray to the lounge. She felt betrayed and furious with Peter for ducking out on an afternoon they had known from the start none of them would enjoy. And she felt guilty, too, because Becky was right. It was her fault.

"Ah, yes," said Dr. Owen getting to his feet as they entered. "Jennifer and —"

"Becky," supplied David. His face told the two girls nothing important had been said yet. "Where's Peter?"

"Gone out for a minute," said Becky evasively.

David looked hard from Becky to Jen. "I thought I just heard him in the kitchen with you."

"I'm sure he'll be right back." Becky's voice expressed a conviction Jen did not share, nor was she sure Becky actually believed her own statement. But David appeared to accept it.

Jen sat behind the teapot. If Becky could be calm, so could she. "Dr. Owen, would you like milk or lemon in your tea? And sugar?"

For the next few minutes Dr. Owen allowed the conversation to wander in a politely aimless fashion from the weather to Aberystwyth, the University, life in Borth. But didn't the Morgans miss living near a city? This did seem a bit primitive. David chuckled and said that, after a few weeks in Borth, Aberystwyth looked like a city to them. Dr. Owen smiled in agreement, but all the while Jen felt he was watching her, and they were all waiting for the real conversation to begin.

Dr. Owen didn't waste much time coming to the point. He had business to transact and wouldn't permit himself to be sidetracked.

"Well," he began, sitting back in his chair, his hands folded. Three pairs of eyes were on him at once. "I don't know if Gwyn told you the purpose of my visit, did he? I do have a reason for asking to come."

"I think we know it," said David quietly.

"That should make this all very much easier then," Dr. Owen said pleasantly. "I've thought about you a good deal since your visit to Cardiff. I was very interested in the *ques-*

tions—ah—Jennifer asked me. She seemed to have something *rather specific* on her mind, and when I spoke to Gwyn last month he confirmed this. As I believe I mentioned at the Museum, objects do turn up in strange places and we can hardly afford not to chase them. So, since I was coming to Aberystwyth, I thought we might just continue our conversation."

"I'm sorry?" Jen struggled to sound as if she'd forgotten it.

"Oh, come. You were far too *interested* not to remember what you were asking about," said Dr. Owen. "It rather sounded to me as if you'd found something that you thought might be of *value*. Of course, no one can tell until it's been examined, but I'm right, am I not?"

"Actually," Jen hedged truthfully, "I haven't found anything."

"Perhaps not. It was your sister or your brother then? You did mention your brother." Dr. Owen regarded her shrewdly. "You asked *specifically* about harp keys as I recall." He turned to David. "I told you then how important the discovery of one would be, didn't I? Yes, I was sure I had. It would be most *unwise* to withhold an object of that nature, but I'm sure I needn't tell *you* that, David. Your background must certainly make you aware of it."

"Yes," said David and looked at Jen.

"Suppose I had found something," said Jen carefully, "and it turned out not to be old. What would happen to it then?"

"Well, if it weren't of interest to the Museum you could keep it, of course. And you can be sure we'd be perfectly honest with you, Jennifer. No question there. If it were an important find, on the other hand, you'd have the satisfaction of knowing you'd *contributed* to the history of the country. Not everyone can do that."

Behind Dr. Owen's calm, pleasant little smile, Jen sensed

a very sharp edge. She had to go with extreme caution; he would see through any deception. "No," she said finally.

"*Good.* I see we're beginning to understand one another. Why don't you just show me this object, hmm? There's every chance I shan't even have to take it back to Cardiff with me. These things frequently turn out to be more quaint and curious than valuable, you know, David."

"I'm sorry." Jen shook her head. "I don't have it."

The smile slipped for an instant, and Jen saw irritation. But only for an instant. "Why don't you get it then while we wait?"

"I don't know where it is." What a relief to be able to tell him the truth!

Dr. Owen frowned slightly. "Have you lost it? That would be dreadfully careless. Perhaps you could think *hard* for a minute?"

"It won't help. I don't know where it is," Jen said again.

"But there *is* such an object?" Dr. Owen had scored one point anyway.

Jen could see no virtue in flatly denying it and fumbling for a cover-up. Dr. Owen was far too clever to accept that, so she said nothing. Instead David interrupted, speaking mildly. He evidently thought Dr. Owen had gone far enough without interference. "I believe Jen understands the importance of what you're saying, Dr. Owen."

"I would hope so, David, but I'm not quite sure. There seems to be no doubt that *one* of your children has found something, and Gwyn seemed to feel it might be of special interest. I've great regard for his judgment."

"So have I," agreed David. "He also feels that my children are capable of taking responsibility for such an object, whatever it is. He has said so to all of us. I can't allow him to have more confidence in them than I do!"

"Up to a point, David, surely, but they *are* children, after all. They can scarcely be expected to judge the value of an ob-

ject that might just *possibly* be thousands of years old. I know
you're their father, but you are also a scholar and you must
understand my point."

"Has Gwyn actually seen this object?"

"No, as a matter of fact he said he hadn't when I asked
him. But he mentioned he'd discussed it with your daughter—
again, Jennifer, I believe. I *am* right?"

Jen gave an unwilling nod.

"So you see."

"I see that you've really got nothing but hearsay to go
on," said David. "In Cardiff I remember your telling us that
nine times out of ten the objects people turn up and bring to
you are simply archaeological rubbish. The countryside must
be full of it."

"Quite, David, quite," said Dr. Owen with exaggerated
patience. "But we do examine every piece that comes in and
occasionally we find a real treasure. How can we be sure until
we see?"

David nodded. "I understand that. You depend upon
cooperation, though, don't you? You can't force someone to
give you whatever he's found, involuntarily."

"Well, not always. That's a rather touchy subject, David,
and I'd as soon *not* get into it with you. Unpleasant, you know.
Naturally, we do depend to a great extent on *voluntary dona-
tions,* as it were. Cooperation is terribly important, not only
because it's far simpler for everyone, but it gives people a
sense of having *done* something. Really, David, all I'm asking
for now is *your* cooperation."

"But I'm not the right person to ask. You must go to the
one with the object."

"There." Dr. Owen made a gesture with his hands, as if
to say exactly so. "One of your children and here I am. If I
seem to be addressing myself primarily to you, it's because I
feel we're colleagues in a sense and I know you understand my
position. I rely on you to make your children understand it.

After all, I'm a stranger to them. However, I'm sure *you* can *make* them bring it forward. I know children love to play games, but this really isn't a matter to be taken lightly."

"I agree." David's tone was cool. "I don't much like the word 'make'."

"Sometimes it does seem necessary. It's only fair to warn you that the Museum does have methods of dealing with those who are uncooperative, when it seems advisable. If it were learned that you were withholding an important specimen from us, there could be rather an unpleasant investigation. Mind you, I don't say there *would* be, but there *could* be. And you'd not have a very strong position, David, as a visitor to Wales. . . . Nor would it seem altogether admirable, shall I say, for a man in your line of work."

"Meaning?"

"You *are* a university lecturer. Someone dedicated to scholarship and all that."

"I would be sorry to see it come down to that," said David shortly.

"Indeed, so should I," Dr. Owen assured him with sincerity. "But this is my *job,* you understand. Normally I enjoy it tremendously—I find it exciting and vital—but from time to time there *are* situations . . . and this is one of them, I'm very much afraid. I don't think there's anything *unreasonable* in my position, do you? I am simply doing my job the most effective way I can. As a parent, I would rather have thought *your* job—"

"My job is to bring up my children the most effective way *I* can," interrupted David. "Part of that job is teaching them responsibility and then trusting them with it. I find it's not easy to learn, either for them or for me. We all have to allow each other to make mistakes, and we're not always as quick as we should be to understand and help. But we *are* learning, Dr. Owen. I'm beginning to have a good deal of confidence in us —I think we'll survive as a family, but only if we can rely on each other. So"—he paused—"I'm going to rely on them now to do what's right. And they can rely on me to help. You've made your case and I'll grant it's a strong one, but I'll tell you in all honesty, I will not stand to see my children bullied by anyone but me."

Jen's heart lifted. She felt like cheering.

But Dr. Owen looked aggrieved. "There is surely a difference between bullying and using common sense, David. You could perhaps call it intervention?"

"Of course. I want to be fair with you, I respect your position. But I truly believe Jen, Becky, and Peter would none of them treat this matter irresponsibly. If I change my mind for any reason, I won't hesitate to *intervene,* as you say. Right now I'm going to leave it to them."

"Not a very professional attitude, David," said Dr. Owen reproachfully. "I certainly hope you don't regret it."

"So do I," David agreed. "I don't think, however, that we'll get any further by pursuing this now." He turned to Jen and Becky who had been listening to the conversation intently. "Do you both understand quite thoroughly what we've been saying?"

Jen pulled herself together. "Yes." Becky nodded.

"Good. Dr. Owen's quite right, I *am* responsible for you —you're minors—so if I think you're getting out of hand," the suggestion of a smile, "I will interfere, I promise you."

With a sigh Dr. Owen stood up. "I'm sorry I can't *really* approve of your method of dealing with this, David."

"So am I." David got to his feet; so did Jen and Becky. "Of course, there's always a good chance we've wasted a lot of breath on an object that doesn't even exist—neither you nor I nor Dr. Rhys has seen it."

The two men exchanged a long, not entirely unfriendly look. "Well, David, I've little time to spare this trip, I'm afraid. I've got some rather pressing business at the National Library before I go back to Cardiff. I hope you feel assured my interests in this matter are purely *professional* if we find we must pursue it further."

"I do," said David.

"Good. And if anything *does* turn up, you can reach me at this address for the next few days—it's a guest house in Aberystwyth. I'll be there until Wednesday. I think possibly once you've had time to *consider,* you may want to reach me."

David nodded. "We may. Becky, would you get Dr. Owen's coat, please?" He and Dr. Owen shook hands.

"Thank you for tea. I hope I'll be speaking to you again soon." Dr. Owen paused long enough to look sharply at each of them, then left, walking quickly away from Bryn Celyn, down the hill to the bus stop. Jen, Becky, and David watched him go.

"What'll happen now?" asked Becky.

"I don't know," David answered. "I doubt very much that he'll drop it, he's too sure of himself, and his arguments are good ones. But he knows where I stand, heaven help me! I only hope I don't live to regret this, as your Aunt Beth would say, I'm sure. I'm only being humorous, Jen, don't frown at me. And where the hell do you suppose Peter's got to this time?"

"You swore—are you terribly cross with him?" Becky asked.

"I have a feeling I ought to be!"

"You can be if you want," Peter said suddenly. "I just couldn't face him at the last minute. I'm sorry. And I didn't tell you where I was going." He made no move to enter the lounge but stood uncertainly in the doorway, his hand on the knob.

"Where were you?" demanded Jen. "And why *didn't* you tell us?"

"You wouldn't have let me go."

"You're right."

"I thought we'd been all through this business of going off alone," said David severely.

"He hasn't been gone very long," said Becky. "He can't have gone far, it's only four-thirty."

"I hate to admit it," said Jen reluctantly, "but we *were* better off without Peter here. It would have been worse if he'd stayed."

David threw up his hands in mock defeat. "What chance does a parent have against the three of you? Why don't we go have a proper tea in the kitchen and forget Dr. Owen for the time being?"

Jen waited until David left them and the three were alone, then got down to business with Peter. Whatever else, she was determined that he should know how his father had stood behind him with Dr. Owen. "He defended you," she told her brother. "He told Dr. Owen that the Key was your responsibility and he trusted you to do the right thing with it. I wish you'd heard him."

Peter made no attempt to hedge. "I couldn't stay. I know it was wrong to run out on you like that, but I didn't even know I was going to do it until the doorbell rang. I might have said just the wrong thing and I wasn't sure of Dad."

"You should have been," Becky said a little impatiently. "He's on your side—*our* side."

"I wasn't sure."

"Well, you can be now. He's trying his hardest to understand," said Jen.

"So are you," Peter said unexpectedly, looking straight at her. "And it will all be over soon, I know it will. I've just got to stay away from Dr. Owen long enough to finish it."

"You've made a good start," exclaimed Jen dryly but without anger. "I hope you're right and it is over soon—it'll be a tremendous relief."

Peter agreed.

Sunday, after dinner, the doorbell rang. David found Rhian on the step, jiggling impatiently up and down. Beyond her the ancient Llechwedd Melyn pickup stood at the curb.

"Afternoon, Mr. Morgan! I hoped you'd be yere then."

"Come in," said David. "Jen? Becky! Rhian's here. We're just finishing the dishes. Is that one of your brothers in the truck? Would he like a cup of tea?"

"Never refuses," said Rhian with a grin and darted back to ask. She returned, followed diffidently by Dai Evans. He wiped his gumboots carefully on the mat and pulled off his cap; he looked huge and awkward in the unfamiliar kitchen.

"Hullo," said Peter, making a wad of his dish towel and tossing it in a corner of the sink. Jen gave an exaggerated sigh and spread it out again. "What are you doing here?"

"We came for you," answered Rhian. "We're off to Ponterwyd, me and Dai, to collect some of our sheep. John Ellis rang the Forestry yesterday to say he'd got some with our mark on, see. They're some of his old lot that Da bought last year and they've gone off home again."

"I didn't think sheep were smart enough to do that," remarked David, putting a mug of tea in Dai's hand.

"Hill sheep. Aye," Dai said, through a mouthful of biscuit.

"They know their own territory," explained Rhian. "Da usually buys further away, but John Ellis Ponterwyd sold up last year and Da's had his eye on them sheep for some time now. Went into building, John Ellis."

"Good stock," offered Dai, swallowing.

"Anyway, I was thinking did you want to come?"

"Can we, Dad?" Becky asked eagerly.

"As far as I'm concerned, if Dai wants to take you all," said David. "Just remember why you're going and don't get in the way. And don't be back late."

"I told you we could use extra rock cakes," said Becky to Jen, as she began to fill a paper bag. "How many?"

"Us and Gwilym. Met him going down to the shop for milk," Rhian answered.

"Leave a couple for my tea," put in David.

"If the weather doesn't worsen and we have time, we might go up Pumlumon after we've got the sheep," said Rhian.

Dai said, "It'll hold for a while yet. Gray but clear with it."

Ponterwyd was a handful of houses scattered on the main road east from Aberystwyth. Dai followed the bus route through Bow Street to Aberystwyth first to leave off a basket of eggs with one of Mrs. Evans's customers, then turned the pickup left along the Rheidol and followed the river. Jen and Becky rode in the cab beside him, the other three in the bed of the truck. It was a novelty for the three Morgans to be driven anywhere, and Jen thoroughly enjoyed the feeling of excitement.

Near the tiny village of Goginan, tucked in a fold of the valley, the road climbed high up the hillside on a series of switchbacks. Rhian, Peter, and Gwilym in the back got a sudden glorious, wide-open view back down the Rheidol toward Aber and the sea: the river snaking across the plain it had carved, the great hills shouldering back from it, patched in dark and light green trees and fields of smoldering gorse, the sprinkling of cottages. Then they were over the crest of the hills and the valley was gone.

The cold damp air felt good against Peter's face. There was too much of it racing past to make conversation possible, so he could sit with his back against the hard side of the pickup and his legs out straight and submerge himself in thought. Rhian was singing to herself, he could see her lips move without hearing the words. And Gwilym's eyes were intent on the gray sky, searching patiently for hawks or buzzards, or with luck, a kite. Peter considered them, the three of them together: how unlike they were. Yet they'd grown familiar to one another and were comfortable. His fingers went automatically to the chain around his neck. It was all woven into the same pattern: Gwilym, Rhian, the Key, his own family, Wales, and a feeling sometimes so powerful it made the back of his throat ache. The pattern was right, it was working itself out. People spent their lives weaving patterns, borrowing bits from one another, but making each pattern different. Peter was part of Rhian's, she was part of his; they overlapped but didn't match. It made him feel old to think that way.

At Ponterwyd, Dai turned left up a steep, narrow road, last paved many Welsh winters ago, that led back into the hills. Gwilym whistled and pointed and, looking up, Peter saw a pair of buzzards, circling slowly just above the horizon, great ragged wings extending in shallow arcs.

The cottage they pulled up in front of stood small and lonely on the bare hillside, its cluster of outbuildings huddled close as if for company. It looked like any of the other hill farms around except that next to it stood a large truck with a flatbed covered with piles of brick and lumber.

John Ellis came out to greet them, surrounded by large, hairy dogs. He was a big pleasant-faced man in overalls and gumboots, with curly red hair. He and Dai made a splendid pair, Jen thought in admiration. Both were the same size, the same age, one dark, the other fair. They were evidently great friends. Dai climbed out of the truck, and they conferred for a few minutes. John Ellis pointed downhill behind the cottage and Dai nodded knowledgeably.

"Come on!" cried Rhian, vaulting down. "We'll all help!"

They piled out, stretching.

"Two of our ewes back in John Ellis's pen," said Dai. "He's seen two more by the river this morning."

"Is that all?" asked Rhian.

John Ellis nodded. "If you'll spread out and work toward the river from yere, we should be finding them no trouble. And I've my dogs to bring them back then."

"Shouldn't take long," Rhian predicted.

"Then we can go on up there." Gwilym's eyes were on the slopes of the mountain Pumlumon, north, rising sharp-cut against the sky.

"It doesn't look like much of a mountain," observed Becky.

"Highest in Cardigan," Gwilym replied.

Peter said, "It looks old."

They spread out as John Ellis instructed, eager to get the job done.

"What do you suppose you do if you find a sheep?" Jen asked Peter, as they set off.

"Stand and yell, I guess." He flashed her a grin.

But it was Rhian and Gwilym who spotted the two strays, both ewes with lambs, huddled uncomfortably in the lee of a gorse bush, fleece matted, eyes wild and blank.

John Ellis sent one of his dogs along to take them back to the cottage. The three border collies were canny sheepdogs, even though they'd lost their own flock. Their instincts were as sharp as ever. John Ellis was too fond of them to think of selling them with his sheep.

At a whistle from him, the one called Gyp streaked off, away from the ewes, belly to the ground, and circled behind them. A short, sharp whistle dropped the dog to earth like a stone. The other two collies sat still beside John Ellis, ears up, trembling with eagerness to be off, but too well-trained to move. At another signal, Gyp began to creep toward the sheep, keeping low and stopping frequently. The ewes were nervous, making short runs first one way, then another. They scented the dogs and people. Then Gyp began to show himself, pushing the beasts gradually uphill toward the cottage, anticipating them each time they tried to bolt the wrong direction.

Coll and Nell were given the task of bringing in the two sheep from the pen by the river, and they were done. But on the way back, Becky found a fifth sheep, half in, half out of a clump of gorse, quite dead. Dai hurried over at her cry of distress and looked at the ewe glumly. "An old one, she," he said, and bent and rolled her over. Half-crushed under the bulky body was a tiny white lamb, less than a day old by the look of it. It lay very still.

"Oh!" gasped Becky involuntarily. "Is it dead too?" It was so new to be lifeless; it had only just started.

Dai gathered it up, his big hands deft and unexpectedly gentle. He was frowning. Then they both saw the lamb's eyes half open. Weakly it bleated—a thin, pitiful sound—and Dai and Becky smiled at each other.

"It's milk she's needing, this one. If we can get her warm and fed, she might do."

"Can I carry her?"

"Aye." With the same gentleness Dai put the lamb in Becky's arms and she was enchanted.

"Bess'll look after you," said John Ellis, when he saw what Becky'd got. "She'll find you a bottle and rubber teat around somewhere."

The kitchen was warm, and very full when they'd all crowded into it. John's wife, Bess, didn't seem at all put out by the appearance of so many strangers, but then she didn't look like the sort of person who could be easily upset by anything. She was a comfortable, calm woman with kind eyes and red, rough hands. She found what Becky needed and showed her how to coax the orphan to drink warm milk from a baby's bottle. Two very small Ellises sat cross-legged on the hearth, watching and grinning like Jack O'Lanterns.

Dai saw the lamb was in good hands and turned to John to discuss dogs; they apparently shared a passionate interest in the subject. There was a man in Ponterwyd Dai was particularly anxious to see called Howell Pritchard, who raised some of the finest rabbit dogs in the county. His best bitch had just whelped, and Dai's heart was set on owning one of her pups. John Ellis was only too pleased to have an excuse to pay Howell Pritchard a visit himself.

"So," Rhian interrupted, "you won't care if we be off for a couple of hours, will you?"

Dai frowned. "You'll be back by tea."

"Aye."

"You going up Pumlumon, then?"

"We might do. We'll go that direction, anyhow."

He nodded. "I'll not come hunting you, mind."

"Are you sure you don't need us still?" asked Gwilym. "We did come to hunt sheep after all."

"And we have done!" exclaimed Rhian. "Them two won't look any more—why should we? More than like, we've got them all now."

At the door Peter paused and turned back. "Becky?" But she was settled happily on the floor near the fire, her arms full of lamb as Bess Ellis held the bottle for it. "I'll stay."

Peter went out after the others. Gwilym and Rhian were arguing amiably about the best way up the mountain, which they referred to as a hill.

"Well, of course, it's best if you go up from Ponterwyd," Gwilym was saying, setting his spectacles firmly on his nose.

"But we're not *in* Ponterwyd then, are we?" said Rhian. "From yere, it's much the best to follow the reservoir round to the right and go straight up. Quicker if you don't mind a scramble. We've not got masses of time, see."

Nant-y-moch, the reservoir, was like a sheet of tin foil blown into wrinkles by a chilly wind. It made a great "U" between the hills where small rivers had incised valleys, then been flooded to make the hydroelectric reservoir. The road met Nant-y-moch at the bottom of the "U" and water spread away from it to both sides.

They turned right off the road along a well-worn track between the shore and Pumlumon itself. Jen and Peter were accustomed to walking with the other two by this time and had no trouble matching Rhian's pace. There were two streams to cross on overgrown footbridges, and they passed a deserted cottage. Jen spotted a kestrel just beyond it, standing on the air, its wings stroking fast, its tail angled downward and fanned to hold it still above some small creature. While they watched it, it closed its wings and stooped. When it rose again a moment later, something limp hung from its talons.

"It's sometimes called 'windhover' because it does that," said Gwilym.

"Windhover," Jen repeated. "That's lovely."

At the end of the reservoir the track led on under a dark, treacherous-looking slide of broken rock. Then at the next stream Rhian started up a footpath that followed the *cwm* onto Pumlumon itself. There was a magical feeling about setting foot on the massive bulk. They had been skirting it carefully until now—they hadn't declared themselves. But once begun, they were committed to climb it. It had none of the rugged cliffs and pinnacles of the mountains further north, above the Dovey, but it had all the ancient force of a true mountain.

The going was steep, but moderately dry, and the path quite easy to follow. The stream came down out of a round little lake, Llyn Llygad Rheidol. Gwilym consulted their map. It lay at the foot of the cliffs that guarded the summit of Pumlumon Fawr, its waters the color of pewter, echoing the metallic sky, but not reflecting it. A patch of white gulls on the far side flawed the surface.

Rhian let the expedition stop to catch its breath here, before making the final ascent, and Gwilym declared he was starving to death. So Jen unpacked the rock cakes and Rhian dug four oranges out of her rucksack; Peter contributed a jacknife, and they settled themselves on a couple of boulders out of the wind. Jen and Peter cut holes in the tops of their oranges and squeezed the juice into their mouths.

"What does Nant-y-moch mean anyway?" asked Jen after a bit.

"*Nant*," said Rhian, "stream. And *moch* is pigs, I think. Mmm. Did you ever make orange-peel teeth?" She slid a piece of peel between her lips and teeth and smiled horribly.

Jen ignored her. "Pig Stream?"

"Stream of Pigs sounds better," corrected Peter,

thoughtfully. "There's a story about pigs in *The Mabinogion,* that book Dr. Rhys loaned me of Welsh myths. One of the heroes, Gwydion, I think, stole pigs from the king in the south and drove them back to his own kingdom in the north."

"*You* sound learned," commented Jen.

Peter shrugged. "He might have brought them through here. That would make the name very old."

"But the reservoir isn't," objected Rhian.

"The name could be older than the reservoir," said Gwilym. "Anyhow, the word is stream not lake. I suppose you could be right, Peter."

"It sounds good." Peter stood up. "Well, come on, let's get to the famous top of this famous mountain!" He flashed a glorious orange peel grin at them and scrambled over the boulders. "To the summit!"

It wasn't much further—over the cliffs and they were on top of Cardiganshire. Spread below, like a giant map, was the country they were familiar with. To the west, it ran out to the gray, hard line of the sea; north, it climbed to the peaks of Snowdonia, lost in cloud: Cader Idris and the Mountains of Eryri. Then, turning south, they could see the rounded humps of the Preselis, where the great blue stones of Stonehenge had been quarried. And finally, to the east, lay England's border and the hills of Shropshire. Ages ago, before Christmas, Jen had traveled through them to Borth. From the summit of Pumlumon Fawr, they could see almost from end to end of Wales and right across it. Small and wild and old, thought Jen, the wind blowing her hair back from her shoulders, stinging her face.

Silently, the four of them wandered about on the mountain top, thinking their own thoughts, while under the thick layer of cloud the light faded and the surface of Nant-y-moch turned black. What subdued color the hillsides held drained away leaving them gray, and down in Ponterwyd the first lights sparked. They made Pumlumon lonelier.

At last with reluctance Rhian said, "We had better be starting down. I did promise Dai, and we will be late even now."

"Yes," said Jen. She started toward the path, Gwilym behind her.

"No!" called Peter. "Wait!" The command was urgent. They all turned to him where he stood, beside the highest cairn, his eyes fixed on something out across the reservoir.

"What?" asked Rhian. There was nothing but darkness moving across the country, but Peter was quite still, intent, his body tense.

"Peter—" began Jen uneasily.

"Quiet, it's coming!"

Again a command. The words tightened around Jen's heart like a cold iron fist. She gasped. No one moved, no one spoke, no one interrupted. In the vast spreading blackness three tiny cottage lights burned bravely beyond the water. And all around Pumlumon the wind prowled restlessly, neither living nor dead. Jen's hands, clenched in her jacket sleeves, were clammy. She stared into the dusk until her eyes ached, searching—for what, she didn't know. It was coming.

An orb of light, bright, steadily moving, white and silent.

"There!" cried Peter in a voice that was not his.

The light came down out of the country, from Foel Goch. The watchers on Pumlumon saw it now in the open, now hidden by forest, lost in a hollow, coming over a rise. It moved like a lantern carried by men, not in a straight line, but following a path through the hills. It was far brighter than any lantern.

Time wavered like reflections in a river—hours, years, centuries, only minutes, which? They could not take their eyes from the light. It reached the far shore of Nant-y-moch and came across the water without faltering as if it knew an ancient path, as if the reservoir were not there.

The wind shifted. It blew up the mountain, and on it came a low rhythmic sound. Jen would have believed she imagined it except that it raised the hairs on the back of her neck. It was a mourning, aching moan.

The light disappeared in the lee of the far shore, and still no one moved. They waited, hardly breathing. For an awful moment, Jen thought the light would come up Pumlumon, right to them, to Peter, when it reappeared, but it moved on only a few paces, then stopped. It hung in the air above the blackness of Nant-y-moch and the sound grew. It rose to an unbearable wailing crescendo, drowning the wind, filling the world until it must burst apart.

Darkness and silence. The light and the wailing were extinguished in an instant and Jen, Peter, Gwilym, and Rhian were alone on the windy summit of Pumlumon Fawr.

Thunder grumbled in the distance, caught somewhere in Eryri. Without a word they turned down the trail, stumbling, hurrying, their eyes still seeing the light, not the path ahead.

It wasn't until they arrived breathless at the track along Nant-y-moch again that they paused.

"What did we see?" asked Rhian in an awed voice. "What was it?"

But none of them knew. Jen glanced at Peter and saw he had no answer; his face was pinched, his eyes uncertain. Up on the mountain, the Key had gone ice cold against his skin. It had burned him with its coldness. There was no song, but there was a presence so strong it seemed to possess him, willing him to understand. He didn't.

"We all saw it—it *was* there." Jen was desperate for reassurance, and Gwilym offered it.

"Yes. We did all see it. But it was Peter first—he knew it was coming. Why?"

Peter did not respond, and with a mighty effort Jen pulled herself together. It was no good asking Peter questions he couldn't answer. "Come on, for heaven's sake. We must be hours late! It's almost pitch black."

"No," said Rhian. "It's not so bad as that. It'll be the storm partly."

As if on cue, the thunder shook itself free and rolled down over their heads, making them jump. "No good to wait for the rain!" She was off again, jogging along the reservoir track, and they had to hurry to keep up.

They hadn't as far to go as they'd expected, for at the paved road they found Dai and Becky waiting for them in the pickup. The sheep were baaing uneasily in the back.

"Where have you been? Clear to Shrewsbury and back, is it?" exclaimed Dai. "Thought I'd have to come after you, me."

"Sorry," called Rhian, swinging herself over the side and in among the ewes. "Pass your pack yere, Jen. That's it."

Peter got into the cab next to Becky, who still held the orphan lamb, and left the others to cope with the livestock. Jen found herself sitting on the hump over one of the rear wheels, across from Gwilym, while Rhian crouched behind the cab.

"If we're lucky, we may yet beat the rain," Rhian shouted over the roar of the engine. The sheep, unprepared for the sudden movement of the pickup, skittered about on stiff legs, staggering in terror. Jen fervently hoped they would beat the rain—dry sheep were infinitely preferable to wet ones.

They almost made it, but as they were turning up onto the Upper Borth road, great hard drops of water hit them, flattening on the roof of the cab and drenching the unfortunates in back. The sheep cried in distress, and Jen felt like joining them, but Dai was stopping in front of Bryn Celyn and the front light was on. Through the uncurtained study window Jen could see her father at his desk. He must have been waiting for them and watching; the door opened before they got to it. Becky relinquished the lamb to Rhian who

climbed in front. Dai was anxious to get his little flock back
to Llechwedd Melyn and shook his head at Becky's offer of
a cup of tea. And Gwilym raced off to his own house, his
windbreaker over his head, leaving the four Morgans alone.

"I was just getting ready to worry," remarked David
mildly, surveying his damp offspring.

"The storm came up so fast," said Jen. "We were on
Pumlumon and didn't get down quickly enough."

"Fast? It's been threatening here all afternoon. You
must have been very intent on mountaineering not to have
noticed it."

"I guess we were."

"I found a lamb," Becky put in. "Its mother was dead,
and Mrs. Ellis taught me to feed it. I didn't go up the mountain, I stayed to look after it. Dai promised he'd look after it
specially for me, and I can see it when I go to Llechwedd
Melyn."

David smiled at her affectionately. "Sounds like a successful afternoon."

"It was. Dai bought a hunting dog, but he can't have it
until it's eight weeks old."

"I hope you found the sheep you went for in your spare
moments. And what was Pumlumon like? Worth the climb?
Maybe I'll get a chance to go up it sometime."

"The view was terrific," said Jen quickly.

"Yes," said Peter. And that was all they'd say.

Peter said, "I've got the answer—if I can just understand it,
Jen."

"You mean yesterday, the light we saw?"

They sat together by the lounge window, the rain outside rattling against the glass. It had rained steadily all day.
In the kitchen Becky and Rhian were getting tea and prac-
ticing the book reports they had to make next day. Frequent
gusts of laughter blew down the hall. Jen remarked that she'd

never found book reports very funny, but Peter refused to be distracted.

"If I knew what the light meant, I'd know what I should do with this." He held the Key in his hands, turning it over and over, tracing its patterns with his fingers.

"You're so sure of that," said Jen.

"Aren't you? You can't possibly believe the light had nothing to do with the Key, Jen. Not even if you want to. It simply can't be explained any other way."

"Well, no . . ." Jen was still reluctant to let go completely and accept Peter's Key. But she was rescued by Becky, who yelled "Tea!" just then. The kettle began to shriek and Jen got up. "We'll have to save some for Dad, I guess. I don't know why he's so late."

Rhian was slapping butter on slices of bread like a bricklayer shoveling mortar, but she stopped when Peter came into the kitchen. Without preliminaries she said, "I told Da about what we saw on Pumlumon yesterday."

"Wish I'd been there." Becky dumped tea into the pot. Peter had told her what happened. It wasn't fair not to when she was so much involved. Besides, it was hardly a secret: Gwilym and Rhian knew.

"Da said he's never seen one himself, but he knows others as have and he knew right what it was, too," Rhian continued.

Peter should have realized someone like Mr. Evans would know. The key to the Key! It was about to fall into Peter's lap. "What?" he demanded. "What was it?"

"Cannwyl corph," Rhian answered, "a corpse candle." Her effect was all she could have hoped, everyone's attention was full on her, and she paused, enjoying herself, then added, "There's all manner of odd things back there in the hills, but then you've been hearing my Da saying that."

"Corpse candle," echoed Becky. "Doesn't sound very nice, what does it do?"

"Ah, then," said Rhian. "It marks the path of a funeral, see. Goes just where the dead one goes and wherever *cannwyl corph* stops, there's where the grave will be. Whoever it is will die within the year, so my Da tells it."

"Funeral!" exclaimed Peter softly. "That's what it was, a funeral procession."

"And the sound—like people wailing," Jen said. "But it stopped in the reservoir. How could anyone be buried there?"

"If you could have heard Da and Aled having at each other over that one last night!" Rhian grinned. "A proper row, that was."

"But if you really saw it," objected Becky, "Aled *has* to believe you."

"Not Aled! No fear. But *I* know I saw it right enough."

"All four of us did," Jen said.

"I wish I had," Becky said again, envious.

David didn't get in until after six. He was tired and wet and sounded discouraged. "What a miserable day!" he exclaimed with feeling. "Almost not worth getting up for it. Peter, your friend Dr. Owen refuses to give up on us, and I'm afraid he can cause a good deal of trouble if he chooses."

"It's none of his business," said Becky. "Why doesn't he just go back to Cardiff where he belongs?"

"But you're wrong, it *is* his business. That's exactly why he can cause trouble about it. Oh, damn this whole mess anyway!"

"Poor Dad," said Jen. "Tell us what happened."

"Gwyn came and talked to me at length this morning. It seems Owen has been making enquiries at the National Library as well as the University. He's also evidently been doing some thinking. I suppose, Peter, you've still got this blasted object?"

"Yes." Peter bit his lower lip. "If I didn't, do you think he'd leave us alone?"

"Of course, he would. It ought to be very easy to convince him—he'd have to believe me. But as long as you've got it, I can't lie to the man, and I wouldn't expect any of you to, either. This is obviously terribly important to Dr. Owen. It's his life in a real sense, and you can't play games with it. I won't let you."

"That's not fair!" Peter's face got suddenly pink. "I'm *not* playing games and I'm not laughing at anyone!"

"I told Dr. Owen that Saturday. If you'd stuck around, you would have heard me," said David impatiently. "But I'm afraid your time's almost up, Peter. He's decided you're the one to talk to. This afternoon he called me and asked if he could see you. Just you."

"Alone?"

"Yes, alone. And I couldn't say no. He's only going to keep on at us until he's satisfied. He meant what he said about the investigation. He could do it and it wouldn't do much for any of us."

Peter stared at his father, rebellion all over his face.

"But that's awful!" burst out Becky.

Even Jen was horrified.

David pushed back his chair and looked at their shocked faces. "All right! You tell me, what's my choice? What have I got to go on? I honestly don't know at this point who's right. I'm not going to be pushed into anything by a man I hardly know and don't much like, but on the other hand I do respect what he represents and I've been trying to teach you that respect. He has a lot of clout, you understand. Dr. Owen knows all the right people, he's got authority, and I'm going to look pretty foolish if it turns out he's right. But that's not important. I've done my best to leave this your responsibility, Peter, and part of that responsibility is facing Dr. Owen. I'm sorry, but there it is. I've told him you'll go in to Aberystwyth tomorrow to see him and I won't listen to any arguments. I have other things on my mind just now. Understand?"

It was an ultimatum, and there were no arguments.

Instead of despairing, Peter was all of a sudden overcome with relief. He had the answer! He understood, it was there, whole, in his mind and he wanted to shout with joy. Dr. Owen didn't matter any more.

"But what are you going to do?" demanded Becky. They heard the study door shut firmly behind David. "How can you go see Dr. Owen if you have the Key? Can you hide it?"

"I won't have to," said Peter. "I won't have it."

"But—" said Becky.

"It'll be gone." He laughed at her astonishment. "Don't you see? I've got the answer—I know what to do with it!"

Jen said carefully, "I don't think I want to know."

"I do," said Becky promptly.

"Jen's right," Peter told her. "It's safer if you don't know right now. Later I'll tell you, when it's over."

"Promise?"

"Mmm."

"Peter, where are you going?" asked Jen.

"Next door. I have to see Gwilym a minute. I won't be gone long." He had his macintosh on and his hand on the doorknob.

The hard part would be convincing Gwilym. Where on earth did he begin, Peter wondered a little frantically. There wasn't time enough to explain the whole story, but he was going to have to explain enough to make Gwilym agree. The strongest bit was the *cannwyl corph,* because Gwilym had seen it, too. And, come to think of it now, he'd seen the Irish boats and the coracle, the men on the track up Foel Goch, the wolf. Lots of the pieces. Peter made up his mind.

Gwilym was alone in the kitchen when Peter knocked; his homework was spread out across the table. He looked slightly guilty, and Peter noticed the book in front of him was open to color plates of salt water ducks. Gwilym hastily buried it under a stack of papers.

"Hullo," he said. "What've you come for?"

"I need help." Peter couldn't afford to waste time, and Gwilym looked a bit startled. So Peter began, trying to tie together for the older boy all the pieces he knew Gwilym had, making a whole story for him. Gwilym listened to the story of Taliesin without interrupting, and Peter struggled to keep the anxiety out of his voice. When he'd finished, Gwilym sat silent for a few minutes, then said, "But what has it got to do with me?"

"Everything!" exclaimed Peter. "I need to borrow your motorbike."

"What?" said Gwilym. "When?"

"Tonight."

"Now?" Gwilym looked at Peter as if he thought him mad.

"Later. About midnight."

"But you can't ride it; you've no license and you don't know how, do you?"

"I'd manage. I wouldn't get caught."

Gwilym shook his head slowly. "It seems a strange thing to want to do," he said.

"I know." Peter was desperate. "But I *have* to. I have to get up into the hills somehow tonight, and it's the only way that's fast enough. I can't walk, it'd take me all night, and a regular bicycle's no good, even if I had one. It's all I can think of. Please? I'll be awfully careful, I promise."

Gwilym frowned. "Why?"

Without answering, Peter took out the Key. It gleamed dully in the kitchen glare; it looked terribly old, alien in his hand. "I found it on the beach months ago. I can't keep it any longer, I have to give it back to its owner. I have to do it tonight, now. If I don't, it'll be lost forever." He put the Key in Gwilym's hand, his eyes met and held Gwilym's. "Please," he said again. "Trust me."

Gwilym's gaze dropped to the Key. He stared at it a long

time, he held it carefully. "It's old," he said at last. Peter nodded. "Very."

"Odd. It feels—"

"Here," exclaimed Mrs. Davies, coming into the kitchen. "Here! What are you doing out at this hour, Peter Morgan? Your father knows where you are, does he?"

Instantly the Key disappeared between Gwilym's clasped hands.

"I just came for a minute," said Peter desperately, "to ask Gwilym a question. I was just going home."

"I should think. Gwilym should be studying and I've a pot of tea to make. No sense at all, you haven't. And you've got the floor all over water with your shoes as well."

"It'll dry, Mum," said Gwilym. "I've almost finished my work anyway. I'll see you to the door, Peter."

On the narrow back porch Gwilym peered out at the rain. "Nasty. What I don't see is why it has to be tonight with the rain and all. Can't it wait?"

"No," said Peter. "I'll have to get there somehow. Thanks all the same."

Gwilym handed him the Key, scowling, deep in thought. "I can't just let you take the motorbike, Peter, not with the weather bad and you not knowing how it works."

"It's all right," said Peter, glumly, "I can understand."

"But what I could do"—Gwilym hesitated—"is take you myself. I'll catch hell if Mum ever finds out." He grinned. "Half eleven late enough?"

Peter's heart gave a wild lurch. "You—you'll *go?*"

Gwilym shrugged. "I've a mind to."

"Oh, Gwilym—!"

"Here's Mum now. Go on before she sees you again or she'll know something's up. It's odd enough you being here at all. Half eleven in the shed."

18

Giving It Back

HALF ELEVEN in the shed. Peter went through the motions of getting ready for bed mechanically, his mind already far ahead. When he got back from Ty Gwyn, Jen gave him a long hard look but didn't ask what had happened. Instead she said, "Dad was given his contract today. He's got to give the University an answer in the next two days, that's why he's so grim. He's worrying about a lot right now." It wasn't an excuse, it was an explanation. Jen wanted Peter to understand.

And he did, but he too had a lot on his mind. He hoped the worrying wouldn't keep David up late tonight. David was tired, however, and pushed them all toward bed earlier than usual.

Becky passed Peter on the stairs as she was going up to brush her teeth. Her eyes asked him a wordless question and he nodded. "Good luck then," she whispered.

There was no chance of going to sleep, of course. Peter lay on his bed fully dressed with the light off, waiting. He heard his father take a bath overhead, then the creak of floorboards as David went into his bedroom, the sound of the door closing, and silence. Jen, or was it Becky, coughed

twice from very far away, and that was all. The clock by
Peter's bed had a luminous face and the hands stood at 10:30.
An hour to go.

Out of the darkness came light and warmth, creeping in
like a rising tide, washing over Peter in gentle waves as he
lay there remembering all that the Key had shown him. Piece
by piece it wove the story of Taliesin before his eyes. But
tonight the Key was silent, as it had been ever since Peter had
seen it lost in the stormy sea. A week—how many hundred
years ago? Fourteen?

The Island in the Lake, and the tall, long-haired woman
who had reached out her hand to a boy and given him the
Key to his life, the bright silver tuning key for a harp. The
miles of road among wild mountains and strange rough men,
across green hills where cattle grazed, through wooded valleys
cut into farm holdings. Firelight in great halls, men's faces
red with warmth and food, the music of harps and the
sound of singing. And Aneirin.

Then the flood. That was part of it, too. The battle on
Cors Fochno in the night. The tiny coracle tossing about on
the ocean. Fear and violence and bravery, all bound up in
one small metal object that ought not to have survived the
battering sea, that might never have been found. Except that
a boy on a beach did find it and keep it for a time.

The story had been entrusted to Peter. He carried it as
Taliesin himself had once carried stories. It seemed unimportant that few people would ever believe him. He knew that
some did, he knew he could trust them. He felt as if he'd come
a long way.

It was twenty minutes past eleven. He turned off his
thoughts abruptly and listened. Silence. Taking a deep breath,
he got up quietly, felt for his flashlight, pulled on his wellingtons, and went into the kitchen. Still no sound. He'd be early,
but he couldn't risk having Gwilym get to the shed first and
think he wasn't coming.

Outside the rain had stopped. The sky was clearing and the wind was up; rags of gray cloud blew across a nearly full moon. Peter was relieved that they wouldn't have to ride the motorbike in the rain. It was a good omen. He touched the Key once—for luck, or just to be certain it was still there?

From the back, Bryn Celyn was dark. So was Ty Gwyn next door. Hugh-the-Bus had to be up early for the first route, and Mrs. Davies was always up to make his breakfast. In the dark, by the shed where the motorbike was kept, Peter was suddenly afraid Gwilym might not come.

A tall dark shape appeared silently beside him. "I think you're mad," said Gwilym conversationally. "Let's get on with it—if you still want to go, that is."

"Yes."

"Right, then. Help me with the door. Move it slow so it won't squeak. Mum would know that squeak."

Together they got the door open and the bike out. It was lovingly polished and greased in spite of its advanced age, and the white L plate on its rear fender stood out in the darkness.

"We'll wheel it down the hill," Gwilym decided. "Don't want to be waking anyone up here."

The engine started a little reluctantly, but Gwilym fiddled with a few knobs by the handlebars, and it settled down at once to a steady putter.

"Haven't had it out in a while. Right. Just you climb on behind me and hold on. It won't go fast, but we'll have that on." He switched on the headlamp. "Set?"

"Yes," said Peter. He closed his fingers tight on Gwilym's windbreaker, out of excitement more than fear of falling off. He was doing it! *They* were doing it! And they were away. It was going on midnight and the roads were deserted, the houses along them dark.

Although Gwilym was right about the bike not going fast, it felt as if they were speeding. There was nothing to protect them from the wind, and the putt of the motor sounded deafening to Peter.

Gwilym took the lane off to the left through Dolybont and over the hill to Talybont, rather than following the main road. In Talybont he swung right, then stopped by the Red Goat. The moon was out and flooded the little green with cold, silver light.

"Well?" asked Gwilym. "You really did mean you wanted to go right the way up to Nant-y-moch? There's nothing back that way, of course. Just miles and miles, empty."

"That's where I have to go."

"Mmm." Gwilym grunted softly. "It's a bit of a lark this far—the middle of the night and us out on the bike like this. Not so bad where there are people, even when they're asleep. But up there it's different." He nodded toward the black hills.

"That's where I have to go," said Peter again.

"I'm not so sure," Gwilym said. "It didn't sound so bad when you were telling me back home, but out here—And what would your dad say if he knew you were out on a motorbike right now? Probably skin you, same as my mum."

"I have to find the place we saw the light Sunday."

Gwilym settled himself back on the seat. "I almost wish I'd never seen that light, myself. I'd not have come at all if I hadn't—I'd be back in bed. Not messing about with something I don't understand."

"We're not messing, we're setting something right." Peter's voice was calm. They'd got this far, he wouldn't let Gwilym turn back.

Gwilym sighed. "Funny, I must believe you. Are you set?"

They pushed off and began the climb back up the narrow road that led into the hills, toward Nant-y-moch. If the country looked wild and lonely by daylight, it looked infinitely more so under the moon. Gwilym and Peter entered it unprotected, defenseless. They were trespassing—humans didn't belong back here. Peter thought, we could be swallowed by the hills without a trace, simply disappear, and no one would ever know what had become of us. It wasn't comforting, but he remembered what he had come to do and felt confident. He didn't know how he would accomplish it yet, but he didn't worry.

About two-thirds of the way to the reservoir, the road took a sharp bend to the right, and at the corner Gwilym turned off for a moment, looking out over the valley toward the place they had killed the wolf. The road came in along the eastern edge of the reservoir, dropping down toward it. Not a light showed anywhere, there were no signs of men. The moon disappeared for a minute, the cloud across it was edged in silver, and when the moon passed out of it, the view ahead caused Gwilym to swerve the bike dangerously. He gave a sharp, startled exclamation.

There was no reservoir.

Where the moon should have been reflected on a long sheet of water, it shone instead on a deep, wooded valley that twisted between the hills.

"God!" said Gwilym softly.

But that was how it had to be. Peter's heart lifted joyfully. "It's all right. Just follow the road."

Instead of skirting the edge of Nant-y-moch, the road ran down into the valley through the trees. It was hard-packed earth and old, very old. One of the ancient, sacred Ways. The funeral procession had come along it, following the *cannwyl corph,* lamenting the death of someone infinitely revered and precious. Someone who had been buried with ceremony among the hills in which he'd lived and found peace.

Gwilym steered the motorbike along the road in silence. Peter could feel him tense and tight, rigid with fear and bewilderment, and wished he could communicate to Gwilym the rightness of what they were doing. He recognized the effort it took for Gwilym to keep going.

They came along the bottom of the valley and ahead of them they saw a bare, rounded hill which, by its shape, identified itself as a place of men: a fortification or a burial mound. Gwilym rode to the bottom of the hill and stopped.

The silence was complete when he switched off the motor; then somewhere off to the left a tawny owl called—a long tremulous, "oo-oo-oo-oo."

Without a word, Peter climbed off the bike and took the Key in his hands. Again it was icy, it felt charged with electricity, once more alive to his fingers. He unfastened the chain and slipped it off and walked up the hill. He was breathing hard, but not from exertion. A second owl called.

On the top of the hill was a single, standing stone. The moonlight showed clearly the symbols cut into it, throwing them into high relief. They were words, and Peter knew what they said without being able to read them. At the foot of the stone stretched a low mound of smaller stones, the length and breadth of a man, a small one. The stones had been carefully placed to make a kind of barrow. It was a grave.

Peter stood looking down at it, alone in the cold light. Taliesin had come here to end his life in exile, but among friends who loved him. He had been buried in this private, sacred place.

And no one in Peter's time would ever find this, the true Bedd Taliesin, for it had vanished. Peter was standing under feet of water.

He knelt on the damp ground at the west end of the mound, and without hesitation he reached out and tugged at one of the stones. His hands knew the right one instinctively. It was rough and solid and he scraped his fingers on it, but it moved easily and without disturbing any other. It left a narrow black hole. He held the Key in his right hand over the empty space and it blazed out bright, not with reflected light, but with its own. The air rang with a song so joyous, so beautiful that Peter cried out aloud and let go of the Key. The light was snuffed. The song died. The stone was heavy in his left hand.

He replaced it and got up. He was light-headed and dizzy, as if he'd stood up too fast and couldn't balance right away.

Gwilym was waiting for him at the foot of the hill. He hadn't moved since Peter left him.

"It's all over," said Peter. "We can go."

Gwilym nodded.

At the head of the valley they looked back, and it surprised neither of them to see the waters of Nant-y-moch stretched across the valley, filling the space they had just ridden the motorbike through.

19

Family Decision

PETER WAS LATE to breakfast the next morning. He'd fallen into bed, exhausted, at half past one, barely managing to kick his boots off first, and had slept hard and dreamlessly for the first time in months. When he woke, it was to find himself all together and clearheaded.

"Not much time for breakfast," David commented, stuffing papers into his briefcase. "Do, for heaven's sake, be on time this afternoon, will you? You're to be in Gwyn Rhys's office at three-thirty."

"I will. You needn't worry." Peter was unconcerned.

"Right," said David. "Good." And he went off to catch the bus to Aberystwyth.

Jen and Becky waited where they were, watching their brother. He was very much aware of them, but he took his time. All the feelings he'd been afraid of yesterday: depression, emptiness, loss—he need not have worried. The Key was gone and he'd done his part exactly right. He gave his sisters a wide, infectious grin.

There was a glimmer of surprise, then Becky grinned back, and a moment later they were all laughing with relief.

"It's gone!" exclaimed Jen.

Peter nodded. "It's where it belongs."

Becky guessed, "Nant-y-moch."

"Gwilym was right about the reservoir not always being there. It used to be a valley with a river through it."

"What about Gwilym?" asked Jen. "Will he tell anyone?"

"No. He's all right. He doesn't want his mum to know what he was doing last night. But it isn't the kind of thing you tell people about anyway, not what we saw."

"You'll tell us," Becky put in. "We know the rest of it. Will anyone ever find the Key again, do you think?"

"I don't see how, even if they drain Nant-y-moch for it."

Jen said, "Then you think he's buried there—under the water?"

"No," Peter corrected her quietly, "I know he is. I saw the cairn—there was a stone for him. Not at Bedd Taliesin, but not far from it after all. This is his country, Jen, that's why he's so strong here."

"I'm glad," said Becky. "Then he'll always be strong here."

Jen went back to what lay heaviest on her mind. "Then you don't have to worry about seeing Dr. Owen this afternoon. If the Key's gone, you can't give it to him. Can you convince him you don't have it?"

"Bound to. It's the truth." Peter's grin returned. "Of course, if he ever finds out what I did with the Key last night, he'll have me put in an institution! But he won't, so it doesn't matter. You know, I'm absolutely starving!"

"Sit down, and I'll get you some toast. Becky, pass the cornflakes, will you? You must have been out half the night." Jen sounded brisk and parental.

"Not really. Did you hear me go?"

"Nope," said Becky. "Not a sound. Did you go on Gwilym's bike? I guessed you had. Was it great?"

Peter nodded vigorously, his mouth full. "Gwilym took me himself."

"Your clothes look rather slept in," said Jen critically, handing her brother a mug of cocoa.

"I bet it was exciting to go off like that in the middle of the night. I wouldn't have minded if I'd had someone to go with me," Becky continued.

"You should have heard Gwilym when he saw the reservoir wasn't there," said Peter.

"I hate to interrupt," Jen said, "but you aren't the only problem we've got right now, Peter."

"I'm not a problem," Peter objected. "Not any more anyway. What else?"

"Dad. He's made up his mind about next year, I know he has, but he won't tell me what he's decided."

"I thought he'd made it pretty clear: he's going to take us all back to Amherst." Peter's voice was curiously flat.

"He hasn't told us straight out. And he hasn't asked any of us what we think, either."

"Well, he ought to ask, of course," declared Peter, "but he didn't the last time, so why do you expect him to now?"

"It's different. We didn't know enough to understand, when Dad brought us, but we've learned a lot."

"Do you want to go back?" Becky asked Peter suddenly.

"Doesn't matter. Dad'll do whatever he wants to."

"That's not fair," said Jen. "He's terribly afraid of doing the wrong thing for all of us. I don't think he's even considered what *he* wants to do. I don't believe he wants to go back yet himself."

"What about you?" Becky asked.

"I don't know what I want." Peter sighed. "It used to be so easy—I just wanted to go home. I suppose I still do, but it isn't the same, it doesn't hurt."

"I want to go home, too," said Jen. "Eventually. Not next year."

"There's a lot to lose if we go," said Becky. "We've started to belong, even you."

Peter emptied his mug. "I suppose I have," he admitted. "But what does it all prove? If Dad's already made the decision, do you really think he'd listen to us?"

"Yes, I do," said Jen. "We all listen a lot more than we used to."

"But he's got some awfully good reasons for taking us back," Peter pointed out. "School and Aunt Beth and his job."

"If we can convince him he wasn't wrong to come here in the first place, we'd have a better chance."

Peter pulled a wry face. "I suppose that's my job—I was wrong and he was right."

"Not wrong," said Becky. "You've changed your mind. If we could just get him to talk to us before he does anything final. Jen's right, he oughtn't to do it by himself."

Peter rolled his eyes and said resignedly, "Oh, well, what's another year of rain and freezing cold houses and a language that's got no vowels and a bunch of kids who don't know how to play football. It's all part of my education."

Becky cried triumphantly, "You *will!* You'll help!"

"I'll try," Peter cautioned. "It's not very likely, you know, but we might as well all be in it together."

"We *are* all in it together," said Jen. "That's the point."

Peter wasn't nervous. He crossed the same dim, hollow-sounding hall that Jen and Becky had crossed months ago when Jen had been searching for an answer Dr. Rhys was unable to give her. Peter came unafraid, ready to meet Dr. Owen.

Becky had offered to come with him as far as the building and wait on the Prom—she knew her father wouldn't want her to go in with Peter. But Peter had told her not to, he was all right.

The clock in the great hall broke the silence into echoes as it struck the half-hour.

"Come," said Dr. Owen's voice in answer to Peter's knock.

"My father said you wanted to see me."

"Indeed yes, Peter." Dr. Owen stood with his back to the window, blotting out the sky. "Sit down, won't you?"

Peter sat on the straight-backed chair in front of the desk.

"Good of you to interrupt your afternoon for me," said Dr. Owen, continuing to stand. "You must have a great many things to do after school."

"No, sir. That is, I don't mind coming." Peter returned the man's gaze composedly.

"Well, there's no point wasting time in any event, is there? I'm sorry you weren't with us on Saturday when I had tea with your father and sisters. I now gather you're the one I'm most interested in seeing. You know, don't you, why I've asked you here? I think you've found something I ought to examine, and I trust we can reach an agreement on it. I'm not quite clear why you feel such reluctance about coming forward with it, but I'm prepared to ignore that. Of course, you realize that I'm here on behalf of the *Museum,* not myself?"

He waited for Peter to speak. Peter said nothing, it was all up to Dr. Owen.

"You do *understand* why we're here?" said Dr. Owen, with a touch of impatience.

"Yes, I do, sir."

"Good. There's no need to feel awkward—provided you do the right thing now. No one will be cross with you. I would hardly expect you to recognize the value of the object you've found, you simply fancied it and put it in your pocket without thinking. In fact, it's probably a very good thing for us that you did instead of leaving it. But now I'm sure you're a clever enough boy to see that you must give it to me—you'll actually be giving it to Wales, you know. It'll do far more good in *Cardiff* than in your pocket."

Instead of resenting Dr. Owen's patronizing words and tone, Peter found himself being slightly sorry for the man. He would obviously far rather be dealing with David than a schoolboy of twelve, but David had granted his son the responsibility, and Dr. Owen had no choice.

When he saw Peter wasn't ready to respond, Dr. Owen went on, "Can you appreciate that the Museum is vitally important, Peter? Wales is a *very small* country and frequently overlooked, but there is a great deal of history in it. Those of us working in the National Museum are trying to pull the history together, as it were, to make real sense of it and preserve it. There are so *few* of us, really, and so much still to be uncovered. It is *essential*"—he paused for emphasis, leaning toward Peter across the desk—"*essential* we each do whatever we can, for the sake of the country. We can't afford to lose any part of it." Peter caught a glimpse of someone else behind the smooth, cool facade, a man who really did care and for whom he felt a sudden sympathy. But he had nothing to give that man, or Dr. Owen either.

"Now." Dr. Owen straightened, sitting on the edge of Dr. Rhys's desk, determinedly casual. "May I see the object? Do you have it with you?"

"No," said Peter, "I don't."

"But you said you knew why I wanted to see you this afternoon," said Dr. Owen impatiently. "I'd have expected you to bring it."

"I couldn't, I don't have it at all."

"Oh, come, Peter, that's a bit *unreasonable,* don't you think? Gwyn Rhys, your father, your sister, all as good as told me you have it."

Peter shook his head. "I'm sorry, but I never have possessed it." He chose his words with care: the plain truth for

Dr. Owen, spoken with conviction. The Key had possessed him, never the other way around.

"There *is* an object. One of your sisters——? No, I can't believe that." Dr. Owen stared thoughtfully at Peter, as if trying to read his mind.

"None of us has it." Peter's mind was clear, his face open. There was absolutely nothing for Dr. Owen to discover. Silence overwhelmed the room.

Aren't there times, Peter wanted to ask, when it would be wrong to lock a thing away from its own world, keep it prisoner in a museum case to be stared at by strangers? What about the history in the hills and rivers and cliffs; how could that be collected and labeled and dated? It couldn't, you had to go into the country itself to find it. Couldn't it be more wrong to break the ancient unfinished pattern than to keep a bit of history from the scrutiny of men like Dr. Owen who meant well but didn't understand that? It was the country that had reached Peter, not the rows of brooches brought out of the Dark Ages, the shards of pottery and carved stones on display in Cardiff. It was the country he'd remember.

At last Dr. Owen turned back toward the window with a baffled frown. From his chair, Peter could see only a rectangle of bright blue, crossed now and then by shining gulls. To himself, Dr. Owen said, "There *was* something . . . Gwyn was excited about *some*thing. I'm *sure* . . ."

"But there isn't," said Peter quietly. Dr. Owen must believe him because he told the truth. "Honestly, we haven't got anything you would want to see."

"Yes, so you keep saying, and I don't think you're lying." He looked down at his hands, examining the fingernails with concentration. "*Such* a pity, too. It would have been quite a find. Too good to be true, I suppose. A *harp key*. Well, I've finished. I'll be on the bus to Cardiff tomorrow— I can't afford to take more time here, particularly if there's no reason. *Time*." He shook his head. "There's so *little* of it and so much that needs doing. There are *thousands* of years still to work on, but I don't suppose you've any concept of thousands of years, have you?"

"Does it matter so much though?" Peter sat forward urgently. "Do you have to fit it all together? I think it would be enough just to touch a piece of it and find it's real."

"No, I didn't think you'd have any concept," said Dr. Owen.

But I do, thought Peter. It mattered to him terribly, but they were on different paths and they would never meet each other. Which was right? Or were they neither? Or both? These were questions Peter couldn't ask Dr. Owen. They didn't understand one another and likely never would.

"No matter. If not today, we'll find it tomorrow, somewhere else. Persistence. We must simply go on *trying* and we'll succeed." He came back to Peter. "No point in keeping you any longer. Give my regards to your father, will you?"

"I'm sorry I couldn't help you," said Peter sincerely. In an odd way he rather liked Dr. Owen. He could afford to now; the Key was safe. "Um, could I just leave a note for Dr. Rhys?"

Dr. Owen nodded absently, his thoughts gone on to something else as he collected a pile of papers.

On a blank index card he found on the desk, Peter wrote: "Everything all right. Peter Morgan" and propped it against Dr. Rhys's penholder. "I'll just go now."

"What? Oh, of course." Thankfully, Peter slipped out of the office; it was done and finished. In his eagerness to get away to the wind and sun, he didn't even see the man standing just outside the door until he bumped into him.

"Ooop!" He checked himself. "Sorry, I—Dad!"

"You're dangerous," remarked David. "I've felt it often recently."

"I wasn't looking."

"I guessed as much."

"Were you waiting for Dr. Rhys? He's not there yet."

"No. You."

"Were you?" Peter was surprised.

"Mmm. You seem to be in very good shape for someone who's just come off the rack."

"It wasn't so bad."

"One or the other of us has changed a great deal in a few months," David observed. "Or both of us, perhaps. Come on, I need a cup of coffee."

The strange, twisted monkey puzzle trees along North Parade were covered with a green haze of new shoots, the wide pavements beneath them crowded with University students and professors, mums with prams and small children hanging like fringe off the hems of their coats. The long afternoon sun still had some warmth in it, though it was past four o'clock. The shabbiness of Aberstwyth was familiar and no longer depressing: the cracked plaster and blistered window frames of the row houses, the chipped paint on doors and smell of frying from the guest houses, the gray net curtains.

How would it seem in the holidays when the students were done with exams and gone and the streets were full instead with people on vacation from the smoky industrial cities of England—Birmingham, Wolverhampton, Sheffield? They'd all walk up and down the Prom and breathe the sea air and buy postcards and ices or lie on the pebbly beach if the sun shone. Hugh-the-Bus said you would hardly know the place, so different it was with all the shops and cafes and cottages open, and the caravan sites along the coast bursting with tourists. Odd to think of strangers walking where Peter and David were walking now, living in Bryn Celyn. Unsettling.

They found seats in the window of a small cafe, where they could sit across from each other and watch the business of the street. David got them two white coffees and Peter loaded his with brown demerara sugar, crunching it on the bottom of his cup with the spoon.

"What happened?" asked David finally. "Will you tell me?"

"Nothing much," answered Peter. "He wanted to know if I had anything he'd be interested in, and I said no. I didn't lie to him; I haven't."

David frowned a little. "Is that the end of it? Was he satisfied?"

"He had to be. I told him the truth and he believed me. He was very disappointed." Peter tasted his coffee, winced, and spooned in more sugar.

"Sorry. I don't suppose you really like coffee, do you? I wasn't thinking. Want something else?"

Peter shook his head. "I was sorry for Dr. Owen, he wanted it so much."

"So it's over—with him, and with you."

"That part is. Dad?"

"What?"

"If we didn't go back to America this summer, what would happen?"

"Did I hear you right?"

"Suppose we stayed another year?"

David sighed. "You needn't worry, Peter, I've made up my mind to take you back."

"No," said Peter. "Jen and Becky and I talked about it this morning after you'd gone." He hesitated, knowing what he was going to say, but not knowing how it would be received. "We don't think it's fair for you to decide for all of us without discussing it."

David sat very still for a long moment, head bent, his hands with their square, capable fingers quiet on the table top. "You don't?" he said at last.

"It's our family, too, Dad. Jen's been running the house for months—managing money and cooking. And Becky's been helping; she's doing well enough with school. They ought to be allowed to say what they think."

"And you?"

"I'm part of the family, too, even though I have made a mess of things. Some of it's my own fault, but some I couldn't help. I'm sorry." It wasn't as hard to say that as Peter had thought it would be.

There was just a hint of a smile in David's eyes when he looked up at his son. "It's much easier for one person to decide than for four to agree," he said.

"Then you get all the blame if you're wrong."

"Or all the credit," David added.

Peter shrugged. The coffee in the cups between them got cold. What was David thinking? That he, Peter, had no right to talk this way after the way he'd behaved all year? But David had been waiting outside the office. He had bought him a cup of coffee. He was listening.

"School's the worst," said Peter. "But I can make it up."

"I know you can," said David dryly. "I've been saying that for months."

"There's a lot I don't know how to explain . . ."

"Then don't try yet. Later, if you need to. Peter, how can I expect all the answers from you when I don't have them myself? The questions aren't easy: what do I do about Jen's school if we stay? She can't have another year like this. What do I tell Beth? And the English Department at Amherst? What are the reasons for staying here?"

"What about wanting to?" asked Peter.

"Even you?"

He nodded. "No matter what we do though, we want it to be *our* decision, not just yours."

Unreadable thoughts flickered across David's face. "You're all so young," he protested mildly. "I can't help thinking of you as my children!"

"We're getting older."

"Almost too fast. You're very persuasive, you know. I'm not at all sure I have much chance against the three of you. There's a tremendous lot to be considered."

"We'll all consider it," Peter pleaded.

"Well," said David. "I spent the afternoon writing this." He took a letter out of his pocket. "I worked hard on it; I was going to walk up the hill and deliver it on the way home. It explains why I have to turn down the University's offer for next year. Now you tell me I can't do it that way."

Peter waited, holding his breath.

"I guess we have to take it back to Bryn Celyn with us and discuss it first."

"Oh." The word escaped involuntarily.

"If we go now, we'll just make the 5:10 bus. Ready?"

"Oh, yes!" Peter cried joyfully. "Yes!"

The 5:10 to Ynyslas Turn was crowded mostly with students—full of cheerful noise. Peter and David had to find separate seats for the ride up Penglais Hill. From the rear of the bus, Peter could only glimpse the back of his father's head between passengers. No promises, no commitments. David hadn't torn up the letter, only said they'd discuss it. But Peter was happy. He watched the rows of houses grind past the window as the bus stuttered up Penglais. At the top a jumble of students piled off, and Peter went up to sit with his father.

Beyond Aber they were once more riding between fields hemmed in by hedges of hawthorn, blackthorn, and blackberry. Bow Street, Llandre, Dolybont. At the Borth post office they climbed out and walked to Upper Borth in the windy evening. Gulls blew overhead, crying, on stretched wings. The lights were coming on behind curtains. The narrow margin that was Borth, a single strand spun thin between the sea and the bog, was beginning to emerge from the twilight—beads of light on a string.

This was not their place forever, but it wasn't a place to be despised, as Peter had once believed. He'd been unhappy here, alone and lonely and resentful. But he'd found something in Borth: a thing more important even than the Key. He had learned that he was part of other people and they part of him and he was glad. He could accept it now.

"Next year, where will we be?" he asked softly.

If David heard him, he didn't answer, but they walked toward Bryn Celyn side by side, so close their arms touched. As they turned up the path, the front door opened, spilling yellow light into the Welsh dusk. Jen and Becky were there, waiting for them.

Primary chief Bard am I to Elphin,
And my original country is that of the Summer Stars;
Idno and Heinin called me Merddin,
At last every king will call me Taliesin.

I have been given the Muse from the cauldron of Caridwen;
I have been Bard of the Harp to Lleon of Lochlin.
I have been on the White Hill, in the Court of Cynfelin.
I have been fostered in the lands of Rheged and Caerleon,
I have been teacher to all manner of men,
I am able to instruct all the Universe.
I shall be until the Day of Doom upon the face of the earth;
And it is not known whether I am man, beast, or fish.

—from The Mabinogion, Taliesin

Author's Note

TALIESIN HIMSELF was a real Welsh bard. He lived during the sixth century, and fragments of his poetry have survived and been translated into English. From the fragments, written down long after his death when Welsh became a written as well as a spoken language, it is known that he was familiar with the courts of men like Maelgwn, Gwyddno, and Urien Rheged—possibly even Arthur's at Caerleon. The story of Taliesin is translated in Lady Charlotte Guest's version of *The Mabinogion,* but it is a fairy tale, a legend that grew around the real man. Perhaps it has its roots in fact; at least so I would like to believe. The poetry in this story is thought to be that of Taliesin and his contemporaries and was translated by Lady Charlotte Guest and William Skene. I have made minor changes in their translations. The life of Taliesin that the Key shows Peter is what I have imagined his real story to be. It is my own version. To my knowledge there is no harp key, and it is not known where Taliesin is buried.

But if you ever travel to Cardiganshire in Wales, you will find the village of Borth as I have described it: caught between the sea and the Bog; and the town of Aberystwyth with its National Library and University. With the help of an Ordnance Survey Map you can even find Bedd Taliesin, Sarn Cynfelin, Nant-y-moch, and Pumlumon Fawr. You'll meet Hugheses and Evanses and Rhyses—but not the ones I've written about—because Welsh surnames are few, and hear Welsh spoken in the shops and on the buses. If you go in the spring you will see primroses and lambs, and unless you're extraordinarily lucky, you will discover that I have not exaggerated about the rain!

Perhaps, if you're there long enough, you will feel the wildness and ancient power of the country, watch buzzards over the hills, discover cairns and hill forts, and understand that there are indeed many kinds of magic.

Nancy Bond

NANCY BOND has spent most of her life in Massachusetts: growing up and living in Concord, going to college at Mt. Holyoke in South Hadley, working in Boston, Lincoln and Gardner. Her three greatest interests as long as she can remember have been natural history, books—especially children's books—and Britain, and she has spent most of her time on one or another or all three. She has worked in the promotion departments of two publishing houses and as a librarian; participated in nature and conservation workshops and organizations; and lived a total of almost four years in the British Isles. Her latest trip there was in 1971–1972 when she studied at the College of Librarianship Wales, in Aberystwyth, for her library degree. It was out of the experiences of that year that *A String in the Harp,* her first book grew.